THE MILLER'S DANCE

The ninth Poldark novel

Winston Graham was the author of forty novels, including *The Walking Stick, Angell, Pearl and Little God, Stephanie* and *Tremor*. His books have been widely translated and his famous 'Poldark' series has been developed into two television series shown in twenty-two countries. A special two-hour television programme has been made of his eighth 'Poldark' novel, *The Stranger from the Sea*, whilst a five-part television serial of his early novel *The Forgotten Story* won a silver medal at the New York Film Festival. Six of Winston Graham's books have been filmed for the big screen, the most notable being *Marnie*, directed by Alfred Hitchcock. Winston Graham was a Fellow of the Royal Society of Literature and in 1983 was awarded the OBE. He died in July 2003.

Also by Winston Graham

Ross Poldark
Demelza
Jeremy Poldark
Warleggan
The Black Moon
The Four Swans
The Angry Tide
The Stranger from the Sea
The Twisted Sword
Bella Poldark

Night Journey
Cordelia
The Forgotten Story
The Merciless Ladies
Night Without Stars
Take My Life
Fortune is a Woman

The Little Walls
The Sleeping Partner
Greek Fire
The Tumbled House
Marnie
The Grove of Eagles
After the Act
The Walking Stick
Angell, Pearl and Little God
The Japanese Girl (short stories)
Woman in the Mirror
The Green Flash
Cameo
Stephanie
Tremor

The Spanish Armada
Poldark's Cornwall
Memoirs of a Private Man

WINSTON GRAHAM

The Miller's Dance

A Novel of Cornwall 1812–1813

PAN BOOKS

First published 1982 by William Collins Sons & Co. Ltd

This edition published 1996 by Pan Books
an imprint of Pan Macmillan Ltd
Pan Macmillan, 20 New Wharf Road, London N1 9RR
Basingstoke and Oxford
Associated companies throughout the world
www.panmacmillan.com

ISBN 0 330 34502 8

5 7 9 8 6

A CIP catalogue record for this book is available from
the British Library.

Typeset by CentraCet Limited, Cambridge
Printed and bound in Great Britain by
Mackays of Chatham plc, Chatham, Kent

*I would like to thank Tony Woolrich
for much valuable help and advice,
especially on the technical aspects
of high-pressure steam.*

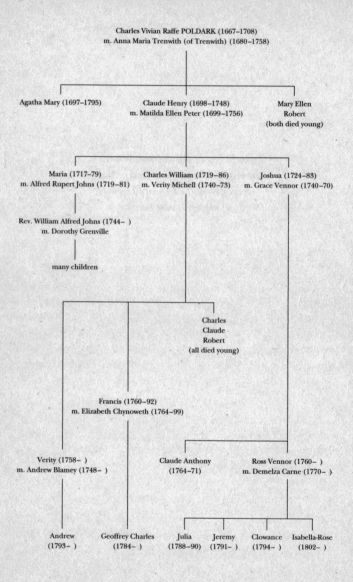

Charles Vivian Raffe POLDARK (1667–1708)
m. Anna Maria Trenwith (of Trenwith) (1680–1758)

Agatha Mary (1697–1795)

Claude Henry (1698–1748)
m. Matilda Ellen Peter (1699–1756)

Mary Ellen
Robert
(both died young)

Maria (1717–79)
m. Alfred Rupert Johns (1719–81)

Charles William (1719–86)
m. Verity Michell (1740–73)

Joshua (1724–83)
m. Grace Vennor (1740–70)

Rev. William Alfred Johns (1744–)
m. Dorothy Grenville

many children

Charles
Claude
Robert
(all died young)

Francis (1760–92)
m. Elizabeth Chynoweth (1764–99)

Verity (1758–)
m. Andrew Blamey (1748–)

Claude Anthony
(1764–71)

Ross Vennor (1760–)
m. Demelza Carne (1770–)

Andrew
(1793–)

Geoffrey Charles
(1784–)

Julia
(1788–90)

Jeremy
(1791–)

Clowance
(1794–)

Isabella-Rose
(1802–)

Jonathan CHYNOWETH (of Cusgarne) (1690–1750)
m. Anna Tregear (1693–1760)

Jonathan (1710–77)
m. Elizabeth Lanyon (1716–50)

Robert (1712–50)
m. Ursula Venning (1720–88)

Jonathan (1737–1806)
m. Joan Le Grice (1730–1804)

Hubert (1750–93)
m. Amelia Tregellas (1751–)

Elizabeth (1764–99)
m. (1) Francis Poldark
(2) George Warleggan

Morwenna (1776–)
m. (1) Rev. Osborne Whitworth
(1764–99)

m. (2) Drake Carne
(1776–)

Conan (1796–)

Loveday (1801–)

Garlanda (1778–)   Morwenna's
Carenza (1780–)   younger
Rowella (1781–)   sisters
m. Arthur Solway

Tom CARNE (1740–94)
m. Demelza Lyon (1752–77)

Luke WARLEGGAN (1715–1800)
m. Bethia Kemp (1716–44)

Demelza (1770–)
Luke (1771–)
Samuel (1772–)
William (1773–)
John (1774–)
Robert (1775–)
Drake (1776–)

Nicholas (of Cardew) (1735–1805)
m. Mary Lashbrook (1732–)

Cary Warleggan
(1740–)

George (1759–)
m. Elizabeth Poldark (née Chynoweth)
(1764–99)

Valentine (1794–)
Ursula (1799–)

BOOK ONE

Chapter One

I

On a grey day early in February, 1812, a convoy was anchored off Hendrawna Beach on the north-west coast of Cornwall. One of the vessels was a brig called *Henry*, and another a sloop *Elizabeth*. Between them floated a lighter with a massive piece of metal lying upon it and protruding over each end like a stranded whale. There were also half a dozen row-boats and a couple of gigs, one of them *Nampara Girl*. The beach was black with helpers and spectators.

February was no safe time normally for any master to hazard his vessel so close upon an inhospitable stretch of tidal sand; but after gales and half-gales succeeding each other through November, December and January, a frost had fallen on the land. It was a light frost, disappearing each midday and coming down again at night – which was the norm for this area – but it meant that the wind had at last dropped and the sea was quiet. For a time it had even been feared they were to be frustrated by the sudden lack of that element of which they had for so long had too much; but after a couple of days the lightest of breezes had sprung up from the north-east and before dawn this Monday morning the convoy had set out from Hayle. It had taken them until noon to get here, which was full tide – though a neap tide, leaving a wide expanse of beach uncovered and much of the sand soft and yielding. The sea was very slight,

3

its hair at the edge in little rolls of curlers hardly big enough to disturb a child.

The distance overland from Hayle, where the parts of the engine had been built, to Nampara was no greater than by sea; but to transport this heavy equipment through the miry lanes and over the rutted moorlands would have taken three times as long and with every possibility of getting bogged down. By sea was quicker and easier – always supposing the right moment was chosen.

The brig had been the first to discharge; since she drew the most water she had to be unloaded into rowing-boats and on to rafts well out; mostly this was the smaller stuff: the brasses, the safety-valves, the piston and piston rod, the cylinder covers, the eduction valves, the catch-pins, the flange bolts and all the working gear of a 45-inch steam engine. The sloop *Elizabeth* had been brought along mainly to carry the boiler, with which she could come closer inshore. Indeed she deliberately ran aground, even on a tide just beginning to turn, confident that when she was the lighter by seven tons she would refloat herself easily.

Ross Poldark, pausing a moment to bite a fish pie that his wife had brought him, stared at the scene and said: 'I have never seen so many people on the beach since the wrecks after Julia died.'

'Don't speak of it,' said Demelza. 'That time . . .'

'Well, then we were young. Now we are not so young. But I wouldn't have it back.'

'Not *that*. Nor all that followed. But I'd like to be twenty again.'

'Well, now we have a son older than that. And working like one demented today.'

Demelza said: 'Julia would have been twenty-two? No, twenty-one. Twenty-two this May.'

Ross swallowed his pie. Since the sloop came in, a broad pathway of sleepers consisting of old pit props had been laid from the bottom of the cliff out to the sloop – not separated as in a tramway, but one sleeper touching the next. The great boiler had been winched down until it rested on a timber frame, which itself stood on eight or nine smooth wooden rollers laid over the sleepers. Immediately it came to rest men had leapt upon the frame and flung ropes over the boiler, securing it to prevent lateral swaying; then they were off and away, manhandling it up the pathway, four men a side while others constantly rescued the rollers from the back and inserted them at the front again. It was not just a question of strength but of delicate balance, for if the rollers were not replaced exactly parallel the whole thing could slew off course and go tumbling into the sand.

Ross looked at the sky. It was leaden and would give them no stars tonight. The sea of course was unpredictable; a heavy swell might develop at any time, presaging wind, not succeeding it. But there were two hours of daylight yet, and once the stuff was unloaded and brought to the foot of the cliff there was no haste. It would be at least two days more before the rising tides reached their piece of cliff. They had all that time to haul it up to its destined site.

'Before you run away, drink this ale,' said Demelza, observing him already fidgeting to be gone.

'Where is Clowance?'

'Down among the others. You could not keep her out of it today. There . . . see her fair head.'

'I see another fair head beside her.'

'Yes, they are often together again these days . . .'

For the moment Ross's mind and memory was still back in that day and night of the 7th January, 1790, when two vessels had been blown in on this beach in a storm and when almost a thousand people, most of them miners, had stripped them in a single tide. The seamen, washed ashore, had barely escaped with their lives, and preventive men and a platoon of soldiers had not been sufficient to halt the wrecking. Desperate with hunger and crazed with the drink they had found, the miners carried all before them, and those who got in the way of their loot did so at their own peril. Great bonfires raged on the beach and drunken figures danced round them like demons from a pit. The sea had been awash with rigging, sails, spars, bales of silk and kegs of brandy, and fighting, struggling men and women. Was it the same people – or some of the same people – who were peacefully unloading an engine for the mine Wheal Leisure which was being re-started on the edge of the cliff? And the hundreds of others who had drifted down from little hamlets around to watch? Ross himself that night so long ago had been half crazed with grief at the death of his only child; and his wife, herself sick to death's point, a waif with wasted cheeks watching him hollow-eyed from her bed.

Now, more than two decades later, instead of being a near bankrupt and a soul bereft, he was fifty-two years of age, no fatter (if anything a little more gaunt), troubled with a painful recurring lameness from a ball wound he had received long ago in America, but otherwise well enough and to a small degree prosperous; a Member of Parliament, who had never distinguished himself in the House but who had established a reputation out of it, so that – for instance – George Canning had written to him a letter received only Friday last; a banker – with very little to contribute as a personal stake but an acknowledged partner in the Cornish Bank of Truro, and gradually profiting from the greater prosperity of the other partners; a mine-owner – of one mine, Wheal Grace, which had been fairy godmother to the Poldarks for nearly twenty years but was now slowly dying on them, and another, Wheal Leisure, in the process of being opened; the part-owner of a small shipyard in Looe, managed by his brother-in-law, Drake Carne; a shareholder in some reverbatory furnaces near Truro; and with a few other little irons in a few other little fires. It all added up to a comfortable existence, except that the dying Wheal Grace accounted for three-quarters of his income.

And beside him, her dark hair lifting and trembling in the breeze, was his wife, his helpmeet, and still, against all probabilities, his love, ten years his junior in everything except wit and wisdom, little changed in looks or figure, but greying at the temples: a sign post she carefully obscured every week with some dye she bought in St Ann's and which Ross pretended not to notice.

On the beach, in the charge of a distraught Mrs Kemp, was their youngest and noisiest, a black-haired ten-year-old of inexhaustible voice and vitality called Isabella-Rose. Near her, momentarily, was their seventeen-year-old daughter Clowance, dressed like a ragamuffin today in a blue fustian jacket and blue trousers rolled up above the knee, fair pigtail swinging as she moved swiftly from one knot of helpers to another. Their eldest child Jeremy, nearly twenty-one, was at present on board the lighter discussing, it seemed from his gestures, the strength and seatings of the windlasses with young Simon Pole from Harvey's Foundry. In charge of the trolley which was to receive the giant cast-iron beam was Ben Carter, grandson of Zacky and potential underground captain of the mine.

Beside Clowance the other fair head Ross had remarked was that of the Viking-like Stephen Carrington. Picked up out of the sea, destitute and half drowned, some sixteen-odd months ago, this sailor had settled among them and had become a notable figure in the villages around. What was more, he had taken a great fancy to Clowance, and Clowance, it seemed, returned the interest.

Last year, following an unexpected visit to London and a later visit to Bowood in Wiltshire, Clowance had turned down an offer of marriage from Lord Edward Fitzmaurice, younger brother of the Marquis of Lansdowne. That she had been *allowed* to refuse such an offer was clear evidence among those who heard of it of the incurable and inexcusable insanity of her parents. As Mrs Pelham said to Caroline Enys, her niece: 'It's not as if he were a gouty old man with a paunch and a weak bladder; he's but twenty-six or seven, with a seat in parliament and the highest connections, and – wonder of wonders in our aristocracy – clean living. Not the greatest conversationalist, nor the wittiest, but not at all ill-looking, and strong and healthy. That the girl should be so ineffably stupid one may set down to childish ignorance, but that your friends, her parents, put no apparent pressure on her to accept him is nothing short of an indictable offence!'

'My dear Aunt,' Caroline had said, 'you must know that my two dearest friends are to me above criticism; but there are occasions, and this is not the first, when I have an unladylike desire to crash their heads together. Pray let the subject drop.'

However much she might rationally resent some of his behaviour, it seemed probable that Stephen Carrington, the unpredictable, tawny-haired man of action and stranger from the sea, helping to build the engine house for Wheal Leisure mine far away in Cornwall, had been the most important factor behind Clowance's personal refusal of Edward Fitzmaurice. No doubt there were other considerations to be taken into account, principally the realization of her special love of Cornwall and of the outdoor life she had lived since she was a child. She would have had to exchange the wild rides on the beach, the bathing and swimming, the barefoot walks over the cliffs, the whole carefree existence of a child of nature for the artificiality of London life and polite society, overheated drawing-rooms and insincere conversation; a young titled lady far away from all her family and friends.

It was on all these matters that Mrs Pelham, and to a lesser degree Caroline, would have had Demelza instruct and reason with her daughter, pointing out that one could not live the life of a gypsy *all* one's life even in Cornwall; that one had to grow up, and probably, eventually, marry and have children, that the possession of wealth, position, influence and a distinguished husband made a difference out of all computation in the world as it was at present constituted, that even for the sake of her future children if not for herself the opportunity to place oneself in such a position *could* not be rejected. But Demelza had not so pressed her daughter and the opportunity was gone for ever.

Instead remained this young man, Stephen Carrington, enterprising, intelligent, virile and unreliable. His very presence made Clowance's blood run thick, her heart beat to a different rhythm. It had not been so with Edward Fitzmaurice. But who was to say in the end which would make the better husband?

The lighter was aground and had been nearly three hours, having run herself into the sand head-on. (She would be refloated about midnight.) The purpose of the long delay was to allow the sand to harden as much as possible before a similar sleeper track was laid from the cliffs –

otherwise the sleepers were likely to sink into the sand under their own weight. This was the really difficult job. The giant cast-iron beam weighed eighteen tons – two and a half times as much as the boiler. A larger timber frame was now being brought along this second pathway of sleepers, with rollers to lay over the sleepers as before. This was altogether too heavy a job for men, and a double team of twelve horses – six a side – waited in harness to pull the makeshift trolley back along the track. Trolley and frame had been left until the last moment so that the minimum weight rested on the sleepers. A score of extra men with sacks, shovels and levers waited alongside to help in case of mishap.

While Ross and Demelza watched, the ropes round the beam began to tighten to near breaking-point as men strove to turn the handles of the low-geared winches. Presently the beam was hanging clear of the deck, which it over-reached at either end. Then the booms swung slowly out while men guarded the chocks hammered into the side of the lighter to prevent it from swaying. On such a foundation there was bound to be movement, but it was slow movement, and as the barge swayed and sank a few inches more to the left so the beam was lowered until it rested fully upon the frame. All was haste then: men lashed the beam into position – though being flat it was less likely to roll than the boiler – then leapt off the trolley as the teams of horses took up the strain and moved the load bumping over the pathway.

There had been a good deal of discussion beforehand about how best to transport the beam, and this way had been chosen as the least likely to run into serious trouble; as Ross approached the straining teams it looked as if there would be no hitch at all. It was slow, exhausting but satisfactory progress, the horses hock deep in sand and difficult to control, with Cobbledick leading one team and Jeremy the other.

Then while still about thirty yards from the cliff, a patch of treacherous sand let them down. It often happened on this beach; there was no such thing as quicksands, but here and there a soft patch would be left, created by a current of the retreating sea and not hardening as it dried like the rest. Here the track dipped a little, and as soon as the weight of the trolley came upon it the sleepers sank too deep for the rollers to have anything solid under them. The horses were halted by the sudden immovability of their load, and a total confusion immediately reigned; the horses backed and reared, Jeremy and Cobbledick clinging on to but not quite controlling the leaders; the trolley slewed and nearly came off the track altogether.

It was Ross's instinct to take charge, but he checked himself. Ben Carter was already making the necessary moves. With eight men behind him armed with pinch bars, he ran forward and they levered the great load on course again while the horses resumed their orderly tugging. Slowly the whole thing began to move, while watchers standing near by cheered; but the rhythm had gone and the forward progression. Now each step was a violent lurch from one slithering roller and one sinking prop to the next. So it went on, with the cliffs getting slowly but agonizingly nearer. Foot by foot, levered and dragged, the beam was drawn towards the towering cliff, while the wooden sleepers dipped and twisted all ways.

In the ebb and flow of people on the beach Stephen Carrington had caught Clowance's hand.

'Where were you yesterday?'

'In church. I do go now and then. And where were you?'

'Looking for you.'

'Not too hard, I'm sure.'

'Why not?'

'Else you might have guessed.'

'What would've been the good if I'd come there? All your family around you.'

'You speak as if they're a plague.'

'So they are when I want you to meself.'

'Well, now you've got me,' she said, looking at her captive hand.

'To little use, I reckon. With half a hundred folk crowdin' around us!'

'And all observing the claim you are putting upon me.'

'Should I not? Must I not?'

'Not in public. Not just yet.'

'Clowance, I'm tired of waiting. We see little or naught of each other—'

'Oh, Friday you came to sup with us. Thursday we talked for time enough at the mine. Tuesday—'

'But that's among *people*. It is not among people that I wish to meet you, as you well know. Why, last year, afore ever I went away, we was more alone than this!'

She wriggled her hand out of his grasp. 'Yes, I suppose.'

'You know well. When can we meet in Trenwith again?'

'Ah. I don't know . . .'

A portly gentleman in a white stock and a black tail-coat but with leather boots over his stockings and knee-breeches came up to Ross. They had spoken earlier in the day when Ross had boarded the *Henry* from *Nampara Girl*. Mr Harvey. Mr Henry Harvey, after whom the brig was named. At thirty-seven, chief partner in the firm of Blewett, Harvey, Vivian & Co. of Hayle, where the mine engine had been built. He was the driving power behind the foundry's rapid expansion. Indeed, soon to be the sole owner, if litigation went well.

He did not personally superintend the delivery of all such engines built by his firm, but this commission had special areas of interest. Firstly Captain Poldark was not just an ordinary mining venturer. Secondly his son, Jeremy, had dented the social traditions of the time by becoming more than half way to practical engineer and by being responsible for the final design of the engine they had built.

'I think all is well now, Captain Poldark. Safely gathered in, if one might say so without irreverence.'

'Yes. We'll get it up the cliff tomorrow.' At the very last the trolley had slid off the track at one side and was quite immovable. But it had done its work. For the last few yards the beam could be levered forward on its own.

'So . . . If I should now take my leave . . .'

'You'd be welcome to sup with us, Mr Harvey. We have all been on a starvation diet today. Indeed, stay the night, if you wish. It would be a pleasure.'

'It would be a pleasure to me, sir. And an honour. But I should neither eat nor sleep peaceable with my three vessels off this dangerous shore. Perhaps another time.'

'Indeed. Your brother Francis stayed with us once before his – his accident.'

'He would have been forty-four this year. I have lost two other brothers and a sister since then. Natural causes with them, of course, natural causes . . . Yes, but strong steam *has* to come in spite of the risks, as your talented son recognizes. I shall watch the performance and duty of this engine with most particular interest.'

Ross looked at the darkening sky. It was like a mourning card.

'I think you're wise to go. There'll be no trouble tonight. But one can't be sure of tomorrow.'

They shook hands. A part of the purchase price of the

engine had already been paid over; the balance was due on delivery, but it was not between gentlemen that this should be discussed. As the sweating horses were relieved of their harness, men at the sea's edge were already beginning to lift the sleeper track. Ross walked with Mr Harvey down to the sea as far as his dinghy, where two men waited to push him out through the frothy little surf to join his brig and return to Hayle.

'. . . Tomorrow?' asked Stephen Carrington.

'What?' said Clowance.

'For Trenwith.'

'It is dangerous. People will see us.'

'Let 'em.'

'*No*. You have not lived here long, Stephen. I would *hate* the whispering, the dirty rumours. It would – contaminate what . . . what I don't wish to have contaminated.'

'Where, then? Where, then?'

'Trenwith maybe. But it would be better about dusk.'

'That suits me.'

'Yes, well . . . But it means . . . more deceit . . . more lying.'

'Not my choice. I would *shout* it out in the open for all to hear.'

Clowance gave a little irritable shrug. It was impossible to explain to him her own mixed feelings, the overwhelming lure of his physical attraction warring with all her loyalties to upbringing, family and friends – with the added weight of little doubts about his attitude towards other women that could not altogether be set aside.

She said: 'Perhaps next week.'

'Too far off. I want to see you tomorrow.'

'No.'

'Then *Wednesday*.'

'*No* . . . Friday I might, perhaps. I could go and see the Paynters, come on from there.'

'What time would it be?'

'About five.'

'I'll be waiting. Don't fail me, will you.'

'I'll try to be there,' said Clowance, knowing well that she would.

II

The winter had been a draughty comfortless one but without severe cold. Its relative mildness had prevented some of the worst privations in the stricken English north; and even in the Iberian peninsula, where each side had gone into winter quarters exhausted after the bloody fights and sieges of the last year, the weather was not so icy as usual.

Throughout a long campaign of desperate battles for hills and bridges and towns in Spain and Portugal one theme had predominated. Wherever Wellington was there victory was. Each of Napoleon's great marshals had taken him on in turn and each in turn had given way, having got the worst of it. Not yet had the ennobled general come into direct conflict with the greatest soldier of them all, but that might occur any time in the next campaign. Although Napoleon still ruled Europe, Englishmen everywhere held their heads higher. Splendid news had come in from the Far East too, where an expeditionary force of 3,500 men under General Auchmuchty had defeated 10,000 Dutch, French and Javanese troops and conquered Java – almost the last and certainly the richest French possession overseas. The picture was changing, for the Czar Alexander was at his most enigmatic and unyielding and Buonaparte was threatening that dire punishments should fall upon the Russians.

At home the King was sunk in his senility and the Prince Regent persisted in his folly of reposing his confidence in his old enemies the Tories and the government of the inefficient and ineffectual Spencer Perceval. Or so the Whigs felt. A year ago when he first became Regent the Prince had abruptly stated that he did not wish to risk making the change of government because his father might recover his sanity any day and be infinitely distressed and wrathful to find his own ministers dismissed. But as time wore on this showed up more and more for the miserable excuse most of his thwarted friends had all along supposed it to be. Having supported the opposition Whigs against his father's Tories all his adult life, the Prince, on the very brink of his accession, had had second thoughts, had held back, trembled on the brink of seeing Grey and Grenville and Whitbread and Brougham in office with the prospect of much-needed reform in England but a patched-up peace with France to go with it. Many straws in the wind might have swayed him at the last moment – even, however minimally, an interview with a certain Cornish soldier – only he knew how far one consideration and another had weighed.

Of course the Opposition, being patriots at heart, had changed their tune about the prospects of Wellington in the Peninsula, and most of them took a more optimistic attitude towards the war than they had done twelve months ago. Yet there were many among them still who pointed out that Buonaparte's set-backs were pinpricks when one observed the extent of his empire. In all Europe only Russia, sulkily obstinate, and Portugal, newly liberated, were not under Napoleon's heel. Half the countries of Europe were at war with England, and none of her manufactured products was allowed to be landed at any port. Ten thousand customs officers existed to see the law observed. Discovered contraband was seized, and often the ships that brought it burned as a lesson to all that the Emperor's edicts must be obeyed.

To make matters worse England was now in trouble with the United States as well. Because of her naval blockade of Europe – preventing the raw materials of war reaching Napoleon – England had claimed the right to intercept and search any ship she found on the high seas. This the Americans both resented and rejected; so, in retaliation, and smarting under old grievances, the Government of the United States had issued a decree forbidding any commercial trade with England at all. This was a killing blow to what was left of Lancashire's trade, for it deprived the mills of their raw cotton; and George Warleggan was glad he had liquidated his unwise investments in the North, even at so cruel a sacrifice. With food double the price it had been twenty years ago, the wages of the weavers of Glasgow were now a quarter of what they had been then.

So would not the Whigs, if allowed to take over now, still see the only realistic way of ending the war in a compromise peace? There had been feelers from Paris not so long ago. Now with a little more with which to bargain . . . France might have Java back in return for guaranteeing the independence of Spain and Portugal. England would recognize France's inalienable rights in the Mediterranean in return for a reopening of the Baltic ports. And so on. It was Ross's recurring nightmare. And not only Ross's . . . In the letter received recently from George Canning:

We miss you [it had said], and need you, Ross. Not just for your vote – though that also – but for some Starch you provide. And military knowledge. You would think the Government inundated with military Information – and so it is. But you speak and argue from a kind of experience – and you have no Axe to grind. You are listened to – if not in the House then outside it in private meetings where decisions of Policy are made. And that is where it is most Important.

Do you read the News sheets? How long do you suppose we may be able to sustain the War, with Revolution pending in the North? Only six of Manchester's thirty-eight mills are left working. The situation is similar throughout urban Lancashire; and these riots in Nottinghamshire where they call themselves Luddites – where will it lead? They gather together openly, these rioters, in towns and villages and ignorantly proceed to destroy the machines they believe have robbed them of work. Of course they must be stopped; but there are already over twelve thousand frame-workers on Poor Relief in Nottinghamshire alone; how can we truly blame them? From what I gather, Perceval and his ministers are bent only on Repression. They are sending a whole brigade of Dragoons up there to bring the county to book, but how shall we fight Napoleon if our troops are needed to fight at home? We *must* give some sort of Help to these starving men and women while yet maintaining a respect for the Law and punishment for those who break it. I intend to press for this, and have my usual support in the House; but

an added vote, an added voice, is of the greatest
importance. We need you, Ross.

Demelza said dismally: 'Shall you go?'

'Of course not. Certainly not yet. I cannot in fairness
leave the opening and management of Wheal Leisure
entirely to Jeremy. I've been too often away, so that my own
affairs have been neglected. I shall not easily forget the
situation I found at Wheal Grace when I came back – was it
nine years ago? God, the time has passed! All that organized
theft . . .'

'It was chiefly Bragg and Nancarrow. It couldn't happen
again.'

'Also,' said Ross.

'Also?'

'Conditions are bad enough here. There won't be
enough grain to go round. By next month people will be
starving in Cornwall too. It's not a pretty prospect.'

'But Mr Canning is very – persuasive. I know how much
you feel for him.'

'Oh yes. Oh yes. He would not be so great a man if he
were not persuasive. You should hear him in the House –
that bearpit! – how, in two minutes after he stands up, all the
noise goes and they *listen*! But this time my duty lies here.'

Demelza wriggled in her seat, not convinced.

'Promise me one thing, Ross.'

'I'll try.'

'Promise that you will not be inveigled into another trip
overseas. It is not right that you should be asked to undertake any more. However much you may enjoy it.'

'What conceivably makes you think I *enjoy* it?'

'Reading that old letter from Geoffrey Charles is what

makes me think you enjoy it,' she said. 'I looked at it again only the other day. You behaved at that battle – that battle of Bussaco – without a single thought for your wife and family! What did Geoffrey Charles say about you? "Biting at the cartridges, leaping like a boy over boulders and dead Frenchmen alike, shooting and stabbing with the best." What a way to act for a man of your dignity and responsibilities! I'll wager Mr Canning would not have done it!'

'Canning is not a soldier . . . When you are in a charge like that you lose the sense of being old and sere and bent with rheumatism. One becomes – uplifted.'

'You're hardly old and sere and, as far as I know except for your ankle, you suffer no rheumatism. But if that is the only way you can be uplifted – by *killing* people . . .'

He rubbed her ear. 'We've had that letter nine months if we've had it a day; you're a little slow to bring the charge!'

'I've been saving it up,' said Demelza.

'Well, have you, now.'

They were sitting together on the sofa in the parlour, each having come from different tasks and each taking ten minutes of the other's company. The great engine beam had just been successfully winched up the cliff, and tomorrow the assembling of the engine would begin.

'Very well,' said Ross, 'I have to admit that I was . . . uplifted. It happened. I dislike – hate – killing as much as most civilized human beings; perhaps more than most for I little enjoy shooting or hunting. I do not for a second believe Geoffrey Charles really enjoys it either. But look at that *last* letter; read it again. There is some strange sense of comradeship that for the moment at least transcends one's better self. Whoever thought that that little boy who was so doted on by Elizabeth (indeed one thought she spoiled him); who would have thought of him engaging in these desperate battles, with all the attendant hardships that he hardly mentions: the hunger, the damp, the fatigue, the loss and mutilation of one's friends . . . and yet seem actually to be *enjoying* himself! There is something rare about the Peninsular army now which adds a dimension to ordinary war.'

Isabella-Rose came into the house shouting at the top of her voice; she did not sound at all angry, just vehement. Mrs Kemp's lower tones followed her up the stairs.

'Just hear that child,' Ross said. 'Is she going to be a singer or a fish jouster?'

'I believe it's just good lungs. Certainly she is the noisiest of the three, and yet born when our life was at its calmest.'

'Anyway,' said Ross. 'I promise faithfully not to go fighting in Portugal ever again. Or anywhere else.'

'Not even in Nottingham?'

'Certainly *not* in Nottingham! I played my part once in putting down a riot here, as you may remember, and the memory still sticks like a bloodstain that won't come out in the wash.'

Demelza moodily licked her lips. 'I think I have a tooth going bad. It hurt last night when I was eating an apple and it has not been comfortable since. I think it has gone poor.'

'Let me see.'

She opened her mouth and pointed.

He prodded and she made a statement that sounded like: 'Ee – ah – ose – ah – ee – ah – ink – ah – all – ee – ike – an – ay – ogers.'

He took his finger out. 'That's a good language but I'll learn it some other time.'

'I was only saying that if I lose my teeth I shall begin to look like Aunt Mary Rogers.'

'Have you finished chattering for a moment?'

'Yes. I have now.'

'Restrain any further thoughts that come to your mind. Just while I look.'

She opened her mouth again.

He prodded. 'Is that it?'

'Eth.'

'You've made the gum sore. A piece of the apple skin must have gone into the gum. The tooth is perfectly sound.'

She closed her teeth on his finger, but not hard.

'Anyway,' he said, having recovered his finger, 'if you look as well as Aunt Mary Rogers at her age you'll be coming along pretty nice. Now you mention it, I *do* see a resemblance.'

'Would you like to put your finger in again?' she asked.

There was a knock on the door and Jane Gimlett entered.

'Oh, beg pardon, sur . . . ma'am. I thought to see if the fire wanted looking to.'

'It does.'

They sat side by side on the settee while Jane built up the fire. Jane's hair is almost white, thought Ross. How long have they been serving us faithfully, she and John? Ever since he had thrown the Paynters out, and that was upwards of twenty-two years. John too had aged. He'd been a journeyman shoemaker before. Presumably they were content to serve the Poldarks for ever, so long as their own strength and health remained. If he, Ross, suggested they should retire on a pension they would be utterly downcast, cut to the quick, supposing that their service and attention had been falling off. Which it had not. So one accepted their service, their loyalty, their wholehearted commitment . . .

'*Thank* you, Jane,' he said as she went out, and she looked up surprised at his tone of voice.

So did Demelza, but said nothing.

Ross said: 'If I feel I have to go to London again in the spring, will you come with me?'

'That I could not. Dare not. Not, that is, unless I take Clowance; and I know she will not leave Nampara again at present. In any case, as Stephen seems settled here, it would only be running away from her problem – to be faced once again when she returned.'

'We can't order our children's lives, Demelza.'

'That is most especially what we have tried *not* to do!' she said indignantly. 'Maybe a little more interference would have been to her benefit!'

He let this pass, aware that he had imposed his own double standards on her and on her children.

'They seem to meet quite rarely, Clowance and Stephen.'

'But when they do you can see that she is moved. Even the way she appears not to notice him.'

'D'you think she regrets refusing Fitzmaurice?'

'*No* . . . She cried a little that first night. I've *told* you, haven't I! I felt *much* for her. It's some dreadful decision for a girl of her age to have to make. A young man so eligible I could have wept myself . . . I don't know if she quite realized what she was turning down. I fear she has inherited from us the expectation that marriages are all-loving and all-successful. We were able to hide our troubles from her when we had them, and she has only seen the bright side – of which there has been a wondrous lot. We have never bickered or quarrelled or been teasy over small things; and when she marries she wants the same!'

'Does she think she will get it with Stephen? He has a strange reputation in the village.'

'I know. It may be just rumour about a man who is easy

in his ways . . . At least she has the sense to hold back. But she's half in love with him – or more than half – and she wasn't at all with Edward Fitzmaurice.'

There was a pause, each wanting to say more but each deciding to leave it there. Presently Ross got up and went to the top drawer in the bureau, took out the last letter they had received from Geoffrey Charles Poldark, came and sat beside her again.

'It's time he was home,' she said. 'I wish he'd take leave. He could stay with us and visit Trenwith at his leisure. It needs him.'

'We have told him all that.'

'Read it to me, Ross. I've forgot the half of it.'

He frowned at the letter, aware that only vanity prevented him from buying spectacles for close work.

'Sabugal, the third of November, 1811,' he read.

My dear Uncle Ross and Aunt Demelza.

I have been tardy in answering your letter of the 12th August, but things of varying interest and moment have been occurring in these parts. Now we are back in our Winter Quarters, as they may be glowingly described, and time will be on our hands until the open season for shooting Frenchies begins again in the New Year.

You ask me to apply for Leave and visit you at Nampara. When I return to England and Cornwall no house shall see me before Yours, and if you are still generous enough to be of the same mind I shall stay with you as long as your Patience lasts. Thank you for that invitation; for Trenwith, I feel, will be draughty with ghosts. I would love to see you all, and have so much to talk of; for it is more than a year now since that happy Meeting before Bussaco. In military ways for me it has been a wonderful year, a year in which after all the retreats and disappointments – even the retreat after Bussaco! – a change has taken place at last and we have been constantly, gradually advancing with great tactical skill. No one in the history of war, I believe, has so brilliantly demonstrated the virtues of *reculer pour mieux sauter* as Wellington. I am reminded of the tide advancing on Hendrawna Beach, as Morwenna and I used to watch it; by little forward and by little back, yet ever irresistible.

I *could* obtain leave now and spend Easter with you – a splendid idea – yet will not; for such camaraderie and kinship has built up here among those officers and men who have survived, that I should feel ill at ease with my Conscience to leave them now, even if only for six or eight weeks. You would not believe how we Esteem each other – even though little is said!

But do not suppose, after the spartan life of this last summer's campaign – and that was spartan indeed! – that we now shall lack all creature Comforts and Entertainment over the winter time. We have in prospect at this moment a series of dances, of festivities, of the new sport of steeple-chasing and the old sport of fox-hunting, of boxing contests and donkey races, and hunting for wolf and wild boar, of amateur concerts and 'professional' suppers which may lack the elegance of the London that I once knew but need fear no comparison in the Zest with which they are performed and enjoyed.

Also, my dears, the ladies here are very sweet and

warm and welcoming. There is a fine line drawn betwixt those whose warmth is restrained by considerations of chaste behaviour and those not. But all are equally gracious – even the nuns! Before I came to the Peninsula I used to expect the Portuguese ladies to be less attractive than the Spanish, but upon my soul, I believe there is little to choose. Perhaps when next you hear from me I shall be wed to one or another of them! I wish they did not have this Popish religion.

Before we retired here for the winter, we had one last splendid brush with Marshal Marmont at a place called El Bodon. I have no doubt that long before you receive this letter your News Sheets will have brought this village and plateau to your attention. But I can only say that, although we were ourselves a little late in the field, through no fault of our own, this was one of the most satisfactory Encounters ever to have been engaged in. It was the usual bloody affair, of course, but an Object Lesson in the way to fight battles when apparently outnumbered. I do believe in future manuals of war El Bodon will have an honoured place.

I have been keeping singularly well, and in a whole year of fighting have not so much as suffered a bellyache or earned a scratch. More of my good friends have gone, but, as I say, a sufficiency remain to continue to sustain me in comradeship and accord.

Again my love to you all.
Ever most sincerely
Geoffrey Charles.

PS. Any news of stepfather George? When we last met, you mentioned that he might be thinking of remarrying, but I have heard Nothing of it. My only correspondent, short of Yourselves, is Valentine, who sometimes sends a note. I received one from him last month, in which he was full of a flirtation he was conducting with someone else's pretty young wife, but he said nothing of acquiring a Step Mother. So I assume George's suit was unsuccessful, or is it still on the Boil?

PPS. Odds heart, I tell an untruth! A Letter from Drake in June. They are *happy*. That is such a *splendid* thing. Him and Morwenna I *must* see when I come home.

Demelza took the letter from Ross and held it crackling in her fingers. Then she got up and put it back in the drawer.

'Perhaps if George remarried, Geoffrey Charles would be more willing to come home, make his home among us again.'

'I doubt if that would make so much difference. Not, that is, while the war lasts.'

'Well, at least thank God Jeremy has not gone.'

'No ...'

Demelza came back, noticing his tone. 'You do not surely wish him to go? ... Do you?'

Ross scowled his discomfort at the question. 'Of course not! Not my only son. But mixed feelings, as you must realize. This is not a colonial war – not a war such as I fought in, which was a mistake from the beginning. This is a war for survival – our survival; and as such must be . . . fought out. If *I* were younger – as you know . . .'

'Yes, I know. But Jeremy's not a fighter – at least not in that way.'

'No, not in that way.'

'But he is working, is he not, for the mine?'

'Oh, indeed! I cannot fault him. He takes more than his fair share of any work that is going. I must admire him greatly for all of it.'

'*Must?*' Demelza said gently.

Ross shifted. 'We have been well enough together these last months. Since he discovered to me his passion for the properties of strong steam – since we had it out together as to why he had concealed it so long, and all the foolish subterfuge of his going fishing – since then we have been in good accord. Really, my love, I mean it.'

'I'm glad. I still think sometimes he feels . . .'

'That he cannot escape from being the owner's son? That I understand. Perhaps if I went away again . . .'

'*No.*'

Ross put his hand over hers. 'At first, of course, I was so angry with him for putting me in a false position . . . And yet, after a time, I felt that more than half the fault was mine. If there is not the communication there should be between a father and a son, surely it is the father who mostly lacks the insight and the understanding.'

'Not always,' said Demelza. 'I have seen you make the effort. But anyway let it be. Forget it – if it is over.'

'It is over. But should not be forgotten, as an object lesson for us both. I mean for him and me.'

Demelza said: 'Even Mr Harvey was telling me what a talented son we have.'

'It is good to know he is so regarded.' Ross added:

'Thank God he seems to have grown out of his disappointment over Cuby Trevanion.'

She turned. 'He hasn't, Ross. I'm certain sure of that. More's the pity. If Clowance is in two minds, Jeremy is not. It's something I know. He grieves for that girl all the time.'

Chapter Two

I

Friday was lowering, with nothing to illumine either sky or sea until late in the afternoon when a red grin appeared in the west where the sun was about to set. At the same time drifting rain moved over the land and a few partial and indistinct rainbows slid across the moorland to semaphore the end of the day.

Trenwith House, that property belonging to Geoffrey Charles Poldark, inherited from his father, long ago dead in a mining accident, looked at its coldest and most neglected as dusk began to fall. Built of enduring Tudor stone and designed with the natural elegance which seemed to come to those forgotten men who generally worked without benefit of architect, it had survived the endless ranting of storm and tempest for three centuries, and structurally it was still sound. A pane or two of glass was cracked, a gutter had rotted here and there and a chimney stack had split. But the roof of giant Delabole slates – put there, one would suppose, by a race of weight-lifters – had cared nothing for wind and weather, and all the granite mouldings, lintels and architraves were as sound as when they had been constructed in the year Henry VIII married Catherine of Aragon.

Throughout this time the house had received the intermittent consideration and neglect of varying generations of Trenwiths and Poldarks who, according to their temperaments or fortunes, had used their home with greater or lesser loving care; but the gardens for the larger part of the three hundred years had received the minimum of attention. This was partly because on a poor, sandy and wind-swept soil gardening was an ill-rewarded occupation, partly because none of the Trenwiths or Poldarks had been notably interested in flowers or shrubs and could find other uses for their usually limited funds. Only, paradoxically, when the house for the first time moved out of the direct care of the family was money and time and attention spent. This was when Geoffrey Charles's young and beautiful widowed mother had married George Warleggan, the black-smith's grandson and a new power in the mercantile world of the county. With Geoffrey Charles still a little boy, George had foreseen Trenwith as his own and his wife's country home for at least the next fifteen years, and not only had restored and refurbished the house with extravagance and excellent taste (chiefly his wife's) but had had the old stagnant pond cleared and made into an ornamental lake, and the gardens laid out and tended like a park.

For a few years Trenwith had glowed under this unex-pected attention, and the gardens, though ravaged by winds, had surprisingly repaid the care and time spent on them with flushes of brilliance and vigorous growth in the hot sun. But high noon had lasted too short a time: in five years Elizabeth was dead in childbirth and George, just become a knight bachelor, could no longer bear the sight of the house; it was occupied by Elizabeth's parents until they died, then the best of the new furniture was moved to George's other home at Cardew, and Trenwith left to the untender mercies of the Harry brothers and their one slatternly wife, who lived in the lodge house and intimidated the neighbourhood with their brutish ways. Geoffrey

Charles Poldark, the rightful owner, was now twenty-seven, but a captain in the Monmouthshires, the 43rd, of the crack Light Division, fighting in Spain, and had not been to Cornwall for five years.

So the house for that length of time, which was since old Mr Chynoweth had died, had lain entirely empty, visited perhaps once a quarter by Sir George just to keep the Harrys up to scratch.

But visiting it occasionally – at first quite openly – Clowance Poldark came. She loved the house and admired her cousin, what little she had seen of him, and being a girl without reservations or second thoughts she saw no reason at all why she shouldn't visit the house just whenever she chose – with or without the knowledge of the odious Harrys. Once indeed by the purest accident she had encountered Sir George himself. He had snarled at her – as being the interfering daughter of his worst enemy – but she had refused to be dragooned or intimidated into leaving – and there was not much physical force that even George could sanction for use on a pretty girl of sixteen with bare feet and fine skin and a luscious bosom; so she had stayed to leave him some flowers and departed in her own time.

But since Stephen Carrington came out of the sea to lure her with his strong arms and compulsive maleness, her visits had become clandestine, secretive, and therefore to her – however necessary – shameful, for she had an instinctive distaste for the least subterfuge. Worse still, it was at her instigation that the secrecy was maintained. He cared nothing for gossip and would have been happy to be seen with her anywhere in the world.

They met upstairs, in Geoffrey Charles's old bedroom, the one he had occupied as a little boy, the turret room, up the three steps and overlooking the courtyard. Some of

Geoffrey Charles's old paintings and drawings still hung on the walls, curling and spotted with damp. The bed and chairs were draped in dust sheets, the faded curtains hung askew in the ebbing light. The house was tomb-cold and still. She was there a few moments before him, and when she heard his footsteps very quietly on the stairs her mouth went dry, something swelled in her body and her knees went weak as if she had already swallowed a love-potion prepared by a witch.

His hand came cautiously round the door; he frowned at its sprained squeaking when he pushed it open; then his face lit up when he saw her standing there near the window in her muslin dress and heavy cloak.

'Clowance! Dear love! There's a good girl! I was afeared . . .'

'What, that I would break my promise?'

'No, but someone might have crossed your will to be here. I know it is not easy for you . . .'

He came towards her, but cautiously, not as he would have wanted to do, hungrily, encompassing her in his arms. Experience of her made him calculating. She was like a bird, for all her sturdiness, easily put off, turned to flight. He put his hands experimentally on her shoulders, kissed each cheek and then her mouth, letting his lips linger but not insist. He withdrew before she did. He drew her to sit beside him on the bed, put his arm around her.

'Are you cold, me love?'

'Did anyone see you come?'

'I've been waiting for this all week, counting the hours.'

She said: 'It's good to be here.'

They talked, while he stroked her face and hands, kissing her gently, smoothing her body under its heavy cloak like someone who had to be reassured and pacified.

She said again: 'Did anyone see you come?'

'Not a soul . . . But I had just to get away from Jeremy. He wanted to talk. I had to hurry back to the Nanfans to take a wash and change me shirt before I came to see me dear love.'

'It's always dangerous,' she said. 'Villages have eyes everywhere.'

'Let 'em see what they want to see.'

'Stephen, I don't wish what we feel for each other soiled by ugly gossip.'

'Then come into the open.'

She was silent, and for a moment he pressed no more, sitting quietly beside her.

He said: 'What's amiss with Jeremy? He's crossed over some girl, isn't he, too? He'll say nothing, but I know it's that way.'

'Cuby Trevanion is her name,' said Clowance.

'Is she pretty?'

'I've never seen her. He met her that time when he went with you to the Scillies and brought your boat in near Mevagissey. When you went away for four or five months.'

'I know all that.'

'Well, he was given shelter by the Trevanions and met this girl then. She helped him out of some difficulty. He won't say what.'

'Maybe I can guess,' said Stephen sardonically.

'Yes, well. He fell in love with her. I don't know if she loves him in return . . .'

'Does she live at that great house? That castle place?'

'Yes. Caerhays, it's called.'

'So twould be a good thing for Jeremy, eh? A fine match, eh? What's the let?'

'Her brother – who's head of the family – does not think Jeremy is good enough.'

'Holy Mary, so that's how the land lies! But I don't follow you! The Poldarks are gentry too! What's he looking for, a duke?'

'It is not so much a question of breeding as of money. For all their possessions, they are desperate hard up. They have overspent on the house and now need Miss Trevanion to marry a rich man.'

Stephen kissed her, moving his lips about the corner of her mouth, lifting her lip with his own. 'Well, dear God, I'm sorry for him! But does not Miss Trevanion have some say in the matter?'

'So far as I can make out she conceives it her duty to do as her brother wishes.'

'Then if she has no more will of her own than that I'd say Jeremy is well out of it!'

'A feeling of family duty takes people various ways.'

It was a significant comment. After a moment he said: 'Maybe him and me are in the same boat.'

'Do you think so?'

'Well, both deep in love with a girl whose family don't think we're good enough for them.'

'My family don't yet know.'

'They must have a fair inkling.'

'Yes,' Clowance agreed. 'They have a fair inkling.'

'That's why they took you away twice – first to London, then to this rich Lord's house in Wiltshire.'

'They didn't take me away. I went of my own accord.'

'Why?'

'Why? Because I wanted to – distance myself from you – try to be more sure.'

'And are you?'

'I think so. Though . . . I still *hear* things.'

'Things!' he said scornfully. 'What do gossip matter? They link me name with every mopsy I so much as look at, let alone exchange a word with over a glass of ale!'

For a change she kissed him. 'I know, Stephen. It is the punishment for being such a good-looking man.'

Slowly now, even under the shelter of her cloak there began the gentle but urgent exchange of love-play. She was as hungry for Stephen as he was for her, and she doubted her strength in the face of his importunities to continue to refuse him. Presently she half stood up, half broke away from him, her clothes untied and unbuttoned, her stockings fallen about her ankles, stood taking deep breaths, half swaying against him.

He said: 'Come here next week, same time. I'll light a fire, make the room comfortable, cosy. This window faces the courtyard. Who could see?'

He thought she moved her head in a negative.

He wiped the back of his hand across his mouth, trying to steady himself too. 'I'm no saint, Clowance, but I'm lost with you like no other ever and I want to be wed to you, and I can't say more. It is me dearest wish. But it can't go on like this. If it goes on like this, one of these days . . .'

'One of these days?'

'One of these days lying rumours will maybe come true.'

'About you and some other woman?'

'Yes.'

She was very still. 'Who is to say it might not be just the same if I married you?'

'It *would* not be, I swear it. For the *need* will have gone! D'you understand me, Clowance? Do you at all? Men are not born to be monks. Least, I'm not, and I reckon most are the same. When you're on board ship, it is a mite different. You're living hard, working hard, maybe fighting; the thoughts and the desires don't come – leastwise if it's women you care for. But here, there's girls in Grambler and Sawle and St Ann's ready for an easy laugh and a joke and then what follows. And here I am eaten up with desire for a girl who won't give way to me! Every time I see you it make it worse.'

'D'you think I am – unmoved? D'you know all that much about women?'

'Maybe not. But a man's desire can reach a point where the need will *force* him to look elsewhere.'

A moon was rising but it gave little light inside this room. She half saw, half imagined the expression on his face, which could look so boyish when it smiled, so mature and experienced in displeasure. She realized the truth of what he said. By offering him a partial love she was putting him in a physically intolerable position. Yet if she gave herself to him without marriage society looked on it as the unforgivable sin. For a poor girl of the parish, of course, it was nothing out of the way to become pregnant by a man before she married: it proved to him that they could have children; and if he refused to marry her and support the child he could go to prison on a bastardy charge. But for a girl of the Poldark class, while the matter would be hushed up and the wedding hurried on, the scandal would be soiling, tawdry; beyond contemplation for her.

Only last month a girl, who it was believed had been going with a soldier lately moved away, had taken her own life because she was pregnant – and been buried at Bargus where the four parishes met, there being no consecrated ground for the suicide. How many other girls concealed their pregnancy, then delivered themselves and put the child over the cliff or down a disused mine shaft?

Yet she loved Stephen and he loved her. If she went on refusing him, whose fault would it be if he did turn to someone else, and she eventually lost him?

Stephen was watching her. 'What are you thinking of, love?'

'I've been thinking that what you said is all true. I must give – must do what you want or promise a date to marry you.'

He put his hand on her bare knee. 'Why not both?'

The question slightly jarred. She shook her head. 'I have been badly brought up, Stephen, that's what it is. My churchgoing has been irregular and not of great conviction, but somehow the commandments have come to mean something to me. If I can avoid breaking the seventh it would also help me to avoid breaking the fifth.'

'Now I am at sea, adrift. What is the fifth?'

'Honour thy father and thy mother . . . I think it is more that than the other which is the chief barrier.'

'Well, then.'

'Well, then. I must still try to play fair to them but no longer play unfair to you. Can I make a promise?'

'If it is a good one.'

'Give me until Easter. What is that? Six, seven weeks. Perhaps it will not be as long as that. You have said – rightly – that my parents have an inkling. Let me make it more than an inkling. Let me try to prepare the way. I can do it. I will have a word perhaps with my father first. If he agrees, if they agree, there will be no more delay.'

'And if they disagree?'

She kissed him. 'There will be no more delay.'

II

A great storm struck the south-west in late February, and four vessels were wrecked on the north coast of Cornwall, one of them on Hendrawna. The riots of 1790, however, were not repeated, and no sailor was lost or molested who could be saved; though the vessel was comprehensively stripped. Wesleyans joined in with the best and with a clear conscience, since this was a traditional way of tempering the struggle for bare survival, and since the struggle was becoming harsher than ever just now. The carcase of the brig was surrounded by horse-drawn carts and panniered mules and men and women and children laden with ladders and sacks and hatchets and saws. Viewed from Nampara, they looked like pygmies about a dead whale. Only Sam Carne and one or two of his most devoted followers were of unquiet mood, and some blamed the wrecking for the outbreak of putrid peripneumonia which began to sweep through the county in the following weeks. It was a scriptural judgment, they implied. Dr Enys was hardly in his bed, and Caroline vehement in her protests at his overwork. She had never, Dwight explained to Demelza, altogether grown out of her early upbringing which looked on epidemics as a useful way of regulating and reducing the surplus population. Indeed why not? Caroline replied; or why did the epidemics occur? To fight them was to go against nature.

Yet for all her talk it was known that she was about to launch one of her winter campaigns to aid the needy.

One thing Dwight noticed was that in the strong and well fed the complaint was little more than a common cold, to be thrown off in a few days. The older he grew, the more he became convinced that, although the rich suffered as many diseases as the poor, they were different diseases. It was like treating two races. Whoever heard of a poor man suffering from strangury and stone, or tympany or gout?

One of the victims of the epidemic was Violet Kellow, who, in her consumptive condition, was quickly laid low and just when she appeared on the mend, suffered a severe haemorrhage. Indeed, although she had that curious tenacity of the young tubercular, Dwight did not think she could survive much longer. Had he known that she had been seen entering the church door in the darkest hour of last Midsummer Eve he would have dismissed the superstition as childish nonsense; but her family and friends, who knew of it, did not.

One of her first visitors, when she was able to see visitors, was Stephen Carrington, who had been seen passing into the church with her.

It so happened that in the second week of Violet's illness Dwight received a message from Place House to the effect that Mr Clement Pope wished to see him. On the Thursday, therefore, after a brief visit to Fernmore to reassure himself of the girl's improvement he rode on to the bigger house.

Dwight had known Sir John Trevaunance, as of course in a sparsely populated district everyone knows everyone else, but Sir John had never been his patient. Of course his brother, Unwin Trevaunance, now Sir Unwin on the baronet's death without issue, had once been half engaged to marry Caroline Penvenen; and neither Trevaunances had taken it kindly when she threw over such a distinguished and coming politician as Unwin to marry a penniless doctor called Dwight Enys. Although a cool, half-spiteful, half-jocular relationship had henceforth existed between Caroline and the two brothers, and they had often met in the hunting field, the social closeness of the early days had never returned. In later years Sir John had become more and more a recluse, and Unwin, having at last married the heiress he was looking for – a girl called Lucy Frant, from Andover, whose father it was said was rich from making army boots – had had less reason to come to see his brother to borrow money.

When Sir John died in 1808 Unwin had lost no time in converting the property into cash by selling it to the austere Mr Clement Pope who, it was said, had made a fortune in the Americas and wished to establish himself socially as an English country gentleman, in company with his pretty blonde second wife and his two rather vacuous daughters. Jeremy renamed the new owner Inclement the First, and his house The Vatican.

Since then public opinion, for what it was worth, had endorsed Jeremy's sardonic reaction. Mr Pope, with his bloodless, austere face, long neck and high collar, spindly legs and precise in-toed walk, exercised an inclement discipline over his two daughters. Although one was now nineteen and the other eighteen, it was believed he had only recently stopped beating them with a strap for the smallest misdemeanour; and even now, though not recently resorted to, the threat was still there.

His pretty young wife was a different matter: he doted on her; when in a room together his eyes followed her wherever she went. But even for her the discipline was formidable.

Although the Cornish gentry were not outrageously clannish, the attempt of the Popes to become a part of the scene had not really come off. However hard Mr Pope tried to be agreeable to the right people, his personality was against him, as indeed were his over-correct manners. ('Like a damned draper,' old Sir Hugh Bodrugan had said after they first met.) This failure was a matter of chagrin not only for Mr Pope, who wished to arrange marriages for his two daughters, but for Mrs Pope, whose natural elegance, left to itself, would soon have overcome any deficiency in breeding.

Caroline had once or twice gone out of her way to befriend them – a gesture which it was difficult to know whether they sufficiently appreciated. Of course she was very much 'county'. On the other hand, they thought, she was only the local surgeon's wife. It was the uncertainty of their manners – or chiefly Mr Pope's manners – in such matters, an inability to know quite how to behave, that was an obstacle to their acceptance in the district.

The ungainly Kate Carter – Ben's younger sister – let Dwight in. Mrs Pope was waiting for him, in Sir John's old study, that pleasant long room which looked down the cove to the sea. She came from beside the curtain, where she had been standing, and greeted him, putting four cool slim fingers into his hand to be bowed over. Then, talking, explaining, she gracefully led the way upstairs, her skirt lapping at each step. Mr Pope, it seemed, had had severe pain this morning early. He had wakened her, but just when they had been about to send for the apothecary the pains had eased. Mr Nat Irby had called at eleven and had made light of the occurrence, but Mr Pope, having heard a good account of Dr Enys's wide physical experience, had thought it desirable to call him in.

The bedroom they entered was dark and stuffy. Heavy velvet curtains, reinforced by lace curtains, kept out most of the light. A slim girl rose to her feet as they entered.

'Thank you, Letitia,' said Mrs Pope, and the girl, with none of her stepmother's grace, ambled out.

Mr Pope smelt of cinnamon and camphor and Peruvian bark. Boluses and draughts were neatly arranged in order of size on the bedside table.

Skullcap askew, he stared aridly at Dwight, clearly not liking the idea of not being the master of any situation in which he found himself, of being beholden or dependent on someone else for an opinion, a verdict, especially, when that someone was of an undetermined social status.

The pains, Mr Pope said, had been over the breast-bone and down the left arm. He had felt a constriction all across the chest and a difficulty in taking a deep breath. He had no doubt whatever that it was the prevalent fever, but he had been persuaded to avail himself of Dr Enys's reputation to confirm this opinion. Still explaining to Dwight exactly what was the matter with him, he allowed his nightshirt to be unbuttoned and pulled down off his bony shoulders. Dwight tapped his chest and back with bent knuckle. Then he took his pulse, which was slower than normal and small and hard. There was no evidence of pyrexia, from feeling the brow or hand. His tongue, for a man of his age, was clear enough, but he had a mouthful of decayed teeth. Resentfully Mr Pope allowed his stomach and belly to be pressed. During this examination Mrs Selina Pope stood by the window wrinkling her smooth brow. She was in pale blue, her hair simply caught at the back with a darker blue bow; navy blue pattens.

Dwight asked his patient to sit up, and tested his kneecaps with a percussion hammer, asked him to stand and observed whether he swayed or trembled. Presently Mr Pope was back in bed, clearly further irritated by all this medical humbug, yet not really wishing to offend or antagonize the husband of Caroline Enys. Dwight made a few notes in his book.

'Well, sir?' said the patient.

'Well, sir,' said Dwight; 'it is perfectly clear that you do not have peripneumonia.'

'Both my daughters have had it. One is still abed.'

'I'm sorry to learn this. It can be a distressing illness, though seldom so serious among the well-to-do.'

'Then what is your diagnosis of this pain?'

Dwight continued to write, while carefully considering what he should say, how much he should say. There was some evidence of dropsy. And the man's teeth ... Dwight had been successful in promoting a new health in one or two of his patients by taking out all the teeth. But he knew the prejudice against this: the accepted course, both among rich and poor, was not to touch the teeth unless toothache made it imperative. When teeth died without toothache they were allowed to remain *in situ* permanently, and people congratulated themselves. But in any case a bad condition of the mouth was not Mr Pope's main complaint.

Dwight said: 'I think you have been over-taxing yourself. You should rest every day after dinner for at least two hours. I will mix you a draught which may prevent a recurrence of the pain, and, if it does recur, another draught to ease it.'

Clement Pope adjusted his skullcap. 'What does that mean?'

'It means that you should not bother with all these potions you have been taking. I intend no offence to Mr Nat Irby, but I believe you are not helping your own health by swallowing so many medicines. I would advise a very light diet, Mrs Pope: eggs and milk and chicken and jelly. Only the lightest of wines or none at all. A little exercise *every* day, sir: a definite walk round the garden or to the sea and back. Be regular in everything and excessive in nothing. If you are troubled again please call me at once.'

'You don't intend to bleed me?'

'In this case it is of no value.'

'What case? What do you suppose the case is?'

'Over-fatigue. May I ask how old you are, Mr Pope?'

'Fifty-nine. No age at all.'

'Oh, I agree. But when one is nearing sixty it may be wise to ease off a little, take life at a slower pace.'

'I believe this to be an unhealthy climate,' said Mr Pope. 'Much of the putrid fever that is about derives or is spread from the malignancy of the mineral effluvia. When I settled here I certainly had not taken these facts into account.'

'You are not at present suffering from a putrid fever. You have over-taxed your strength. You must rest more, that is all. Living a quiet and ordered life will help you a great deal.'

Pope said irritably: 'In what way do you suppose I do *not* lead an ordered and quiet life? As you must know, I am *retired* here. I manage my property, look to the education of my daughters, accompany Mrs Pope on social visits. Since I broke my collar-bone two years ago I no longer ride to hounds. I retire to bed sober. I seldom over-eat. I become angry only at the most flagrant disobedience. My life is most placid and well regulated.'

'Quite so, quite so.' Dwight's eyes flickered towards Mrs Pope and away again. It was not his business to speculate on what the relationship was between them and whether Mr Pope felt himself under an obligation to accommodate his pretty young wife in other ways besides accompanying her on social visits to their neighbours. 'Well, Mr Pope, I believe your heart to be over-tired, to have been under some strain, and for that the best medicine – better than any I can prescribe – is light exercise with ample rest.'

Presently he was walking down the stairs with Mrs Pope floating beside him.

'I'm sorry,' he said, 'if my diagnosis has somewhat upset your husband. I thought not to say more, but came to the conclusion that if I left him unsatisfied he would disregard my advice.

'Totally,' said Mrs Pope with a slight smile. 'He can be a very stubborn man – and a difficult patient. But are you sure it is his heart?'

'One can seldom be sure of anything, Mrs Pope. Medicine is mostly guesswork, which becomes more accurate with practice. I would have thought . . .'

'Yes?'

'I would have thought the symptoms were completely typical of an anginal condition. But they could also be caused by stone in the gall-bladder; or even by a form of dyspepsia in which the food comes back into the gullet instead of being properly ingested. We can only wait and see.'

Dwight was shown out, as he had been shown in, by Katie Carter. Katie did not exactly tower over Dwight, but seemed to as she handed him his cloak because tall, big women always appear bigger than they really are. Dwight of course knew almost everyone in the district and they knew him. He had first treated Katie for a summer cholera when she was nine and had seen her a couple of times medically since. Katie smiled at him broadly now and dropped his hat, then almost dislodged her cap as she stooped to pick it up. Strange, Dwight thought, that she should be so clumsy where her brother was so deft.

Strange too that Mr Pope should insist that his indoor staff should be entirely of women. He was like a thin little sultan ruling over a harem. But at the moment, Dwight was sure, the sultan was sick.

III

Dwight had not yet left the grounds when he saw ahead of him a blond-haired man walking up the hill at the far side of the valley in company with a thin gangling youth whose manner of walking on tiptoe was easily identifiable. The first was Stephen Carrington, the second Music Thomas, the oddest of the three odd bachelor brothers who lived next to Jud and Prudie Paynter in Grambler. Music worked part time, or as much time as he was allowed to, as a stable-boy at Place House. He was good with horses and was paid three shillings a week for his trouble; for the rest he got a midday meal there and that was enough. Stephen had a spade over his shoulder.

As Dwight came up they both stopped and turned.

'Good day to you, Stephen, good day, Music. Are you both going my way?'

'Marning, sur,' said Music. It was actually evening.

'Dr Enys,' said Stephen. 'Good day to you indeed. You bound for Grambler village?'

'Near enough.'

'I'm going part way but have a message for Sally Chill-off in Sawle.'

'I be gwan that way, sur,' said Music, beaming. 'I be gwan right 'ome.'

Dwight slowed his horse to keep pace with them. It was this companionableness that endeared him to the villagers. He had not changed a degree since he was an unsophisticated, barely fledged boy of twenty-four, living in Captain Poldark's tiny Gatehouse, with no experience of doctoring except what he had learned from books and as a student in London, and very little more experience of women or human nature either. Now, forty-nine years of age, widely experienced, correspondent of famous men, called up to London sometimes for consultation, it was rumoured, and married to an heiress and living in one of the big houses, he still made time to slow his horse and chat.

'If you wonder for me spade,' volunteered Stephen, 'I work two days a week on St Ann's pier. It is in a poor way after the storms. Many of the granite blocks is part dislodged.'

'I doubt they'll ever make it secure against the worst gales,' Dwight said. 'There's not enough of a natural barrier provided by the cliffs. At least not from the north-west. The wind brings the waves directly in upon it.'

'He'll never stand,' said Music in his thin alto voice; 'the wind bring the waves directly in upon him.'

'I came round this way,' Stephen said, 'to leave a message for Music. Music works in the stables at Place House, y' know.'

'Yes, I know.'

'His brothers be going to take out their boat tonight – they have her at St Ann's – but Art has taken this fever that is abroad, so he can't go. They want – John and his mates want Music to take his place.'

'Gwan fetch my gear,' said Music. 'He'm all over to Grambler, you. Brother say, be over by sundown. Can just do that, I reckon.'

Dwight looked at the sky. 'There's wind about somewhere.'

Music smiled. 'Nay, tis narthin'. He'm only dappled

mackerel, sur. He'll pipe up for a while when the sun d' drop, but twill all be over in a hour or two.'

'Wish I was going with 'em,' said Stephen. 'I've never had aught to do with fishing but I'd like a night afloat.'

'Shall you go back to sea in the end?'

Stephen glanced at Dwight to see if the question was loaded. Concluding it was not, he said: 'It depends, Dr Enys. Sooner or later maybe. But living here, it is like being at sea.'

'On the whole I prefer to be a landlubber.'

'You can hardly call yourself that, surgeon.'

'What d'you mean?'

'Well, you being once in the Navy.'

Dwight laughed. 'It seems a long time ago.'

The direct track to Sawle Combe came into view, and Stephen went off down it, spade on shoulder, his gait, it seemed, a little more rolling for the talk of being afloat. Music's gait continued as of a man making a carefree way through a minefield.

'Surgeon.'

'Yes?'

'That's what Stephen Carrington d'call ee. Surgeon. I like that. Could I call ee surgeon too?'

'If you wish.'

'You bein' once in the Navy, sur.'

'That's true.'

Dwight watched Stephen disappear down the hill. He wondered why Stephen had seemed a little over-anxious to explain his presence near Place House. Why should he? What did it matter? Or was he imagining something that hadn't been there?

'Surgeon.'

'Yes?'

'What's amiss wi' me, surgeon?' Music Thomas asked, smiling.

'Amiss? I don't know that anything is. Are you not well?'

'Oh, ais. Brave. Sur. Surgeon . . . Ha! Sur be short for surgeon, eh?'

'If you like to look on it that way.'

'I don't mean to be insolent, sur. You d'know Parson Odgers? . . . You d'know what he d'say 'bout me once? He say I be in the front rank of the insolent squad. Tedn my intention, like! Tedn my wish to be in the insolent squad! It be just that I don't always knows just 'ow to be'ave, see?'

'Of course.'

'So if I d'say surgeon when I didn't ought to, tis not a wish I 'ave to be in the insolent squad . . .' He tiptoed a few yards in silence. 'Sur, what be amiss wi' me?'

'You haven't told me what is wrong with you?'

'I never 'ad no sickness in me life, not *ever*, see? But folk d'laugh at me! Boys d'jeer. Girls . . .' Still smiling, Music swallowed his large adam's apple as if he had a quinsy. 'Even Brothers. Both on em! They treat me like I were half an eedgit! Mebbe I aren't a one for schoolin', but I aren't a lubber-head neither! I think to myself, mebbe surgeons know.'

They went on a way without further conversation. Dwight glanced at the young man. He was about twenty, and outward signs were that he had not yet come to puberty. He was altogether an unusual figure, with his walk, his tall stooping weedy figure, and his voice; and country villages seldom took kindly – or silently – to the unusual. Dwight had always looked on him as a hollow young man. There was certainly nothing wrong with his counter-tenor voice when it soared in church, but in speech or in laughter it sounded false, empty of feeling. Sometimes too his eyes were empty, hollow, as if sentience had left them. One knew the look so well in the young man or woman who walked crooked and dribbled at the mouth and had fits: there were enough of such about, products of a brother–sister or father–daughter parentage, or of a midwife's mishandling at birth or any other of a dozen misalignments. Dwight had always put Music down as a borderline case: demonstrably odd but not quite a simpleton. He had got himself into mischief once or twice but so far had kept out of the hands of the law.

But this question he was putting . . . Some simpletons, in Dwight's experience, were sensitive enough; but to them it was the world that was at fault, not themselves. It seemed that Music felt that the fault was in himself and vaguely detected the causes. It put him in a different category. And if Dwight was not mistaken, it was something new. As if he had only just come to realize his peculiarities.

'Do you shave, Music?'

'*Well* . . . more or less, sur. Most times I cut'n off wi scissors. If I go Barber 'e d'make game.'

'Your voice has not yet broken. That is unusual in a man.'

'Drop 'n on the floor and scat'n to jowds,' said Music with a secret smile.

'When you walk, why do you not put your heels down?'

'When I were a tacker I walked on some 'ot coals. When it 'ealed over twas tender for so long I got into this way o' walking.'

'So if you got into this way of walking you could get out of it?'

'Couldn' now,' said Music, a cloud coming over his face.

'Why not?'

'Couldn' now.'

Four small boys were working a field with two teams of

oxen and were chanting their usual encouragement. '*Now*
then, Beauty, *come* on, Tartar; *now* then, Britain, *come* along,
Cloudy; *now* then, Beauty, *come* on, Tartar; *now* then, Britain,
come along, Cloudy.' They could have been young novitiates
at their plainsong. Then one of them spoiled it by seeing
Music and whistling rudely through his fingers.

Dwight said: 'In this world people – folk – do not like
what is different from themselves. To be happy perhaps it is
necessary to be as nearly like everyone else as possible. Do
you follow me?'

'Ais, I reckon.'

'Because you are different they make fun. It is – a form
of ignorance, but you cannot change it. But perhaps you
can change yourself. Have you ever tried to talk – deeper,
more in the back of the throat?'

'Nay.'

'Try. You don't need to – what is it? – drop it on the
floor and scat it to jowds. A man I knew once in London
had just such a voice as yours for singing, but in speech his
voice was as deep and firm as the next man's. It might be
worth your trying.'

'They'd laugh the more.'

'Possibly. But they could not laugh so much if you altered
your way of walking too.'

Music's attention appeared to be straying, as if the act of
concentration could not be sustained too long. Or perhaps
it was because Dwight's replies were unwelcome to him.

'When I walk on me 'eels,' he said, 'I d'feel like a duck.'

'Perhaps you would for a while.'

'Ducks d'walk on their 'eels. Quack, quack! Same as 'ens.
Same as geese.'

'Human beings – most of them – use both heel and toe.
That's the important thing.'

They would soon be in Grambler village. Dwight said: 'Well, I must be getting along.'

'Surgeon.'

'Yes.'

'What's amiss wi' me?'

'I've told you.'

'Just that?'

'I can't be sure. I would have to examine you.'

''Xamine me? What do that mean?'

'If I looked at your feet I could probably tell you whether there was any malfunction – whether there was anything wrong with the ligaments of your feet which made it impossible to use your heels. That sort of thing.'

After a moment Music said: 'I got feelins just like normal.' And laughed in embarrassment.

'Good. Well, try what I have suggested. If you make no progress come to see me and I will see if I can advise you further.'

Music touched his forelock and stepped back as Dwight urged his horse into a trot along the muddy stinking lane that divided the cottages. Music rubbed his long nose and watched him go. Then gingerly he lowered himself on to his heels as if afraid something in his feet might break.

As Dwight went on he guessed he had scared the young man off for life. Any talk of an examination was enough to frighten the villagers away, especially if they did not feel ill. It was like the threat of the knife.

All the same, Dwight reflected, if this did not occur and Music persisted with his questions, the sort of simple examination he had in mind would have to take place in the presence of some other doctor or apothecary. Otherwise, Dwight knew the sort of stories that might spread.

Chapter Three

I

On March 1 Mary Warleggan, née Lashbrook, died. She was eighty. Her long life had spanned the rise of the Warleggans. Her small money when he married her had enabled Nicholas Warleggan to finance his first enterprises, and she had lived to inhabit a mansion near the river Fal, a splendid town house in Truro, to see her son one of the most powerful and most feared men in Cornwall, a Member of Parliament, a knight and an owner of a pocket borough.

A simple woman whom riches had changed little, content with the simple pleasures of life when her husband and son allowed her to be, slow, intensely superstitious, warmhearted in a village way, wanting no thoughts beyond the comfort and sustenance of her family, ambitious only when told to be, and then with reluctance, she died slowly but without pain, her last conscious thought being regret that the conserves were not keeping as well as usual (had they not been boiled long enough?) and that she would never now see her beloved little Ursula in her first ball gown. On March 5, the day after the funeral, Sir George rode to see Lady Harriet Carter and, finding her at home, proposed marriage.

He said with a thin smile: 'It may seem a little hurried to come to you in this way so close on top of a bereavement, but it is not a wife I mourn. She ... went long ago. I flatter myself – I trust not unduly – that during the last half year we have come to an understanding of each other which will not cause this request to seem premature or abrupt for any other reasons. I am not, as I have told you, yet in the affluence I would have liked to be before I spoke to you. Thanks to unwise speculations in the Manchester district, undertaken—'

'Yes,' she said in her husky, drawling voice, 'you have explained why you undertook them.'

'It may be five years before I am as prosperous as I was before; but there is no *risk* now, no likelihood of my remaining anything but well-situated in a modest but substantial way; and you, I know, have made it clear that money could never be the deciding factor in your choice . . . My mother's death – so grievous as it is – leaves Cardew without a chatelaine. I would ask you to take it – and me.'

She did not smile at this but lifted her black eyebrows. 'Are you inviting me to be your housekeeper or your wife?'

He was not put out. 'Both. But you should know by now how earnestly I would wish you to be the latter.'

'Do I? Should I? By what means? Have you ever expressed, except in words, such an ambition?'

'In what other way would you wish me to express it?'

'*Well* . . .' She smoothed her frock with strong, well-kept fingers. 'I know that we are supposed to be members of the genteel landed gentry – would you so describe it? – but however reticent such a class may be – and observation of it suggests to me it is not really reticent when it comes to the point – the functional processes of humanity still prevail. Have you ever kissed me – tried to kiss me – on the mouth, I mean? Is there not a distinct hazard that the closer contact implicit in my becoming your wife might turn out to be distasteful to you when it was too late to change – or distasteful to me, even? For women have just as strong preferences as men, and are not, as I have pointed out, always swayed by thoughts of material advantage.'

He looked at her carefully, but she was staring out at the wind-tossed day. He suspected that, now it had come to the point, she was making a token show of reluctance, of resistance. (Her thoughts, on at least one other occasion – last Christmas – had seemed to be perfectly clear.) She was a woman like any other, and as such was the subject of whim and errant impulse, which could soon be overborne.

Yet could he be absolutely sure? Perhaps his manner *had* been stiff. Unprogressively punctilious. In dealing with the daughter of a duke he had tended to remain on his best behaviour. How change it now?

'Very well, Harriet,' he said, 'if you will stand up I will certainly do my best to convince you that we are not – distasteful to each other.'

'Why should I stand up? Do you not think a kneeling attitude would be more suitable for this occasion?'

He almost did; and then suddenly was certain she would esteem him less if he accepted her suggestion. So he got up and took her hand. She looked up at him with a contemptuous glance. He pulled her to her feet. As they were kissing she suddenly laughed, so that her breath was on his cheek. Then she kissed him back.

'Well,' she said, 'I suppose it is no worse than a cold bath. One can get used to it.'

One of the giant boarhounds snoozing near the fire looked up and gave a throaty cough, like a lion.

'Quiet, Pollux,' said Harriet. 'He is not used to seeing his mistress handled by a man. They were but puppies when the infamous Toby was alive.'

George eyed the two dogs with distaste. They were something he had not quite bargained for when he made the first approaches to her. He disliked dogs on principle. (There was also another strange animal with great eyes, tiny but ugly, that swung sometimes from the curtains.) No doubt they could all be kept in the stables after the wedding.

'The first of May?' he said. 'Would that be suitable?'

'I believe you are mentally opening your diary. Close it and let us talk for a while.'

'More talk? Certainly if you wish. But what is it you want to talk about?'

'Anything. Nothing. Do you not ever indulge in *bavarderie?* . . . Idle chatter,' she hastened to explain.

'Of course. Not perhaps when I am waiting for an answer to one of the most important questions of my life.'

Even now he could not exaggerate, say it was the *most* important. The most important had been on the 14th March, 1793. She moved a little away from him, which was not difficult for he had taken his hands off her shoulders when the dog growled.

'Tell me, George, why do you have such a fearsome reputation in Cornwall? You have never shown a sign of earning it in my company.'

'Fearsome? My name is respected! It's impossible to be enterprising, progressive in a county such as this without making some enemies. But they bark and snap to no account.'

'My aunt tells me your name creates fear and apprehension in some circles. Small traders, mining venturers and the like.' In fact her aunt had said nothing of the kind. (At an earlier stage she had said: 'If you intend to marry an upstart, why don't you at least choose one with the *makings* of a gentleman.')

George said: 'I trust you asked your aunt if I had a fearsome reputation with women.'

'No, I did not, and I don't suppose you have.'

'Perhaps you would prefer it if I were a notorious rake.'

'Having been married to one, perhaps not. Rather am I anxious to assure myself that once we are married you will not just write me down as an item in your ledger book.'

This was rather near home, and he was conscious that his face was showing annoyance. With an effort he wiped it off.

'No, Harriet, I truly love you, and ask you to marry me for that reason only. I never thought to remarry until I met you. Since then it has been my consuming wish. Even though you despise money—'

'Very, very, very far from it!'

'Even though you say you are not affected by the sort of affluence your husband can claim, if you suppose me to be a man much preoccupied by his financial affairs, then as a part of that supposition you must equally admit that I risked – and lost – a great fortune in order to have a better claim to your hand. You cannot have it both ways, Harriet!'

She smiled. 'You know women always want it both ways. But I take your meaning. And am suitably impressed. Did you say the first of May? What day of the week would that be?'

'I have no idea.'

'Could the engagement be kept secret for another month?'

'If you wish it. But . . .'

'I do wish it. But if that is adhered to, then may I say, dear George, that all this is agreeable to me?'

They embraced again. And again the dog growled. George found the embrace a far from unpleasant experience. She had a feminine-feeling body – more so than might have been supposed by her robust manner and neck-or-nothing attitude both on and off the hunting field. It pleased him. In little more than eight weeks he would have this woman sharing his bed, in a nightdress which would soon be taken off, and he would possess, with all the pent-up passion of his fifty-two years, the daughter and the sister of a duke. He was very glad that he had held his tongue this afternoon when tempted by her delicate jibes to reply in kind.

Careful and cautious to the extremest degree, as soon as he became engrossed with Lady Harriet, he had employed his friend and lackey, lawyer Hector Trembath, to make due inquiries not merely into Lady Harriet's life but into the life of her antecedents. Trembath had exceeded his instructions by going far back into the history of the Dukes of Leeds, but he had come up with some very piquant items. For instance, that the family fortunes of the Osbornes had been founded by a poor apprentice clothworker who had jumped off London Bridge into the Thames and saved his employer's daughter from drowning, subsequently marrying her and inheriting the clothworker's money. Or, for instance, that the first Duke of Leeds had been a highly dislikeable man, described as an inveterate liar, proud, ambitious, revengeful, false, prodigal, corrupt, and covetous to the highest degree, the most hated minister, some said, that had ever been about King Charles II.

When nettled by her little sarcastic darts he had been very tempted to mention some of this to her – pointing out that not all of her family for all their eminence were above the criticism that they cared for money and power. Now he was very glad he had held his tongue. It was not the spirit in which to enter into the marriage contract.

Besides, if the occasion arose, the information could be utilized at some later date.

II

On the same day, March 5, another marriage was being discussed.

Ross said gently: 'And you have just come to this conclusion?'

'About two weeks ago, Papa. But I have been waiting for – for a favourable opportunity. You have been in Truro, and then to Tehidy, and . . .'

'Does your mother know?'

'Not for certain – I'm sure she suspects.'

'So you came to me first?'

'I told Stephen I would.'

'Should he not be here? Surely it is his duty to ask for your hand.'

'Yes. He'll do that, of course. But I felt I wanted to speak to you first – break the news . . . which may not be good news for you and Mama.'

'Why should it not be?'

'Well, Stephen is – has no money; and as you know, he has no proper employment. He . . . has no pedigree – oh, I know you don't want that as such – you and Mama are above that – but if *I* had a daughter I should want to know *something* of the parents of the man she was going to marry. Stephen himself knows little. I think you *all* like him in a way. But perhaps not enough to wish him to become one of the family.'

'But you love him?'

'Yes.'

'Then surely is that not sufficient?'

'You're very sweet, Papa. Is that how you truly feel? Is that how you will be to him?'

Ross glanced away from her earnest gaze. Flicking through his mind, like the scenes of his life before a dying man, went memories of twenty years of fatherhood: the ineffable trust, the endearing love, the family squabbles, the uninhibited laughter, the intimate but sometimes prickly comradeship. And now she was in love – with a stranger. Not merely a stranger to the family, for anyone she married would be that, to begin at any rate (the closer one's family was, the more it risked in disruption), but a stranger from a distant county whose views and opinions from now on would automatically rank as more important to her than all the ties and loyalties of childhood. Was there even this evening a hint of hostility in her? – as if nature demanded a cleavage at this point, a clean fresh break between the old and the new, like an insect, a butterfly breaking away from its chrysalis. Something inherent in nature: one forced one's way out from the enclosing confines of family, turned one's back, marched on.

'If I am being sweet to you,' he said, 'as you say I am – then you cannot expect me to be as sweet to him. You are my eldest daughter, much beloved; I must test him in any way I can to be sure that he cares as you care. If I light a fire under him it will be for your good. I *must* know, be positively convinced, about the way he regards you and how he is going to maintain you.'

She was silent, still looking at him. 'What could he say that would convince you?'

'I don't know. I shall wait to hear.'

Clowance got up, picked up a primrose that had fallen out of a bowl, replaced it. She wanted to say much more, talk to her father, explain, argue with him, tell him every-thing she could, if necessary in an emotional outburst. His quiet acceptance of the news, though a vast relief, left her with not enough to say. There was a sort of vacuum. She wanted to fight Stephen's battles for him.

'He's thirty,' she said sternly.

'And you're not yet eighteen . . .'

'Papa, he's the only man.'

'The only one you have seen so far.'

'I believe,' Clowance said, 'Mama was not yet eighteen when she married you. And I do not believe all her life she has ever looked elsewhere.'

'But once,' said Ross.

'Oh?' Clowance was suddenly alert.

'And then but briefly. It was unimportant.'

'Well, then. That is what I mean.'

'It does not follow. But it could follow. I would be happy – happier – if I felt sure of him; not of you.'

'These silly lies that are spread about him . . .'

'I hadn't heard them.'

'Any woman – any man – takes a risk in marriage. It's the risk we want to take.'

Ross got up and began to draw the curtains. 'Well, I suppose it can be a while yet.'

'Not long, if you will permit it, Papa. We have waited already.'

'Waited!'

The sudden steel in his tone made her jump. 'Well, it seems so to us. There was the first few months he was here when you did not see him at all. And then there has been another eight months now. I . . . have tried to be sensible. Have I not? You must admit it! I think it was first sight with us both. But I went to London with Aunt Caroline a year last January – and then to Bowood this last July. Both times I tried to see it as a way of proving to myself whether I loved him or not. Both times it was the same.'

'He came here to supper twice while you were away in July.'

'Yes, he told me. It was kind of you to ask him. But was it because . . .'

'Yes, mainly. Though he is Jeremy's friend and might have come anyhow.'

'It was then that he invested in the mine, wasn't it?'

'In spite of my warnings. He's a very personable young man, intelligent, a quick thinker. It seems he should have done more with his life. Opportunities, of course, do not come easy when one has no connections. Perhaps when – if – he has a stabilizing influence, a different kind of ambition . . .'

'When can you see him?'

'See him? Not tomorrow. Any time Thursday. In the forenoon would be best. Tell him to come to the library. We shall be undisturbed there.'

Clowance moved across and kissed him. 'You will tell Mama?'

'Of course!'

'I mean tonight.'

'Certainly. We have few secrets from each other, and this is the last subject . . .'

Clowance smiled. 'That is the way I wish it to be between Stephen and me.'

'Tell him to wait on me at eleven.'

II

'What was she?' asked Ross. 'A schooner?'

'Yes, sir. Tops'l. Quite small.'

'How small?'

'About eighty ton.'

'And commanded by?'

'A Captain Fraser. Out of Bristol.'

'Had you been with him long?'

'Twas our second voyage. He was a Scotsman, hard, red-haired, not the type to cross.'

'But not a very good sailor?'

'Why d'you say that, sir?'

'Running his vessel aground on Gris Nez. Even if there was a storm at the time.'

'No, sir, the cannon shot that killed Captain Fraser carried away our foremast, and the whole mass of yards and stays and shrouds came crashing down, so that the vessel yawed and near went on her beam ends afore they could be cut away. We did our best to claw up into the wind, but in trying to escape from the Frenchies we'd closed the land, and sea and tide was too much for us.'

'You never heard in Bristol of any of the others being saved?'

'No. I think they was all lost.'

'How old are you, Stephen?'

'Thirty.'

'You've been at sea all your life?'

'Nay, I worked on a farm when I was a lad. Then for a short while I was a coachman to Sir Edward Hope, who lived just outside of Bristol. That's when I first saw the sea and the ships. I walked the docks, narrowly missed being pressed and instead got away in a brig sailing for Canada. After that—'

'Why did you leave Sir Edward Hope's service?'

'It was not for me.'

'In what way?'

'Little chance for promotion. And I thought one day to be me own master.'

'But you haven't become that?'

'Tisn't easy, as you yourself have said, pulling yourself up wi'out influence.'

'Are you for an indoor or outdoor life?'

'Outdoor, for preference. I always have been. Couldn't stand going down a mine. But I'm – just keen to get on – for every reason.'

Ross walked to the window. It was raining again.

'You are thirty, Stephen. You must have had attachments such as this before.'

Stephen looked at his questioner warily. 'Attachments I'll not deny. Never one such as this. Never one to be deep in love.'

'Have you ever heard of Charles Dibdin?'

'Not so far as I know.'

'He writes popular songs of the sea. They were much in vogue in London a few years ago.'

'Oh?'

'I remember one in which a sailor is supposed to be singing. The words are: "In every mess I find a friend. In every port a wife." Has that ever applied to you?'

Stephen flushed. 'As God's me witness! That's unfair!—'

'Why is it unfair? Might it not have been natural—'

'D'you think I'd come here asking for your daughter's hand if I was already wed?' His tone was rough.

Ross said: 'You might have been married and your wife died. These things can happen. If you consider you have the right to ask for my daughter's hand, I consider I have the right to inquire.'

Stephen swallowed, ran a hand through his hair. For a moment he had looked a big formidable man, the muscles and veins of his neck tightening.

'I'm sorry, Captain Poldark. You have a right. The answer's no. I don't have a wife in any other port, and never have had.'

'Good ... Tell me, if supposing you were to marry Clowance, how would you expect to support her?'

'*Somehow*, wi' me own hands. All me life I've never lacked for work. Just now, as ye know, I'm part time at the mine, and I'm two days a week at St Ann's helping repair the quay. Tis all a pittance, of course, but I'll find something different. Give me a little time.'

Ross said: 'I must tell you, Stephen, I'm not a rich man although it may seem so to you – by comparison, that is. I have a number of interests here and there in the county but they are all small. On my mining interests my prosperity – or lack of it – largely depends; and of the two mines I own, one is just paying expenses and liable to do less than that soon; the other is not yet in operation.'

'Next week, is it?'

'Next week?'

'For opening Wheal Leisure.'

'Yes, I expect so.'

'May that bring luck to us all!'

'Indeed.'

Silence fell.

'I wouldn't look for charity from you ... I've always supported meself, and, God willing, I can support Clowance too . . . Maybe not the way she's used to living but she says she don't mind that.'

'Nor, I imagine, would she,' Ross said drily. 'Clowance has ever been one to live simply.'

'Then can I expect you to say yes?' Stephen asked.

Ross moved to the side table and poured two glasses of French wine, recently run in from Roscoff. He brought one across to Stephen, who was on the point of refusing it and then changed his mind.

'I think I must consult Clowance's mother before we go so far. I think there is no need to rush anything. We've known of course for some time of your attachment for Clowance and hers for you, but the idea of an early marriage is quite new. To us, if not to you. Let us talk of this a while before making any precipitate promises. Come to supper tomorrow. Let the matter be in the air, so to speak, for a week or two. I will talk to Clowance again . . . Taste this wine. It has been kept in barrel, they say, for three years.'

Stephen tasted. He would have liked to stand up to this tall bony limping man and tell him his day was past, that he and his wife and people of their age were all back numbers, that the present and the future belonged to folk like himself and Clowance, that he was going to have Clowance whether or no, her whole body – every pale, firm, curving inch of it – and her whole mind, so that what he said she believed and that everything he did was right – and even her soul if need be. That if her father and mother put obstacles in their way they would be brushed aside like ornaments on a mantelpiece, splintering into little bits of china on the parlour floor. That he only had to crook his finger and beckon and Clowance would follow him anywhere, and to hell with the consequences.

He tasted the wine and held his tongue. He knew the strength of the Poldark ties, and he didn't want to snap them if it was not necessary. He genuinely loved Clowance and wanted her to be happy, and he sensed that she could not be totally happy if she married without her parents' approval. So in all ways it was better to conform, so long as they agreed to the marriage. Captain Poldark had great status in the county, if not all that much money, and he pleaded poverty too easily. To become the son-in-law of a Member of Parliament and a banker *must* sooner or later open doors. He, Stephen, wanted to be nobody's lackey or errand boy, and nothing would please him better than to make an entirely fresh start – and a home – for his wife independent of *any* help or favour. But if not, then the help or favour would probably be forthcoming, sooner or later.

So long as the wedding was sooner and not later.

IV

'Oh *no!*' said Clowance, a week later. 'I'm not eighteen till November!'

'It will come,' said Ross.

'Oh, Papa, that is impossible!'

'Why?' Demelza asked.

'Don't you see? I know I am *young*, but this – this has come upon me. It is not something . . .' she lowered her head . . . 'it is not something that can be *contained* so long as that!'

Demelza eyed her tall blonde daughter, and it was in her mind to tell her that she was so ineffably young she might well wait two years and come to no hurt, leave alone a mere eight or nine months. But the memory of her own early life with Ross was still too sharp in her mind, too vivid to ignore. How could she reprimand or lecture from such a base?

Ross said: 'Let us just go through it again. Tom Jonas having just died, Wilf is looking for an assistant at the mill. This will be hard, heavy work, but it will be local and outdoors, and as Wilf is childless it may lead to better things. At least it is the most suitable employment I can suggest at the moment. I am, as you know, against the idea of a son-in-law taking work with his wife's father: it leads to friction . . . even if I had anything to offer. The one thing I *can* offer is the Gatehouse. Where Dwight Enys once lived before he married Caroline. That is a pleasant small house and will do very well for you both—'

'I know, Papa, and thank you—'

'But if Stephen begins with Wilf Jonas next month – and I think that can be arranged – he can go into the Gatehouse on his own and see how he fares as a miller. By November he will have had a chance of getting the house in order – for it is in poor shape at present. Milling is a profitable business, and even one who is merely employed there – to begin – will not be badly paid. By November Stephen will have been earning seven or eight months. He will have a home ready for you to go to, and at least just enough money to maintain you. If need be, I can then add something to it to help you set up a home of your own . . .'

Clowance stood there, firmly planted between them, young, graceful, vulnerable, supremely honest.

'I do not know what Stephen will say . . .'

'What *can* he say?'

She did not answer her father's question, though she knew the answer. If Stephen chose not to see the reason of her parents' conditions and made it a condition of his own that he could not wait that long, then she would give herself to him – not in holy wedlock but in the mildewed dusty grimness of Geoffrey Charles's old bedroom, with the spiders and the wood fire and the damp sheets warmed by their nakedness. That was what she knew would happen, but she could not explain this to them, either as a reason or as a threat. Whatever had happened to *them* when they were young, it was too far away to have any relevance to the present.

She said: 'Could it be midsummer instead?'

'Why midsummer?'

'That would be a year since he returned. It would still give him time to establish himself in the Gatehouse, to have been working with Wilf Jonas for several months. It is not so – so *horribly* far away as November.'

Ross looked at Demelza. Demelza said: 'Why do we not see how Stephen feels about working for Jonas? The rest of the suggestions too. If he agrees, let us see how long it will take him to get settled. In the end we might all be agreeable to some compromise – say late August? Or perhaps after the harvest? I was at the Gatehouse last November, took the key, looked around. It is in very poor shape. There is rot in the floors, and many slates have gone. All this would have to be done before *you* could go to live there. Even Stephen might prefer to continue to live with the Nanfans for a while. But it would give him an incentive, both of you an incentive, to repair and prepare. September, I think, would be a good time.'

Clowance picked at the skin in the palm of her hand. There had been a thorn there yesterday. Stephen had taken it out. She had enjoyed being hurt by him.

'I know you are trying to be kind – both of you . . . and

thank you for being so thoughtful. Would I be – could I be officially affianced to Stephen then? Soon. It might help. He would feel he was not being just put off, delayed. A promise would mean there would not be more delay.'

There was a pause. 'At Easter?' Demelza said to Ross.

'Very well,' said Ross slowly. 'Easter it shall be.'

When Clowance had left he said: 'You weakened the stand we agreed on last night.'

'I know, Ross; I'm sorry. November is really no time to wait; but, do you ever remember when you were a child, each night when you went to bed was like a little death? Tomorrow morning was a month away. Well, Clowance is not a child, but even at her age three-quarters of a year seems half a lifetime. I felt of a sudden that perhaps a half-way-between date would make her happier, and if it is to happen, two extra months will not stop it.'

Ross began to walk slowly about the room, picking up an ornament here, a book there, replacing them, without any particular awareness of what he was doing.

'A lot of sensible men would forbid the marriage altogether, leave alone becoming involved in discussing when it should take place!'

'I know,' said Demelza.

'You know? And yet . . .'

'You're not that type of man, are you. You have never imposed that sort of discipline on your children. I think, Ross, we have to accept facts.'

'You know I caught him out when I was questioning him about the sinking of his privateer? I said he had run aground at Gris Nez, and before he had said the Scillies. He didn't correct me . . . But to be fair there was another point in my question, and he may have been more concerned to answer that and so have overlooked the other.'

'At least,' Demelza said, 'she has not run away. We are all being very civilized so far.'

There was a thoughtful silence.

'You think there could be a risk?'

'If we forbade the marriage . . . and if she cares enough.'

'It would be a way of finding out.'

'Not a pretty way.'

Ross crouched on his heels to poke the fire – then straightened up as that position hurt his ankle. He stirred the coal from a bending position. The firelight flickered on his face.

Demelza said: 'Does all this not make you feel *old*?'

'Old?'

'Prosy. Cautious. Elderly! If we cannot sensibly forbid, yet we have to counsel prudence. Advise care. Make them wait. I – I never thought it would be like this!'

'How did you think it would be?'

'*Joyous*. Us joining in. You and I. Have we not always been ready to take a risk? I thought I would throw my arms round my son-in-law's neck and cry "Welcome! Welcome!"'

The light died off Ross's face as he shovelled coal on and watched the grey smoke rise. 'My case is no better. Nor my ease. If I am able to agree that they shall marry, then I at once become parsimonious by offering him only the opportunity to start with Jonas. With all my connections in the county I should find something better for him than that.'

'Perhaps you will later.'

'Yes . . . perhaps I will later. To be grudging is a disagreeable sensation, particularly towards someone so – so ungrudging as Clowance. It's *her* life, *her* judgment. I cannot believe that a man she chooses is undeserving of our love and support. But in the circumstances it seems right for them both that they do not begin their married life too easy.'

Demelza was silent for a few moments.

'When I was at Bowood last year,' she said, 'the ladies were talking about some rich young lady, who at eighteen had married a man they described as "worthless". I have no means of judging how they calculated worth, of course! But I remember a Mrs Dawson who was there – she said: "We all know, unhappily, what a hand, a man's hand, whosoever's it may be, can do to a virgin's body, how it can enslave." I remember exactly those words. She said: "Intellect," she said, "the mind, the spirit – they're forgot. It is as strong as any spell, and between good and evil there is little difference of choice." That's what she said. I – have thought of it many times since.'

Ross looked up sharply. 'What are you suggesting?'

'Nothing, my dear. Only that when people fall in love, merit, goodness, kindness are not what tis always determined by. And we cannot think for others. We cannot feel for others . . .'

He stared at her still. He knew his wife well and wondered whether she was being quite frank with him, whether there was something behind her words.

He said: 'I wish we had not given way about November . . .'

In fact Demelza was holding back something she had heard only that morning, and painfully, at that gossip shop, the Paynters' cottage. Prudie, having drawn Demelza out of earshot of a sulphurous Jud – who was complaining that rain had been dripping on his bald head all night – confided apologetically that she had heard a rumour, a whispering, a cabby bit of rumour which was here and there in the village. She didn't know whether she did ought to say nothing about'n or to hold her clack, but sometimes twas best to mention dirty spiteous lying dungy gossip, and then it could be nailed to the bud. The gossip was, and begging pardon for mentioning it, was that Miss Clowance and that foreign chap had been seen entering and leaving Trenwith. Mind, if twas true there was certain sure naught to'n, and anyway twas sartin to be a cabby lie, but she did just feel she did ought to mention it, like.

Demelza thanked Prudie but made no other comment, passing it over as if she thought it of little importance. But privately she instantly believed it, and this had brought her change of attitude. She thought she read her daughter correctly and believed her still to be cháste, but she could imagine the strains she would be under, not only from Stephen but from her own temperament.

She would never mention Prudie's remarks to Ross. Somehow she must drop a hint to Clowance to warn her *never* to go there again – not for all the tea in China – for if this rumour got to her father's ears there would be all hell to pay. You could seldom predict how Ross would respond to a given situation, but this one you could see from a mile off. He would be likely to kick Stephen out of the house. (This unfairly, for it could only have been Clowance who had led him to Trenwith. But Ross, unable to raise a hand to his daughter, would take it out on her suitor instead.)

It was strange, Demelza thought, that in such a reaction it would not be moral outrage that spurred Ross to anger – he would undoubtedly believe whatever his daughter told him – the unforgivable thing was that they should have been meeting at Trenwith. She could imagine how he would feel if George wrote to him and said: 'My servants, Tom Harry and Harry Harry, recently surprised your daughter, Miss Clowance Poldark, in compromising circumstances with one of her paramours, some seedy sailor, trespassing upon my property in the house of Trenwith. Would you please inform her . . .'

Such a situation would be insupportable to Ross, a humiliation for which he would never forgive either Clowance or Stephen. Thank God that had not yet happened. Certainly these visits, for whatever purpose they were undertaken, must instantly be stopped.

Chapter Four

I

Wheal Leisure was opened on Wednesday, March 25. During the last two months all the parts of the engine delivered on the foreshore had been winched up – the great pieces with agonizing slowness and care – and assembled under Jeremy Poldark's supervision.

The original main shaft of the mine was about fifty yards from where the engine had been built, and there had been some who argued that not to make use of it for the engine was a terrible waste, since a new shaft meant three months of back-breaking toil for a dozen men; but Jeremy had refused to consider it. The original shaft was too narrow, and although it began perpendicularly, after about ten fathoms it began to incline, as the miners had followed the lode at an angle downwards. To have a bend in one's pump rods sixty feet below ground was something Jeremy refused to consider, though he knew it was often done. Further, the placing of the engine on this platform of ground a short distance from the main site enabled it to be built about 40 feet lower. There was no need ever to raise the water to the surface, only to the height of the lowest adit, which winter and summer emptied its yellowish stream on to the beach at the foot of the cliff; and a saving of height as they went deeper meant a saving of strain on engine and rods.

The pump rods now installed were fir poles such as might have been used for the masts of ships, but square instead of round. These poles were clamped one to another by long iron plates, fitted on all four sides of the wood and secured by cross bolts, so that they were held firm and straight and formed a single rod with the top end attached to the beam of the engine. Guides had been fitted at intervals down the shaft to prevent the rod from swinging or bending under the strain. Today the new engine would for the first time lift these heavy rods out of the deep bowels of the pit and then, at the top of the stroke, allow the rods to sink back under their own weight and by their pressure force the water up the columns of parallel pipes step by step and cistern by cistern until it reached the adit level where it could run away safely to the beach and the sea.

The nine-foot-square shaft was divided all the way down by a partition of stout wooden planking, the smaller half of which would be used for drawing up the ore by means of buckets or kibbles, these being of iron plate and rounded like coal scuttles so that they should not catch against projections as they went up and down. The larger half of the pit contained the pump rod and also the ladders by which the miners climbed up and down to and from their work. The ladders would further be used for inspection and repair of the rods and pipes.

About eight that morning, before people began to gather for the opening ceremony, Jeremy walked up to the mine with Horrie Treneglos and Stephen Carrington. As he had expected, Dan Curnow and Aaron Nanfan were already there, but after a few moments the others went outside to inspect the painting of windows and doors, which was still in progress. It gave Jeremy a chance of walking round the engine house on his own.

On the ground floor opposite him was the boiler he had ordered from Harvey's seven months ago, now built round with heat-resistant fire-brick forming a double flue underneath; above it but more centrally placed was the cylinder, jacketed in a padded container of varnished elm bound with brass rings; surrounding it were the valve gear, the wheels and levers of the exhaust and top regulators, and the steam gauge – this last not being clock-faced but rising and falling like a thermometer. A table and two comfortable chairs completed the furnishing of the room where the engineer would spend most of his waking life.

The only second-hand piece of equipment being used was outside the engine house: a smaller beam Ross had bought from a failed mine, and which they were utilizing as a balance bob. This invaluable contraption consisted of a see-saw beam attached to the free arm of the main beam, with a large box at the other end containing stones and lumps of iron and lead to give it a calculated weight. Gravitation was not only strong enough to pull the pump rod down, it also raised the heavy balance box. When it came time for the engine to do its work of pulling up the rod, the weighted box, drawn by gravitation towards the ground again, lightened the engine's load.

Up the stairs Jeremy went to the middle chamber where the cylinder protruded through from below and the polished sword-coloured piston-rod reached further up into the floor above. He remembered the struggle they had been at to get the great beam into place: it had been winched by block and tackle, hung from sheerlegs, up the outside of the engine house and swung in through an aperture in the beam wall before being lowered on to the bob stools.

There had, of course, been a trial start yesterday, and everything had gone according to plan; but one still had a feeling of responsibility, of apprehension. Soon the fire, having been lighted yesterday and damped down overnight, would be raked and the damper opened. Shortly after that the boiler would begin to sing as it raised steam.

About eleven a.m. people began to collect, many of them with no specific interest in the mine – except that a stone of prosperity dropped into a pool of poverty sent out ripples – but more with the same wish to be present at any occurrence that would provide a show, as they would have gone to watch a good catch of pilchards, or a hanging. At eleven-thirty the choir from the church, with instruments, assembled outside the engine house, and then Captain and Mrs Poldark and their two daughters, and Mrs Kellow and Mr Charles and Miss Daisy Kellow and Mr and Mrs John Treneglos and a half-dozen others of the gentry.

At eleven forty-five the choir sang, and played, 'Jesus shall Reign Where'er the Sun'. Parson Odgers, escorted by his wife to make sure that he didn't forget what he was doing and wander off on the beach, said three prayers, and Sam Carne followed him with two. It was the first ceremony at which Mr Odgers had ever consented to appear on the same platform as Sam, for he looked on Wesleyanism as a foreign and infidel faith only a degree less deadly than Catholicism. But Ross, who would have been quite agreeable to the shortest possible opening ceremony, and an entirely secular one at that, knew that his workforce would not be happy without the blessing of both church and chapel, any more than they would without the upturned horseshoe nailed over the door. So he had 'persuaded' the Odgers to fight their prejudices in the interests of commercial and spiritual goodwill.

When all this was done Ross and Demelza climbed to the third floor of the engine house and out on to the unrailed wooden platform – or bob plat – high above the groups of people below. Ross shouted out his short speech while Demelza stood beside him, her hair ruffling in the wind. From here she could see the whole three-mile length of Hendrawna Beach, the sand tawny and hard in the hazy sunlight, the swell thundering in in the distance like an undisciplined cavalry charge. Smoke blew away hurriedly from two chimney tops of Nampara. Mary Gimlett had been washing sheets; they semaphored messages and flapped and tied themselves round the line.

Below, this house – this engine house – was brand-new and handsome. The doors and window-frames were painted scarlet; the window-boxes, which later would be filled with summer flowers – marigolds or geraniums – were at present bright with the daffodils she had picked yesterday from her garden. (Couldn't see the garden from here for the shoulder of the chimney.) How would it all look a year hence? The brickwork darkened with smoke, coal dust in niches of the yard, ochreous stainings on the stone walls; but still reasonably smart, still reasonably tidy – though there was a depressing tendency among most engineers to let the congealed dirt and grease collect in the house where it was not important, so long as the working part were kept oil-clean and bright.

But what of the products brought up? All her life, it seemed to her – or all that part of her life worth living, since she came to Nampara – had been bound up, coloured, influenced for good or ill, certainly for richer or poorer, by the progress of these mines that Ross owned. First this one, Leisure, when she was still a servant in the house; she remembered a dinner Ross had given to mark the decision to open; strange, impressive, bewigged elderly gentlemen had attended it – she had long forgotten their names but not the inquiring, knowing glances that had come her way;

then, when she was married, the struggle to keep the Warleggan influence from gaining control of it; Ross's impulsive – or it seemed impulsive – decision to re-open Wheal Grace. His cousin Francis's death in it; the further tragedy of unwatering Wheal Maiden just over the hill; the enormous enduring prosperity which had come to them as a result of the discovery of the tin floors at Wheal Grace.

'I cannot name this mine,' Ross shouted into the cool, windy, sunlit air, 'for it is already known to us all. But I will re-name it Wheal Leisure, and the new engine I will name Isabella-Rose.'

He lifted the bottle of white Canary wine and broke it over the beam, and as the liquid glittered and spilt in the light air there was a cheer from the waiting people.

Below, Jeremy and Curnow had raised the steam to seven inches on the scale. With the outer cylinder fully warmed and steam escaping gently from the small valve of the waste pipe, they now opened the steam regulator, blew out the air, then shut the regulators and repeated this at intervals until the gauge had fallen to four. Then Jeremy opened the exhaust regulator and the injection valve at the same time. Gradually the piston began to slide and the beam above it to move: to avoid too violent a stroke while the load was so light he shut off the regulators again; the piston continued to slide downwards and the engine's valves emitted a sudden sharp click as the steam was cut off. The pump rods now took charge, and their weight, acting on the pump plungers in the shaft, began their perpetual task of thrusting the water in the pit upwards towards the adit level. While Tom Curnow adjusted the four valves which regulated the distribution of the steam Jeremy went to the foot of the stairs waiting for his father and mother to come down to witness the ever-recurring miracle of a modern fire engine at work.

II

The customary dinner had been eaten, the toasts drunk, most of the guests had left. Unlike his father, who named the mine he opened after his wife, Ross had been unwilling to re-name this mine Demelza. He had a feeling that only one person, one object in the world merited that name. It was fine to call the engine Isabella-Rose; Bella was flattered and everyone else was pleased.

Ross had spread his net wide, and everyone connected with the mine had been invited to the dinner. Stephen and Clowance sat side by side and few could doubt their attachment for each other. All the same it was still a week to Easter and Ross did not make an announcement. As soon as he could, Jeremy slipped out of the house again and walked back across the beach to Wheal Leisure. Already, he noted with pleasure, the yellow water gushing from the adit at the foot of the cliff had doubled in volume since this morning.

As he climbed the cliff he could hear the engine stirring inside its house with a measured breath and a grunt. It was like a great animal waiting to get out. Even in a stationary engine such as this, Jeremy had the feeling that what he had created had a life and a character of its own. And a temper.

He went in, stood for a while in the warmth watching it all work: the steam rising round the piston, the valve levers clicking up and down, looking like swans' heads as they automatically opened and shut the valves. *Grunt, pause, breath . . . grunt, pause, breath.* About three hundred gallons of water was brought up per minute. The engine had thirty tons of rods to lift. *Grunt, pause, breath . . . grunt, pause, breath.* What a majestic thing.

But imagine, just imagine this same engine, smaller and differently constructed but incorporating the same principles, the piston on its side or offset at an angle, so that the rod instead of animating a giant beam and pump could be connected to the crankshaft of the two back wheels of a road vehicle! It was all there. Somehow it was all there. One only had to adapt and adjust and overcome problems of weight and friction. That genius Trevithick had done it more than once, before he had gone off pursuing other hares . . .

Dan Curnow came trotting down the stairs, oil-can in hand.

'All right, Dan?'

'Everything going proper, Mr Poldark. I reckon she's settling down handsome.'

He set the can aside, wiping his hands on a rag, opened the fire door. Glowing heat came into the room. He riddled at the coal so that ashes fell into the bottom semi-circle of the furnace, added new coal. As he was doing this Ben Carter came down the stairs.

'Hullo, Ben. Didn't know you were here still.'

'Just looking around,' Ben said. 'Is it all over?'

'What?'

'The dinner.'

'Yes. Pretty well. You off home now?'

'I reckon.'

Ben had declined the invitation to dinner on the excuse that it was important the first day to observe the effects below ground. Jeremy was not sure whether this excuse was a valid one, for he had himself been down as far as the sump immediately after the opening to see that everything was working satisfactorily. In fact much of the rest would take several weeks to arrange: the change-over of duties below ground; the intake of the newly engaged tributers who would have to strike bargains over the ground they mined; the allotment of pitches to them as the deeper levels were dug and drained and paying ground, one hoped, uncovered. This last could necessarily only be a gradual process, following blasting and laborious pick and shovel work.

Of course Ben notoriously was not one for the social occasion. And this particular social occasion he might have found particularly trying. He was silent as Jeremy walked part way home with him, but as they reached the ruins of Wheal Maiden he stopped.

'You've come out o' your way.'

'I prefer to be out,' said Jeremy. 'I can't settle yet. It's not every day one sees an engine come to life.'

'Aye,' said Ben. 'Your design too. Tis something to take pride in.'

'My design, yes. But with a lot of advice from practical men.'

'Practical men? You're one yourself!'

'Practical engineers, then. But yes, it is my over-all plan they've built to. As soon as I leave you I think I shall go back yet again just to make sure it is still working!'

Ben laughed but without humour.

There were lights in the Meeting House.

'Do you ever go in there?' Jeremy asked, nodding towards it.

'What, me? No. When I pass, though, as I do each day now, I cann't help the wondering.'

'Wondering?'

'What your uncle d'see in it all.'

'Oh, Uncle Sam . . . it is his life. You're not a member of their Society yourself, Ben?'

'Oh no. I don't reckon I believe nothing o' that trade.'

From here you could still see one or two lights at Wheal Leisure, but there were more at Grace, where the changing of the cores was in progress. As they stood there two men came up over the hill, figures moving against the lights, tramping on their way home to Grambler village.

'Well,' said Jeremy. 'See you in the morning.'

'Jeremy.' As he half turned.

'Yes?'

'Is it true that Clowance is to be betrothed to that man?'

So it was out now. 'Stephen? Well, yes. That is the arrangement.' Jeremy kicked at a stone, knowing the hurt he was giving. 'I believe it will be official next week.'

'Ah . . . I see.'

Inside the Meeting House they were singing a hymn.

> 'Oh Christ, Who art the Light and Day
> Thy beams chase night's dark shades away.'

Ben said: 'My mother was attacked by a madman when I were a few months old. That's where I come by this scar. My father, he died of a gangrened arm when he were put in prison for being after a pheasant on Bodrugan land. He was twenty-four. My grandfather died of miner's phthisis at twenty-six. Any of these here things I can see as part of God's pattern more easier'n I can see Clowance Poldark wedding Stephen Carrington.'

Jeremy could think of nothing to say. He knew the depth of Ben's feelings and related them to his own for Cuby.

'It is hard for you, Ben. I'm very, very sorry.'

'Maybe if I speak more you'll think tis just the jealousy of it; but I suppose you d'know he's been carrying on wi' Lottie Kempthorne? And she's no better 'n she should be and her father betrayed the village to the Gaugers. You know that, don't you. And there's Violet Kellow. What do ee think of Violet Kellow? Twas wi' she that he were first seen when he come back 'ere last Midsummer Eve.'

'Yes. I know.'

'Do ee also know he visit her every week even now? Every Friday eve around seven.'

'She's sick, Ben.'

'Aye. But how sick?'

Jeremy was silent, remembering a visit he had paid last week. Violet had been brilliant, thin as a rake, cheeks flushed with fever, blue eyes twinkling, sparklingly witty. How sick? Ben had asked.

'God knows, Ben. I think we have to give him the benefit of the doubt.'

'Do we? *Do* we? Well, twas Lottie in November, I'll swear. An' livin wi' the Nanfans . . .'

'The Nanfans are honest folk – aside from being relations of yours. They'd not allow him to touch Beth . . .'

'Not if they know, I'm sure. But who d'know? There's been rumours.'

'There's always rumours, Ben. But don't think I don't know how you feel.'

'Nobody knows how I feel,' said Ben roughly. 'Maybe I'm not good 'nough for Clowance. That's easy to see. But *him* . . . That's what grates like a knife on a bone every waking hour. Every waking hour.'

III

Valentine Warleggan, home for the Easter holidays before his last half at Eton, had written to Jeremy and Clowance inviting them to the Great House to spend the day with him on April 14, which was the week after Easter. 'There are', he wrote, 'the Shamrock Players performing each night in the Assembly Rooms and Monday night promises a good programme. Doors open at six but we can get reserved chairs, so there will be time to dine comfortably first, sup after, and lie with us the night. My father', he added, 'will unfortunately be here and proposes a small *Party* for the occasion, but it will be, I believe, mixed young and old, so I think it will not altogether be too dull a Company. Pray do not tell me you cannot come because you are lifting potatoes or carrying corn or something else equally and infinitely rural!'

Jeremy and Clowance had been to Cardew one day just before Christmas. George had been away but they had met his mother and also his daughter, Ursula, and numerous other amusing people Valentine had gathered together. The visit had been a success. Ross and Demelza, naturally enough, were concerned that the friendship between their children and Valentine Warleggan should not become too close, especially between Valentine and Clowance, who were of an age; but the true reason for this anxiety could not be spoken of to anyone, so their lack of enthusiasm for the friendship was in danger of being misinterpreted by their children as an old-fashioned resentment against an old-fashioned enemy.

Approached on her own while Ross was in Looe, Demelza used his absence to make her point.

'Lovely. Have you seen the players advertised?'

'No. Valentine has the knack of discovering these things in advance,' Jeremy said.

'Well, it will be some nice for you both. It is years since I was at a play ... There is just one thing. As you know – though – I am sure you do not approve it – there is this feeling betwixt Sir George and your father. I know it is little to do with you ... but I think, I believe, that your father would be happier if you did not spend the *night* with them. I think it should not be difficult to make other arrangements.'

'Did you not spend the night there once yourself?' Clowance asked. 'You told me you did.'

'Did I? ... Well, yes, I suppose I did; but that was long ago, before either of you was born. And it was before the feeling between your father and Sir George ran so high. Indeed, what happened that night helped – just helped to begin – to make the breach more serious.'

'What did happen that night?' Clowance asked.

Demelza hesitated. 'Well, if you really wish to know, I suppose there is no reason why I should not say ... Your father and Sir George's cousin, a man called Sanson, played cards together – long into the night – gambling – we were risking far more than we could afford, almost everything. In the end your father caught Sanson cheating and took him by the coat-tails and threw him in the river.'

To Demelza's surprise they both laughed hilariously. Jeremy said: 'You had all the fun!'

'Well, I can inform you it did not seem all that so very much like fun at the time!'

'But did you get your money back?'

'Oh yes. On the spot!'

'All the same,' said Jeremy, 'it doesn't really affect Valentine, does it, now? Do you really wish us to refuse?'

'No, no, *no*! Go by all means. But I think your father would be happier – as I should – if you did not sleep there. I'll write to Mrs Polwhele. She has always said you may stay with them if you wish.'

'And Stephen?' said Clowance.

Demelza hesitated. 'Have you time to write to Valentine before?'

'Oh yes . . . But I do not think Stephen has quite the right suit for such an occasion. In fact I have already mentioned it to him.'

'And what does he say?'

'He says he will come if I feel he should. But that he will not mind, as our engagement will be so recent, if I leave him behind.'

Demelza would not be drawn. 'Then you must do as you think best, mustn't you?'

'Yes,' said Clowance. 'I think the right thing this time is if I just go with Jeremy. It will avoid complications.'

Stephen was late that evening. He found Clowance in the library.

'Sorry, sorry, sorry,' he said breathlessly. 'I been helping Will Nanfan with his lambing, and the last one was difficult.'

She kissed him. 'It does not matter.'

'Strange,' he said; 'strange it is to me after all these years to be helping wi' the ewes again. Long ago when I was a lad of ten I was expected to be there all hours to fetch and carry for Farmer Elwyn when lambing time came round. I used to go to sleep standing up in the middle of the day!

. . . I thought to repay Will Nanfan wi' something besides money for the way his wife have looked after me all these months.'

She said again: 'It does not matter.'

Stephen looked round the library appreciatively. The last time he was in here – to be examined and questioned by Ross – he had been in no mood to admire the furnishings. And before that scarcely ever properly, for, in spite of their attempt to include it in their everyday life, the Poldarks tended to congregate in the old parlour, or in the dining-room, which had once been Joshua's ground-floor bedroom. The library, built – or re-built – in the first flush of their prosperity from Wheal Grace, still remained something of a withdrawing-room for special occasions. Though out of style with the rest of the house, the light pine panelling with its fluted cornice and the Grecian motifs on the high plaster ceiling had improved with maturity. Persian rugs bought in London, applewood claw tables, sofa tables, books in shelves going up to elegant arches, heavy damask curtains, the tall Cummings clock, the fine cut-glass vases, the silver candlesticks, all spoke of money and refinement and good taste. The only inevitable concession to the climate was a damp patch in one corner, which Ross was always meaning to get repaired.

'Handsome room,' Stephen said.

'Yes . . . And private, compared to the rest of the house.'

Private, in that they were alone? he thought; but such meetings had to be frustratingly chaste even by Clowance's subtle standards. Such meetings were a temporary solution which could be permitted to last only a little while. Clowance had passed on what she thought fit of the message, that Trenwith henceforward must be out of bounds, though she pretended to him that the idea was her own.

'You never talk about your life, Stephen. Your early life, I mean. Don't you realize I'm anxious to know all I can about you?'

He smiled. 'Even the bad parts?'

'Even the bad parts.'

'There was plenty of bad parts to begin. I was a little raggamuffin, out at elbow – and sometimes backside too! – hungry, always hungry. Me mother was bonny, grey-eyed – a *strong* woman, but Father left soon after I was born and she'd to fend for herself. D'you know what it's like to fend for yourself when you're a woman and penniless, and with a squalling brat to carry around? First thing I remember she was scrubbing woman at the Coat of Arms near Evesham. She gave me no love – I was just a blamed nuisance – but I'll say this for her, she didn't give her favours to any man for money, nor easily at any time. When I was four she got this offer: man called Adam wanted her for his stage company in Gloucester. As I say, she was handsome, big, strong. He wanted her – maybe more ways 'n one, I don't know. But he didn't want *me*. What was she to do?'

There was a pause.

'You can't drop a four-year-old down a well like you can a four-week-old. Maybe she wished she *had* done. It was too late. She knew a woman called Black Moll. Not a savoury name, eh? Moll wasn't savoury neither. I'll not forget the smell of her.' Stephen wiped his hand across his mouth. 'You'd never believe, she was on the side of the law. She worked at a sponging house in Tewkesbury. Know what that is?'

'I can guess.'

'No, you can't. Not if you don't know. It is a place where debtors be kept before they go to court and to prison. She had two brats of her own. She said she'd take me.

Mother promised to pay. Don't know if she did. I never knew . . .'

'What happened?'

'We-ll . . . I stopped two years. Most times I had to steal to eat. Then I ran away. Nobody cared.' Stephen peered out at the day. 'Look, there's snowflakes, at *this* time o' year. Let us go and take a second look at the Gatehouse before dark falls. There's half an hour.'

'Tell me the rest. I want to know.'

In the distant parlour – and because the library had been built on it did sound distant – Isabella-Rose was trying to sing. Even from here it was discordant.

'When you're barely seven and you've no one to answer for you, you're liable to get picked up, sent to a House of Correction . . . Or maybe sent to prison for stealing an apple. That's what happened to me.'

'Sent to prison?'

'That's right. Oh yes. Didn't know you had a gaolbird for a suitor, did you. Only a month, first time, first offender. When I come out – came out – they put me in charge of the Overseers, who sold me to the coal mines in the Forest of Dean. I worked there near a year before I ran away. Then I lived wild for a bit—'

'You worked in the mines?'

'Yes. Had me eighth birthday down the Avoncroft Coal Mine.' Stephen paused and rubbed his chin, which rasped. 'Funny, you're the first I've told. First ever. I tell people I've never *been* down a mine. I told Jeremy that. I went down Wheal Leisure last year, just to see if it was the same. It was. The shivers took me, reminded me of old times. Funny, I always pretend. Pretend to meself often as not. It saves bad dreams.'

'But at *that* age . . .'

'Yes, I'll say that for Cornish miners, they don't take children underground, not till they're ten or eleven and then only as willing learners. I was put to draw a truck. In harness, like a pony – or more like a dog. The tunnel I drew the truck through was often so small a bigger lad could not have done it. The truck runs along iron rails from the place where they hew the coal to the foot of the shaft, just like in a Cornish mine, see, but there they use children to draw it. They put a belt round your waist and this is clamped to a chain betwixt your legs, so as you pull it it chafes your legs and rubs 'em raw. One day when we're better acquainted I'll show you marks I've got.'

Clowance said: 'You were like that – a year?'

'Give or take a month. You lose count of time. But I gave 'em the slip one day and headed into the forest. I was scared to stop running for a long time because if you got caught you not only got beaten, you had chains riveted to your ankles and wrists and you never had 'em taken off, night or day. But I was lucky.'

'Lucky . . .'

'Well, yes. Twas summer so I could live wild. It isn't so hard when there's fruit growing. I lived well enough till winter came on, then I began to give out. Village called Harfield, not far from Dursley, I went to a farm begging. Last place they'd set the dogs on me. This one, woman came to the door, took pity on me, gave me a crust. Black-eyed, Jewish-looking woman – but she wasn't Jewish, just Welsh, name of Elwyn. When her husband came in I thought he'd kick me away from his fireside, where I'd wheedled me way; but the woman persuaded him to let me stay the night. I stayed seven years. They were good to me. After their fashion. Mind, I worked from dawn to dusk seven days a week. But after the mines it was heaven. *And* I got learned to read and write, learned to be a farmer. Or a farmer's boy. Mebbe I should've stayed. They'd no children. Mebbe if I'd stayed I should've inherited the farm. But I didn't. One day I journeyed to Bristol and saw the sea.'

'Weren't you a coachman for a time?'

He looked up. 'Your father's been telling you that? Aye, for Sir Edward Hope, near Bristol. But it was no good. Couldn't settle once I'd seen the sea.'

'Will you ever be able to settle?'

He smiled and looked at her. 'Can I ever want to be away from you?'

'It's easy to say that now!'

'I know. Who can promise anything? Certainly I can't change me nature. But would you want me to? I certainly wouldn't want to change yours.'

He sat beside her and kissed her, let his lips run over her face. 'You're a wonder to me every day, Clowance. The more I know of you the more I think this. What a wife you'll make me!'

'I only love you,' said Clowance. 'That's all.'

'And God's me life, I dearly care for you—'

The door burst open and Isabella-Rose projected herself into the room with the speed of a Congreve fire rocket. She stopped short on seeing them, all brakes squeaking.

'*Clowance!* And *Stephen*! Ooh ... I didn't know. Mama didn't tell me you was here. Damn me! What a lark, eh? I thought you only kissed at party times!'

She was in pink dimity, with shiny scarlet ribbons in her black hair. She was the most like Demelza of the three children, with the long legs and the eyes and the quick movements of her mother. But the eyes were not so softly dark and her voice was hoarse. At this stage one could only guess whether she would grow into a raving beauty or miss it all by a mile.

'Damn me!' she said again. 'I'm interrupting, ain't I.'

'Bella, you should not swear,' Clowance said.

'Well, old Mr Treneglos was here yesterday, talking to Papa and he said "damn me" or "stone me" every time he opened his mouth. If he can, why not me?'

'Because you're not grown up. And because it's not ladylike anyhow.'

'Who wants to be a lady?' asked Isabella-Rose. 'And I'll wager Stephen swears, don't you, Stephen, eh, what?'

'Often,' said Stephen.

'Did you hear me singing? It was a song I made up all by myself, about a snail. I'll sing it for you sometime, Stephen!'

'Thank you, me darling.'

'What a lark, kissing in the library!' said Isabella-Rose. She retreated to the door. 'Will that happen to me when I grow up?'

'Aye,' said Stephen. 'If not before.'

'Stone me,' said Isabella-Rose. And went out.

They stared at each other, annoyed at the interruption, then broke out laughing together.

After a minute Clowance said: 'Have you never heard of your mother – not ever since you were four?'

'I heard *about* her once or twice, when I was on the farm. She was with the players. They came twice to Dursley. But Mrs Elwyn thought play-going was sinful.'

'Even to see your own mother?'

'I didn't tell her.'

'Why not?'

'They thought I was an orphan. Twere better left that way.'

Clowance looked at his face – so close to her own. She looked at his hair, his eyes, his mouth.

'What are you staring at?'

She said: 'You were underground – in those conditions – at eight. I can scarce believe it.'

'It happens all the time. Not many are so lucky as me.'

'It – hasn't stunted you. You're big – and strong.'

'Farming did that.'

'The thought of you in the mine scares me.'

'It does me, even now, if I think of it. So I don't think of it.'

'I shouldn't have asked.'

'Maybe you should. Maybe it's better not to pretend.'

She held his arm. He was frowning. It was the first sign of vulnerability she had seen in him, and it made him more than ever dear to her.

She said: 'And before that – to go to prison at seven for stealing an apple!'

'Four apples, to tell the truth. Of course I'd stole before then – all the time I was with Black Moll.'

'And since?'

'Privateering is a sort of stealing, isn't it. Legalized piracy, some call it.'

'It's not that sort I mean.'

'I'd steal to get you!'

'You haven't had to.'

'No . . . No . . . Glory be. Glory, glory, glory be.'

'Amen.'

He put his hand over hers. 'What *is* going to happen on Sunday?'

'Oh, nothing much. Nothing important. We shall just have supper, just the family, with Dr and Mrs Enys, who are our oldest friends. I have said, no fuss, no toasts, just a friendly meal; thus it will be done.'

Stephen said again: 'Let us walk as far as the Gatehouse while the daylight lasts.'

IV

Badajoz was invested on March 16. The great fortress had changed hands twice before; this time the British were determined to have it for good, and it was estimated that the siege might take a month. In fact the final assault began – and one which was to be the bloodiest battle of the war – on Easter Sunday. Only an hour after supper finished at Nampara, where the Poldarks rejoiced in, or at least marked and celebrated, the betrothal of their eldest daughter to Stephen Carrington, all hell broke loose around that distant Spanish fortress as the British, starved by their government of proper siege equipment, attempted to force the walls by hand-to-hand assault. Geoffrey Charles Poldark, Captain in the Monmouthshires, was among the leading assault troops to face the mines, the grenades, the powder barrels and the murderous crossfire which was to decimate the attacking army. Five thousand men fell that night. But in Nampara a fire crackled cheerfully in the parlour; well fed, the men comfortably sipped their port and stretched their legs, the ladies chatted and gossiped. Isabella-Rose, up late for the special occasion, was being suitably well-behaved and restrained, though she cast envious eyes at the spinet. Superficially at least one could not have imagined a more homely and restful scene. There was no psychic bond, no spiritual link to span the distance and set up the smallest alarm to tell them that one of their flesh and blood was in direst peril. The bell might toll, but none could hear.

Demelza thought: he is nice-looking and he will fit in; already he is easier of manner, less tense, since we said yes. They *are* in love with each other; she knows her own mind; I was two years younger than she is when I knew mine. We *must* find him something better than Jonas's Mill soon; but I expect Ross is right, let him begin so; anyway he won't be easy to fit in, for he has no learning; Judas, I feel queer.

Dwight and Ross were discussing the changes in medical attitudes that had been taking place. More and more the apothecary had grown in importance these last years, and a two-tier system of service had come into being. The poor and most of the middle-classes now employed the apothecary first. Physicians and surgeons devoted much of their time to the rich, or were consulted or called in by lesser folk if the case were sufficiently grave or sufficiently interesting. Dwight – 'Naturally!' interposed Caroline – refused to follow this pattern. He continued to go everywhere in the village, not caring whether he was paid or not, and so had built up a reputation – for which he cared nothing – and a sense of trust – for which he cared a great deal.

'I hear Mr Pope is coming brave again,' Demelza said. Then she raised an ironical eyebrow. 'Beg pardon, I know we are not permitted to ask.'

There was a laugh. Dwight said: 'When I was there on Thursday who should be calling on them but Unwin Trevaunance.'

'Unwin?' said his wife. 'I did not know he was in the county!'

'Staying with the de Dunstanvilles, it seems. Originally, of course, he sat in the Basset interest.'

'You never told me he was here,' said Caroline. 'How

deceitful of you! Does he have his wife with him? I've never yet met her.'

'I would not think so. It seems he is here on business.'

'When was Unwin ever not?' said Caroline. 'Even when he was courting me!'

There was another laugh.

Dwight said: 'I could start a news sheet with the gossip I hear. The story about Unwin is that when he sold the property to the Popes he did not sell the mining rights.'

'It's a common practice,' said Ross.

'Well, some prospectors wish to begin excavations near Place House, I'm told. Chenhalls from Bodmin is behind it and Unwin is putting in money. Mr Pope objects, as it is too near the house and he says it will ruin his property.'

'The old smelting works have long spoiled his view down the cove,' said Demelza.

'Yes, but they're more or less picturesque ruins now, and the vegetation has quite recovered.'

'I remember riding there once to see Sir John Trevaunance,' Demelza said. 'It was when you were – at Bodmin. The smelting works had only just been opened, and it straggled all down the side of the cove, with reverbatory furnaces and the like, and great volumes of smoke and heat and the men looking pale and ill from the fumes, and mules carrying ore down to the quay.'

'Was that for refining tin or copper?' Stephen asked.

'Copper.'

'Why was it abandoned?'

Ross said: 'It was begun to smelt copper in Cornwall instead of having it all sent to South Wales, where they had a monopoly. I was one of those along with Sir John who believed it could be done better here. I was wrong.'

'So was George Warleggan,' said Dwight, 'when he took

it over after you had withdrawn. It must be the only occasion when he has made a bad speculation.'

'Until recently,' said Ross.

'Indeed, yes,' said Dwight with an inflexion in his voice which raised eyebrows. He went on: 'But this projected mine at Trevaunance: they say it would be almost at the front door of Place House.'

'Can Mr Pope do nothing to stop them?' Jeremy asked his father.

'He might make things difficult – denying them access to water, questioning their right of way. But I don't think any court in Cornwall would be sympathetic towards a land-owner who tried to impede mining ventures. If I were Unwin,' Ross added, 'I'd offer Mr Pope a small interest in the mine. It has been done before. It is quite astonishing how a man's aesthetic senses are dulled by a possibility of profit.'

Another laugh. Stephen thought: they're nice enough folk, good folk, good *living* . . . not one of 'em's drunk tonight, except Jeremy. But is this the way to live when you have money? It is middle-aged. *They're* middle-aged, most of 'em. Yet it's not all been smooth and easy for them, not always. That man last night in Sally's telling about when Dr Dwight Enys was held on a smuggling charge. And these two, Clowance's parents: he with his gaunt, tight-drawn face, she with those eyes. Not always so quiet. Ross Poldark, it was said, had once been nearly hanged for insurrection or some such. And they whispered she was a miner's brat. That he took leave to doubt. He hadn't seen any miner's brats around looking like her. More was the pity.

Well, it was all over now for all of them anyway. Clowance even said her father intended to resign his seat in Parlia-ment at the next election. Country squire riding to hounds.

But he didn't even ride to hounds. Country squire, gouty and purple. His father-in-law. Dying off in a year or two.

Four cool fingers in his the only contact tonight. Polite society. Hell and damnation. He wanted this girl beside him with all the adult passion of a male stag in rut. It made it no better that she was now promised to him. Worse, rather. September? . . . Almighty Christ, what was he supposed to do till then – dance attendance on her and eat sweetmeats like a eunuch?'

They were still talking about illnesses.

'And Violet Kellow?' he heard himself ask.

There was a brief pause.

Dwight said: 'Violet? Stephen, I'm afraid . . .'

Caroline finished the sentence. 'Dr Enys seldom talks about his patients, Stephen, even to me. It is one of his peculiarities, no doubt dictated by Paracelsus or Hippocrates or one of those sages of the past. His predecessor here, Dr Choake, who used to live where the Kellows now live, was quite different. Indeed he made his every visit a cosy chat, in which one learned all about the kidney complaints, gouty humours and bowel movements of one's neighbours.'

Another laugh.

'Seriously,' Caroline said, 'if I may venture a personal opinion that owes nothing at all to my medical husband, I'm afraid she is not long for this world.'

'So am I,' said Stephen.

Conversation continued, but he was aware that the four fingers he had been holding had been withdrawn from his hand.

Chapter Five

I

On Monday the 14th Jeremy and Clowance rode into Truro and met Valentine and his party and went to see the play.

The party was a little larger than they had expected, but made up, as Valentine had prophesied, of old and young. The 'old' were Lady Harriet Carter with her friend the Hon. Maria Agar, Sir Unwin Trevaunance, Major John Trevanion; the young, apart from themselves, were the two Trevanion girls, Miss Clemency and Miss Cuby. It was not the most adroit of groupings, but neither Sir George nor Valentine was to know that Jeremy and John Trevanion had mortally insulted each other at their last meeting.

They dined at the Great House – which was not nearly so great as its name – and walked across to the theatre a few minutes before seven.

It was over ten months since Jeremy had seen his love. She was dressed in green velvet tonight with gauzy sleeves, and lace at the throat and wrists. She wasn't really *pretty* – he had told himself this over and over again to try to ease his own heart; and the view of her tonight instantly reconfirmed the truth of this. She was not even pretty like Daisy Kellow. Her hair was nearly straight, her skin olive, her face too round. It made not a whit of difference: she turned his heart over. Her every movement and expression was like magic to him, making his blood beat fast, his tongue stumble over the simplest phrase.

He did not sit next to her at dinner, nor at the theatre. He cursed his ill-luck at meeting her again, but at the same time knew himself newly alive. As for her brother – they had so far successfully avoided each other altogether, even in this small party.

The Shamrock Players, who may or may not have had some affiliation with Ireland, were performing *The Tragedy of the Gamester, or False Friend.* They were also to give *The Milliners* and the farce entitled *The Village Lawyer.* Sir George had taken one of the two boxes.

The theatre, which was crowded for the performance, had now been in service for nearly a quarter of a century. It was the only one, it was claimed, in England to have been specially built so that it could be used also as assembly rooms for balls and receptions. It had three small galleries where the noisy rabble congregated and sucked oranges and threw the peel about and sometimes interrupted the actors. Most of the wooden floor which was utilized for balls and dancing was lifted away for the stage performance, and the pit sat on benches arranged on the earth floor underneath. This effectively lowered them about two feet below the level of the performers. The stage consisted of a section of the original wooden floor which had not been removed, and this extended to the right and left to make two boxes, for which the richer gentry were able to pay 3s. each to sit on cane chairs and watch the acting at close quarters.

The interior of the theatre only measured some sixty-odd feet by half as wide, so intimacy was achieved on all levels. When someone as famous as Mrs Siddons came, even the benches were removed from the pit and people stood shoulder to shoulder for the show.

Although the ten chairs in their box were set close together Jeremy again had no direct contact with Cuby, being divided from her by Clowance and Valentine. Earlier, in the Warleggans' home, she had flushed at the sight of him; they had exchanged stiff bows and several times before dinner been drawn into the same conversation. But there had been no personal, private exchange. Hardly an exchange of glances. Cuby's eyes seemed able to look anywhere except into Jeremy's. She moistened her lips and joined casually in the talk, occasionally smiling. Then in the way that Jeremy so heartbreakingly remembered, the sulky mouth broke the barely observable dimples into enchanting crescents, and the whole face lit as if with some electric charge.

When the first half of the performance ended there was an interval before the farce began, and most of the audience pressed out into the entrance hall to take the air and to buy lemonade and sherbet and a new drink called ginger-beer which was becoming the fashion. Unfortunately this vestibule was tiny, and the movement of many people so overcrowded it that procession either backwards or forwards was minimal. The older members of the party had stayed in the box, where drinks would be taken to them.

So they came together, almost pressed together, while Valentine was attending to the requirements of Clowance and Clemency.

Jeremy said: 'I hope you are enjoying the play.'

She looked up at him as if he were a clumsy stranger who had trodden on her dress. 'Not very greatly.'

'Why not?'

'I do not care to be *stared* at.'

'Who is doing that?'

'You are not watching the play at all! You can hardly know what it is about!'

'I have a fair notion. Is it not . . .'

'Not what?'

'Is it not about a young lady who showed preference for a man she knew and then changed her feelings at her brother's request?'

'That play has yet to be written. You should attend to the stage.'

'Perhaps the farce will suit me better. That may be more true to life.'

Cuby looked at the glass of lemonade he was offering her. 'Thank you, you may drink that. I'm not thirsty.'

'You did say lemonade? Is this another change of feeling? But your brother is safely out of earshot.'

She turned to thrust herself away from him, but people hemmed her in. 'I did not suppose you could be so needlessly offensive.'

'Needlessly? Do you think I have no need, no cause?'

She was about to reply when the voice of someone beside her, louder than the others, shouted:

'Leave us open they doors, Enry, cann't ee? Tedn proper dark yet.' Someone shouted back: 'Couldn't, you. They'd never disjoin them as has paid from them as has not!'

Jeremy said: 'If I am bitter, tell me why I should not be.'

'Because you see only one *side*.'

'You have never given me help to see any other!'

'I had hoped it was not important to you – that it would all soon be forgot.'

'Well, it has not been.'

'No. No, I see that . . .'

'Is that all you can see?'

'You cannot expect me to discuss it in the middle of this crowd!'

'Why not? Nobody is listening.'

She took a deep breath. He offered her the glass again.

'Tell me your side,' he persisted. 'I would like to understand it. I would like to be enlightened.'

She took the glass from him, sipped it, but more as if it were some poison cup. 'You accuse me – insultingly – of changing my feelings at my brother's command. You cannot be sure what my feelings were! And who *says* they have changed?'

'Then what am I to think?'

'Think – believe – what I told you last at Caerhays. Think of me as well as you can – that's *all*.'

'I think you're beautiful.'

They both knew then that the emotional wound was wide open again.

'No!' she said quietly but very angrily. 'No, that's not *it*! That's not the way to try to *understand*. I am not weak, I am *strong*! I am not wanton or frivolous, only *hard*. I . . .' She threw her head back. 'In fact, I intend to marry money.'

'So I have been told.'

She stopped. 'You know that?'

'I have been told so.'

'Well, it's true. Who said so?'

'It doesn't matter if it's true.'

'Who *said* so?'

'The same person who told me your family was near bankrupt over this stupid castle Major Trevanion has built; and that they were looking to you to retrieve their fortunes.'

She turned on him. 'And if it is true, who is responsible? Not just my brother, who gets all the blame! From the age of sixteen, when this castle was being planned, I wanted it too! When I saw the plans and sketches I was enchanted. So was Charlotte. So was my mother. So were Augustus and Clemency. We *all* bear responsibility! The cost has gone *far* beyond our expectations. I told you of the landslip. And there have been many more mishaps. We *jointly* bear the blame.'

'But it is *you* who must sacrifice yourself for money.'

'Oh,' she shrugged, suddenly cold, 'who is to talk of sacrifice? I may yet find some pretty man with a fortune whom I may come to care for far more than his moneybags.'

'As you once cared for me?'

'Oh, *you*.' She half laughed contemptuously. 'You're just Jeremy and by then will be *long* forgot.'

'You're making much of this forgetting. D'you suppose I can forget? I'm in love with you. I love you. I *love* you, Cuby. Does that mean nothing to you at all?'

'Stop it, I tell you! Be quiet! Shut up!'

People were pushing back towards the auditorium.

She saw his face. 'I'm *sorry*, Jeremy.'

'For me or for us both?'

'I am sorry for having allowed myself to like you too much.'

There was a germ of comfort for him here among all the bitterness and jealousy and distress.

'So you do still care.' It was no longer a question.

'What does that *mean*? It can mean anything. Let us go back now. I still wish to – to watch, to enjoy the play.'

'Cuby . . .'

'No more now, please.'

'Cuby, you *do* care. Can you deny it?'

'I am not in the witness-box!'

'Can we meet afterwards? After supper perhaps.'

'*No!* If I'd known you would be here I should not have come!'

'To talk. For ten minutes only.'

'No!'

'Ah,' said Valentine, pushing his way through and smiling his brilliant, crooked smile. 'Are you joining us again? Clemency and Clowance have gone already, anxious not to miss a word. Brighten up, Cuby, for the Farce. I believe you have taken the Tragedy too much to heart.'

II

There was another entr'acte just before nine, but Cuby did not budge from her seat. When it was over, and they came out into the mild windy April night, with the carriages and the chairs and the lanterns waiting and winking outside in the square, it was only four minutes' stroll back to the Warleggans', so the five young people dismissed one carriage and walked, stepping carefully here and there to avoid the pools and the horse-droppings and the heaps of refuse, talking and laughing among themselves, making their way from High Cross to St Mary's Church, down the slit of Church Lane, into the new broad Boscawen Street and thence to Prince's Street, where the Warleggans' town house was up the steps on the right.

They supped, but on far sides of the table. Major Trevanion this time sat directly opposite Jeremy, but they looked stiff-faced at each other and avoided conversation. Fortunately the table was broad.

The Trevanions were spending the night with the Warleggans, but faithful to Demelza's preferences, her children after supper would have to ride a matter of three miles up the hill to Polwhele. Jeremy again cursed his luck, for the Trevanions would leave for home early in the morning, and there would be no chance then. And Cuby was clearly intent on avoiding a further meeting tonight. Yet now the awful wound was open again, something he felt *had* to be resolved. Some peace of mind, some hope, or some death.

Then by chance, just when he was despairing, he caught her in the hall as she came slippering down the stairs. Of course she moved to pass him but he barred the way. The drawing-room door was half open only just behind him.

'Let me pass,' she whispered intensely but he did not move.

'I asked for ten minutes.'

'*No!*'

'Five, then. Tell me, explain to me, a little more of your thinking in this matter. After all, do you not owe me that? You say you would – sell yourself merely to preserve a house – not an ancient and beloved family seat which has sheltered ten or twelve generations of Trevanions, but a castle, a new castle, a beautiful but somewhat ridiculous castle – on which your family has insanely overspent itself.'

'*Yes!* If you wish to put it so unpleasantly. That is no worse a reason than many people marry for. Certainly I should never rest easy if I married for preference only and went away somewhere to some other part of the country and watched from afar as the house and the grounds and all the other lands were sold and the Trevanions vanished from a countryside where they had lived for so many centuries! For *that* is what will *happen,* and I should have contributed to it!'

'And Augustus and Clemency? Do they also have these noble ideals?'

'Why are you so objectionable? Clemency, yes, she does. Augustus . . . I cannot say.'

'You think that if he finds a young lady with a pretty fortune he will be likely to hand over most of it to enlarge the affairs of his eldest brother. I rather doubt it!'

She did not reply.

'Of course,' Jeremy said, 'his name is still Bettesworth . . .'

She said: 'Good night, Jeremy. And goodbye. There are many pleasant girls who would make as good a wife for you as I would. I urge you to find one.'

'The difficulty is', he replied, 'that I have found the one I want. Be she pleasant or unpleasant, I still want her.'

Her pearl-ivory skin was darkened rather than coloured by its flush.

He said: 'When I knew – when I was told it was money that you wanted and not breeding I was somewhat more disgusted even than before. To want someone of higher estate, if fastidious and arrogant, was yet understandable. This willingness to auction yourself for money . . .'

'If you don't let me pass I shall call out to my brother!'

'Call out! Go on. Call out!'

She did not.

'So,' said Jeremy unmoving, 'I thought I would cut you out of my life – forget you – as you seem always to be urging me to do – set the sour page aside as a lesson in the futility of – of trying to judge human nature – of its shallowness, of its worthlessness, of its disenchantment . . . Until by misfortune I met you again today . . .'

There was a bray of laughter from the room beyond. It was Unwin Trevaunance, who always laughed like that.

Jeremy said: 'Now, having seen you again, I discover my mistake in supposing you *can* be forgot. On whatever terms, I am still tied . . . So now . . . so now I think, how much would you want, Cuby? If you are for sale, what is your price?'

'Coming from you,' she said in a low voice, 'could anything be more insulting?'

'No, I don't see that. I'm in the market. I want to *buy*

you. I'd rob a bank to buy you! Tell me how much you would cost?'

She began to cry. It was totally without noise. Just tears coming out of her eyes and running down her face. For some moments she did not even try to brush them away.

'Ten thousand?' he asked.

She said: 'Oh, Jeremy! Please take yourself away to *Hell* and leave me alone!'

III

All those who were leaving had left. The dark, vivid sister of the Duke of Leeds had departed with the Hon. Maria Agar, with whom she was spending the night. Having accepted a postponement of one month to his first marriage, with disastrous consequences to his happiness, George looked with an element of unease on his future wife's insistence on continuing secrecy about his second. In fact, as he had pointed out to her this afternoon, there could be little secrecy remaining. The banns had been published for the first time yesterday in the church of Breage in which parish Lady Harriet was at present living, so anyone attending prayers there would be bound to know. Her aunt, Miss Darcy, obviously knew. Maria Agar knew. Caroline Penvenen knew. And the household of Cardew could hardly be given less than three weeks to prepare for a new mistress.

She had patted his face and said: 'Do you want a big wedding with three choirs and five hundred guests and a great marquee?'

'You know I do not! It is the very last thing. But that is not—'

'Nor do I. This way – nobody speaking about it until a

week before – a quiet, simple ceremony – the fewer relatives and friends the better. Is it not more dignified, for us?'

'Yes, I agree. But—'

'Then pray do not be a sulky boy.'

It was so long since he had been called any such thing that he was not quite sure whether to be flattered or annoyed. But she had her way.

The one advantage of the secrecy was that Valentine need not be told until he was back at Eton. Disciplined by his father last year for over-spending and for having been rusticated for a half for immoral behaviour, Valentine had this year been noticeably more circumspect and the tensions between him and Sir George had lessened. But there was still a disaffection between them. Many boys go through a cynical, world-weary, disillusioned stage which means only that they are unsure of themselves and are having difficulty growing up. Valentine's was more deep-seated and enduring than that, and often he made George uneasy and irritable with his thin handsome good looks and sharp sarcastic tongue. Sometimes in their quarrels the old suspicion had reared its head in George and he had had difficulty in keeping to the oath he had sworn on his dead wife's body that he would never again give room to the old corroding doubt and jealousy which had ruined the last years of their married life.

Elizabeth, by giving birth prematurely to her daughter, had reinforced and made concrete all her angry denials about the birth of her son. George, at her death, had totally accepted them. And in the intervening years he had adhered to his belief that Valentine was truly his son. He still did not really doubt it even now, but he wished the boy would exhibit some more solid Warleggan traits, like his sister Ursula.

It could be said that he bore most resemblance in bearing and manner to his half-brother, Geoffrey Charles Poldark, at that age. In the days when Geoffrey Charles was living under his roof George had found him a constant irritant and a thorn. At the time he had blamed the Poldark blood of his father, since nothing ever good, in George's view, came from that poisonous strain. But possibly, since Elizabeth was mother to them both, the fault lay at least partly with the Chynoweths. Old Jonathan had been an ineffectual nonentity all his life; but Elizabeth's mother, herself a Le Grice, had been a determined and difficult woman, so one might trace the contrariness and perverseness to her. It was the most acceptable explanation.

Anyway, George would be saved the necessity of explaining or at least announcing personally his forthcoming marriage. A letter was altogether different. When Valentine came back it would all have happened; everyone would have settled down and a new pattern be firmly established.

After the Trevanion girls had retired, only the three older men were left in the drawing-room on the first floor, drinking port and stretching their legs towards the fire.

Sir Unwin Trevaunance, who had left Tehidy this morning, was catching the coach for London tomorrow at eight-thirty, so he said he was sleepy and would leave the other two to their own devices.

'You've told us little of your own project,' George said. 'I trust it augurs well.'

'Fair enough,' said Unwin. 'The advance in copper prices makes the venture the more promising. I doubt not I shall be down again before long. It's a pesky distance to travel. When I sold Place House I thought, that's an end to those interminable bone-rattling journeys.'

'Except that you still sit for Bodmin,' said Major Trevanion.

'Oh, pooh. Who cares about that? There's no election pending.'

George said: 'And you find Mr Pope amenable to the idea?'

'Not at all! He's as stubborn as a horse with glanders. I'd damn his eyes if twere not for that pretty woman he has somehow enticed into being his wife. God knows, I wonder what happens to women sometimes! Morsels as tasty as that *hide* away when you're looking for a wife and then they turn up *married* to old men as thin as asparagus tips, and with a good deal less juice in 'em, I would suppose.'

'It is possible that money and possessions play an important part,' observed Trevanion drily.

'Oh yes. Oh yes. Alas, alas.'

'So what do you intend to do?' asked George.

'About what?' Unwin looked startled, as if his secret thoughts had been surprised.

'About the mine?'

'Oh, *that*. Well, go ahead, of course! He cannot stop us. There's not a court in the land that would find for him . . . How's your mine doing, by the way? That one I see smoking each time I go to Place House.'

'Spinster? Only moderate well. We cleared a small profit last year, but costs are ever rising.'

'What made you close Wheal Plenty just along the coast? Good copper, wasn't it?'

'High-grade ore. But it is the sort of mine that yields abundantly only for a time. Once such ventures show signs of being mined out, it is essential to shut them down to save the loss you know will be coming.' George narrowed his eyes. 'As we have done before. Wheal Prosper, for instance. And Wheal Leisure.'

'That's been opened again, though, hasn't it? By the Trenegloses. And the Poldarks.'

'Much good may it do them,' said George spitefully. 'Copper never improves as you go deeper.'

'Well, we shall hope to find ore at shallow levels. The signs are good ... We're wanting a name for the venture, by the way. Do you have any thoughts?'

'Wheal Pope?' suggested Trevanion, and laughed loudly.

'If you are interested,' George said, 'we might have surplus materials from Wheal Spinster. We have some track and ladders from the west shaft that we are closing down. We could agree a price.'

John Trevanion, on whom the port was having a deleterious influence, pursued his own line of thought. 'If Wheal Spinster, why not Wheal Virgin, eh? Or Wheal Wife? Or Wheal Widow.' Another gust of laughter.

Unwin stared at him, as if taking his proposal half seriously. 'Chenhalls wants to call it some fancy name – Hannah, I think, after a mistress he once had. For my own part, since your nearest mine has closed, George, I thought we might call it West Wheal Plenty.'

'Plenty?' said Trevanion. 'Plenty of what?'

Unwin smiled. 'Of all the things we most desire, my friend. And now good night to you both. I must be up betimes.'

IV

Left alone at last, the two remaining men changed from port to brandy and talked for a while. The only other active person in the house was Valentine, who on the third floor was making successful advances to a young kitchen maid who had recently been engaged. His father might think him too tall, with over-thin shanks, one slightly bowed, and a long nose down which he permanently took a sour view of the world; but she found his dark good looks and gentility and cheerful, charming confidence quite overwhelming.

In the drawing-room Sir George kicked at the fire to make it blaze. 'On the subject we have so far scarcely discussed, Major Trevanion, I have to tell you that the sort of advance you had in mind, made virtually without security, must attract a high rate of interest.'

John Trevanion shook himself out of his semi-torpor. This was too important a matter to debate with a fuddled brain. 'Surely the land . . .'

'Already mortgaged. However, let us not quibble. The thousand pounds that my bank is advancing this month, with a further thousand next, should help to tide you over the immediate crisis. Am I not right?'

'You are right. And I am obliged. Nevertheless it will only be a temporary alleviation.'

'Well, it will hold the position for the time being. Possibly until the end of the year?'

'I doubt that. I have other commitments, such as—'

'Not, I trust, wagering on horses.'

Trevanion's florid face went a deeper red. As always, his moods were quick-changing, unpredictable. Had he not been so heavily in hock, not only to this damned banker but to a dozen other folk, he would have stalked out of the house.

'You will, I trust, appreciate,' said George, who realized he had expressed himself without tact, 'that were this a normal loan against property I would not presume to utter a word as to how you used it. But, totally unsecured as it is . . . You will appreciate I have to answer to my partners.'

Trevanion grunted. 'I thought this advance was from your own pocket.'

'Half only. Naturally if money were easier at the moment I should have been happy to shoulder the burden myself. But – may I be quite frank with you?'

'I thought you always were.'

George chose to ignore this impropriety.

'Until recently, I should explain, I have had very extensive investments in the North of England, which have been hit disastrously by the continuance of the war. Had the Prince Regent been an honourable man . . . But no matter. Suffice it to say that during the last year or so I have been liquidating these investments in order to concentrate all my future interests in this county and in Devon.'

'Didn't know that,' said Trevanion, eyeing his host warily.

'So let us for the moment be content with a move which will prevent a deterioration of your position *this* year. Eh? Until the end of the year, don't you think?'

'If you say so,' Trevanion acknowledged.

Sir George crossed and uncrossed his legs, turned over the couple of bright new guineas he always kept in his fob pocket. He weighed the priorities in his life. His marriage would involve him in much new expense, no doubt of that. Already, since his mother died, Cardew had been redecorated, worn furniture replaced, part of the stables rebuilt to accommodate Harriet's horses, the drives rolled and repaired, new ovens in the kitchens so that food could be served hotter. When Harriet was installed she would no doubt want to change some things to suit her own taste, possibly to buy more hunters, to have, perhaps, a better light carriage for her personal use.

In the meantime he was involving himself voluntarily in shoring up the shaky foundations of Major Trevanion's life. More money to lay out. Money at risk. Not of course that it was more than a bagatelle compared to what he had risked and lost in Manchester. But it could mount up. And as a *result* of his losses in the North he was still very short of liquid capital. That was the galling thing. All the same, there was a handsome prize at the end of this. As a possibility. Only as a possible possibility. Did one voice any such thoughts at this stage or allow the situation to brew for a while? Would any harm come of broaching it now? Could the idea be any worse for a preliminary airing?

'More brandy, Major?'

'Thank you.'

Liquid blobbed out of the decanter into the two glasses.

'Not only has my financial position been tightened by my losses in the North but I am expecting shortly to be married again . . .'

Trevanion frowned into his brandy as if it held some explanation of this surprising news.

'Indeed?' he said eventually. 'My – hm – congratulations.'

'Thank you.'

'Is it someone I know?'

'The extra expense involved in such a situation must clearly be my first responsibility. But in a year that situation will have stabilized itself, as will my own position.'

'Isn't *that* your own position?'

'I mean,' said George with a hint of testiness, 'my investment position.'

'Ah, I see. Yes.'

'Therefore it would be wise for us both to look on next year as a time when something more substantial might be done to help you.'

'Yes, yes, if you say so. As I've told you, as you well know, I walk a tightrope. One bill comes due on top of another. Some cannot be discounted; so they say. Others—'

'How old is Miss Cuby?' George asked.

There was a brief, taut silence.

'What?'

'Miss Cuby. Your sister. How old is she?'

'Cuby? Twenty-one last month. Why d'you ask?'

'A most charming girl.'

'No doubt. No doubt. I think so, yes.'

'She must be much sought after.'

Trevanion swallowed some heartburn in his throat. 'Oh? Well, maybe, yes. She's very *close* to me, you know, Cuby is.'

'I've no doubt.'

'*And* she has been an invaluable help in looking after my young children.'

Silence fell again. Trevanion looked at his glass. 'Good brandy, this. It was run, I suppose?'

'It was run.'

Some drunken wastrels began quarrelling in the street below. It was one of the problems of town life; one could not withdraw oneself far enough from the vulgars.

'Cuby has been closer to me than anyone since my darling Charlotte died. She is a very proud girl.'

'Who would not be in her position?'

'We speak – she and I speak much of the future together. She feels my situation keenly.'

'As any warm-hearted girl would.'

'Ah yes. No doubt.'

'Valentine,' George said. 'Valentine was eighteen in February.'

So far as George could determine, Trevanion's expression did not change. He wondered if the coupling of

119

the names did not register; or if they came as a complete surprise to Major Trevanion; or if they came as no surprise to him at all. Even at the end of an evening of drinking it was impossible to tell. Trevanion was no fool. Nor, did it seem, was he willing to make any of the running.

'Valentine', George said, 'has excelled himself at Fives at Eton. He has also rowed extensively and is expecting to do well at St John's, Cambridge. His tutor spoke highly of his mathematical abilities.'

'A fine lad, I'm sure.'

'My only son.'

'You have a daughter?'

'She was twelve last December. We gave a big party for her then at my country seat of Cardew.'

Trevanion stretched his legs further towards the fire. No one can sprawl more successfully than a man with a long ancestry.

'Is your son to come into the banking world?'

'He is educated to be a gentleman. If he enters banking he will probably operate in the way de Dunstanville does, governing through his partners.'

'Cardew will go to him, I suppose?'

'I had thought to include it in the wedding portion for my daughter.'

'In which case he will lack a country seat?'

'One can be got.'

'Ah yes, well . . .' The Major looked carefully at his empty glass and it was refilled. 'If you'll pardon the question, Sir George, how old are you?'

'Almost fifty-three.'

'And I'm not yet quite thirty-two . . . You tell me you are going to remarry?'

'Shortly. Yes.'

'Is your wife – your future wife – young?'

'Quite young.'

'So you may have issue. I mean further issue.'

'Quite possibly. But that would involve a dispensation far in the future.'

'Not so sure. A woman will soon start seeking proper provision for her children.'

'There should be enough for all.'

'Oh, well. So you say. Maybe you're right . . . You know your own business best . . . I must confess I'm damned disinclined to remarry myself. Charlotte was an angel – specially in the way she put up with me – and I can see none to take her place. Of course I would accept a marriage – nay, jump at it – if that way I could see myself out of this financial mess. But what widow, a suitable woman, would bring a portion of twenty thousand?'

'Twenty is a lot of money.'

'Yes.' Major Trevanion finished his brandy again. Each glass, George noticed, who was not keeping pace, went more swiftly than the last. 'So . . .' There was a pause.

'So?' prompted his host.

'So, failing such a widow or suitable woman . . .'

'Some other solution must be looked for, if such can be found.'

'Yes . . . Well, yes. That's what I would want.'

It was coming near to the point. George waited but the other man did not speak. He was staring with slow-blinking eyes into the fire. In the end George went on.

'Such as one of your sisters marrying money?'

'Such as that, for instance. If it could be arranged.'

'It would be very difficult to arrange a match which would be suitable to her and suitable to yourself.'

'I don't see why. Caerhays is big enough for two families

if need be. Or, if it came to the point, I might in a few years be prepared to withdraw to a dower house, which would leave Cuby's husband master of the most beautiful house in Cornwall.'

'Yes ... Yes ...' George's lids drooped, to hide his satisfaction at the way things were now going; at the way, in the last resort, some of the proposition and some of its most important details were being squeezed out of Trevanion himself.

'But is it not the *most* beautiful, Warleggan, is it not? Nash, damn him, has all but ruined me; but nothing else compares to this castle he has put up: you have to admit it! Lanhydrock, perhaps. Cotehele. I doubt if either matches it for sheer elegance and beauty.'

'I would not quarrel with what you have said.'

In a further silence each digested the other's meaning.

'Well,' said Trevanion at last.

'Well,' said George.

'Yes, well ... I must say—'

'Let us wait a little,' said George. 'Let us see how circumstances develop. Valentine is as yet only about to go up to Cambridge. There is no reason at all, of course, why he should not take a wife while still studying; but I think we should look at the situation again towards the end of the year.'

Major Trevanion finished his brandy but this time did not extend his glass for more. In spite of his blurry voice and appearance, the amount of alcohol he had consumed had not really affected his judgment. He had no particular relish for the company he was in, and in happier times would not have sought it. Nor would he have entertained doing any such deal with Warleggan as now was in the air. The thought of a relationship by marriage with one of this

Warleggan family offended him, and his conscience stirred. His sister – his younger sister – was his companion and confidante. When she was very small he had been like a father to her. He had seen her grow and bloom into a very attractive young woman. Since Charlotte died everything unfairly had piled up on him, and he spoke freely to Cuby of it all. Often they walked by the sea together discussing his problems. She was already like a mother to his little boys, responding as it were, as he had, to a bereavement. Altogether she was a remarkable young woman, and as such deserved better than an arranged marriage of this nature.

But a recollection of his present debts and the accommodation bills due quelled the stirrings of doubt and conscience. Who else was available to save him from a debtors' prison? – for that was what loomed. Even an escape to Europe, which he had more than once contemplated, was not really practicable while this tyrant ruled there. Who else and what else? Even though he did not wish to marry again he would have done so – as he had just said to Warleggan – if there were available some rich widow. None such existed. Given five years he might have gone into London society, scoured the shires, offered his great house and ancient name as his side of the deal. But no one would give him five years. Only through the piecemeal support of Sir George Warleggan was he to be vouchsafed one year – or part of a year.

Of course if his filly, Honoria, won the Oaks . . . And if he had the confidence to wager heavily enough . . . Warleggan, knowing his passion, his other passion, had made it a condition of the loan . . . But would he ever know? Certainly he would know if Honoria *lost.* And all his family had been at him recently to debar himself from such gambling. His own mother. Cuby even. Cuby . . .

George – he supposed he must learn to call him that – had frowned sharply at the mention of £20,000. But he hadn't declared it impossible. That was what was needed. That would really set the family up again. Somehow, if it came to the point, this amount would have to be guaranteed – possibly paid over in full before the marriage took place. A dowry in reverse. Promises alone, understandings, verbal agreements, could never be enough. He would eventually have to make that clear. It must all be down in writing.

Perhaps Cuby would not at all be averse to the idea and the deal behind it. She seemed to feel almost as much for the property and the name as he did. And young Warleggan was a very handsome chap in a narrow-eyed way – at least as personable as that lanky, insolent, Poldark whelp – who had turned up tonight again – and certainly better mannered and better educated. No doubt it took only one generation to make a gentleman. Anyway she was not being asked to marry some gouty old drunkard.

'Do you think,' George asked, his mind just as clearly still on the same aspect of the same theme; 'do you think that if we provisionally agreed some such arrangement, Miss Cuby would willingly become a party to it?'

'Ugh – ugh. She is very sensible of my wishes. In fact I am sure she would see the wisdom of the arrangement. But your son?'

'Valentine', George said, 'has suffered the disadvantages as well as the advantages of being a rich man's son. So he has been brought up not only to expect luxury but to need it. He is a truly charming, wholly delightful boy, as you will have observed . . .' He paused.

'Yes, yes,' said Trevanion impatiently.

'Though a little wayward, as most boys are. There have been occasions in the past when our opinions have differed.

When it has not been important to me I have given way. This makes for give and take in a family. But when it has been of prime importance to me *he* has given way. *Always*. If it is a choice between obedience with luxury and disobedience without it, he has always chosen luxury.'

At this moment on the third floor the new kitchen maid was saying: 'Oh, Master Valentine! *Oh*, Master Valentine!'

Chapter Six

I

Violet Kellow said: 'So you have deserted me! That is perfectly plain.'

'Nonsense, old darling,' said Stephen, 'you know I'd never do no such thing.'

They were in Violet's bedroom at Fernmore. Stephen was sitting beside the bed, holding her hand. He had taken the opportunity of Clowance's absence in Truro to pay Violet an extra visit.

'But it is true! No wonder I am sick, ill, languishing, like a flower left out of water. Jilted! And almost at the altar. All those sweet promises you made!'

'I know, I know.' Stephen shook his head in regret.

'I have decided what I shall do,' Violet said; 'I shall die before you marry and then come to haunt you at the altar; so that when the parson says: "If any man can show just cause why these two shall not lawfully be joined," I shall shout: "I am not a man, nor even a woman any longer, but a *ghost*! ... and I can tell you *dreadful* things!" And Clowance will swoon – I hope – and you will be driven from the village – as you richly deserve.' Violet coughed: a thick deep-seated rustling cough which seemed too heavy for so frail a person.

'So long as you don't haunt me on my bridal night,' said Stephen.

'I'm almost *sorry* for that girl – even though she has

thrown herself at your head. Anyway when she marries you she'll get what she deserves!'

'You know what you deserve,' said Stephen. 'A smacking. Which you'd get if you was not so sick.'

'Touch me and I shall cry out!'

'What, for more?'

She looked at him, her fine blue eyes paler for her illness, and presently they began to fill with tears.

'Hey!' Stephen said on a different note. 'What's this? We were joking. Weren't we?'

She took her hand out of his and fished for a handkerchief. 'Oh, leave me alone! It is nothing.'

'Violet, me old dear, really – I didn't mean to offend you.'

'It's *nothing*, you fool!'

'Tell me.'

'Well, don't think I'm crying for *you*!'

'I should trust not!'

'Well, you know now.'

'Good.'

'You're just worthless, good-for-nothing, gallows-fodder, Mr Carrington.'

'Thank ee for the compliment.' He hesitated. 'Well, I must say I've not seen you like this before.'

'And won't again, I assure you.'

'What's amiss with you?'

'Pray do not be embarrassed. See, it is all over.' She dabbed her eyes and smiled. 'Forget it.'

'Trying hard,' he said.

'Now make me laugh – if you can.'

He did not try but sat picking at his fingernail, his head lowered. 'You'll be all right,' he said.

'Do you think so?'

'I'm sure so. With the warm days you'll come brave again.'

She said in a low voice: 'I don't want to die.'

'Who's ever said anything about it excepting you – and then in *jest*? Look—'

'I *do* look! And it is there, isn't it. So very, very close. D'you see, I shall never grow to be old so I don't know how I would feel then; but at least I should know I had *lived*. I could count so many days, so many years – which must somehow have brought *some* fulfilment – fulfilment we – we are born into the world to enjoy – or at least to experience. But I – so far yet I've had *nothing*.'

'Oh yes, you have, old darling, you've had a lot of fun. For instance—'

'Stop trying to *comfort* me! I can't *bear* you! I suppose *you* never think of it, do you – so strong and healthy – what it must be like to die, to be nothing, not to feel or see or think again . . .'

'Not so long ago,' said Stephen, 'less'n eighteen months gone I lay on a raft after the *Unique* was wrecked. Me and a lascar. We drifted. No food, no water, getting weaker. I thought then. I reckoned I was going to slip my wind. I prayed . . . first time for years.'

'But you had *hope*.'

'Well, and don't you? Look you, for Heaven's sake—'

'No,' she said. 'I have no hope.'

He took her hand. 'What's got into you today? It isn't like old Violet—'

'No, it isn't like old Violet, is it – who always has a bright smile and a jest. Well, just now and then I lose it. Because I see my end in my mother's face. Dr Enys tries to be cheerful; he smiles and says this and that; but I know what he has told them behind my back! Nothing has got into me today, you

128

fool, but what has been there since before Christmas – only I've *hid* it – and now I can no longer hide it. So just for a minute I'm – not such passing good company . . .'

The tears began to start again. He sat on the bed and put his hand on her cheek and pressed her head against his arm.

'There now. Have a good cry if twill help. Or curse me, if that helps more.'

'Curse you,' she said. 'Curse you, you great blundering, unfeeling, stupid male beast!'

'That's right,' he said. 'That's right.'

'And now no doubt you'll not come to see me any more.'

'Of *course* I will!'

'*She*'ll not let you!'

'Nay, she's not mean-natured like that.'

'You don't have to be mean-natured to be jealous. She's always been jealous of me, ever since last Midsummer Eve.'

'I'll tell her. I'll explain.'

'Do you love her?'

Stephen hesitated. 'If I say yes, you'll hate me more. If I say no, you'll dub me a liar. What do it matter, old darling?'

'It matters to her!'

'I promise I'll come and see you still – every Friday – till you're well again.'

'*Well* again. D'you know, Stephen, it is most strange . . . A while ago I sowed some mignonette in pots so that they should bloom outside my window. You will see them if you go into the conservatory. They are already sturdy plants. But I wonder every day what colour they will be and if I shall ever know. It is most – frustrating.'

'Now you're sorry for yourself.'

She pushed him away, instantly reacting to the challenge. 'So would you be, you clumsy oaf! Really, I'm sorry for

Clowance Poldark. She comes here to see me and sits there simple and sweet, and Lord knows what she thinks she's caught! Tis like a little girl going out with a fishing net and coming back with an octopus!'

'Now I know you're feeling better,' he said. 'I always make you fell better, don't I. Dr Carrington, they should call me.'

'Surgeon Carrington with a bloody knife, that's you! Plunging it into the hearts of innocent girls, one after the other! Go away, you irritate me beyond endurance!'

'I'll come Friday, old darling,' he said, kissing her averted face. 'I promise I'll come again Friday.'

II

Downstairs Stephen ran Paul Kellow to earth behind the parlour in the small room Dr Choake had once used as his dispensary. He was writing at a desk piled with accounts books and littered with pamphlets, bill-heads, folded maps, bills of consignment.

'Intruding?' Stephen asked.

Paul put his pen aside and swung his swivel chair. 'Pray intrude. If you gave me two pennies, which I doubt you possess, I'd gladly drop this for the rest of the day.'

'What are you about?'

'Drafting an advertisement for the *West Briton* announcing a change in our routes in West Cornwall for the summer months.'

'Expanding them?'

'Reducing them. The Cornish are too damned slow to appreciate the benefits of easy travel.'

Paul Kellow had had his twenty-first birthday last week,

an occasion which had gone unmarked, ostensibly because his sister was so ill. Paul was slim and not tall, with rather effeminate good looks, but his dark sleek hair, sallow skin and composed and confident manner would have passed him for twenty-seven or eight. When Dr Choake died, Polly, his lisping wife, had moved smartly into Truro where whist was available every afternoon, but instead of selling Fernmore she had let it to her cousin by marriage, Mr Charlie Kellow, who was associated with new coaching enterprises in Truro and Penzance. Good sense would have suggested that he and his family were better accommodated nearer the centre of their business, but it was whispered that because of the relationship and because they were chronically short of money Mrs Choake had allowed them to take Fernmore at a peppercorn rent.

Nothing they had done since they came had dispelled the impression that they were hard up. Dr Choake would have been deeply offended to see his old house so neglected, with its bare pretentions at the best of times to dignity and gentility. In his day he employed eight servants – now there were only two, one indoors and one out; and although the two girls, Violet and Daisy, were at home with their mother all day, the curtains were shabby, the furniture threadbare, the garden littered and untidy.

Such were the Kellows, cursed with a tubercular strain and a chronic shortage of money, blessed with good looks and a supreme belief in their own importance in the world.

'How did you find her?' Paul asked.

Stephen shrugged. 'Depressed. That's not common. What does Enys say?'

'He says there's a large cavity in the right lung and the left one is now affected. He thinks the next haemorrhage may kill her.'

'D'ye reckon she's come to know that?'

'Not from us, she hasn't. But then maybe she reads between the lines. It is not difficult. After all, it was the same with Dorrie – the year before we came here. Violet saw it all then.'

Paul went over to a keg of beer lying on a trestle in the corner of the small dark room. However short of some things, the Kellows were never without the essentials. He brought back two brimming mugs.

'I'll never forgive that parson.'

'What parson?'

'The one at Dorrie's funeral. Trevail. He was so drunk he damn near fell into the open grave. I wished he had, and broke his neck.'

They drank together. A bell was tinkling somewhere in the house. It was Violet ringing for their solitary maid.

Paul said: 'Well, I have to congratulate you, eh?'

'Thank you. Yes, thank you.'

'You've won yourself a fine girl there. When's the wedding?'

'Not fixed yet.'

'Twould be nice if it could be a double wedding.'

'How d'ye mean?'

'Well, Jeremy is very warm for Daisy. I think he'd take her tomorrow if she'd have him.'

'And won't she?'

Paul allowed a frown to wrinkle his smooth brow. 'You can never tell with her. She's wayward.'

'Ah,' said Stephen, disbelieving.

'I believe you're going to work for Wilf Jonas.'

'Aye.'

'When d'you begin?'

'Week after next.'

Paul finished his ale.

'Wilf's a sour puss. You won't find him conversational.'

'So I've noticed.'

'Another one?'

'Thanks.'

As he came back again Paul said: 'Still, it's a beginning, I suppose. I would have thought the Poldarks could have done better than that for you.'

'I seek no favours.'

'But still. Of course, if you're *satisfied* . . .'

'I'm marrying the girl I want – that's the main thing to be satisfied about, isn't it?'

'How's the mine going?'

'The mine?'

'Wheal Leisure.'

'Nothing of note. Tis early days. Or so I'm told.'

'I heard two old miners at the Bounders' Arms, night before last; they'd both worked in Leisure twenty years ago. They reckoned she was played out.'

'Captain Poldark doesn't think so. Nor Jeremy. Nor Ben Carter.'

'Ah . . . Ben Carter. You want to watch out for him, Stephen.'

'For what?'

'On account of his being moonstruck for Clowance. I reckon he thinks it's the worst day's work we ever did, fishing you out of the sea.'

Stephen did not reply for a while. He did not fancy Paul's manner this afternoon. The two tankards of ale Paul had just downed were clearly not the first, and it was making him cross-grained; he seemed to want to pick, to scratch, to rub things up the wrong way. But Stephen was not going to meet him at his own game. He wanted something and hoped he might be able to get it.

'Paul, would you be interested in a venture?'

'What sort of venture?'

'Something that needs an outlay.'

'What of, money?'

'Among other things.'

Paul gave a harsh laugh. 'Enlighten me about the other things.'

Stephen fished in his pocket, took out a crumpled cutting from a newspaper.

'I was reading the *West Briton* Saturday. It is a useful paper, like – you learn a lot about the county. When I come here first I thought there'd be plenty of opportunity for someone like me. Are you Cornish?'

'Yes.'

'Well, I kind of thought them a bit slow.'

'Thanks.'

'I think maybe they're not so backward where money is concerned. And yet – look at this.' He extended the piece of paper. 'Penzance lifeboat for sale.'

Paul frowned at the print. 'What is there about that?'

'Did you know they had one?'

'I can't suppose I ever thought.'

'No, well they have. They've had it for ten years. Built by public subscription. Everyone real proud of it. But it has *never* been used. Never once.'

'It doesn't say that here,' Paul observed.

'No, but it's true. Know why it has never once been used in all these years? I can make a good guess. Can't you?'

'Well, unless . . .'

'Unless the folk there better prefer the wrecks to drift ashore, eh? I'd guess that was the reason, wouldn't you.'

Paul shrugged. 'Why are they selling it?'

'To discharge a debt. It seems it sits in this shed day and night, year in year out, and the rent of the shed has mounted up and up and no one to pay it. Once the lifeboat was bought, there was no money left for aught else. So I'm told.'

'Who told you?'

'Never mind, it is the truth.'

Paul got up and thrust his hands in his pockets. 'Been to see it, have you?'

'Yes.'

'When?'

'Yesterday. I borrowed a pony from Jeremy. It was too late to get back, so I slept under a hedge.'

'Is he in this?'

'No. Not yet. It would not be much use anyway. He has spent what small money he ever had on this road vehicle you have been attempting to build in Hayle. Save for what his father gives him monthly, he has no money. He's told me so before.'

'Well, *I've* none,' said Paul. 'What have you got?'

'Ten pounds maybe. Since I came to live here the money's slipped away.'

'And what notion have you in your head?'

'I thought to buy her.'

'What, the lifeboat?'

'Yes.'

'You're witless. Whatever point—'

'Only to sell again.'

Paul stared at his friend.

'You think she'd sell again?'

'Soon enough, I think. Not maybe in Penzance.'

'At a profit? . . . What's she like?'

'She's not a vessel I'd want to keep meself, not for the purpose I'd have in mind. But she's a fine boat of her kind. Near on 30 feet long by 10 beam, and can row ten oars double banked. Stern and stern alike, and with a curved keel such as I've not seen afore. She's not been well kept; but I went over her careful. Everything essential is Bristol fashion – well, she's never even been afloat! They say she cost a hundred and fifty guineas, and I'd not disbelieve that.'

'Paul!' a voice called. 'Are you there, Paul?' It was Mrs Kellow's voice.

Paul shut the door on it.

'What would you have in mind?'

'Go down Thursday for the auction – with money in me pocket – enough to buy her if she was going cheap.'

'What makes you suppose she will?'

'No one seems *interested*. If I had forty guineas I could buy her, I'd guess. And at that price she *would* be cheap.'

Paul's eyes roved back to the desk, to the cash-box. Then he shook his head. 'I could borrow ten from the box . . . maybe twelve. There's no more in there. And my father'd be raising the roof within the week. We're skinned out, Stephen, you and I. Unless you can rob some poor old lady you'd best abandon the idea.'

III

The same evening while the two older children were still away and Isabella-Rose had retired conversationally to bed, Demelza told Ross that she was with child again.

Ross put his pipe carefully down on the mantelshelf. 'Good God!'

Demelza said: 'Yes, indeed.'

'Almighty God, I never supposed . . .'

'I don't think we can blame Him.'

Ross got up, looked at the accounts book he had been about to tackle on his desk. Priorities, perspectives had suddenly changed.

'When?'

'Oh . . . maybe November. Before Christmas anyhow.'

'Have you been feeling unwell for some time?'

'A couple of weeks. It is passing now. I shall feel brave now. I always do.'

He stared at her – this dark-eyed, witty, warmly perceptive, earthy woman who had been his loving companion for twenty-five years, a woman who, at rising forty-two, still attracted straying glances from men whenever she went into company.

'I didn't expect this!'

'The old women say it's a good thing – to have another baby at my age.'

'*Your* age! You're a mere child yet.'

'Yes, grandpa. I . . . hope the others won't mind.'

'What others?'

'Jeremy and Clowance, of course. They may think it a little inopportune. Is that the right word?'

'I'll knock their heads together if they show the least sign of thinking that. But . . . how will it affect your megrim?'

'May stop it. Should not anyway do it any *harm*. Ross, having babies is natural in a woman. It does not have any permanent effect – on their health or on their ordinary ailments.'

'I'm not so sure,' he said, thinking of all the women he had known who had died in childbirth. 'Have you told Dwight?'

'I haven't *seen* him. You are the first one to hear – of course.'

He took up his pipe and began to fill it. It was not done very expertly tonight. Every time this happened with Demelza it got worse. Each time he found he had more to lose. He had hoped it would never occur again.

'I'm very selfish,' he said. 'I think only of you.'

'That doesn't sound selfish.'

'Well it is. Because the older I get, the older we both get, the more I *depend* on you.'

'I know that, Ross. At least, I feel it so also. It operates both ways. But in what respect will this alter it?'

He hesitated. 'Not at all if it is as the others have been.'

'Well, then. That is how it shall be.'

He held his tongue, not wanting to damp her with his own fears.

Presently she said: 'I wonder what we shall call him.'

'Him?'

'Shouldn't that be? On average. We've had three girls and only one boy.'

'As God is my judge,' Ross said, 'I'll be well past seventy before the child is of age!'

'Never mind. You are not so yet. I am – delighted.'

He looked into her eyes. '*Really?*'

'Yes! Oh yes! It – puts the clock back. One is – young again!'

'How strange,' he said. 'I have never thought of you as anything but young.'

'We'll call him,' she said, 'Vennor. Or Drake. Or Francis.'

'Why not Garrick?' Ross suggested, and dodged the cushion she threw at him.

But he was not amused. There was no laughter in him at all.

IV

News was now reaching England of the fall of Badajoz. The great fortress had been taken at bitter cost. Wellington, it was said, had wept in the greyness of the early morning, knowing so many of his best officers slain. Even the great General Craufurd, commander of the Light Division, was dead. And afterwards a terrible sacking of the town which, legitimate though it was according to the bitter rules of war which decreed a garrison must surrender after the first breaches had been made or suffer the full penalty, nevertheless went far beyond all humane licence. Wine ran everywhere, doors were blown off, old men murdered, women raped and robbed. The newspapers in England were discreet but the hideous stories spread.

Was Geoffrey Charles alive? No news of individual casualties or survivors had yet come through, except for the names of the senior officers who had fallen.

Jeremy, racked and strained beyond his endurance by the encounter with Cuby, decided on his first day home to go to Hayle. Short of the engine at Wheal Leisure, which anyhow was at present working without particular problems, this challenge at the Harvey works was the only counter-irritant he knew. Paul was not available so he persuaded Ben Carter to ride with him. The mine could go hang for a solitary day.

In the last six months Jeremy's visits to Hayle had been infrequent – far less often than when he went by sea and had to employ the subterfuge of apparently going out for a day's fishing. This was not because of any loss of interest in the idea of developing a steam-powered road carriage but because he had staked his pride on producing a suitable steam engine for Wheal Leisure. His father had agreed – albeit with unspoken elements of doubt – and this had now been done. But while it was being done, both during the manufacture at Hayle and the erection of the parts on the site, there had been little time for secondary issues. Now perhaps they could be taken up again. In fact, they must be taken up again – or he must find some other preoccupation to take his mind off Cuby.

When the two young men got to Hayle they spent an hour or so going over the basic construction of the carriage. Central to it all, of course, was the Trevithick boiler, built to the design of the master himself, though for another purpose, probably for a thrashing machine like the one he had more recently designed for Sir Christopher Hawkins. It had been found, cobwebbed and dirty, in a corner of the foundry, and Jeremy had at once seized on it and finally had been able to buy it for his own purposes. It seemed to him at the time of its discovery heaven-sent; but on his more recent visits he had realized there were certain disadvantages to its use. The chief of them was that instead of its being designed to fit a proposed road carriage, the road carriage itself had to be designed to fit the boiler. This had seemed at first a minor obstacle, since the carriage they proposed to construct would only need to be lengthened by two feet to something like ten feet overall in order to accommodate the boiler. Richard Trevithick himself on several occasions had done just this sort of thing, namely used one of his engines constructed for a stationary purpose to move a carriage on wheels. At the moment a few more difficulties were emerging, chiefly to do with the fact that you cannot manipulate or alter cast iron once it has been cast. The cylinder and many other working parts would necessarily now have their situation predetermined.

Still, progress was being made. With the help of two workmen loaned by Mr Harvey, the wooden frame of the engine had been constructed and the wheels were to be made and fitted next month. Other parts were in process and would be assembled as they were required. The fourway steam cock was to be worked by a rod from the cross-head; side connecting rods were to be attached to this cross-head at the top and would activate the crank pins fixed in the driving wheels. One of these driving wheels would have a spur wheel cast with it to be driven by a gear fixed to the crankshaft.

Jeremy was not above learning from any source, and he had spread out on the bench before him drawings he had borrowed from Lord de Dunstanville, made by William Murdock, the Scottish engineer and inventor, who had been Watt's agent in Cornwall until 1799. These admittedly were of a model only; but it had been built and had *worked* as a model, and Lady de Dunstanville herself remembered seeing it in action some years before Trevithick's first engine had run. Jeremy had also copied out some designs he had found illustrating work by William Symington and James Sadler.

This was all a bit out of Ben Carter's depth, but he was

someone to talk to and Ben had a shrewd practical approach to the work that was often useful.

They were making calculations as to the size of the fly wheel when a voice said behind them:

'Well, my dears, making proper progress, are ee?'

A big shambling man, tall even by Jeremy's standards, with intent blue eyes in a gaunt but fleshy face, black hair streaked with grey that looked as if it had not seen brush or comb for a week, a blue drill shirt open at the neck, a wide leather belt holding up shabby breeches, grey woollen stockings and patched boots.

Jeremy recognized him instantly, and swallowed with shock.

'Mr Trevithick!'

'Aye. I know you, boy, don't I? Met you last in London when you was a tacker. Came a ride on my engine, you did. You and your father and your mother. Mr Jeremy Poldark, eh?'

They shook hands, Jeremy's thin sensitive hand disappearing in the bear-grip of the older man. Ben Carter was introduced.

Trevithick had aged much in six years, and he did not look well, but he talked with all the verve and vigour Jeremy so well remembered. After a few moments he turned and stared at the partly completed construction behind him.

'What're we about here, then, eh, my dears? I think I recall that boiler. A father always recognizes his child. Twas made here five or six years gone, but never have I seen him so smart and shiny. Never used yet, so far as I know. Putting him into an exhibition, are ee?'

Jeremy explained, though he was pretty certain that Trevithick knew all about it. Now the Cornish inventor was back in Camborne it was unlikely that Henry Harvey, who was his brother-in-law, had not mentioned the sale of the boiler to Jeremy and Jeremy's ambition. Indeed it was not unlikely that, Trevithick happening to turn up that day, Harvey had suggested he should go into the works and see for himself.

Embarrassed at allowing his hero to see the construction in so rudimentary a state, Jeremy stumbled over the explanation. Trevithick put one or two questions, then asked to see the draft drawing that Jeremy himself had prepared. He fumbled it in his big fingers, screwing up his eyes the better to apprehend the fineness of the sketches.

After a while he set it down on the bench and there was silence.

'Nice drawing,' said Trevithick. 'Proper sketching. Proper job.'

'Thank you,' said Jeremy.

'Wish I could do 'em as tidy as that. Me, I was never so neat. I belong to scribble and scrawl.'

'To good purpose,' said Jeremy.

'What? Oh, aye. Yes, I'd agree on that . . .'

Another silence. Trevithick thumbed his chin, which rasped for lack of a recent razor. Then he slowly shook his head.

'It won't do, Mr Poldark.'

Jeremy looked at him inquiringly but did not speak.

'It won't do,' said Trevithick.

'In what way, sir?'

'The boiler. Tis all wrong.'

'It is your own boiler, Mr Trevithick. You have just said so.'

'Oh, tis my boiler sure 'nough.'

'It is one you designed for – for thrashing, I believe. Isn't it? I thought it just the high-pressure boiler we needed. Is there something wrong with it?'

'Not *wrong*.' Trevithick rubbed his chin again. 'Not for its purpose. But for your purpose, tis too *big*, Mr Poldark, that's all.'

'I don't understand. You have often—'

'Well, I tell ee. And there's none who knows better.'

They waited. Trevithick screwed up his eyes again.

After a few moments Jeremy said: 'That one you built in Pen-y-daren in Glamorgan . . . did it? . . . Have you not said often that there is little difference betwixt a boiler you have designed for stationary work and one which moves?'

'Quite true. Quite true. In principle there's little to choose. What matters be the power you generate.'

'So is that not—'

'Wait. Wi' a moving machine that is necessary, but that be not all. Look ee at that there boiler again, boy! Regard it. Fill it with water. My Pen-y-daren engine weighted upwards of five tons. This would be more. And Pen-y-daren was on *rails*.'

Jeremy had flushed deeply. Ben Carter was staring at Trevithick as if he didn't take in what was being said.

'I'll tell ee about the Pen-y-daren engine, boy. I built it for a wager. That ye may know. Sam Homfray, the iron-master, wagered five hundred sov'reigns that I could build an engine which would haul a ten-ton load for ten miles down the Tramway. And so I did. Twould have pulled *thrice* the weight. Easy! We did it in four hours. We should have done it in half the time but the rails kept *breaking* or *spreading* under the weight. See? The weight was too great. What d'you suppose would happen to this machine ye are building on the common roads of Cornwall? Twould be bogged down every hundred yards! And the tramroad you ran on in London, the Catch-me-who-Can: d'ye know why twas abandoned? Because the rails kept breaking.'

'But . . . you succeeded in Cornwall – eleven years ago.'

'Oh yes, my son, and could again – and more so. *More* so. But who wants it? Who'll *pay* for it?'

Because he did not know what else to do, Jeremy began picking up and folding away the designs of the other engineers he had been examining.

Trevithick said: 'That's a Murdock drawing, isn't it? Good man, Murdock. Might have done a deal for steam travel but Watt would not *let* him. Dog in the manger. *Cat* in the manger, Watt is. Oh, he's an engineer, an inventor – I give ee that. Separate condenser. Clever in his way. But cautious, canny, suspicious, niggardly, *mean* . . . What has he done for the boiler? He found it a hot-water tank. He left it a hot-water tank. Or *would* have done. If he had his way twould never be anything more. Know what he said 'bout me, eh? Said I deserved hanging for introducing high-pressure steam!' Trevithick laughed. 'D'ye know he once tried to get an act passed through Parliament forbidding the use of high-pressure steam! Did ye know that?'

Jeremy listened to the clank and bang of a distant hammer.

'But you still *believe* in steam travel?'

'Bless you, my dear, of course I do! Twill come – and at not too distant a date. But wi' small boilers, ever *smaller* boilers. Higher and higher pressure. A hundred and fifty pounds! If ye are ever to produce a boiler to run an engine on the roads ye should have one no bigger than a big bass drum – such as ye might see in a military band. Why, the one I built in Coalbrookdale nine years gone – twas not dissimilar from that! Four foot diameter, cylinder seven inches with a three-foot stroke – working forty strokes per minute, needing three hundredweight of coal per four hours, and working a *miracle*. So they said, all the other engineers. They said twas *impossible* such a small boiler should work so much steam! D'ye know, twas then I first turned the exhaust steam up the chimney and found that the harder the engine worked the greater the draught up the chimney, and so through the grate, the hotter the fire would burn!'

Jeremy said miserably: 'So this boiler, you think, is no use.'

'Nay, boy, tis a handsome boiler if put to its proper purposes ... But not for providing power for a vehicle for the common roads.' Trevithick glanced at Jeremy. 'Ye could use it as a specimen, no doubt – up and down a few hundred yards? ... Twould attract some attention. Or if ye are set upon doing something, seeing as you have got so far, maybe ye could approach those infidels running the Por-treath–Poldice tramway and see if they can be persuaded out of the use of horses. The machine ye are building no doubt would work there – if the rails was strengthened.'

'Have you approached them yourself?'

'Nay, I have other fish to fry.' Trevithick took a deep breath. 'This building of Plymouth breakwater ... And the high-pressure beam engine for Dolcoath ... And the plunger pole high-pressure engine ... And I have plans for a vertical Barker's mill to drive a ship ... Then there's a cultivator to think on. And an improved thrashing machine. Nay, I can spare no time for road travel. There's no *money* to it, Mr Poldark. As for you, you're a gentleman and can afford the money to experiment. But me – not long since adjudged a bankrupt – I have better fish to fry.'

There was silence. The distant hammering had stopped.

A workman went past with an empty wheelbarrow. A sudden rainstorm lashed upon the dirty window of the foundry.

'Well, Ben,' Jeremy said. 'It seems we have been making fools of ourselves . . .'

'On the contrary, boy.' Trevithick gripped his arm as he was turning away. 'This be a new age just beginning. Doing what you've done be valuable experience. You start off 'gainst most other folk with a head start! You've a talent, I can see that – the way even in those drawings ye've foreseen obstacles and made provision for 'em like not many would do . . . Look ee . . .'

'Yes?'

'Let's see those drawings. Got ink, have ee?'

'No. There's this pencil.'

'Right. Mind if I draw on the back?'

Jeremy shook his head.

'Now look ee here.' Trevithick began to sketch in broad lines, but with the clumsiness of a child. 'This is the type of engine ye need. Like this, like this, like this. Not just a boiler wi' water but a boiler wi' *tubes*. Many tubes with the water in 'em. Many, many tubes. Like a man's intestines, see? Ye build it small, *small*, wi' endless tubes top and bottom wi' the fire box in between. Then ye put up the pressure to maybe two hundred pounds per square inch! Then ye've got nigh on *limitless* power in a small space – and *light* in weight, light in weight, see . . .'

'Yes,' Jeremy said. 'If—'

'That's the boiler of the future, boy – especially when it has to go on wheels, has to travel. There's one drawback yet . . .'

'What?'

'If I was building that now, who's to make the design sound enough, accurate enough? There's no one here –

yet. Twill *come*. But tis not the design that's lacking, tis not the *idea*; tis the execution. This be a constructive problem, boy, not an inventive one. *I* can do the inventing. Others have to carry it out . . . Maybe in London or the Midlands – precision making – like making watches and clocks. That's what we need. But we haven't got it yet. They're improving every year. Tis only a matter of time. A decade maybe. Maybe less. Then you'll have your horseless carriage, boy. And I shall ask permission to be the first to ride in it with ee!'

Chapter Seven

I

Soon after her return from Truro Clowance met Stephen at the Gatehouse. She told him about the play as they wandered hand in hand round their future house. When Dwight had occupied it he had made it a comfortable little house and had kept one servant. They looked up now at the castellated turret where the two main bedrooms were, stopped and peered in through the narrow gothic windows of the parlour. It was all decayed but superficially so. Like Trenwith, it was built of granite and even the Cornish weather could do little to hurt it.

'I'll move in in two weeks,' Stephen said. 'These here rooms are good enough, and I can work on the rest better if I'm living in. The summer is coming, and I'm not one to shrink at the first touch o' damp.'

'I'm sorry it is not better, Stephen. Not better for you.'

'I'm sorry tis not better for *you* – but as for the rest, why ten years ago this'd have looked like Windsor Castle to me!'

She squeezed his hand. 'Can you get along with Wilf?'

'He's no great talker, is he. Just nods and grunts. A miller I used to know near Dursley, he was just the same. Mebbe I shall get that way, nod at you, grunt at you when I want anything.'

'You'd better! But Wilf's *amiable* enough.'

'Amiable? I wouldn't go so far as that. No harm in him, I'm sure . . . His wife's got more to her than he has.'

'Mary? Trust you to notice. She's a great church worker. Don't know what the Odgerses would do without her. Pity they have no children.'

'Captain Poldark spoke as if this might advantage me, but Wilf's no great age at all. Doubt if he's more'n ten year older than I am. It will be long afore he is likely to have thoughts of retiring.'

'It is a beginning, Stephen.'

'Yes, it is a beginning. I believe after all I would have gone down a mine again to get you.'

'Well, you haven't had to, have you . . .'

'D'you know what I did Sunday and yesterday while you were away?'

'No?'

'Didn't Jeremy tell you I borrowed his pony? Well, I went so far as Penzance. It was a long way – for the pony – so I spent the night under a hedge. Got back only in the forenoon of yesterday. Clowance . . .'

She looked at him. 'Is something wrong?'

'*No*. Not betwixt us . . . Clowance, do you have any money of your own? Cash.'

'A little. How much do you mean? Shillings or pounds?'

'Pounds.'

'Is it for the Gatehouse? To pay for repairs?'

'No. Oh no.'

'But you want it for something?'

'How much do you have?'

'In the bank, thirty pounds. Out of the bank, six pounds five shillings.'

'Would you lend it me?'

'All of it?'

'All of it.'

'Of course.'

He stroked her hand. 'There's trust for you. How soon could you get it?'

'I could get the six pounds at once. It is under my bed. The other I would have to withdraw from the bank. I would have to go into Truro, or send someone in. When did you want it?'

'Next Monday at the latest.'

Clowance pulled at her hair. 'I believe Zacky Martin is going in on Friday for my father. He is the sort of man who would do it quietly – as a favour. Or do you not mind my father knowing?'

'I mind. You see . . .'

'What?'

'I have invested in Wheal Leisure, as you know. I bought me two shares, for forty pound. But when the engine started there was another call. They'd warned me when I first invested but I took the risk. Well, that second forty pound drained me out. Doubt if I've more'n ten pound left in the world. Now I want to borrow some, and your father'd not approve of me taking it from you.'

'Well, I'll ask Zacky. I know he'd do that for me. How would you want it?'

'Cash if possible. Some notes will do if they're Bank of England. But all guineas would be best.'

'All right,' said Clowance. 'I'll ask Zacky in the morning.'

There was a low wall beside the front gate, and he pressed her gently against it, kissed her.

'Don't you even want to know what I want it for?'

'Of course. I am dying with curiosity. But I know you will tell me in due course.'

He kissed her again. '*Wonderful* girl. I'll tell you now.'

Which he did.

II

By chance a fierce gale blew up towards the end of the week, shattering the quiet of the April weather, totally destroying Demelza's garden. It was when she stood at the window watching her flowers being maliciously beheaded one by one . . . that was the only time in her life when she was thoroughly irritable. The whole family knew and understood this and walked carefully in her presence. It was so ghastly to Demelza because the wind never stopped, not until every petal had been twisted off and was gone. Obscene stalks waving in the wind were left. It was as if the climate derided her efforts, brought things on with sunshine and mild air and then, like an evil child, in one day destroyed the lot.

A particularly bad time in Penzance, for an earlier wind from the E.S.E. had induced a number of vessels to shelter in the Road; then the wind veered to S.W. and blew a full gale, catching them on a lee shore. The few that had been lucky enough to attach themselves to the pier of the harbour were able to warp in, but the rest had to cut their cables and run upon the sand. The few who attempted to weather the gale fared no better. Among those lost was the *Gauge*, John Aldridge master, from Bideford to Deptford with timber for the navy; she ran on the August rock with five of her men drowned in full view of the spectators on the shore. The *Nimble*, with Adam Gribble as master, from Cardiff to London suffered a like fate – though with fewer casualties; as did the *United Friends*, Henry Geach master, from Swansea to Fowey, the *William Charles*, Edward Amery master, from Jersey to Swansea; the *Nancy*, Joseph Jolly master, from

Bideford to Plymouth; and the *Nettle*, Arthur Morris master, from Falmouth to Fowey. This did not take account of the vessels wrecked near by.

Nevertheless the lifeboat came under the hammer on the Wednesday, as advertised, and was knocked down to two young men, strangers to the town, for twenty guineas.

Unaware of the connection between any of these events, Ross found himself irritated by the sudden disappearance of his future son-in-law. Stephen had borrowed Will Nanfan's pony on the Monday – as a change from borrowing Jeremy's – since when nothing at all had been heard of him. Wilf Jonas, who was expecting him to start work on the following Monday at seven a.m., found himself without his assistant. Clowance told the first lie she had ever told her parents when she informed them that she didn't know where Stephen was. (But perhaps it was only a half lie, for she was not asked if she knew what he was about, and as to where he was, he might be in Penzance, which clearly was where he had been going, but that was half a week ago.)

What no one particularly noticed was that Paul Kellow had disappeared at the same time as Stephen. It was of course customary for Paul to be away from home and to be away for more than a week at a time, and the Poldarks often did not meet the Kellows for longer than that. Only Clowance, visiting Violet on her sick bed, heard her speculating as to where her rogue of a brother had disappeared to, and accordingly put two and two together.

So the mystery remained, and the first to see the two when they returned was Dwight Enys.

III

On the following Thursday, which was April 30, Caroline had been out riding all afternoon and evening, and came in fresh and glowing to find Dwight already returned and Sophie and Meliora waiting for a bedtime story.

She breezed in, kissed all three of her beloved in turn and breezed out again, resisting the heartrending cries of her young and calling over her shoulder: 'Supper in fifteen minutes, Dr Enys.'

So he shortly joined her and they ate codfish with shrimp sauce, mutton steaks with frilled oysters, a plain lemon pudding.

She said: 'You have set your face against coming tomorrow?'

'Well, Harriet doesn't really want me! At least, she doesn't *need* me. She's *your* friend, and they especially desire a quiet wedding.'

'You know I never like going to functions without you.'

'I know. But Myners will be with you . . . You must not even go at all if the weather is still bad.'

'I told her that. Miss Darcy, of course, invited me to spend two nights, but I said no. The ceremony is at noon, which means I should leave soon after nine. Be back about six.'

'It's a long day.'

'You know I like it. I was born to live half my life in the saddle.'

They ate a while in silence.

'Do you think it will be a success?' he asked.

'What, the marriage? My dear, I don't know. They are

such *opposites*. Yet I suspect that in spite of everything, she
has a slight feeling for him, which will help. She has never
said so much, but reading between the lines – or, rather,
into the pauses – I get that distinct impression. And he is
very much taken with her. You know what a really impossible
snob George is. Yet it may be more than that . . . Elizabeth
was always delicate – a lady in the best sense. Harriet, if I
may put it so, is *indelicate* – a lady in the worst sense – and
this surprises and delights him. How long it will last, of
course, I cannot tell. At least I do not feel yet to blame for
so flagrantly contriving their re-meeting here.'

'I hope it will work – if only for her sake. Perhaps a *little*
for his. It is not pleasant to see any individual, however
undeserving, so much alone as he has been since Elizabeth
died.'

The servant took their plates away.

Caroline said: 'Was the mutton not tender?'

'Darling, I ate a splendid dinner not many hours ago.
Don't fuss me as if I had just got out of that French camp.'

'You remind me of that time . . . Well, what has your day
been? I dare not comment or you will think I am still
applying Malthus to the daily doings of Sawle.'

He laughed. 'Sawle has been much as usual . . . One or
two patients, as usual, slipping away. One new patient I did
not expect.'

'Who was that?'

'Do you know the Thomases? John, the elder brother.
The younger ones are called Art and Music.'

'Is Music the one in the choir?'

'Yes. A trifle . . . simple. Though by no means a simpleton. He asked me a couple of months ago if I could help
him.'

'In what way?'

'He has not developed. The voice and the walk. Other things. It seemed to me a plain physiological defect; it happens sometimes: some malfunction of the blood or of the glands; one can never tell. Some of my colleagues would blame it on the humours.'

'What did he want?'

'To know if I could tell him why he was not normal. It is a most unusual sign, for anyone to ask. He has changed much in the last twelve months. Today I asked *him* why he had changed, and he told me why. He has a fancy for a girl.'

'Good lack!' Caroline said. 'I did not suppose him to have inclinations of that sort.'

'Nor I—'

'And who is the fortunate woman?'

'Ben's sister. Katie Carter. She is a parlourmaid at the Popes', where Music works in the stables.'

'Does she know?'

'I don't think so. Though women, if I'm not mistaken, generally do.'

'I did,' said Caroline. 'But then we were of a higher perceptive standard. I hope.'

'Well, he came to me this afternoon, asked me again. It occurred to me that sometimes – once in a hundred times – it is the mind that blocks development of the body. Something has happened to you in the past, and in return your mind will not accept change, development, responsibility. So you remain – frozen, unable to live an ordinary life. That is how it is sometimes.'

'And Music?'

'I don't know. He came today. To be on the safe side I invited Clotworthy to be present ... As far as I can tell

Music is normal. There is no evidence of atrophy or underdevelopment. Nor is there evidence ... He told me he walked that way because he had burned his feet as a child; but there was no sign of any scars or burn marks. It again suggests something in the mind.'

'So how can you help him?'

'I have given him exercises to do. For the voice. For the calf muscles.'

Caroline took a sip of illegal claret. 'You may spoil his church voice.'

'May well. And do no good otherwise. But . . .'

'Have you spoken to his brothers?'

Dwight paused, spoon over pudding. 'No. But it is a good thought. I'll try John sometime. He is the most responsible of the three.'

'Who knows?' said Caroline. 'You may make a man of him yet.'

'Well, it pleasures him to try. That he should *want* to do something to help himself is half the battle. If he sets his mind on something – as I am sure he has never done before in all his life – who knows what may be the result?'

Their manservant had coughed behind his hand. 'If you please, sur, there be two young men asking to see you, sur, just arrived at the door. Medical I think tis, sur.'

'Did they give a name?'

'Yes, sur, Mr Paul Kellow and Mr Stephen Carrington.'

'Paul!' said Caroline. 'This is strange. Shall we not ask them in for a glass of wine?'

'If it is medical,' Dwight said, rising from his chair, 'perhaps I should see them first. Will you excuse that? Then if they are so minded they can drink with us afterwards.'

Downstairs in the hall the two young men were seated

on chairs, looking fatigued. Paul had a stained bandage round his head and another round his right wrist; Stephen had a leg held stiffly in front of him.

After a few minutes mud-stained and blood-stained clothes lay on the dispensary floor.

Dwight said: 'You came all the way from Plymouth like this?'

'Not in one day,' said Paul. 'We left Plymouth yesterday and slept at Falmouth. We had to go to Penzance today to pick up our ponies, and as there is no coach on that road we had to travel by wagon; and so we have rid home this evening. It has been a sore ride.'

'Well,' said Dwight, wiping his hands. 'This musket wound of Carrington's is the most in need of attention; but the ball passed through the fleshy part of the thigh and there is only a slight inflammation. Musket balls, if they don't carry anything in with them, are usually sterile. I'll dress it and you can see how it is tomorrow. When was the wound made?'

'Monday eve,' said Stephen. 'Paul's injuries too.'

'His are not serious,' said Dwight. 'Those heavy bruises and cuts on the head will in all likelihood give you no trouble after a couple of days' rest. This sprained wrist also . . . You have been in a fight?'

Stephen laughed. 'That's what ye might call it, I reckon. I'll give Plymouth a wide berth in future.'

'Amen,' said Paul.

Dwight wrapped up a piece of bandage and put it away.

'We was up in Plymouth on business, Dr Enys,' said Stephen. 'Simple, innocent, honest, commercial business, when we meet some gentlemen who strove to persuade us to join His Majesty's navy.'

'Press gang?' said Dwight.

'Press gang. Correct in the first instance. Well, Dr Enys, that was not in my mind, nor in the mind of Mr Paul Kellow here. They said yes and we said no; and this disagreement led to a show of arms and a show of resistance. Hence these wounds we've suffered. Hence His Majesty be short of two sailors, such as he would greatly have liked. But I dare swear that certain members of the press gang are also suffering bruises and injuries as well.'

Dwight laughed. Now that they had been somewhat cleaned up, there was an air of gaiety about these young men, as if their adventure, now the danger was past, had stimulated them. That or something else.

'I'll give you a mixture of Peruvian bark,' he said. 'Take it three times a day until the wounds are healed. In the meantime, my wife would wish you to drink a glass of canary with us.'

IV

It had in fact been a desperate and bloody encounter.

Stephen had taken Paul with him, not so much for the twelve pounds he was able to 'borrow' from the cash-box as because Paul was well known in certain quarters in Penzance, and if Stephen's *bona fides* were called in question Paul could no doubt find people to vouch for him, and this might be in other ways than for the colour of his gold. When in fact, after standing for half an hour in the dusty parlour of the Union Hotel with two dozen other assorted men of varying degrees of respectability, the lifeboat had been knocked down to them, something still had to be done beyond paying for the vessel. Arrangements had to be made either for her semi-permanent storage in the harbour area

– with payment in advance – or she had to be taken elsewhere, to some more lively port where there would be a better chance of a quick re-sale.

'The weather was good,' Stephen said, telling it all later to Clowance. 'There was this lull after the gales, so I looked around. One or two likely lads were hanging about the harbour, hands in pockets, holes in breeches, chewing plug. So I say to Paul, the place to sell this vessel is Plymouth. They'll build up the deck, rig her out, and she'll be useful for all manner of work. Someone will snap her up there, I say, it's just a morning's sail for us, or a few hours' muscle if the breeze takes off. And you've friends in Plymouth too, Paul, I say, who'll know the ropes. These likely lads, they'd not be above crewing for a guinea. If there's no change in the sky by morning . . . So he says, why not? and this is what we did.'

'And you re-sold her?'

'It took near on four days – longer'n I'd expected – to find the right interest. But we did in the end. Two youngsters went with us; as it turned out we had no need to row; I paid them a guinea each and their fare home. They were full of joy. Did not stay, of course. Took wagons back to Penzance next day, so *they* came to no harm. No harm at all. Wish it'd been the same with us, but oh, well, it has worked to nobody's disadvantage as it has turned out.'

'How did you become involved with the . . .'

Stephen's face clouded, then he grunted and smiled. Fundamentally an honest man – that is, honest in his personal relationships – he had no wish to tell Clowance anything but the stark truth; yet he knew he must tell it with tact.

'I reckon I was to blame. More to blame, that is, than

Paul. When we'd been paid the money and counted it and made sure it was all there and settled up and rubbed our hands with glee, I say to Paul, avast, we'll travel home in style, let's book on one of your rivals and go home first thing in the morning. So we went round to the Royal Hotel and found the *Self-Defence* was leaving at eight a.m. for Truro, with connections to Hayle and beyond. We'll go the whole way, I say, and spend another night maybe at Penzance, I say, pick up our ponies and ride home! So Paul says, agreed. Did you know they've given up almost the same routes, him and his father and their partners?'

'What routes?'

'Those we took home.'

'Well, no, I didn't.'

'Well, it is the same except that their coaches started from Torpoint. The route hasn't paid, and Paul was watchful to see how their rival worked from Plymouth. It is Paul's view that passengers prefer to go aboard at Plymouth and cross the river on the coach; sooner that than cross for themselves and board a coach starting from the other side. That's as maybe, and it don't concern me, except that Paul wanted to spend the night at the Royal and the evening there too, talking to folk and finding out what he could. Well, you know me – or do you? I hope so, m'dear. I've never disguised from you that I do things on the impulse of the moment, like – small bit reckless – unruly, as you might say. And I was happy at the deal I'd done! So though I was content to lie at the Royal I thought the evening would be tedious and I better preferred an inn I'd heard tell of in Plymouth Dock. I thought to go and have a mug of ale, and so Paul agreed.'

'And find two girls?' Clowance suggested.

Because in fact that never had been in his mind he was able to look more shocked. 'As God's my judge! If you've no better feeling for me than that!'

'A little,' said Clowance, patting his hand, but feeling warmer, more reassured for his indignation.

'Well . . . we were there no more than an hour when the door burst open and seven or eight press men rushed in. Two officers. For a couple of minutes all was riot, but the gang had muskets and it looked a lost cause. Can you imagine how I felt?'

'Go on,' she said quietly.

But here he had to go carefully. His mind went over the memory of that scene. The low-raftered taproom, the mugs and glasses on the bar, the two sweating tapsters, a one-legged man on a stool in the corner playing his accordion, two mangy dogs that had crept in, a group of sailors from a frigate, a blind man keeping time to the sing-song with his empty mug, two drunks in a corner asleep on the sawdust; noise and smoke and heat and the untuneful voices. And then the sudden invasion, the snapping off of the song, the shouts, the quick rush round the taproom to cut off escape, the officers' voices, shouted commands; two or three scuffles, one involving Paul who shoved back at one of the press gang, protesting he was a gentleman, and got beaten over the head for it.

'Go on,' she said again.

'I never been pressed. You know that, Clowance, don't you. Though more than once I been near. I never been caught – not ever since that first time with the apples. It is not a pretty feeling to be caught. Now here was I, this night of all nights, with a bag of gold in me pocket – half of it belonging to *you*, half of it taken unnecessary and in me pocket with the rest. And . . . you waiting; that was worst of all. *You* waiting. If I gave in this time I lost all!'

He winced as he moved his leg.

'When I was aboard the *Unique* we was always fair game then. The men who sail in privateers are most often the best sailors, see. The Navy never picks up landlubbers if it boards a privateer. I tell you, we would often dread the sight of a British frigate more than we would a French. But I've never been *caught*. Now . . . Well, the inn was crowded – luckily for us. It took time to line up the men they'd captured, see what they'd got in their net. Behind me was the door out of the taproom into the parlour beyond. One sailor with a musket guarded it. You know that knife I carry?'

She stared at him, wide-eyed. 'Yes . . .'

'It doesn't need to be opened, you know, it is on a spring as it draws out of its sheath. Well, I had to give it to him . . . Paul was next me nursing his broken head, but as the sailor went down I pushed Paul ahead of me through the door. The others of the gang couldn't shoot, else they'd have hit the other men in the room. We went through that door and the room beyond like death was after us. As it was. They started shooting when we got out – I got this then; twas lucky it did not stop me running. That part of the town, by the river, is a maze of alleys. We turned and twisted, no breath left. Tis funny how you're not a coward till you start to run. Then your liver turns to water . . . It did to me, all those years ago, running from the pit. I felt as if I was running away from that coal-pit all over again . . .' Stephen shifted his position once more. 'They did not follow far – else they would have lost the rest of their haul. Somehow we found our way to a pump. I tore a piece off me shirt, stopped the bleeding, tied it; Paul was not so noticeable then as he is now – the cuts and bruises have come out – we patched ourselves up, decided to brazen it out and claim our room at the hotel. Nobody noticed. Wednesday we caught the coach. I'll confess I was relieved to see the end of Plymouth. They might well have searched and found us.'

Clowance got up, went to the window, then turned and looked at him from a greater distance. Nearness to him always distorted her judgment.

'And the sailor?'

'Which one?'

'The one you . . .'

'Oh, it was but a light jab. He was already starting to climb upon his feet before I slammed the door in their faces.'

She said: 'You should never have gone!'

'To Penzance? To Plymouth? Or to the tavern?'

'What am I to answer to that?'

'Clowance, m'love, it is in me nature to take risks. I was brought up rough – as you know. Life for me has always been – a fight. A sort of a fight. If a cat grows up wild, tis hard to tame it. Do you badly want to tame me?'

She shrugged. 'I'm not sure.'

He smiled at her, showing his broken eye tooth. But his look warmed her. There was no fight in him so far as she was concerned.

'Being pressed is always a risk a man runs who lives in a port. Especially a seaman. That I should have thought more closely about. I promise I'll think more closely next time.'

'Is there to be a next time?'

'Maybe not. Not likely, is it, when I've got so much to lose?'

'You did this time.'

'Yes. I confess it. I'm guilty. But I didn't think so far

ahead. I didn't see the risk. At least . . . all's well that ends well.'

She half smiled, not sure. 'Is it?'

'Isn't it?'

'If you say so, I suppose it is.'

He got slowly to his feet, took a bag out of the inside pocket of his loose jacket. 'Here's your money, m'love. Thirty-six pounds. When we're wed maybe I'll take your money; but till then I'll only borrow it.'

She looked at the bag but did not put out a hand. He set it down on the table with a clink that clearly gave him satisfaction.

'And best thanks to you for the loan. I sold that lifeboat for eighty pounds. What d'you think of that? Fifty-nine pounds *profit*. Hoare and Stevens cost me two guineas each; Paul twenty. Then it cost me around five pounds for food and drink and travel. That's a nett profit of around thirty pounds. And your own money back safe and sound. Now will you give me a kiss for it?'

Chapter Eight

I

George Warleggan and Harriet Carter were united in Holy matrimony at noon on the 1st May, 1812, in the church of Breage, near Helston. Sir Christopher Hawkins gave the bride away. The Reverend Richard Knava, who happened to be Vicar of Luxulyan thirty-five miles away, but held also the benefices of Breage, Germoe, Cury and Gunwalloe, performed the ceremony. He was a portly man and a second cousin of the bride, and did well out of his five livings. A wedding breakfast was held at Godolphin Hall. Harriet's aunt, Miss Darcy, had been persuaded to relax her disapproval of the marriage for long enough for the guests to be entertained and for the meal to be taken. The Duke and Duchess of Leeds, brother and sister-in-law of the bride, had not travelled from London to attend the nuptials. This would have been a sign of family affection and approval which even George could not have expected.

All the same there was a fair smattering of distant relatives who appeared to have made their home in the West Country, and they were a formidable group. All seemed excessively tall, long-nosed and arrogant. Although George was a knight and a man of power and distinction both in the county and out, they made him feel uncouth.

George, who really wished the wedding to be as quiet as possible, and who had by recent bereavement been excused the necessity of inviting his mother, had for obvious reasons made an exception for Major John Trevanion and his two sisters – also for about a half-dozen people with whom he was involved in some business deal or other and who, he knew, would be flattered to be asked. His uncle Cary had been informed of the occasion but not been invited, for the refusal would have been blunt, automatic, and probably not polite. His son Valentine, as planned, was at Eton, and he had written to him to appraise him of the event late enough to be sure that the letter would not arrive until the wedding was over. His daughter, Ursula, was better at home on this occasion, he had decided. Ursula had not taken too well to the idea of having a stepmother to rule over her. But they would all soon, no doubt, settle down together.

One guest who irritated him by being there was Lady Whitworth, with her big voice, her dewlaps, her button eyes and her powder-crusted skin. She arrogantly presumed on a tenuous relationship with them both. (Being herself a Godolphin she was of course a distant relative of Harriet's.) But since her large and bumptious son, the Revd Osborne Whitworth, had been killed when his horse bolted, she had striven to maintain this other connection, which existed only on the strength of George's first wife's cousinship with Whitworth's wife, that shy, short-sighted, high-breasted, long-legged girl who had now married into the Poldark family. The marriage between Osborne Whitworth and Morwenna Chynoweth, which George had engineered, had been a disaster from the start, and the sight of Lady Whitworth, booming and blinking and fanning herself and putting on – when she could – a proprietorial air towards him, was a constant annoyance and a reminder of the whole sordid sequence which George would have been glad to forget.

Still worse – and certainly uninvited here today – was the

solitary outcome of that miscalculated coupling: John Conan Osborne Whitworth – known as Conan after his great-uncle – a burly short-sighted pallid boy who looked as if he hardly ever saw the daylight and whose hair was so close cropped and finely growing as to resemble mouse fur. Shortly to be sixteen, he had put on an inch in height since last year and lost a couple of inches round the waist. His interest in food, however, had not abated. Had he recently been rescued from some desert island on which he had lived for years on a diet of coconuts and lugworms, he could not have been more concerned at the wedding breakfast not to be turned empty away. He gave George an uncomfortable feeling of looking at the Revd Osborne Whitworth all over again – for they now closely resembled each other – but in some ways worse, for Ossie, give him his due, had had manners and a presence. And his brain, when its attention was not turned to lust or preferment, had been a good one. He had enjoyed food and drank well, but neither to excess in a time when excess was the norm. Had he had the good fortune he constantly contrived for, he would have made a tolerable bishop.

After the breakfast two carriages were waiting for Sir George and Lady Harriet Warleggan. Followed by her maid in a phaeton with luggage and personal belongings, they would bump and lurch over the narrow rutted road to Helston and from there take the new turnpike for Truro. Five or so miles before Truro they would turn off right, over the creek and up the hill to Cardew.

There there would be no one waiting for them but little Ursula and her governess and an eager, well-drilled and well-paid staff. He meant to impress his bride, even though in the nature of her breed and upbringing she was unimpressionable. For eighteen months he had been waiting for this day. It should not pass unmarked. Great fires would be roaring in the withdrawing-room and in the dining-room. Another in the bedroom. A hundred candles would burn where a dozen were customarily used. A choice meal would be served, light and savoury, with the best French wines. Nothing should be spared. A nuptial fit for a knight bachelor preparing to mate with the sister of a duke.

All very different from his marriage to Elizabeth. But one must forget that . . .

He looked at his new bride. There was a hint of hardness in her face, an aristocratic harshness which seemed to have become more perceptible to him since he moved among so many of her tall hatchet-faced kinsmen today. Either their manner had rubbed off on her or it had alerted his perceptions to the similarity. Not that she was not handsome – quite beautiful in some lights. And *young*. By his standards very young. She had put thirty on the certificate, and he hadn't the least doubt it was the truth. *Mature* and yet still *fresh*. Ideal. They sat opposite each other in the carriage but he began to want to touch her. His possession now. No nonsense about it. He thought of moving over beside her, of stroking her cheek, her neck. Yet it was beneath his dignity to behave like an amorous boy.

'I have brought Philbert,' said Harriet.

'Who?' George stared at her. 'Oh? . . .' This was her pet, a strange horrid little beast, smaller than a squirrel, which seemed to come alive when night fell. 'Where?'

'He is with Camilla. In his box. He will not disturb us.'

George shifted uneasily. 'Can Camilla deal with him?'

'He is especially attached to me. But I'm sure he will not bother you.'

'I am none too used to having animals roam about the house.'

'Well, I'll promise not to bring Dundee further than the hall.'

George stared at her and then laughed. Or it was as near to laughter as he ever came. 'For a moment I thought you were serious.'

They jogged along. The countryside was not yet at its best. To a Londoner the trees would have seemed unnaturally late, but in the farthest west, though hedgerow flowers were well in advance of the rest of England, trees held back their leaves as if fearful of the next gale. The day had begun dull but was brightening; glimpses of the sea showed beryl blue between declivities in the low cliffs.

George began to realize he wanted this woman badly. He had so often successfully subdued his impulses over the past years that it had not occurred to him it would be different now. It was different now. She was sitting there in front of him. Belonging to him. And he knew what was to come.

She said: 'The groom will bring over Castor and Pollux tomorrow.'

He rubbed his chin. He would need shaving again before tonight. They were just about to enter the little town of Helston. From here the road would be better – far less chance of the coach overturning. The horses fell to a walk and began to pull up the cobbled main street, the coachman clucking to them and flicking his whip. Small granite houses watched them pass. A knife-grinder stood in the gutter, one foot carelessly in a trickling rivulet as he worked his machine with the other. Four ragged children fell in beside the coach, two each side, walking with hands extended. Three lads were fighting and a housewife was shouting at them. A stage coach was filling up outside the Angel. Those travelling outside were well muffled.

'What did you say?'

'When?'

'About your dogs.'

'They are coming tomorrow.'

'My house will be full when they arrive.'

'I fear they are part of the entourage. That was agreed.'

'Of course.' But not that they should roam rampant anywhere through Cardew the way they had done at Polwendron.

'After all, my dear George, think how much more agreeable it must be for you that you have to put up only with two boarhounds and a galago when instead I might have come to you trailing a half-dozen whining children such as those we have just passed.'

She was looking casually out of the window at the last cottages of the town, the chimney of a mine smoking, a train of mules, a great mountain of rubble almost spilling on to the road. The wan sunlight fell on her firm features, fine skin, brilliant jackdaw black hair. What time was it? He did not like to look at his watch but he judged it to be about six-thirty. In two hours it would be dark. They would probably arrive at Cardew about eight. Then it would be at least four hours after *that* before they had bathed, changed, supped and climbed the stairs again. Roughly, one might estimate, five hours from now! He looked at her and wondered if her legs really were rather thick, as he had long suspected. Not pale and very slim like Elizabeth's, but probably dark-skinned and over-heavy below the knee. He did not mind. She was a dusky woman and the daughter of a duke, who had this day given him the right to explore.

She raised her eyes, was surprised at what she saw, and had the grace to lower them again under his hot glance.

II

A week or so later Paul Kellow met Jeremy and asked him if he thought Captain Poldark would loan his father five hundred pounds. Jeremy was startled, and looked it.

Paul said sulkily: 'You may think it a bit steep, but after all we *are* neighbours, aren't we. My father and Captain Poldark have often met socially, and then there's *our* friendship: you and Clowance and Daisy and Violet and I. We've been together a lot these last few years. There's the work we've done together on this horseless carriage at Hayle ... And there's your special friendship with Daisy. Naturally we wouldn't ask if the situation were not serious.'

'What is wrong? Conditions of the day?'

'We have over-extended. You know how it is with innovators, men with new ideas – ordinary people are so hidebound, can't see the advantages of new things. It's a dead county anyway.'

'You mean the routes you have opened—'

'*Three* new ones in the last year. All needed. All contributing valuably to communications. But people aren't awake to what they are being offered! Perhaps in another couple of years they might become accustomed to a regular service, a coach leaving at a fixed time once a week. But the poor are used to wagons and contrive so to travel, the rich ride or hire post-chaises. By the time they have changed their habits it will be too late.' Paul laughed huskily. 'Or too late for us. No doubt second-class carriers coming along after will reap the benefit of our enterprise.'

'That's a pity. If—'

'Look at the mail coaches,' Paul said. 'Just look at them! They compete on the same main routes but they are exempt from tolls! We on the other hand have to pay dearly at every turnpike gate, which means we must charge more or run at a loss! Not enough people are willing to pay extra for day travel. It is a dire situation, I can tell you!'

'I can only ask my father. But would it not be more proper for Mr Kellow to call?'

'I thought our friendship closer and therefore would make the request justifiable.'

'Yes. Yes, I see.' Jeremy stirred the ground with his foot. He would have appreciated it more if Paul had not made it sound as if the Poldarks were in some way responsible. And it was not true that his father and Paul's father had often met socially: an occasional handshake when their visits to Sawle Church coincided; passing the time of day if they came upon each other on road or track. He happened to know that his father didn't care for Mr Kellow. On the whole he took his father's side.

Everyone was short of money, it seemed.

'You don't like my asking,' Paul said sharply.

'Of course I'll pass the message on. If anything comes of it, then I'm sure my father will want to talk it all out with yours.' He added: 'I wish Wheal Leisure were yielding better – then it would be easier.'

'Nothing yet?'

'Oh, something. It's all thoroughly cleaned and drained now but the quality of the new ground is poor.'

'Anyway, the Poldarks have done well out of Wheal Grace for years. I should not think such a sum too hard to find.'

Jeremy did not reply. They were near Sawle Church. Fernmore was close by.

'Why do you not come in?' Paul said. 'Daisy is always looking for you and you have been noticeably absent since Easter.'

He had. During the early months of the year he had kept up his light flirtation with Daisy, skating quite agreeably on thin ice. His re-meeting with Cuby had killed all that stone dead. With Daisy he now felt he could only take her into the nearest hayfield and settle for her and arrange a marriage, or keep out of her sight.

'Thanks, but I . . .' A friendly excuse escaped him. Anyway, what was there for him at home? What was there for him anywhere? 'Very well, thank you. How is Violet?'

'She coughed blood again last week but has a remarkable way of coming round. Inspect her for yourself. She will love to see you too.'

It was nearly dark before he was able to get away. His father had been out but was likely to be back by now. Jeremy wondered whether to bring up Paul's request tonight. It was an awkward thing to be asked and he was not sure that Paul and he should have been employed as go-betweens. But when creditors pressed . . .

He had often noted the shabby comfort of the Kellow home, as Stephen had observed it earlier. Both girls spent money on dressmakers and Paul was always well-clad and well-shod, but Mrs Kellow invariably looked harried and overworked. With the property only rented there would be nothing to offer as surety for loans or to sell if a crisis became too severe. And that startlingly bright invalid; what would happen to her?

His father and mother were just finishing supper and he slipped into a chair with an apology for being late, telling them where he had been. They talked in a desultory way over the meal. Clowance, it seemed, was out with Stephen

at the Tablegloses. Last Saturday's newspaper had just come
with further details of the triumph of Badajoz, but there was
still no word from Geoffrey Charles. Friction with the
United States was becoming more and more frequent as
American ships tried to run the blockade and came into
conflict with the British Navy. The paper reported an action
which had taken place in the Bay of Biscay, 'Sparring by
accident,' they called it, between an American frigate and
an English brig of war, in which thirty had been killed in
the English ship before the action broke off. The paper also
carried advertisements for American vessels which had been
captured and condemned as prizes, now up for sale together
with their cargoes.

'It is like striking sparks near gunpowder barrels,' Ross
said. 'Any moment one might blow up.'

'You mean war with America again?' Demelza said.

'There is a probability. Many US Congressmen, I'm sure,
look enviously at the open spaces of Canada and its unde-
fended frontier. Our troops out there are minimal.'

'I suppose there's nothing we can do,' Jeremy said.

'I believe we should repeal the Orders in Council and no
longer attempt to enforce the blockade so far as American
ships are concerned. In any case they don't have a large
enough merchant fleet to sway the balance of the war
decisively.'

After a silence Jeremy said: 'D'you know . . .'

They waited but he did not go on.

Demelza said: 'I hope you are not going to say what I
think you are going to say.'

Jeremy smiled wryly. 'Perhaps so.'

Ross frowned. 'Is this a game I'm not privy to?'

Jeremy said: 'I shall be twenty-one next week. Maybe it's
time.'

'I don't think it is ever time,' Demelza said.

'Well, Mama, I ask myself. The fire engine I've built is working well – there are no immediate flaws, praise be – though the mine so far has produced no results. I cannot see that I am especially *needed* here.'

Ross stared at his son and knew what they were talking about. With a shock of surprise he realized his own immediate feelings. As a matter of principle he welcomed the idea. As a matter of practical application he found he disliked it.

'I think we are coming to a crisis in the war,' he said. 'I doubt if the outcome will be influenced in any way by anything you may do now.'

'That would be a poor argument for anyone ever going to fight,' Jeremy said.

Now the words were out, but it was no better.

'Is it seeing Miss Trevanion again?' Demelza asked with less than her usual tact; but her emotions were too deeply involved for finesse.

Jeremy flushed. 'To an extent, yes. But that is not all. I did not tell you, either of you, that when I was at Harvey's last week Richard Trevithick was there. He came in unexpectedly. I think Mr Harvey had told him what I was about and he came to see what we were doing . . . He tells me that the boiler I bought is unsuitable for a road carriage.'

After a moment Ross said: 'That surely need not mean . . .' He stopped.

'It means that I have been making rather a fool of myself, Father, though Mr Trevithick was kind enough to deny it. It means, in effect, that the boiler is far too big to use in a horseless carriage on the common roads. The roads, as he points out, would not take it. The damned thing would become bogged down, or the wheels would break.'

Demelza said: 'But in a year or two the roads may be improved. After the war . . .'

'Oh yes. But when shall that be? Mr Trevithick was also kind enough to sketch for me the kind of boiler that would be needed to make such a machine practical; but he says that as yet there is not enough engineering skill to manufacture it.'

Ross cut into his pie but did not eat it. 'So?'

Demelza said: '*He* made it run on a road.'

'Yes, for a triumphant experiment, that is all. He says there can be no money in it – certainly not for years.'

'But what of rail?'

'Ah,' said Jeremy, and also began to pick at his food. 'Mr Trevithick had the same idea – perhaps by way of consolation. That, of course, was not my object in making this machine; but yesterday morning I rode over to Poldice mine to see if the venturers would be interested in a steam engine working the tramroad from their mine to Portreath harbour. They are not. They see it as impracticable, dangerous, and more expensive than horses. I pointed out the success of Mr Trevithick's tramroad experiment in Glamorgan. They pointed out that it is no longer working . . .'

They ate for a minute or two in silence. Then Ross said: 'I believe Francis de Dunstanville has a considerable interest in Poldice. I wonder . . .'

'No, Father . . .' Jeremy stopped and smiled, though there was not much humour in his face. 'I think this has to be resolved without anyone's influence – kindly though you mean it. It may very well be that the Poldice people are talking commercial good sense. What does seem to emerge is that I began this road machine with more enthusiasm for the idea than knowledge of the difficulties. Perhaps I am a little ahead of my time – though this set-back will not deter me from trying again very soon. It only seems that the very soon need not be immediately . . .'

There was another heavy silence. Demelza glanced from one to the other of her menfolk.

'In the meantime . . .?'

'Well, that is the point. This training I do with the Volunteers. Are the Volunteers not really a home for shirkers? While I could persuade myself that the things I was doing here were of sufficient importance . . . Now one has succeeded and the other failed . . . One thinks: oh, the war will be over this year, then the war will be over next year. But now, if the Americans come in . . .'

'That will scarcely affect it,' said Ross. 'If the Americans come in it will be a major mistake on their part – and on ours. But they are too far away to exert a decisive influence. The war will be won and lost in Europe.'

'Which, I think, is where I belong now.'

Demelza looked again at Ross, who was still eating, but absent-mindedly, as if he had no taste for the food.

'Jeremy,' he said, 'I think you should wait a little.'

Both Jeremy and Demelza were surprised at this.

'Why?'

'What I said is literally true. If you were to go now, I could no doubt buy you a commission in the 62nd Foot or some associated regiment. But by the time you were trained I believe the crisis will have come and gone. I think it to be very close.'

'And if it does not come?'

'Then I shall not stand in your way.'

'And you, Mama?'

Demelza's eyes brimmed unexpectedly; both men

observed them and were embarrassed at the unusual sight. She blinked the moisture impatiently away.

'That I do not know, my son. We shall have to see, shall we not, when it is nearer the time.'

'Ais, my dee-ur,' said Jeremy, trying to defuse the situation; and then: 'Well, Father, when we need that steam whim, I already possess a boiler which will suit it most admirably. That means we are almost half way with the engine.'

'May it come soon,' said Ross.

Jeremy had forgotten the other matter. 'What do you suppose Paul Kellow asked me this afternoon?'

They did not try to guess, so he told them.

Demelza said: 'Caroline told me last year they have borrowed money from Dwight too.'

'The devil they have! Did she say how much?'

'I think it was five hundred pounds. They asked for more, offering in return a part share in the business, but Dwight refused that and made a straightforward loan. It was Mrs Kellow who approached Dwight one day when he was visiting Violet.'

'Are we being offered a share in the business?' Ross asked ironically.

'It wasn't mentioned. Maybe there's not much business left to offer.'

'Kellow seems to employ his family on these distasteful jobs. Is he not man enough to come himself?'

Jeremy said: 'I told Paul if you entertained the idea that his father should have to come and see you.'

'Quite right.' Ross looked at his wife, who had now recovered from her temporary weakness. 'It's a mite difficult, isn't it.'

'Hard to say no – when we remember what it was like.'

'At least we did not borrow from friends.'

'Nor you wouldn't ever let me try neither.'

Jeremy glanced from one to the other. 'Was it as bad as that?'

'Worse,' said Ross. 'We sold some of the furniture – all the stock – your mother's brooch.'

'What, the one . . .'

'One very like it,' said Demelza.

'I don't see *that* sort of poverty,' Ross said. 'All the same I should not sleep very comfortable if those two girls – particularly Violet – were turned out. Whether it was my direct fault or not, I should feel . . . Two years ago, of course, it would have been much easier for us.'

Jeremy said: 'I bear responsibility for ever re-opening Wheal Leisure.'

'So you do,' said Ross. 'But once you'd suggested it, I couldn't get it out of my head either.'

'And the Kellows, Ross?'

'Well, I can certainly do it; though I confess it goes against the grain feeling the money may be emptied into a bottomless pit. Did Paul say what they were trying to do to save themselves?'

'Oh yes. They have cut out two unprofitable lines altogether. Two others are running once weekly instead of twice. Paul himself is to do more driving, at least as a temporary measure. They hope to dispense with six men altogether.'

'And that will make the difference?'

'They hope so. I can't say more than that. Perhaps Mr Kellow can explain.'

Mr Kellow in due course did explain. It was a rather distasteful interview. Charlie Kellow had none of his son's premature dignity. He breathed stale spirits – to which had been added fresh spirits – over Ross. (Ross had a particular aversion for the sort of person who stands too close to you while he talks and pursues you relentlessly as you edge backwards.) Mr Kellow had a splendid array of figures which were elicited to prove that stage-coaching was in its infancy in Cornwall and that Kellow, Clotworthy, Jones & Co. were the best organized, best staffed and best equipped to take advantage of the expansion when it came. All they needed was working capital, enough to sustain them through the present recession, and they would be happily launched on a long and successful career.

Ross felt there was a sizeable element of truth in all this, in the sense that if this damned and interminable war ever ended there was bound to be a large extension of the turnpike road system in the West Country, and with it an expansion of coach, carriage and wagon traffic. What he was not sure about was whether this half ingratiating, half resentful, red-nosed, pot-bellied, shabby man was the one he could personally have picked to take advantage of it. But there it was. This man, chiefly because their respective sons and daughters were friendly, was the man he was being asked to help. Indeed this man, if the dice had fallen differently, might have become Jeremy's father-in-law. Might *still*, he supposed! Was it a total impossibility even now?

He offered Mr Kellow a loan of £500 for two years interest free. It represented something like three weeks less for Wheal Grace to work if the decision was finally taken to close her down.

Mr Kellow accepted the loan with no sign of hesitation, though with a certain dignity of manner that hitherto had been lacking. Ross also suspected there was a gleam of regret in his eyes because he was thinking that as the request had been met in full he should initially have asked for more.

III

On May 11 Jeremy received a short note from Valentine, writing from Eton. 'I have just heard from Geoffrey Charles, a note writ with his left hand. He has asked me to let you know he is alive and recovering. He was wounded thrice at Badajoz but is hoping to rejoin his regiment in a matter of weeks. His right arm was pierced and he says he was lucky to retain it, but at present it makes writing tedious so he asks to be excused. He sends his most faithful love to you all ...'

IV

About five o'clock that afternoon when entering the lobby of the House of Commons to make a speech on the industrial unrest in the North, Mr Spencer Perceval, barrister-at-law, Prime Minister of Great Britain, was shot dead by a man called Bellingham, a Liverpool broker who had been ruined by the recession.

Chapter Nine

I

The Bounders' Arms was a small inn not far from Sawle Church on the lane leading to Fernmore, where the Kellows lived. In the 'seventies and 'eighties of last century, under old Joe Tresidder, brother of the Jonathan Tresidder who had once been chief shareholder in Wheal Radiant, the inn had done good business and been a popular meeting place for miners. But the closing of Grambler Mine in November '88 had been a mortal blow from which it had never recovered. The proliferation of casual ale-houses and kid- dleys, where much smuggled liquor was drunk, had made matters worse, and when Joe died there was no one to carry on. So the old tavern had lapsed. For a while it had been occupied by two prolific but unstable families called Hoskin and Bartle. (The best of the last had worked at Trenwith for a time.) Then epidemics and poverty had carried them all off either to churchyards or to poorhouses and the place had remained in the possession of a cousin of the Tresid- ders. She had recently sold it to Ned and Emma Hartnell, who had opened it again as an inn and were hoping to live there with their two children and to attract enough custom to make ends meet.

In the last few months it had done well. There was an opening for the slightly superior drinking place, and the Bounders' Arms, though very shabby, was big enough to offer two private rooms where the better-off could drink and talk in privacy and a degree of comfort. This was what had first attracted Jeremy Poldark, Stephen Carrington and Paul Kellow, and they met there now and again.

Jeremy had complained angrily to Stephen about being omitted from his scheme to buy the Penzance lifeboat. Stephen had said: 'Don't you see I am already depending on the Poldarks enough? ... Because I'm to be your brother-in-law I could not ask for your help just as if you already were that. Could I now? Don't you see?'

'No, I don't.'

The loan Clowance had made him was still a secret between them. 'In any case, could ye have been so long absent from your home and from your mine?'

'The mine could well dispense with my attentions. I believe now that my cousin Valentine Warleggan has the right idea when he supposes that his father never sells anything of value . . .'

'Well, maybe another time we could do something together.'

'Will there be another time?'

'There's always things turning up – believe me. It's a matter of keeping your eyes open, being ready to take a chance.'

Jeremy looked at his watch. 'Paul is late. D'you think he's coming?'

'I haven't seen him for a week. He's been away.'

'I know. Stephen, I've been seriously thinking . . .'

'Of what? Some other way of making money?'

'Of taking a part in the war. I'm twenty-one. My father went when he was eighteen. His father bought him a commission as Ensign in the Duke of Edinburgh's Wiltshire Regiment—'

'Why?'

'Why? . . . Why did he go? I think he was in trouble on some smuggling charge and—'

'Ah! That is interesting. He was not above breaking the law when he was young.'

'*Everyone* breaks that law, Stephen . . . We have just had news of Geoffrey Charles – that's my cousin who owns Trenwith. He has been wounded three times at Badajoz; and here I stay making ill use of my time.'

'Do you want my opinion, Jeremy?'

'If you want to give it.'

'I think you'd be crazed.'

'Maybe.'

Mrs Hartnell came into the private room with two tankards of ale. She was a tall handsome youngish woman with brilliant black eyes and fine dark gypsy-like hair. She was twenty years younger than her husband who, until he inherited a little money from an aunt, had been head footman at Tehidy. The young men liked her because she was always gay and cheerful of manner and would chat to them, leaning with a forearm against the door-jamb, or exit discreetly if she felt they wanted to be alone. Jeremy reflected whimsically sometimes that, but for a quirk of fate, she might have become his aunt.

When she had gone Stephen said: 'Fighting on land is a loon's game. Even if you don't get cut apart by a cannon ball or lose an arm or leg, you end up with *nothing*, no money, no reward, scarcely a thank-you. You see 'em stumping around everywhere, raddled, ruined men with nothing to show for all their hero's talk. If you were to fight at all – which I wouldn't advise – the Navy would at least give you an outside chance of prize money. Mind, fighting at sea is maybe bloodiest of all; but there's the chance you'd not be penniless at the end. All the same . . .'

'What were you going to say?'

'If you have to go to the war, why not in a privateer?'

'That's not going to war in the right sense.'

'Well, I tell you you've just as much of a chance of fighting the French as you'll find in Wellington's army; but there's some money to it.'

'I think there's something more to this than money. Anyway, I have none to invest.'

Stephen said: 'Only last month the *Percuil*, a privateer out of Falmouth, recaptured a rich silk ship from Valencia that a French privateer was taking in to Cherbourg. A sharp fight and she was theirs – they brought her in to Falmouth. They say the value is eighteen thousand. Think of the prize money on that!'

'I've no idea what it would be.'

'Well, three thousand at the very least. Maybe twice that if they played their cards proper.'

'I have no *money*,' said Jeremy again.

'None at all?'

'After Trafalgar, to celebrate the victory, my father gave fifty pounds each to Clowance and myself to do with as we wished. I kept my little nest-egg in the bank in Truro, having no need for it, since we were given everything we wanted and generous pocket money as well. But last year, by arrangement with Harvey's, I bought a Trevithick boiler from them and other parts – at half price because they were building the Wheal Leisure engine. Most of the fifty pounds went then . . . But that has now all come to nothing. I could as well have thrown the money in the sea.'

Stephen raised his eyebrows at the bitterness of Jeremy's tone. 'You have your shares in Wheal Leisure – like me.'

'Yes, my father gave me them, for what they are worth: in any event I could not attempt to realize on them.'

Stephen said: 'I think maybe *I* should've kept me money for investing in things I understood. But at the time I was thinking too much of Clowance, thinking maybe of standing well in your family's favour.'

Paul came in. The bruises on his face were now mere discolorations; if his cut head was sore he gave no indication of it; though he looked worried and self-important. He carried in a tankard of ale he had already bought at the counter. He had a newspaper under his arm.

'Have you seen this?' He spread out the newspaper on the table. Without elaborating he proceeded to read it out: '"Bitter fight in Plymouth Dock. Naval rating stabbed to death in struggle. Armed Pressmen from HMS *Arethusa* entered the Ring o' Bells Inn, Plymouth Dock, last Monday Eve, looking to press recruits for His Majesty's Navy. Although a number of likely seamen were collected, some put up a sturdy resistance, and in the struggle which ensued one of the press gang, Seaman William Morrison, aged twenty-six, received knife wounds in his abdomen from which he has since died. The miscreants escaped, and those enlisted for the Navy have not been charged."'

Stephen read it through a second time. 'Well, well, a surprising likeness to our little affair. And the same inn!'

'It *was* our affair,' said Paul.

'Stuff and nonsense! All that happened two weeks ago.'

'This paper is a week old.'

Stephen picked up the paper and looked at it, as if suspecting it a forgery. Then he took a long drink of his ale.

'I never used my knife enough to cause nobody a fatal injury. This is altogether another affray.'

Paul looked expressively at Jeremy. His face was rather grey.

'Funny,' added Stephen softly. 'I always read the newspapers. They're worth the sixpence ha'penny just for the local news. Funny I never saw that.'

'It will not be funny if they ever trace us,' said Paul. 'There were people a-plenty in that tavern took a fair view of us before the pressgang came in. You remember, you were leading the singing. That shanty – how does it go? "A leaky ship with her anchor down, Her anchor down, her anchor down! A leaky ship with her anchor down, Hurrah, me boys, Hurrah!"'

'Ah, well,' said Stephen, ruffling through his hair, 'if it be truth, which I doubt – they exaggerate these things to sell the paper – if it be true, then we are a long way from Plymouth Dock; and maybe for the next few months we should stay a long way from Plymouth Dock, just to be on the safe side. I suspect he died of something else, this sailor, and they put it down to a pinprick in the belly. There's no accounting for how cunning these Navy folk can be. Trying to make out . . . But even suppose . . . Well, just suppose . . . What would you have had me do, Paul?'

The question was suddenly as hard as a bullet.

'What?' said Paul.

'What would you have had me *do*, eh? Give at the knees like a seasick calf? Would you better prefer it if you was afloat now in some naval frigate with a cat o' nine tails as the only yea or nay? Would you? Just tell me that.'

'No,' said Paul sulkily, withdrawing from what had been an accusation. 'It was the only thing to do – what you did. But I thought to warn you to keep quiet about this venture. The fewer know of it, the less the risk. The news spreads, you know. Many people have seen you limping about, and me with my bandaged head. We've made little effort so far to keep it quiet. Escaping from the press gang is like escaping the preventive men – something to brag of. But not when you kill an able seaman of the British Navy.'

In the silence they could hear noisy drinkers in the main bar joking with Mrs Hartnell. Jeremy put his forefinger on the table and rubbed over the damp circle where his mug had been.

'Since I'm not in this – though wishing until five minutes ago that I had been – I'd say you were nearly half safe. This paper's more than a week old. No one round here seems to have noticed the connection. I don't suppose you ever mentioned the Ring o' Bells to anyone, did you? No, well, the chances are no one else will think of it. Paul is right, though: say no more now to anyone.'

Stephen grunted. 'I gave the man the merest dig with the point. If it is true, his guts must have been ready to spill. But I still believe it be half invention.'

They sat for a while, sipping their drinks, chatting about other things, though with the memory of the newspaper item lying between them, just as if the paper had not been crumpled up and thrust back into Paul's pocket.

Paul said: 'How is the milling, Miller?'

'Well enough.'

'I don't see flour in your hair yet.'

'Soap and water's cheap.'

'You were due to start that Monday.'

'I was.'

'Wilf would not be pleased.'

'Nor was he. Said I'd be paid only half a week for half a week's work.'

'What did you say?'

'Said I'd never expected more.'

'All the same,' said Paul, 'you won't be free to take time

off whenever you fancy, not from now on. Not even when you become Captain Poldark's son-in-law.'

'I'll take no favour that I can't pay for.'

Paul had a waspish side to his nature. It was seldom allowed to show in his dealings with Jeremy, but quite often where Stephen was concerned. Though Paul had never really made up to Clowance, he would have liked the prestige he now saw coming to Stephen. This gibing was a form of jealousy perhaps, or it could derive simply from anxiety about the dead sailor. However much Stephen might have saved the day by his ruthless act, the consequences would be obvious if they were ever traced.

After a while Stephen pulled the bell to summon Mrs Hartnell.

Paul said: 'One thing that night in Plymouth I did see. Though it is useless knowledge, or knowledge that cannot be taken advantage of.'

'Share it with me,' said Jeremy, 'since I'm party to most of your secrets.'

'Oh, it is not at all a secret. It is in the line of observing, what I observed that night and on the following day. With my head and cheek split open and my wrist sprained I was not in the best condition for sleep. No doubt the Miller fared better.'

'I doused meself wi' brandy,' said Stephen. 'When you have a flesh wound it is better to be in a drunken stupor than to stay feeling pain all night.'

'You snored, I know that. God, how you snored! Well, I finished your bottle and still did not sleep. You see, I never was a pirate, used to thrusting with his cutlass . . .'

'Hold your gab,' said Stephen.

'. . . and even then I felt more than a little miscomfortable about the prospect of pursuit. So when dawn came I got up and sat in a chair by the window. This looked out of the back on to the yard, where the coach was stationed that we were to join at eight. There were three coaches there, but I knew the *Self-Defence* we'd booked on by its gold trim. At seven the ostlers were out seeing to the horses. At seven thirty the messengers came carrying two steel boxes. These were put into the safe box under the guard's seat and padlocked in. After they'd got their receipt the messengers left and the coach was harnessed and driven round to the front door of the hotel for the passengers to begin boarding.'

Jeremy said: 'What is especial about that?'

Paul grunted. 'Well, that's all it is, really.'

Emma Hartnell came in.

'Like to wet the other eye, would ee? Come 'long, Mr Poldark, not keeping up wi' your friends, eh?'

Jeremy drained his mug. 'There we are. That satisfactory?'

She laughed and went out, the three glasses clinking.

'What do you suppose was in the boxes?' Stephen asked.

'Money, of course.'

'Why of course?'

'The shape and size of 'em. The way they were carried. And they were both marked *Devon & Cornwall Bank.*'

'Did you see how far they came?'

'Truro.'

'You never spoke of it at the time.'

'Most of the journey I conjected that my head was about to lift off. It is only since I have been thinking back on it . . .'

'What for?' Jeremy asked ironically. 'Going to turn highwayman?'

Paul shrugged. 'Of course . . . No, I was just surprised, that's all, thinking of all that money – and not in a mail coach either.'

'Why was it not being sent by mail coach?' Stephen asked.

'That puzzled me at first. One of the two men who met the coach at Pearce's Hotel I know by sight. I've seen him in Warleggan's Bank. He's called Blencowe.'

'Well,' said Jeremy. 'Warleggan's Bank and the Devon & Cornwall Bank are now in partnership. It was in the paper last year. I expect now and then they send money back and forth. Though why by that coach . . . I mean why by the *Self-Defence* . . .'

'Ah,' said Paul, 'that is not so hard to explain. Warleggan's have put money into it. Didn't you know? Into the company, I mean. The *Self-Defence* and three other coaches were started a couple of years ago by Fagg, Whitmarsh, Fromont, Weakley & Co., but last November they ran into difficulties when the recession grew worse, and Warleggan's bailed them out. So all the Warleggans are doing is patronizing their own firm.'

'Well, I don't see much edge to your story,' said Stephen. 'Mail coach or private firm, there's surely little risk. Is that what you're thinking about, the risk? This is a law-abiding county, ain't it? Highwaymen keep to the prosperous lanes. And there were three men aboard: two coachmen and an armed guard! A light post coach no doubt travels faster than the mail coach – and by day at that.'

'All the same,' Paul said, 'to Hell with the Warleggans. It is since they breathed money into the concern that it has been undercutting us. You know the results. Or you do, Jeremy, for not long ago I told you of them. That line, that service, we abandoned in February.'

Emma came back, carrying the three glasses on a tray. The noise in the taproom had died down, and she looked as if she might be willing to stand and gossip; but seeing the preoccupation on the faces of the three young men she put the glasses down, winked cheerfully at Jeremy and went out again.

There was a pause while all of them drank deeply, and when conversation resumed it was about local matters.

But presently, almost absently, Stephen said: 'Any idea how much cash there might be in the boxes?'

'On the coach, you mean? Oh ... some of it would probably be paper. As for the rest, it depends whether it was silver or gold, doesn't it. But the size of the boxes and the way the men were carrying them ... It must have been an amount. One thousand, two thousand, who knows?'

Stephen whistled. 'Phew...'

'It's no good, Stephen,' Jeremy said with bitter amusement. 'Don't forget you're marrying into a respectable family. You can't do any of this privateering on land, you know. Else you might find yourself accidentally swinging from a tree.'

'A risk he already runs,' Paul pointed out.

'And you. And *you*,' said Stephen. 'I have read somewhere that it is the law that if one man commits a crime in the company of another, the other is held equal in blame.' He turned to Jeremy. 'You may have your jest, Rat's bane. All the same, if there was a way, I do not think I should turn it down out of a sense o' piety. Would you? *Would* you, now. We could all do with money. You've told me yourself—'

'I know what I've told you,' said Jeremy sharply, for he had not said anything to Paul about Cuby, lest he spread it to his sister.

'Well, then.'

'Well, then,' mocked Jeremy. 'I could do with money. But not on those terms.'

'Nay,' said Stephen. 'You're right. Not on those terms.'

'What terms?' asked Paul. 'D'you mean moral terms? Would you argue that taking money from a bank is as wicked as robbing widows and orphans?'

They both looked at him.

'No,' said Jeremy eventually. 'There may be many degrees of wrongdoing. But it doesn't make any of 'em right.'

The conversation from being barely more than casual had shifted its ground. More responsible than anything said was Paul's dark face.

'You'd do something if you *could*?' Jeremy asked incredulously. 'Is that it, Paul? D'you mean it?'

'I don't *know*. Maybe. There's so much injustice in the world, inequality. Money is always in the wrong hands. Fortunately the opportunity does not arise. At least I suppose it is fortunate. I cannot pretend I would not be tempted.'

'Oh, so would I,' said Stephen. 'Two thousand pounds! For half that I could buy a privateer, equip her, crew her. There's so much to be picked up off the French coast. I know.'

Jeremy said: 'This whole discussion is witless ... Let's drink to some practical idea.'

'Amen,' said Stephen, leaning back with a sigh. 'You can set your mind at rest so far as one thing goes, Jeremy. I'll not turn highwayman. I might have done to gain Clowance. But that's all gained. I made a little money this month legitimate. There's naught illegal about buying and selling. I'm sorry about the pressgang, but who was to know that that would happen? Anything legitimate I'll be glad to try . . .'

Paul took a long draught of his ale. 'Damme, one can't help wondering, though.'

'What?'

'Of course I agree with Stephen. No black masks for me. But ideas, once they've started, they won't leave you alone.'

'What ideas?'

'I know coachmen. I've been dealing with them for years. I know how they like their liquor. Some of 'em can hardly sit their seats by the time the journey is half done. I can't help wondering, just wondering if the coachmen and the guard of the *Self-Defence* ever get down together – at Torpoint, or at Liskeard, or at St Austell. If they ever go in to the inn together. And if so, who guards the coach.'

BOOK TWO

Chapter One

I

Ross left for London on May 23. George Canning had written:

This has been a great tragedy. As you know, Perceval and I have for some time been estranged and I confess to have had bitter disagreements with his policy; but in truth he was a man with whom one could *not* be at variance *personally*; and our rivalry has been a rivalry of Circumstances which neither of us could command – certainly not one of choice, still less of enmity. His greatness lay perhaps not in his breadth of Mind but in his shining Integrity; and I doubt if any other politician of our generation would have been so sincerely mourned. Not one of the speakers, and I was among them, could give a dry utterance to our sentiments in the House the following day.

As you may by now have heard, the grief of his colleagues has not been matched in the North. The starving Mobs everywhere have rejoiced at his death, blaming him for all the bitter Privations they have been suffering, and his Assassin is exalted as a hero. The drums and revolutionary flags have been out, and only a strong show of troops and militia can hope to prevent a general Rising.

In the same month, ignoring the advice of Cambacérès and Talleyrand that he should not fight Russia while 'the Spanish Ulcer' was still festering, Napoleon Buonaparte turned his back on the smaller and unimportant problems provided by Wellington, and travelled to Dresden where, with Marie Louise, he held court and obtained the submission of the various kings and princes of Europe. Then with 600,000 men, he marched on Russia. Four weeks later, when he was approaching the River Niemen, the United States declared war on England, not knowing that the British Government had just revoked the Orders-in-Council which provoked the war. After a pause to regroup, the French crossed the Niemen, and four days after that occupied Vilna, from which the Russians had already fled. How much further would they go?

Meanwhile the delicate *contre-danse* in the English House of Commons was taking its course with due ceremony and total lack of urgency. The acting Prime Minister, Lord Liverpool, had got nowhere with all his days of negotiation and consultation, so after a defeat in the House he resigned, whereupon the Prince Regent sent for Lord Wellesley. Wellington's elder brother had had the idea of inviting some of the simmering and disgruntled Whigs to join him in another 'Government of all the Talents', but since they were of the view that all the talents reposed in their own ranks and anyhow now thoroughly distrusted any administration which did not give them authority over the Prince, they refused. Then Lord Moira had a shot, with equal lack of success; though for a few brief days it looked as if he would succeed not only in forming a government but in offering Canning a position in it that he considered worthy of his gifts.

But at the last all was frustration and failure again; and

in weakly desperation the Regent invited Lord Liverpool back to try once more. The Lords Grey and Granville and other leading Whigs suspected this was not desperation at all but part of a wickedly calculated manoeuvre of the Prince's to get what he had really wanted all the time – a continuation of Perceval's ailing and ramshackle administration which would contrive to dodge the Catholic question and yet pursue the war with some show of vigour.

In the middle of all this consultation and hedging and backing Ross found himself more and more uncomfortable yet more and more involved.

It seems, love [he wrote to Demelza], I must always be making an excuse not to return; yet it is no excuse, for I truthfully feel I cannot desert George at this juncture. Now that he has failed to accept Liverpool's offer he justifies his refusal, in private, so endlessly that I perceive he is already regretting it. Much as I regard him, I confess an impatience with him now. Even the Prince Regent, who once so much disliked him, appealed to him to sink his differences with Castlereagh and others and accept Liverpool's offer – but all to no avail.

Well . . . however long-winded, this is my Swan Song. I do not believe an Election can be long delayed when Parliament reassembles, and after that the great and the good George will see less of me, I swear, than the rich and wicked George spinning his webs in Cornwall.

I have seen the Prince a half-dozen times, and he is always very courteous to me, though I fear the one time we met last year I was not as courteous as I should have been to him. They say that after the accident to his Ankle while dancing he has had to take 250 drops of laudanum a day, and also hemlock, just to get three hours sleep!

I received Jeremy's letter last week reporting a failure to find any Quality Ore in Wheal Leisure. You must tell him – or leave him read this letter – that it is very Early Days as yet. I have known one mine near East Pool where the Venturers prospected for two years before they struck profitable ground. Of course we could not sustain that – and sometimes now I wonder whether my decision was wise to keep the majority of shares in the two families; it bears heavy, but you know my reason.

Time is racing on, and I have already been away too long. I hope Jeremy behaves in a sensible way in all things; and take care also, please, for yourself and your Third Man. I do not as you know wear my heart on my sleeve in family matters, and no doubt Compliments and Love Tokens from me have fallen upon you as thick as snowflakes in a hot summer; but all the same I charge you to be circumspect in all things regarding your general health and safety. Preferably do not climb trees – even little ones; do not attempt to carry the spinet under your arm; nor argue with the cows; nor fall off your horse; nor leap up the stairs more than four at a time. All these things are *Inadvisable*.

In due course I shall be with you. Until then I subscribe myself your Ever Faithful if Frequently Absent, Husband.

II

On a Thursday in July, Stephen, parting from Clowance as the short darkness began to fall, said he would see her on Saturday as usual. He had taken to riding, and on these long summer evenings there was nothing they enjoyed more than galloping across the beach to the Dark Cliffs and back. This could be at some tides a hazardous undertaking, and twice recently they had had to dismount and lead their horses up across the sandhills and past Mingoose before they reached home.

'What of tomorrow?' Clowance said, gently stroking Nero's sweaty neck.

'Dearest, ye know we never meet on Fridays.'

'Tomorrow the tide will be just right. We can walk through it as it recedes and have a glorious gallop back.'

'Yes. Yes, I imagine. But twill be little different on Saturday.'

'We shall have to wait then for the tide to go.'

'. . . We could leave an hour later.'

She said: 'Are you going to see Violet?'

Stephen's horse rattled its bridle and snorted. He said: 'Yes.'

'Why do you not miss it for a week?'

'She is mortal sick, Clowance.'

'I know. But she has been sick a long time. This Friday arrangement is claiming something she has no real right to. Go Sunday morning.'

'She will be expecting me tomorrow.'

'And that is more important than meeting me?'

'*No.* Of course not. But it has become a sort of – of a pact.'

'Do you think she has a right to any sort of pact?'

'Of a certainty not. But it is just that I have – promised – every Friday.'

Clowance sat her horse, fair hair blowing in the inevitable breeze.

'Then I will come with you.'

There was another silence. Stephen said: 'Dear heart, you should know what I feel about you. If you don't, I have been sadly lacking in conveying me feelings. But when I go see Violet Kellow it is – something different. Of course I don't *love* her. But it has been a sort of pretence – make believe – that I do. It is – a joke. She don't even believe it herself. But she pretends to believe it – just like I do. So we meet Fridays. I sit for an hour or so talking, holding her hand, cheering her up. She's a dear soul – in a brittle way. Soon she's going to break . . .'

Clowance said: 'So you will not allow me even to come with you – so that you can protest your undying devotion. I would clearly be in the way.'

Stephen hesitated. 'Yes, me dear, you would,' he said at length.

As she was about to turn her horse he caught at the bridle. 'Clowance, show a mite of sense! Ye're too big a person to feel that way! Violet is mortal sick. It is not as if I was carrying on wi' some village girl, Beth Nanfan or the like. Even—'

'How do I know you're not?'

He stared at her. 'You trying to pick a fight with me, dear heart?'

'No, but I would like to see this straight. I would like—'

'No matter what ye'd like, ye'll never see it straight if you've no trust in me at all!'

'Well, there are still rumours enough.'

'Such as what, do you suppose?'

'You go to the kiddleys – especially Sally Chill-Off's. You go to the Nanfans'. It seems to me you go anywhere there's a chance of a village girl.'

She tried to get her bridle free but he held it very firm. Nero rolled his eyes and snorted and was not happy with this restraint from outside. Stephen's horse was also trying to back away.

Stephen said: 'Listen to me: I don't go back on friends, whoever they may be! Nanfans was very kind to me while I lived with 'em, and still are. Beth's a nice pretty girl and I like her. But so do I like Will and Char, her father and mother. D'you think they'd be friends along of me if I was carrying on with their daughter while being promised to you? And as for Sally's . . . there's folk in there I've come to know over this last year or so – including old Tholly, who's a rogue if ever there was one; but he was a friend of your *grandfather*'s! Never stops talking of the Old Cap'n, as he calls him. Regular devil he must've been.'

Nero, either prompted or on his own initiative, tossed up his head and nearly unseated Stephen, who lost his hold. But Clowance could see his face in the half dark.

'Specially with women,' he said. 'Your grandfather was a devil with women, according to old Tholly. No woman was safe, Tholly said. There was so many wronged husbands, it's a blamed wonder old Joshua ever died in his bed. That's what Tholly says.'

Clowance's temper flared. 'I don't know what Tholly says and I don't care! If my grandfather was a devil with women and you seem so much to admire him, perhaps you had better go follow his example!'

She dug her heels into Nero and galloped through the gate towards the stables. Stephen began to follow her, and called her name but she would not look back. As Matthew Mark Martin came running out to help her dismount Stephen cursed under his breath and turned his horse away. He began to make his way up the track past Mellin Cottages to his lonely home at the Gatehouse.

III

When he reached Fernmore the following evening he wondered if this weekly visit was really worth a row with Clowance. Yet he was angry and resentful towards her for what he saw as her arrogance, and his resentment was the greater for still feeling, in spite of the engagement, a niggling sense of inferiority which was an insult to his manhood. All the same, were the Kellows *that* important to him? Daisy anyway was in Truro today visiting her aunt, Mrs Choake; Paul was in Falmouth with his father; and Mrs Kellow only waited to see him upstairs before asking if Stephen would 'see to' Violet for a few minutes while she called on Mrs Odgers, the parson's wife. Although no one could be more devoted to Violet than her mother, she clearly saw Stephen as a regular and reliable visitor whose arrival was a chance for taking a welcome break.

However, Violet was the main object of his call. He went up the stairs, and Violet was looking better. Last week she had looked sick to death, but she was lively today, better coloured, and the sore on her mouth had disappeared. It crossed Stephen's mind that perhaps Clowance was not altogether mistaken in supposing that Violet had been – and by implication would be – sick a long time.

Yet once they got talking together he perceived that Violet's cheerfulness was surface-rooted.

It began with the usual banter. 'Stephen, my pet, we are alone at last! You have come to claim your rights as a bridegroom!'

'That's for sure, old darling.' He kissed her. 'I told your mother not to come back for two hours. That should be long enough, shouldn't it? Shall I draw the curtains?'

'Please.'

He laughed and held her hand. 'You look five times the girl you was last week. Been taking your turnip broth regular? Before I know where I am we shall be walking the beach together!'

She shook her head. 'You know that could never happen now. You've sold your soul to another. However much Miss Clowance may see fit to allow you to call here, she would not take kindly to any beach promenading. Nor would I in her shoes . . . But she has small need to worry. I'll never see the beach again.'

'Oh, now, come now—'

'Oh, now, come now,' she mocked. 'It is easy for you to sympathize, for you care little or nothing for me.'

'But I do, I care the greatest of a lot. Otherwise, I would not—'

'The greatest of a lot,' she said. 'What does that mean? The greatest of a lot. Where do you find these phrases? They sound more suitable to an effete drawing-room than what might be bandied about among pirates roving the seas with cutlasses and the like.'

'Privateers,' he corrected. 'You would learn to know the difference if you was ever captured by one or the other.

And I've never used a cutlass yet – though I'm often tempted to when I come to see you.'

So it went on, harmless, lightly insulting banter mixed with half-serious, half-cynical declarations of affection. It was a form of conversation Violet had excelled in even when well, and these meetings with Stephen, who played her at her own game, brought the sparkle out in her again. But only for a short time. Presently she lay back on her pillow, porcelain eyes exploring the day.

'This weather, Lud, it is so humid; it feels as if the clouds are sitting on the housetops like little fat elephants. Thank God Dr Enys permits me a window open. Mama would keep me in a sealed room for fear the fresh air would set me coughing. Put that drumble-drain out, will you, Stephen. He has no business in here, and he irritates me.'

Stephen gingerly picked up the rosebud on which the bee had briefly settled, carried it to the window and shook it. The bee would not let go and began to creep up the stalk of the flower. He dropped it.

'I believe you are frightened of insects! A big man like you!'

'Drumble-drain,' he retorted. 'Where do you get such phrases? Drumble-drain. They sound more suitable to a speary old Cornish fishwife than to an effete drawing-room.'

'*Touché* . . .' She sighed. 'D'you know, Stephen . . .'

'What?'

'No matter. I had better not say it. Tell me about your work as a miller. Does it prosper? There are two men in the choir in church and I confess I have never known which of them is Wilf Jonas.'

'Wilf has a birthmark behind his ear that spreads down the back of his neck.'

'Alas, I never saw their necks so close! I confess I never

tried! Well, tell me what you have been doing. Are there any more lifeboats for sale?'

He gave her a brief account of his doings over the last week. He had the faculty of being able to present quite ordinary happenings in a way that was never dull to the listener. It was the gift of the gab, as Ben Carter called it. It entertained Violet for a few minutes. When it was over she offered him a sweetmeat. He took it and they chewed in silence.

'Mrs Pope came to see me yesterday.'

'Oh, did she. That was a neighbourly act.'

'I could not quite determine whether she looked on it as a social visit or whether she accounted it part of her duty to the sick poor.'

Stephen guffawed. 'That would not suit you, Miss Violet, would it. Well, mebbe you have to excuse her, with a husband like she's got. A leaky old drainpipe.'

'You always excuse pretty women,' Violet said. 'I've noticed it before.'

'Of course. That's why I excuse you. But think on it, what must life be like for her, tied to a sick old man?'

'Do you know what she said yesterday? She said, "When I go into Cornish society now without my husband, and it is known that he is old and ill, it exposes me to the impertinences of many idle young men." I so wanted to laugh!'

'So would I.' Stephen brooded. 'D'ye know, from the look of her, I would not have supposed that she would have resented such impertinences at all!'

'She has too careful a sense of her own position, that is the trouble.'

They ate another sweetmeat together.

He said: 'What were you going to say, Violet?'

'When?'

'Just now. You began to say something and then broke off.'

'Oh, that. I dare not tell you.'

'I reckon there's nothing you daren't tell me. Nothing *you* daren't say to a man!'

She smiled enigmatically out at the dark day, a hint more colour in her face.

'I would have you know I was brought up a lady – much more so than Mrs Pope – however low I may have dropped from that estate by falling in love with you.'

He laughed again, but a little less certainly. Joke and truth were interwoven but one could not discern the balance, the proportion of the mix.

'Now, now, old darling, that's enough of that. One of these days I might take you serious.'

'You'll take me serious when I'm dead,' Violet said.

'If you're going to be morbid I'd best be going.'

'Yes, you had,' said Violet, 'if I say what I was going to say, for it will scare you more thoroughly than the drumble-drain. Be off with you now. Run away, little boy, and go buy another lifeboat.'

He took her hand. 'Say on. Go on, shock me. See if you can. What's wrong? Tell your old shipmate.'

She took her hand away. 'What's *wrong*?' she said lightly. 'Oh, nothing much. Nothing important. I'm going to die, that's all. As I said to you a few weeks ago. Of course, it means nothing. People die every day – nearly as many as are born. The only person to whom this death is important is *me*!'

'If I—'

'Now *wait*. I said to you a few weeks ago, that what upsets me is I have known so little, done so little, experienced so little. How much *can* one have lived at twenty-two? I have never been to London, I have never been at sea, I have never had a lover, I have never had a child, I have never fully grown into the world before it is time to go out of it. All this, dear Stephen, I bitterly and most passionately resent!'

Some jackdaws were chakking on the roof just above the bedroom. The light from the window briefly darkened as they took it into their heads to fly away. The beat of their wings seemed to create a flutter of air and the curtain stirred.

'Violet,' said Stephen. 'That's a bad view, that is . . . I *am* kind of shocked—'

'No. That is not it. That is not the shocking part. This is what I was going to say to you. I am a virgin.'

He looked at her in puzzlement, half grinned. 'Well . . . we never ventured that far, did we.'

'Nor has any man.'

'Well . . .' he said again. 'That's good. Leastwise . . .'

'Leastwise it is not good. I have never known what it is to have a man. That is not good. But in the misty days of last year I thought there was still time.'

'Of course there's still time—'

'Don't, please, lie to me. I know there is not.'

'Well,' he said once again, and smiled at her.

'Well,' she said. 'Yes. Is it not an embarrassing subject?'

'But surely not shocking.'

'Not yet.' She moved an inch or two away from him, again taking her hand from his grasp. 'I imagine I am repulsive to you now, am I not?'

He stared. 'I don't quite see—'

'My face is still pretty. I examine it each morning for flaws and I find few. But my body has lost much weight since a year ago when you put your hands upon it in the church. It has – wasted. I do not suppose you could bear to touch it now.'

He still stared, his mind slowly adjusting to what she was saying and what she was implying.

'It is a pity,' she said, 'that it is too late for me to know . . .'

'Know what?'

'Is that not a stupid question?'

'Oh yes. Oh yes . . .' His face had flushed. 'But you don't surely mean . . .'

'Why should I not mean?'

'Well, old darling, you're serious sick.'

'Mortal sick.'

'Now, now. But whatever way you see it—'

'So I am sick,' she said. 'Mortal sick, I believe. And what of it? That is precisely my meaning. I really think I rather love you, Stephen. Not much. But enough to pass for the real thing. It is an unladylike confession – even unmannerly – but I will not retract it. If I were ever to experience the sensation of having a lover, a man, I do not suppose I would ever think of choosing anyone to give me that experience better than you. Now are you shocked?'

He felt unable to move from the chair beside her bed. The birds had gone. The heavy afternoon dreamed in silence.

'Violet,' he said.

'Yes, Stephen.'

'Violet, I'm not shocked – not that way – because I know ye do not mean it.'

'Of course not. It was the veriest joke.'

'No, I know twas not *that*. But you have to try to understand . . .'

'Understand what?' She pushed limp hair away from her brow.

'Well. Try to understand—'

'That you are engaged to marry Clowance Poldark?'

'That was not what I had the mind to say.'

'It is very strange,' she said. 'It's a woman's place never to propose – only to accept or refuse what is put to her. But one of the few advantages of mortal illness is that these restrictions are waived. So I feel in a position both of great weakness and of great strength. Pray answer me and say exactly what you think.'

He sat back, spread his hands. 'Really, old darling—'

'Please do not call me that.'

'Really, Violet, you are not suggesting . . .'

'Should I not? Why should I not?'

'Maybe sometime in the future . . .'

'I have no future.'

'When, then?'

'Now, of course.'

'Now? At this moment?'

'Could there be a better? There is no one in the house, but there is a bolt on the door, if you wish to be double sure.'

He suddenly stood up. 'Holy Mary! God's me life! It would *kill* you!'

'And if it did?'

'I'd feel a murderer.'

'Is it just thinking of yourself, or is it an attempt to discover an excuse? . . . But of course, it is not that at all! You find me repulsive.'

'Not so! But can you imagine – if you *died* next week . . . You are shaping up splendid this week. By next summer you may well be quite recovered.'

She moistened her lips, coughed quietly into a handker-chief. 'Do you not suppose I have the clearest possible memory of how Dorrie, my elder sister, died? The terrible

pains in her chest, the lack of breath, the flow of blood.
Do you imagine that I entertain the least hope that it is
not all going to happen also to me? – is indeed already
happening! If by any act of my own I were to shorten that
agony, should I for one moment regret it? Incidentally—'
She stopped.

'What?'

'Do you know what a woman's courses means?'

'Surely.'

'Well, I have not suffered one for almost a year – so that,
if this were to happen now, and I, ungrateful wretch, were
to survive the experience, and indeed to survive and
recover, there would be no risk of a bastard child or a
paternity claim. So your suit with Miss Clowance Poldark
would remain unassailable.'

'Almighty Christ!' said Stephen, clutching his hair.

After a moment Violet said: 'I do not believe you have
had Clowance yet.'

'Shut up!'

'Village girls . . . I do not believe that they will have been
easy in these villages that almost *belong* to the Poldarks. The
scandal might ruin your chances.'

He scowled at her. 'I shouldn't never have supposed you
would say such things.'

'Well, it is quite rational, is it not? No doubt you have
your fun when you are away. But I do not believe you can
have been inundated with offers such as this. So, it cannot
be altogether to your discredit if you consider it. As for me,
well, I . . . I seek an experience which only you can give me.
You must once have felt a strong attraction for me, if our
encounter in Sawle Church a year ago is anything to judge
by. Whatever happens, I swear to eternal silence on it. Soon
the grave will close my mouth. You once wanted me . . .'

'Yes,' he said. 'I once wanted you. But—'

'Well,' she said, 'examine my body if you will. It is frail but clean. I can only offer it to you. If you reject it, please go now and leave me to my tears.'

He came very slowly over and laughed and sat on the bed. 'You she-devil,' he said.

'Please draw the curtains.'

'You little she-*devil*,' he said.

She shook her head. 'Don't blame me, Stephen. Please don't blame me.'

He put his hand on her arm. 'Me old dear . . . How *can* I? Not *now*? Some day later when you are feeling better, *stronger*. We could maybe make arrangements.'

'My mother will stay gossiping for at least another hour. Lecky has gone into Sawle, and anyway if she came back would not come up unless I rang. And I am feeling much better today. So for me it is now or never. You must tell me if you find me repulsive, Stephen.'

He looked at her. 'I'll swear it isn't *that*!'

'Then what is it? Loyalty to Clowance? Right enough. But she can never know. Or are you so embarrassed and upset that you could *not* make love to me today?'

After a long pause he wiped his hand across his mouth. 'No, I reckon it wouldn't be that neither.'

She said: 'I believe I am totally shameless.' She pulled back the sheet. 'You see, my legs have not shrunk so much. They, I would have thought, could not be an ill sight to an interested man . . . Kill me if you like, I swear to you I should be entirely without regret.'

He stared at her a moment longer. Then he got up and drew the curtains over.

'It is so warm today,' she said, stretching. 'It is so warm.'

Chapter Two

I

In late July Valentine Warleggan, just home finally from Eton, wrote to Ross and Demelza telling them he was making a few courtesy calls in their district on Thursday next and would be spending the night with the Trenegloses. Might he take the liberty of inviting himself to sup with them at Nampara? He hoped to arrive about seven.

It put Demelza in a dilemma. Ross's absence provided an excuse for a refusal; but she was out when the groom delivered the letter, and Valentine had hardly left time to reply. He was obviously counting on a welcome and would be offended if he did not receive it – offended even by a letter and such a lame excuse. After all, Jeremy and Clowance had been to Cardew last year and to the theatre as his guests at Easter. Need she be embarrassed by his controversial presence at this late stage in their lives? But for this, his first visit, his very first visit to Nampara, she would have preferred Ross to be at her side.

It was a problem she could not even explain to Caroline, who was her normal confidante at such times. All she could do was ride over and ask Caroline and Dwight to come to sup with them on Thursday too. She also sent an invitation to Horrie Treneglos and asked Clowance to be sure to ask Stephen. Clowance, who had been going around with a face like thunder, said she would try.

'What is amiss?' Demelza asked. 'Have you had a quarrel?'

'I am not so sure it is as bad as that. Sometimes we do not altogether agree.'

'So then you disagree.'

'Well, yes. I – have not spoken to him for a week.'

'That's a fine way to begin! Is that how you expect to conduct your married life?'

Clowance muttered something in reply.

Demelza said: 'If he has done something you don't like, or you have done something he doesn't like, why do you not go and see him and have it out? The sun shouldn't go down on one's wrath, you know.'

'It is well for you,' said Clowance. 'You and Papa are different. You never seem to irritate each other, get on each other's nerves . . .'

'My dear life,' said Demelza, 'everyone quarrels sometime. Your father and I have quarrelled in the past – have we *not*! – but then it has been over *big* things; and big things, thank God, are rare. Life is too short to allow little things to fret.'

'How do you know when a thing is big?'

'You'll know, I assure you . . . *Is* this big?'

Clowance shrugged. 'I don't suppose so. But sometimes, so often, the point seems to become a matter of principle.'

'And neither will give way?'

'I think it *is* really rather important.'

'Do you want to talk to me about it?'

'No . . . Oh, I don't know. One of the things I object to is his wish to spend every Friday evening with Violet Kellow . . .'

Demelza was surreptitiously letting out a frock, but none of her children bothered to inquire what she was doing. It was early days yet but she didn't want to be caught unawares. Becoming large was the only part of child-bearing she hated.

217

'Violet is some sick,' she said. 'Dr Enys has been to her twice this week.'

'I know. And that makes me feel ashamed. But it's the way in which it's done. He – he seems to think going there is more important than anything else. Then he began to sneer at my family.'

Demelza looked up in surprise. 'What? In what way?'

'He was repeating stories he'd heard of my grand-father. Papa's father, I mean. Of course we've all heard something about him; but Stephen was gloating, as if what my grandfather did made the family come low, made me come low.'

Demelza said: 'You must warn him sometime. Tell him to be careful to say nothing of that nature in front of your father. It would not matter if it were true or not. He would go out, either through the door or the window.'

Clowance half laughed. 'Just at the moment one part of me would like that.'

When she had gone Demelza put away the frock, and then Isabella-Rose came in, and naturally after that there was no time for rational thoughts. Demelza wondered if Clowance were a little too fond of her father, too fond, that was, for the good of her coming marriage. It wouldn't be unlikely for Stephen to be jealous of the relationship and so be not unwilling to cast slurs on her beloved father's father: as near as he could get to tilting at Ross himself. Not a pretty manoeuvre; but then people in love often felt too deeply to choose only genteel weapons.

The following day, which was the Wednesday, she rode over to Mingoose to see Ruth Treneglos and on the way home she saw Stephen working on the dry-stone wall outside the Gatehouse. It was evening and a brilliant remote sky was cloudless except for a few cherubs and elephants flushing fatly in the sun's path. She called to him and he looked up and dropped his hammer and came over.

'Mrs Poldark. There now, what an honour! Have ye come to see the house again?'

'No. To invite you to supper tomorrow night. Valentine Warleggan, whom you'll remember by name, is coming, and I thought you should meet him.'

'There now. Thank you. What time would that be?'

'I believe he is coming at seven. But we shall sup as usual about eight.'

'Thank you.' He looked down at his hands, which were brown with the sandy soil. 'Does Clowance know I am to be asked?'

'I did not consult her. As you are engaged to marry, I should not have supposed she would object.'

He laughed without amusement. 'No, that's true, isn't it.'

There was a pause. Demelza said: 'Have you ever built a Cornish wall before?'

'No. I'm trying.'

'It is a skill,' she said. 'There are men here who would show you.'

He laughed again. 'I reckoned perhaps I could do it meself. Maybe I'm learning me mistake.'

'Sephus Billing,' said Demelza. 'He helps us sometimes with the hay, and at harvest. He is not . . .' She paused. 'He would not pass the simplest scholar's test. But no one can build a Cornish hedge or wall like him. He learned it from his father, who learned it from *his* father. It is a skill.'

Stephen straightened up, frowned at the cherubs in the sky, which were altering their shape. 'Mrs Poldark, I suppose you know things is not quite what they should be betwixt me and Clowance just now . . .'

'I – got that impression, yes.'

Stephen picked up a stone and threw it far across the moors. A rabbit, unexpectedly disturbed, flashed his white scut at them before disappearing into his burrow.

'I think it is all me own fault,' he said.

'Have you said that to her?'

'I've had little opportunity.'

'Perhaps you'll have the opportunity tomorrow evening.'

He said: 'I think it has been all me own fault.'

She patted the pony's neck to keep him quiet. 'About seven then.'

'Mrs Poldark,' he said, as she made a move.

She settled her hat and tightened the rein.

'I may not be the sort of man you would have wanted for Clowance, eh?'

Demelza looked at him, at his masculine sturdiness, the strong throat showing over the open shirt, the mature reckless face with its cleft chin, the tawny hair.

'Clowance makes her own choice,' she said pleasantly.

'And for that I count me luck,' he said. 'Often enough I count me luck. But it is not in me not to get out of step sometime. That's the way I was born. Maybe it's the way I was bred too. I never saw me own mother after I was four or five. I was brought up by an old woman, and then ran away, and the rest . . . It makes a difference.'

'I never saw *my* mother after I was seven,' said Demelza. 'She died.'

'Did she? I didn't know. Was you on your own?'

'No, I had six brothers to look after.'

There was a pause.

'Younger or older?'

'All younger.'

'Did your father marry again?'

'Not until much later. Not until I was about to marry Captain Poldark.'

'So – you looked after your brothers as best you could . . . I suppose you got a nurse.'

'*Nurse*,' said Demelza. 'We did not have enough to *eat*. My father drank all his wages.'

Stephen picked up another larger stone, weighed it in his hands. 'I reckon I must ask Sephus Billing about this.'

'I reckon you should.'

Stephen said: 'Is it not in your nature, Mrs Poldark, to get out of step sometimes?'

'If I do,' said Demelza, 'it is not in my nature not to be able to say sorry.'

'Yes,' said Stephen. 'Yes,' and put the stone back on the wall. 'Thank ye, Mrs Poldark.'

The soft dying sun had found its way among the curly clouds, and the bare moorland bloomed in its light. Demelza hesitated to leave on that note, wondering if her reply assumed a superiority she did not intend. This gave him time to come up to her, put his hand briefly on hers.

'If I marry Clowance . . . when I marry Clowance, I reckon I shall be double lucky. Double lucky that she has a mother like you. You're so young-seeming – and yet so wise. Thank ye for that.'

His look of frank admiration was uninhibited.

She said: 'We shall expect you tomorrow, Stephen.'

II

Demelza need not have been concerned about Valentine's visit. The little party she had arranged went without hitch, and the chief contributor to its success was Valentine himself. Tall and elegant in his stork-like way because of the thinness and length of his shanks, dashingly good-looking if one ignored the narrowness of his eyes, he could hardly have looked less like George Warleggan if nature had tried. But in all manner of ways, if not exactly in looks, he resembled Elizabeth: gesture of hand and movement of head; the light timbre of his voice which was little heavier than his mother's warm contralto tones; the smile that creased his cheeks could have been hers.

Unaware of Mr Clement Pope's illness, he had written to Mrs Selina Pope inviting himself to dinner. Mrs Pope had not chosen to put him off, and he had arrived there and after a few minutes of embarrassment had decided to make the best of it – since that apparently was their wish – and had dined there alone with the three women. What charming girls Miss Pope and Miss Maud Pope were – particularly Maud, with that golden hair; he could swear if it were unloosed it would fall to her waist. His eyes glinted as he said this, as if picturing a scene in which he participated in such an event. No, he had not seen Mr Pope at all. It seemed that he had good days and bad days and this was one of the latter. It was some fatty condition of the heart, they said; or – begging Dr Enys's pardon – what Dr Enys said. Though anyone less *fat* than Mr Pope it would be hard to conceive!

He was sure he would find Cambridge a tiresome place to be after Eton; it was such a dashed disadvantage being so far from London. He wished his father might have sent him to Oxford, since that at least was much nearer Cornwall. He pictured himself for the next three years spending a large part of his time suffering the oppilations and vertigo of travel in smelly and bug-ridden coaches.

How beautiful, he observed, Clowance was looking. All

Cornwall would be jealous of Stephen – whom he had only just had the pleasure of meeting – my warmest congratulations, sir, for having gained such a rose. The rose and her future bridegroom muttered the appropriate replies, but to Demelza it was clear that there existed between them only the sort of truce that occurred between the British and French after a battle: an agreed suspension of hostilities while the dead and wounded were attended to.

Valentine, in answer to Demelza's inquiry – prompted by her own thoughts – told them he had had another brief letter from Geoffrey Charles, who was learning to write with his right hand again. He assured all his friends in Cornwall, did Geoffrey Charles, that he had lost nothing, no finger, hand, or other part of his anatomy; it was only that the fingers of his right hand had been part paralysed and that holding a pen took a little getting used to again. He had recovered, apparently, the use of his trigger finger more rapidly than any other. That morning Valentine told them, before he visited the Popes, he had called in at Trenwith. What blackguards and ruffians those Harry brothers were, allowing the place to fall into such disrepair. How his father ever came first to employ them he could not imagine, unless, on the assumption that ugly pigs can grow out of pretty piglets, they had been less surly and uncomely in their youth. In which case one wondered that his father *still* continued to retain them. He and Geoffrey Charles, he had to confess, had not got on too well together in the old days, but he was looking forward to the time when he returned and threw those two blackguards out. After all, he and Geoffrey Charles had the same mother, and that was the strongest link in the world, eh, Cousin Demelza. Fathers mattered less, or had done so to him. His father, especially, being what he was.

'Being what he is?' said Jeremy.

'Well, a thought *nouveau riche*, cousin, wouldn't you say? If that's not filial in me, pray forgive. I mean it in the kindest way. Or do I? At least he has had the taste to marry two women of infinite breeding.'

'I hope they're happy together,' Caroline said. 'I mean your father and Lady Harriet. I have hardly seen them since the wedding.'

'To tell the truth, Mrs Enys, hardly have I! It is but a week since I returned – in the company of Blencowe who had been sent to escort me! No side-slipping was I to be allowed this time! Accompanied across London too, eyes carefully blinkered to avoid the sights and sounds of temptation! Then side by side for five dreary days in a lurching coach with not a word or a thought in common. I would as soon have had a Methody for company! . . . Cardew? Well, yes . . . I must confess there is an elegance to the house now that of recent years it has lacked: merely to see Step-Mama taking her long strides about the place raises one's body heat . . . As for my little sister Ursula, I do not think she is used to her new mother yet, but she much enjoys her new mother's animals. These great hounds – or whatever they may be – look as if they could eat her for supper any day, and I believe Papa suffers anxieties on that account; but Ursula treats them like puppies and they behave to her as if they were.'

'I wondered about the dogs,' Caroline murmured.

'Yes, well you might. Last Friday, the day after I returned, we was all in the summer parlour with Unwin Trevaunance and Betty Devoran and others, and Castor and Pollux were as usual beside their mistress. My father went over to speak to her privately a moment while the others were being served tea, when Castor – or was it Pollux? – turned suddenly, I believe because there was a bluebottle in his ear, and his great haunches quite undermined Sir George, who went down with a thump on his backside! I tell you, had I not been afraid my allowance would be totally cancelled, I would have split myself with laughter!'

'Don't ye get on with your father?' Stephen asked bluntly.

'I wouldn't go as far as that, my friend. We live in the same house from time to time. He supplies me with the education and the money I need and only occasionally reminds me that he holds the purse strings.'

'What are you going to be?' Stephen asked.

'A gentleman. I may later go into Parliament. My father owns a borough and would no doubt favour his son in a few years' time. I'm sorry Cousin Ross is not here or I would ask him how much profit he had found to it.'

'It depends how you regard the office,' said Dwight.

'And a gentleman regards it as a privilege and not as an opportunity for advancement? I take your meaning.'

'Not all gentlemen by any means see it that way,' said Caroline with a laugh.

'Well,' said Valentine. 'I must judge for myself. Perhaps I shall be in the army instead. If the French emperor subjugates Russia and then, having secured his flank, turns upon us we shall all be in the line of fire – or suing for peace.'

'Soon I shall go into the Navy,' said Horrie sleepily. 'Like my brother. N-no one can defeat us while we hold the seas.'

'First, dear boy, you must learn to hold your liquor . . .'

There was a cough at the door. John Gimlett had come in, and beside him was Paul Kellow.

'If you please, sur—'

'Paul,' said Jeremy, getting up. 'Welcome to our little supper. A glass of wine? Pray sit down.'

The window in the dining-room faced south-east, so in

the evening the light in the room became shadowy though it was still full daylight outside. Therefore for a moment or two it was not easy to see Paul's expression as he came in at the door. But his voice was grim.

'Thank you, but I must not stop. I have been for Dr Enys and was told he was here . . .'

Dwight dabbed his fingers on his napkin and got up. 'Is it Violet?'

'Yes, sir. She has lost a deal of blood and is in much pain . . .'

'I'll come at once . . .'

'John,' Demelza said, 'will you bring Dr Enys's horse to the front.'

'Yes, 'm.'

'Paul,' said Jeremy. 'Shall I come with you?'

He shook his head resentfully. 'It would do no good. I am sorry to break up your little party.'

Demelza glanced briefly at Stephen. He was facing the window and his face had deeply flushed.

Clowance unexpectedly said: 'Would you like to go, Stephen?'

He stared at her in surprise. 'What? Well . . . I don't think it's – me place . . .' He tried to discern how she meant the suggestion but could not.

Clowance said to Paul: 'Is she . . .'

Paul nodded. 'I think so.'

Jeremy took a glass of wine to Paul, who sipped it until John Gimlett returned. Dwight looked at his wife, smiled round at the others. 'Thank you for a delightful evening. I'll come back for you, Caroline. If you grow tired of waiting, no doubt someone . . .'

'Of course,' said Jeremy. 'I'll see her home.'

The two men went out.

'I'm afraid I am not *au fait* of the seriously sick on this coast,' said Valentine. 'As instance my intrusion on the Popes. Is this some other friend?'

Demelza began to explain. In the middle of it Stephen got to his feet.

''Scuse me,' he said. He looked again at Clowance. 'If it's that bad, maybe I should . . .' He put his hand over Clowance's, squeezed it. 'I'll be back, love. I'll be back.'

'Borrow my pony,' said Jeremy, but already Stephen was out of the room.

After an awkward pause Demelza finished her explanation. The others ate their strawberry and cream pie and drank their white wine, all except Horrie Treneglos who was asleep. Valentine, having returned to the subject of the Popes, now launched on a further description of their merits, particularly of Maud, to whom it was clear he had taken the greatest fancy. Indeed he risked becoming a bore on the subject. But it was difficult to tell whether he was insensitive to the atmosphere or well aware of it. At least he sustained most of the conversation until it was time to leave; and by then the party had become more cheerful again.

Whatever he might or might not feel about Maud, it did not prevent his kissing Clowance and Demelza and Caroline familiarly on the mouth. The fact that the two latter ladies were both just old enough to be his mother meant they were old enough not to resent it; but in both cases it was not a respectful salute. When a tall handsome boy of eighteen kisses two handsome women of early middle age as if he would like to know them very much more intimately, it is quite hard for them not to be both amused and indulgent. Any other reaction would savour of the prudish or the self-important.

At the door he said: 'I like this area. God's kidneys, it is more robust than the south – downright. After all, I was born here. I like the pounding of the surf on the beaches, the barrenness, the brilliant skies. I would much like to inherit Trenwith. That, alas, could only ensue from the decease of my half-brother, which I should be the last to wish. Long live Geoffrey Charles, the only warrior in the family! That is, apart from Cousin Ross. I trust *he* is staying close to London this time and not adventuring overseas unknown to us all! ... Well, thank you for a handsome supper. Come along, Horrie. Wake up! Wake up! Can you walk? Can you ride? Perhaps the fresh air will do him good. By God, it *is* fresh as well. This wind that's got up is as sharp as a surgeon's knife. July, did they say? How far is it? Couple of miles? If you can only get him up into his saddle, no doubt his horse will know the way. And I will follow like a true disciple. Come along, Horrie, bestir yourself! Up, up! There, how's that? Oops, make sure he does not slide off the other side! Farewell, Poldarks all. If we ever find our way to Mingoose I forecast I shall sleep well, even without a wench to company me.'

III

Stephen did not return that night. Nor did Dwight. Jeremy rode home with Caroline soon after eleven-thirty. Violet died at two a.m. Stephen held her hand to the last. She was buried in Sawle Church on August 2, almost six weeks too late to fulfil the prophecy of her appearance with Stephen at the church on Midsummer's Eve, 1811.

Chapter Three

I

On August 10 four young men met in the summer parlour of Mingoose House. They had just walked back from Wheal Grace where they had talked to the accompaniment of the slither and clack of the engine as it breathed and hissed and sucked; they had gone from the comfortable warmth of the engine house into a wind so strong that it felt as cold as winter. There was no sea to speak of except for the whitelicked surfaces of shallow waves, but so gusty and uncertain was the wind that they staggered like shaky automata towards the first deformed hawthorns that sheltered Mingoose House.

There they sat about a newly lighted sea-coal fire and warmed their tingling fingers. Horrie Treneglos, Jeremy Poldark, Stephen Carrington, Ben Carter. Horrie was leafing through the cost book.

He said: 'We're almost out of coal. And cash will soon be running short. By the end of the month we shall have to make another call.'

Jeremy said: 'Does your father know we're here?'

'Yes. Yes, he does. But he said he'd leave it to me.'

Jeremy grunted. Mr John Treneglos's personal interest in the mine, though he had substantially invested in it, was minimal. It was Horrie's plaything. John was happier with his dogs and his horses.

'Well, it's almost a month to the next shareholders' meeting. Shall we last out that long?'

'Have to. Borrow a bit. Anyway we can decide pretty much about what we want today, except to minute it. We hold the majority of the shares.'

'When is *your* father coming back, Jeremy?' asked Stephen.

'We expected him two weeks ago. Don't know what is keeping him.'

Horrie said to Ben: 'Zacky not well again?'

'Oh yes. I called in for the cost book. Tis just that he don't reckon to come out in this wind if it can be avoided.'

They listened to the fitful boom of the unseasonable weather. Mingoose House had always been poorly maintained, and one felt that the unexpected strain of this summer gale was too much for it to bear. Like Demelza's garden. People had steered clear of her again today.

Stephen said: 'Eighty pound of me own money is already sunk in this venture. Me *own* money. I'd not want to see much more go.'

Jeremy said: 'The expensive time is over. From now on it is just the miners' wages – a third of them are on tribute anyhow – and coal, and maintenance. We're using less than half the coal at Leisure that we do at Grace – or nearer a quarter, relative to the duty performed. A call of, say, ten pounds a share at the end of this month would see us through pretty well another three months. By then the returns should have picked up even if we're not in the richest ground.'

Stephen grunted. 'Well, I could manage twenty pounds, I suppose.'

'Getting wed is no easy time,' said Horrie with a grin.

'It is not that so much as a feeling that I may well be throwing . . .'

'Good money after bad?' said Horrie. 'That could be true. But it was ever so with venturers. Few are lucky straight off. Faint hearts never won, etcetera.'

'What is your opinion, Ben?' Stephen asked.

They very seldom addressed each other direct. But Stephen, now that he was surer of his position in the community, and particularly of Clowance, was not above making the occasional approach.

'Ye should come down wi' me sometime and I'll show ee. I've been vanning samples all this week, and there's naught to give us lively encouragement yet.'

'What does that mean, for God's sake?'

Jeremy diplomatically intervened. 'You break up the ore stuff with a bucking hammer; then you put the crushed ground on a vanning shovel and cove it with water. A skilled man swirls it around, letting the water run off and adding more, until he can flip up the best of what's left into what we call a head. Then you judge from that what value there is in the ground.'

'And the old lodes?' asked Horrie.

'What ye saw last month. We've done better wi' they than wi' the new ground. The east one going down from thirty fathoms is far the best still. The old men picked out the eyes of it but left a fair amount of good ore unworked. The south lode at thirty is also fair. We fetched up nigh on twenty tons of red copper ore from the east lode for the four weeks up to last Friday, and from the south lode about seven tons of poorer quality copper, five tons of zinc, small amounts of tin stone and black tin, and a smattering of silver.'

A dog was scratching to get in. Horrie opened the door to admit a young spaniel that went into ecstasies of welcome, his backside corkscrewing with joy.

'You can always sell your shares,' Horrie said to Stephen,

who was still frowning at his own thoughts. 'That's if you really feel you don't want to meet the call.'

'Would *you* buy them?'

'Get down, you beast! Stop your slobbering! ... Would I buy them? No, for I have enough. But you could put 'em up in one of these auctions. There's one at Gray's Hotel, Redruth, next week; I saw it advertised. You could sell 'em next month. I've no doubt they'd still bring a fair price seeing the mine is so new.'

'I'd buy them,' said Ben, 'if I had the money.'

They all looked at him. His eyes under their black level brows flickered with antagonism; but again Jeremy turned the obvious intention of Ben's remark by saying: 'Well, if our underground captain feels like that it is a good sign. This sort of thing can be a long haul.'

'Oh, I'll go along,' said Stephen. 'I'll go along. I'll say it again, I was always one for a gamble, and by the fortunate chance of my little adventure in Penzance and places I can find the money. All the same, I wish twere showing better. It is very well for those that invest nothing.'

Jeremy put a warning finger on Ben's arm.

'We'll settle for ten pounds a share, then. Subject to approval of the other shareholders next month. I think we should enter it down accordingly.'

Three of them had a glass of mountain – Ben was a non-drinker – and the meeting broke up, Ben to return to the mine and Horrie to go out to the stables to find his father and acquaint him with the facts he should have been present to learn for himself. Jeremy and Stephen walked back towards Nampara. They staggered drunkenly across the sandy moorland, the wind gusting and stabbing as they went.

Jeremy said: 'Was it all right with Wilf Jonas?'

Stephen smiled with his lips only. 'He does not ever take kindly to me absence during working hours, but he is used to it now. Ye see ... I benefit because I'm one of the Poldarks. Or almost one. That's how it is, like.'

'Will you come in now?'

'Thank ee, no. I can still put in two hours extra, and that will appease him.'

'And Clowance?' said Jeremy.

'Eh?'

'Is it all right between you two again?'

'Oh yes. Oh yes.'

'You sound doubtful.'

'Nay. It is healing over. And now poor Violet is gone, there is no longer the cause.'

They came to the gate of the garden.

'Clowance is at the Enyses' now, I think.'

'Yes, she told me that.'

Jeremy said: 'What was your real feeling for Violet?'

Stephen shrugged. 'She was one of those girls it is hard to resist. Don't you find Daisy much the same? Headlong. Headstrong. Devil-may-care because they feel the devil is after 'em. A challenge ... Yes, poor soul, I cared a little. God rest her.'

'It was hard for Clowance.'

'Yes, I know.'

'Especially hard because Violet's illness made her feel mean – that her jealousy was mean.'

'Yes, of course I know.' Stephen was getting restive but Jeremy went on.

'Don't expect her to be the same about any other, will you.'

'What any other?'

'Any other girl. Any other woman.'

'Holy Mary, that's my business. And hers. What's it to do with *you!*'

Jeremy would not be outfaced. 'I'm her brother. And, I imagine, your friend. I know her pretty well. I'm just saying, I'm just making the observation, that she'll not stand for it. Not with anybody else. She has a very strong personality under – under her simple-seeming ways. Not before marriage. Nor after.'

A gust of wind thrust them both against the gate.

Jeremy said: 'You've got a way with women, Stephen. Men too, to some extent. But women. I've watched it. It's a talent. Wish I had it. But it doesn't – that talent doesn't always make for the best husband. When you've been married a year or two and the newness has worn off – all those handsome girls – girls like Beth Nanfan, and pretty young wives – and Lottie Kempthorne . . .' As Stephen was about to say something he added: 'I wouldn't want to see Clowance hurt. Or angry. And it would be both.'

Stephen said: 'Thank you, Uncle Jeremy.'

Jeremy flushed. 'Take it which way you want.'

They stood a moment unspeaking, then Jeremy unlatched the gate and went in.

Stephen said: 'You done anything more about the steam carriage?'

'What more is there to do?'

'Well, it seems to me your Richard Trevithick can't know everything in the world.'

'It's not just Trevithick *saying* it won't work. Once he explained, I could see it wouldn't work. I could see he was right. That's what stopped me in my tracks.'

'But his did work, you say.'

'Yes, for a limited time. With a limited objective. I've told you.'

'So what're you going to do?'

'Nothing – for the time being. *Think* about the carriage. Maybe try to see Mr Trevithick again.'

'And in the meantime?'

'In the meantime what?'

'Oh, nothing.' Stephen shrugged. 'Well, I'll be getting along.'

'Yes.'

'Jeremy.'

'Well?' He stopped again.

Stephen kicked at a stone. 'I want Clowance for wife, d'ye know. That's something different even to me – different to invalids with pretty faces, or pigtailed handsome young women who I fancy the looks of, or easy doxies like Lottie Kempthorne. It's different.'

'I'm glad.'

'But, Jeremy, when Clowance marries me she becomes me own wife. She'll become a Carrington – not a Poldark no longer. She'll have to fend for herself. Not even her brother, dearly as I like him, will be allowed to interfere.'

They looked at each other.

Jeremy said: 'So long as Clowance is happy you can rely on that.'

II

Ross came home by sea. The Channel was considered fairly safe at the moment; despite Napoleon's claim to have an invasion force still ready and fifty battleships a-building. So long as he made war on the Czar and personally led great armies eastwards, his Channel threats could not be taken too seriously.

All the same, they travelled in convoy as a precaution against the single marauding raider.

Just before they reached Falmouth they heard of another great victory achieved by Wellington in Spain. Four years after Sir John Moore had left it, the British had returned to Salamanca and completely destroyed the French army there. Marshall Marmont was gravely wounded and four of his divisional commanders dead. The French had fled the battlefield, leaving some fifteen thousand casualties and a further seven thousand taken prisoner. The news was flagged across a hundred yards of water by a British naval sloop carrying the news to London. Cheering broke out from one ship to another of the convoy, like fire spreading, as the news was passed.

It was late in the afternoon when they put into Falmouth. Though he did not land in the town but at once hired a jolly boat to take him across the harbour to Flushing, Ross could see that a transport was about to leave; the streets were full of redcoats, and he could hear the bugles. The government was being faithful to its policy of risking invasion and denuding England of regular troops to supply the overseas armies.

In Flushing, where the Blameys now lived, Verity welcomed him with surprised delight. The years had dealt kindly with his cousin: her almost white hair showed off her still good complexion and unlined face, which had become more handsome than anyone could have predicted thirty years ago. Andrew, retired ten years from the packet service, had become a burgess of the town and was still occupied as adviser to the Post Office on matters dealing with the repair of packet vessels. He *had* aged, being slower of movement and speech than when Ross had last seen him.

Ross accepted the invitation to lie there, and they supped

together talking of old friends and exchanging news of families. Young Andrew, their son, was now a junior officer in the packet service. He was not at present at sea but was from home tonight. After Verity had left, Ross and Andrew senior stayed on talking and smoking. They looked up where Salamanca was on a battered old map of Spain and speculated whether Wellington, still greatly outnumbered and with no local recruitment to call on, could ever really carry the war into France itself. And how could the Czar stand against Napoleon? How soon before he sued for peace?

It was midnight before Ross went upstairs, eyes pricking with sleep, and he was surprised when there was a tap on the door as he was pulling at his neck cloth.

Verity edged herself into the room, a half-smile of apology on her face. 'I have only come for ten minutes, Ross. You must be dropping.'

'Not dropping. But I thought you were abed.'

She said: 'I know you'll be off early in the morning . . .'

He looked around. 'This chair . . .'

'No, you sit there. I noticed you limping again. I'll sit on the bed.' Which she did. 'I am so delighted about Demelza!'

'Yes . . . So is she.'

'You must not be anxious, Ross. This is what I came to tell you. I wish I could have had at least two more children. For some reason it was not to be. You're so lucky!'

'I'll esteem myself that at Christmas. But of course another child will give her great joy . . .' He paused and smiled. 'Tidings of great joy, eh? . . . I suppose that is it, isn't it – even in so minor a form. Women feel like that.'

'And you'll feel like that too.'

'Not that some of my present children do not raise other emotions than joy in me from time to time!'

'Tell me more about Clowance's attachment. And Jeremy.'

They talked for a while. Then Ross said: 'And your young Andrew? You said he was not at sea but was away for the night. Something in your voice. And his father's look. Do you have problems too?'

'Well, yes.'

'Is it just that, from worrying over the safety of one Andrew you now turn to worrying over the other?'

'No. Not quite. Though of course I'm concerned for that too. But it is when he is ashore I worry about him most.'

'Where is he tonight?'

'Cardew, I suppose.'

'With the Warleggans?'

'There or at their house in Truro.'

'Is that to be regretted so much? Naturally I would not want to go, but Jeremy and Clowance have been there and have come to no hurt. Valentine invited them.'

'It is Valentine he is friendly with.'

Ross took his neck cloth off and folded it, put it on the table beside his chair.

'I did not know you ever saw any of them – not since Elizabeth's death.'

'I didn't. We didn't. I have never cared for George, and Geoffrey Charles being still away ... But about a year ago Valentine called here when Andrew was home, and a friendship grew up. Since then they have been meeting whenever it has happened that they have both been at home.'

'I don't think I have seen Valentine for about five years. He was at Jonathan Chynoweth's funeral. Well, is it so wrong they should like each other? They are almost of an age.'

'Andrew is about a year the elder. But Valentine's is the

influence . . . Even before he met Valentine Andrew was too fond of drink. Perhaps we are especially careful, nervous, because of his father's history. Andrew senior, because of what it did to him, looks on drink as he would the Devil; so we have little liquor in the house; but Andrew junior often comes in tipsy. It is the cause of great trouble between them . . . Being in the packet service since he was seventeen has meant of course discipline while he was at sea, and I used to urge his father to ignore it, saying everyone, every sailor – *almost* every sailor – drank heavily when they came ashore.'

Verity stopped, seemed uncertain how to go on.

'And it has increased, this drinking, since he met Valentine?'

'Oh yes. But not that only. Valentine, although he is constantly complaining about being kept short of money, has in fact an enormous allowance; far more than Andrew can hope to keep up with. They go together to the cockfights in Truro, wagering . . . Do you know the Norway Inn?'

'At Devoran? Yes.'

'They meet there, five or six young men, to play cards and dice. They are all well-to-do except Andrew. He is already deep in debt.'

Ross rubbed his eyes. 'Surely it is just the usual thing – youth, with too much exuberance. You know, I expect, that twice I had to bail out Geoffrey Charles.'

'No, I didn't know. I hope you're right, Ross. Perhaps you think I am being too – concerned about such a small thing?'

'No. It is not all that small. Whom is he in debt to?'

'Moneylenders chiefly.'

'Oh. That's always more difficult.'

Verity slid off the bed. 'I'm keeping you too long now. But I so seldom have a chance of talking to you, Ross. We are separated only by eighteen miles and yet – Of course you are so often away. I do not know how Demelza can stand it.'

'She shall stand it less in future. I have promised her. And you. If you want to see me send only a note. Is it a question of wanting to settle his debts now? I could help.'

'No, I would not let you. You have told me about your mines. Anyhow, we are not badly off. Andrew senior came out of his active service with a nest egg, and of course he still works from time to time. It is a question if we settle this debt whether young Andrew will not simply run into another.'

'Well, tell me if I can help in any other way. Could I talk to him? Would that be of use?'

'I don't know. But thank you, Ross.'

'I'll come over any time you ask.'

Verity ruffled her hair. 'You haven't seen Valentine for some years, you say. He is not at all like his father.'

'He was not when last I saw him,' Ross said drily.

'He's very good-looking. Very debonair – as of course Geoffrey Charles was at his age. But otherwise there is no similarity. Geoffrey Charles's elegance and sophistication were of a young man going through a phase. One – enjoyed it. Valentine's is something darker, I think more twisted. He is strung up, nervous, yet in command of his nerves. When he comes here he looks at me very much – and treats me very much as a woman.'

'Who would not?'

'But I mean one of his age! He looked at me as if he would wish – as if he would wish . . .'

Ross made a gesture of understanding. 'Not at all like his father, as you say.'

'. . . He seems to resent George. Of course it is not

uncommon for a son to wish to be free of his parents at that age. But Valentine sometimes speaks as if he is in a stranglehold! I do not believe George is anything but generous to him.'

'Well, I would not personally relish being at George's beck and call.'

'Oh, *you* would not, no! But Valentine . . .' Verity walked to the door and put her fingers on the latch. 'Do you know, in those early days, Ross, when Elizabeth sometimes would come over to see me and bring Valentine with her; d'you know, I used to think – when Valentine was about eight or nine years of age – I used to think he was like you . . .'

There was a pause. Ross crossed his legs the other way.

'This ankle is trying at times.'

Verity said: 'It was one of those strange coincidences, without reason, without purpose. I just thought the colouring, the hair, the eyes, the set of the head . . . But now . . . now there is a different impression – equally stupid, if you know what I mean.'

'Of course I don't know what you mean.'

'Now he is not at all like you. He is far too *narrow* a young man to be like you. His eyes are close together, his way of walking, with his thin shanks, his *agreeableness* which doesn't quite ring true . . .'

She had flushed.

'So?'

'No, I know you will think me equally stupid, but he reminds me of your father.'

His eyes were lidded, their expression not to be guessed by any movement of the face.

'Nothing you say is stupid to me, Verity. But it would have to be so described by a genealogist.'

'Of course.' She was anxious to agree. 'But sometimes I

have a superstitious feeling that blood is not all. Valentine was born in Trenwith, where the Poldarks have lived for two and a half centuries. It was a strange birth, premature, under a total eclipse – the black moon as they called it – Aunt Agatha was a dominant influence in the house. I know of course he has no Poldark blood – but do you not ever feel that spiritual influences, psychical influences, can have a profound effect upon a child?'

Ross said: 'You remember my father better than I do, Verity. In some ways, that is. Being a year or so older and at a distance of a few miles, you could take a more detached view. And of course I was absent for the last few years of his life.'

'Your father', Verity said, 'was always of a kindness to me. But he had a wilful wildness, a rebellious disposition in a way quite different from yours. You are against authority when it seems to be – to be imposing its unfair will upon the rights of others. His wildness seemed to be for the pleasure of provocation.'

'And you think it is in that way that Valentine seems to bear some resemblance to him? Surely many young men . . .'

'Not in the same way. Or so it appears to me. He'd lend anyone a smiling hand on the way to perdition.'

'Well, that's a good recommend for your sister-in-law's son!'

There was a long silence.

Verity said: 'While your mother was alive your father's wildness lay in abeyance – like a wildness soothed. When she died so young . . .'

'He was always *hard* with me,' said Ross reflectively. 'It took some perception – which as a boy I lacked – to realize that he was at all fond of me. I remember when I was twelve I caught pneumonia. The surgeon – it was the one before Choake – Ellis, was it? – he said I was going to die. I remember hearing my father shouting quite hysterically at Prudie, swearing she had given me unaired sheets to lie in. I remember thinking: "Lord help us, he *likes* me!"'

'Poor Ross.'

'No, no. Perhaps all that gave me a stronger instinct to survive. I think really he was much more vulnerable than we give him credit for. After Mother's death he was rabid. For women, I mean.'

'Yes, I know.'

'I wonder sometimes now if that was partly to counteract the hurt, the loneliness. At the time, of course ... Fortunately he made most of his assignations at a distance. Only the disorderly ones came to stay.'

Verity made a face. 'No doubt with Jud and Tholly Tregirls dancing attendance.'

'With Jud and Tholly, as you say, dancing attendance. Tholly usually brought a woman of his own. Jud, with Prudie breathing down his neck, had to be content with getting drunk ... Perhaps my own respectability has been a move against all that.'

'Respectability? Oh yes, in a way. But not many would have agreed with that description of you twenty years ago! Or ten. As you surely know.'

'Well, now I am a tabby cat, warming himself by the fire, full of conformity.'

'If you are beginning to talk nonsense it is a sign I have outstayed my welcome. Good night, my dear.'

He got up and kissed her. 'Really, though ... are you suggesting that among other ill features Valentine has picked up through being born in a Poldark house under a black moon, is a similarity with my father in his preoccupation with women?'

She pushed him a little away. 'Now you make it sound as stupid as it no doubt is! All I can say to you is that when Valentine called that first time and sat and talked and eyed me and eyed Janet when she brought in the tea, and the way his bright tense looks impressed themselves on me, I had an uncanny feeling of being taken back thirty-five years and seeing your father smiling at me across the table – just as he did more than once in those distant days. It was a strange experience. I felt cold.'

Chapter Four

I

Ross and Demelza supped with the Enyses.

Ross said: 'Yes, I know I deserve all the obloquy for staying away so long but it was a desperate situation. You've no notion. It was not only for Canning's blue eyes that I remained . . .'

'The obloquy', said Caroline, 'is of your own imagining. It's just that we prefer you here.'

'All this political manoeuvring . . . Of itself it is embarrassing enough but it would, I believe, have found its own level – have stabilized itself – had there been a stabilizing influence at the centre, i.e. the Regent. But the Prince was in a dire state and has been all through the negotiations: heavy with drink or laudanum, bursting into tears when asked for some grave decision, almost in convulsions of fear over the letters he has been receiving.'

'Letters from whom?'

'Oh, anonymous. Or signed "*Vox Populi*". Or "An Enemy of the damned Royal Family". Threatening the same fate as Spencer Perceval if Bellingham died. And then, when he was executed, promising revenge. It's true, of course, that there have been many placards in the north of England offering a hundred guineas for the Regent's head. Some even in the south. It cannot make for an easy mind. But many feared he was going the way of his father.' Ross looked at Dwight. 'We discussed that possibility once before, you remember. At the Duchess of Gordon's ball.'

'I remember,' Dwight said, 'and the painful choices open if in fact the country had two insane monarchs on its hands.'

'Princess Charlotte,' said Caroline, 'a minor, with Uncle William as second Regent. Or would he be third?'

'Has there been talk of an election?' Dwight asked.

'Parliament will be dissolved later this month.'

'And are you quite determined not to seek reselection?'

Ross said: 'I'm quite determined not to stir from this county again while Demelza is as she is.'

Demelza smiled slightly. 'You see. He is wavering.'

Ross smiled back at her. 'She knows my dilemmas.'

'Make us free of them,' said Caroline.

'They would be tedious. And there would be much retracing of old ground.'

'If we cannot bear it we'll serve you notice.'

Silence fell for a few moments. Demelza stirred at a movement of her child.

Ross said: 'Every sensible instinct informs me that I have been a member of parliament long enough. I am not an effective member of the Chamber. Sometimes I have been of use behind the scenes, and sometimes, though rarely, I have been useful in committee. But in the main my justification has been in these commissions overseas. I have felt that they have been of value. But now they are finished. I am getting increasingly lame for the most active work; in any event I have done my share, and I promised myself and I promised Demelza that there should be an end to it. There is no altering that and no wish to alter it.'

Caroline passed a sweetmeat to Demelza.

''Kyou,' said Demelza, and sucked thoughtfully, her dark eyes reflecting some light from the evening window.

Ross said: 'I told Falmouth last year that I should not be standing for his borough again. And that was my wish then and is still. It is only in this last visit to Westminster that I have again had qualms of conscience about the unfinished business.'

'Which means?'

'Since Perceval died I have realized all over again how tenuous is our will to continue to make war. The Prince is a broken reed, more concerned about his debts and his mistresses than the effort to defeat Napoleon ... It is the same crisis that came up when the Prince was made Regent. It has never altogether gone away. I gather that during July he did in fact invite Grey and Granville to form a government, but their terms regarding the composition of his household were too high, so it came to nothing. Nevertheless, the risk is always there.'

'So you think you might serve another term?' said Caroline.

'No. But I could have wished to leave it all at a better time.'

'Well, there is nothing to stop you from changing your mind and carrying on.'

There was a pattering of feet in the corridor and the cries of little girls. Caroline frowned, but not with much rancour.

'Do you ever wish', she said to Demelza, 'that you could harness your children to a horse whim or some other useful machine so that their energies should not be altogether wasted?'

'Frequently,' said Demelza.

Dwight said: 'If you didn't stand this time in the Boscawen interest you could do so in the Basset. De Dunstanville would find you a seat.'

Ross took a sip of tea, which had just been served. 'Unfortunately, my views and Francis's are totally opposed on the subject of rotten boroughs! I could hardly accept his patronage and then advocate the abolition of the parliamentary seats he controls!'

'That is what you do for Lord Falmouth.'

'Yes. But in the first place I stood in his interest to serve his ends – or his father's ends – which were to get rid of George Warleggan. At least twice since I have offered to resign, and he has refused; so one can assume, I conject, that he found some advantage in the situation – though it has clearly not been a material one. And just as clearly, because of this, I have never felt muzzled or constrained in what I did or said. If I took a Basset seat I should feel constrained. Indeed, de Dunstanville feels more strongly against the need for reform than the Boscawens do. Our friendship, his and mine, was clouded three years ago when there was so much agitation in the country and I supported Colman Rashleigh and the others.'

'I remember,' said Caroline. 'Dwight was very hot for your cause.'

'Still am,' said Dwight, 'Though no doubt any change will have to wait for the end of the war, like so many other things – especially those of advantage to the North.'

'Not only to the North,' Ross said. 'When one thinks that any four of our Cornish boroughs – take, say, four of the rottenest: East Looe, St Michael, Bossiney and St Mawes – that any such four return as many members to Parliament as the cities of London and Westminster together *and* the whole county of Middlesex, which have something like a million inhabitants between them and contribute about a sixth of the total revenue of the country ... well, it turns representation of the people into a sorry farce.'

'Francis de Dunstanville, bless his little heart,' said Caroline, 'would argue that representation of the people is best carried out by those educated for the task, that government by the mob would end in the loss of more civil and religious liberties than we have at present, and that bare-faced impudence joined to ignorance always outweighs and triumphs over modest truth.' She turned swiftly to Demelza: 'Save me. Spare me from the crushing retorts of my husband and my best friend. You know how tender I am when severity is shown me, so easily bruised. Pray think of some other subject to bring up quickly before they have drawn breath.'

'But this is such an interesting subject,' Demelza said. 'I am listening to Ross making up his mind!'

Eventually Ross said: 'My mind and my wish is *not* to stand again, and that is how it will be. It's only among friends that I admit to taking a backward glance.'

Caroline said: 'And when is Clowance's wedding to be?'

'Oh . . .' Demelza exchanged a glance with Ross. 'In October sometime. We haven't fixed a date yet – or they haven't. But I should think Saturday the twenty-fourth.'

'And you? Will you be about eight months by then?'

'A little less if your husband is to be believed.'

'It will be a Christmas present, then!'

'I'm arranging for the mistletoe,' said Ross.

'Old Meggy Dawes always insisted on rowan berries. In fact,' said Demelza, 'I shall be not a small amount embarrassed at Clowance's wedding lest some onlooker mistakes me for the bride.'

The others laughed.

'It's a well-established Cornish custom,' said Dwight.

'Seriously,' said Demelza, 'I wish I was further away from my children – my grown-up children – while this is happening to me. They are both being engagingly sweet about it; but I would better prefer them to go off to some retreat until it is over. I shall not endure to have either of them *near* the house while I am in labour.'

'Well, at least by then Clowance will have a home of her own. And Jeremy, I am sure, is not above taking a hint. Still seriously,' Caroline added, 'is it going well between Clowance and Stephen?' There had already been a sharing of confidences.

Ross said: 'He's working hard, both at the mill and on the cottage. I confess I would like the young man if he did not wish to become my son-in-law.'

Demelza said: 'There seems just too little *ease* between them – at least when they are in company. There doesn't seem enough companionship. They are deeply in love but it is a prickly love. There is much of that about, of course; I see it in many couples all through their married lives. An edginess. I never understand it. But *before* marriage it is less frequent. I wonder if marriage will help to cure it for Stephen and Clowance or if, in time, when the passion is burning less brightly, they will find each other intolerable. I wake at nights and think about it.'

Caroline said: 'My dear, you can only live one life, and that's your own. Leave them be.'

'That's what I tell her,' said Ross. 'But it does not prevent me from feeling the same.'

Demelza said: 'I know how you blame us about Edward Petty-Fitzmaurice . . .'

'Nonsense. Forget that I ever spoke reprovingly. It was not so meant . . . As I grow older I think we must all learn to become fatalists about our children. Errors of omission are always easier to forgive oneself than errors of commission. You have done less than normal to direct your children's lives. So you bear *less* responsibility, *less* blame if things go wrong ... Was it the Spartans who relinquished charge of their children at an early age? Possibly that is the best solution of all.'

The long evening light was dying.

Caroline said: 'Shall you be at the races next week?'

'Where, at Truro? I fancy not.'

'I think I shall go. If I can persuade Dwight to take me. It will be interesting to see what they make of it.'

'Jeremy is going,' said Demelza. 'One of the younger Boscawens is making up a party.'

'Oh?' said Ross. 'I didn't know. Where did he meet him?'

'I think it was at Caerhays.'

Myners came in. 'Dr Enys, sir. There is a messenger from Place House. Mr Pope is sick again, and his wife has sent for you. Do you wish to go, sir? Shall I have your horse saddled?'

Dwight rose. Over the years, from the gentle young physician Demelza had first known, he had become lean-faced, rather austere. The time in the French prisoner-of-war camp still left its indelible mark. 'It seems we cannot eat together without my being called out. Believe me, there are many evenings when Caroline and I are beautifully undisturbed.'

'Take a brandy before you go,' said Caroline; 'it will be more sustaining than tea; and if I know the Popes' hospitality, you are not likely to be offered anything supportive there.'

So presently the three were left alone, and Dwight's horse crunched over the pebbles down the drive and out into the darkling twilight.

II

The Truro races were held on the last Tuesday in September. It was a new venture. This year the Bodmin autumn meeting, normally held in the first week of the month, had been cancelled because of litigation pending over the land on which the races were held, so some worthy citizens of Truro, not to be denied their sport, had decided to hold a scratch meeting three weeks later. A piece of flat land had been rented from a farmer near Penair, temporary fences set up, a course marked out, two stands erected. Most of the competitors who would have appeared at Bodmin had agreed to come to Truro.

Driving rain throughout the previous week was enough to damp anyone's ardour, and the constant traffic of preparation turned all the lanes into liquid mud, but when the day came a mass of vehicles of all sorts and condition were to be observed struggling up the various hills towards the venue.

The morning weather looked like turning the day into a disaster. A pall of cloud, the colour of coal and sulphur, loured over the scene, threatening torrential rainfall if not thunder. Although there was little wind, the clouds kept sidling around and breaking and filling like warships shifting their ground to take better aim. Now and then a spot as big as a six-shilling piece would fall, splitting and spreading into a drying star.

But then, about eleven, as if an appeal from Ossie Whitworth's old church had found a miraculous way through, a shaft of sunlight broke up one of the clouds, bits of cerulean blue showed through the rents, and the whole monstrous company shuffled off. By noon, when the first race was due to begin, the crowd basked in high summer.

In the end almost all the Poldarks went. Jeremy joined John-Evelyn Boscawen's party. Boscawen had hired a wagonette for the occasion, and all nine of his guests were young.

Ross decided to ride in, but nothing would persuade Demelza to accompany him. 'You must know by now how I mislike myself when I look like Sir John Trevaunance. It is the only part of having children that I detest. It will soon be over now. Have patience.'

'I could well take a vow of abstinence when I see you put to so much strain and inconvenience just to satisfy my appetites.'

'Don't take a vow that I shall persuade you to break. For abstinence is not in *me* yet.'

'It would be a good name, wouldn't it,' Ross said. 'Abstinence. Abstinence Poldark. But would it be for a girl or a boy?'

Demelza said: 'Don't you think Indulgence would be better?'

'Or Incontinence,' said Ross.

'That might be too near the truth!' Demelza put her hand on his arm. 'Serious, Ross, why don't you take Isabella-Rose?'

'Bella? Would she enjoy it?'

'She would adore it. Take Mrs Kemp too. There are likely to be ponies for sale and Bella has been promised one for her birthday.'

Ross thought if the occasion offered he might also buy himself a new horse, as Sheridan was failing. At this stage Clowance said she had no intention of being left out and went to see Wilf Jonas to beg a day off for Stephen.

Jeremy had half expected to find Cuby one of the party,

and indeed she was there, together with Clemency and Augustus. Most of the others he knew slightly or well. Nicholas Carveth and Joanna Bird were among them, as was John-Evelyn's sister, the Hon. Elizabeth Boscawen. Valentine Warleggan seemed of the party and not of the party, since he was riding a horse himself today and was in the company of two or three other young men, among them Jeremy's cousin Andrew Blamey.

When the invitation came Jeremy had written a refusal, thinking to avoid another hurtful confrontation. Then he had torn it up and spent a restless night and written an acceptance. Until he made the decision to leave Cornwall, or came to some conclusion about his arid and frustrated future, was he to avoid all contact with society or his fellow men just for fear it might involve him in this dread encounter? Why should he dread it? He knew that he loved Cuby and only Cuby, and that there would never be anyone else like her; but already he felt as if his soul had been ground into the mud because of it. Would he feel any worse, *could* he feel any worse as a result of meeting her again?

It also occurred to him that in the disastrous encounter of Easter he might have been guilty of serious tactical error. Precisely because he felt so deeply about her, as if his very life were at stake, he had glared at her, bullied her into tears, showed his heartbreak and his bitterness and anger. Might there not be another way to treat this young lady? After all, she was wed to no one yet. Affianced to no one. Major Trevanion could hardly keep her under lock and key all her life, releasing her, a willing victim to his cupidity, only when the right suitor broke cover.

So when he came to the wagonette and saw her sitting there in a plum-coloured velvet frock (which didn't in the

least suit her black hair but in a wicked perverse way only
enhanced her beauty) he bowed over her hand with his
best and most ingenuous smile, as if he were an old friend
who really liked her, rather than a spurned lover who
wished her either in his bed or in hell. Her troubled look
changed to one of slight surprise, as he was challenged by
Augustus, who immediately fell into easy conversation with
him about London and the progress of the war, and the
odds that were being offered today. With tact Jeremy drew
her into the conversation, and he made a special set at
Clemency, whom he dearly loved and admired except in
the one way that mattered. So the initial embarrassment was
lifted. Jeremy even went so far as to enquire if Major
Trevanion were here today, to be told that he was sharing a
barouche with Sir George and Lady Harriet Warleggan and
Miss Maria Agar.

It was indeed a remarkable scene that stretched before
them in the burgeoning sunshine. It seemed that every
form of vehicle known to man had been utilized. There
were carriages filled with elegant ladies, a fine smattering of
the Brecon and Monmouth militia in their black and scarlet,
farmers in respectable carts, tradesmen with their wives and
daughters in gigs and broughams, sporting gentlemen on
high-mettled mounts, boys on cart-horses, decorated wagon-
ettes, dung-carts with plough boys, donkeys and mules
carrying miners and buddle boys, and a great concourse
moving about on foot. The brilliant day turned what would
have been a sodden quagmire into a scene of joviality and
colour.

There was also an additional reason for joviality and
rejoicing today; for news of yet another military victory had
just come in, not this time from Wellington or the Peninsula
but from far-off Canada. There the Americans had pushed

a strong expeditionary force into Canada under General Hull, and in mid-July Hull had crossed the narrow channel between Lakes Huron and Erie, and led a strong force of militia into upper Canada, intending to take possession of the whole country in the name of the United States. But failing to maintain his momentum and surrounded by an unfriendly wilderness, he had decided to return to his base at Detroit. There that genial mountain of a Channel Islander, Major General Isaac Brock, having a thousand miles of frontier to defend for Britain and only fourteen hundred men to do it with – of which two-thirds were Indians or untrained volunteers – had decided to seek out the would-be invader, had himself entered United States territory, laid siege to Detroit and then captured it, together with 2,500 troops, a number of officers, and 25 guns.

When at last Jeremy could get a word really alone with Cuby he said: 'I have made a new resolution.'

She did not look at him. 'But it is not the New Year.'

'Does that matter?'

'It depends upon the resolution.'

'My resolution is to continue always to admire you but never to rebuke.'

She put up a finger and carefully looped a strand of hair behind her ear. 'That would be a welcome change.'

'It has happened. I assure you.'

'Pray how has it come about?'

'I have grown older – and less earnest.'

'And no doubt have found some other young lady better tempered than myself.'

'On the contrary. Without bringing into question the matter of tempers, good or not good, I can assure you that it is not so. No other lady, young or otherwise.

Her eyes transferred themselves briefly to his face,

searching it for a few quick seconds for evidence of sarcasm, double meaning, hidden bitterness. She found none and looked away.

After a silence she said: 'What is your fancy for the one o'clock?'

'*Pretty Lady.*'

'I don't *believe* there is any such—' She looked down at her card. 'Oh yes, there is. I – hadn't noticed.' A half-apologetic smile flickered around her face. 'Do you know the jockey?'

'No, but it is entered by Lady Bodrugan, so I think it will have some good blood.'

'Your cousin Valentine is riding in the two-forty-five. *Larkspur.* We ought to put a guinea or two on him.

He was very pleased by the 'we'. 'Let's put a guinea or two on him. Let's share five between us.'

The boy in charge of the wagonette was summoned and asked to go round among the more fashionable of the other coaches to see if any lady or gentleman would accept such a bet, against a horse of their own choosing, the bet to be void if neither won.

After that young Boscawen came up, and conversation became general again. But later Jeremy talked to Clemency and then, gradually, to Cuby again.

'That is my father over there, crossing in front of the yellow coach now.'

'The tall dark man, with the older woman and the little girl? Who are they?'

'My youngest sister and her governess. Isabella-Rose. And not so little! She is ten years of age.'

'She's vastly pretty. I consider her quite charming.'

'You would not think her so charming if you heard her sing. She sounds like a choirboy whose voice is breaking!'

'Your mother is not here?'

'No . . .'

'Nor is mine. I think she is becoming a little mopish. We should have persuaded her to come, Clemency.'

'She swore it would be wet. And far too many of the lower class.'

'Whereas the sun is positively tropical! And the lower orders are keeping their distance beautifully!'

Except this one, thought Jeremy, but just bit off the words in time.

'Do you not also have another sister?' Clemency asked.

'Oh yes. But she is almost eighteen. She is here today too, with her future husband. I cannot at the moment see them. I expect they are off on their own.'

III

Stephen said, 'In a month now, me beauty. Less than a month. Less than four weeks. Less than twenty-eight days. How many hours? I can't count. But one has almost gone already since we came to this affair.'

'Are you not enjoying it?'

'Of course. I like being with you. And this crowd . . . Sometimes I wonder if Cornwall's properly alive. Folk hide in their houses, peer out suspicious from their doors, go about life in secret. This shows the other side, shows they can enjoy themselves proper when they feel like it. It is like a beehive, isn't it, only more colour . . . All the same, I reckon we could be putting the time to better advantage.'

She squeezed his hand. 'Soon we shall have leisure for our better advantage, as you have just pointed out. Have patience.'

'It is all very well for you.'

'Why? Why should it be? Why is it different for me?'

'Because – well, you have your family all round you – you're living the life you've always lived. With your father and mother and family. I'm – on my own.'

'It doesn't make that much difference, Stephen. Surely you must know how quickly I want the next month to pass.'

'Why did your mother not come today?'

'Is it not obvious?'

'Is she ashamed of her condition?'

'Of *course* not! Has she not a right to her preferences?'

Stephen bit at his thumb. 'I wish you was in that state.'

'What, you'd prefer to marry me when I was with child?'

'Not exactly. But I wish there was reason. I wish we'd made love.'

'It is all to come.'

'Not all, thank the Powers.'

'No . . . not all.'

They had wandered off behind the stands to where a group of gypsies had made their encampment. The two young people were quickly surrounded by children begging and older children trying to sell them pots and pans. Stephen waved them irritably away, and presently took Clowance's arm to steer her back the way they had come.

'Anyway, if you was like your mother is I'd be surer of you.'

'Still not sure of me?'

He looked at her, and his expression cleared. 'Oh, more or less.'

'Perhaps that way *I* would have been, been surer of *you*.'

'Oh no.'

'Oh no?'

'No. Y'see, I'm a villain at heart. To have a pregnant

woman at the altar rails – it would not affect me at all if I'd the mind not to wed her.'

'I'll remember that. How fortunate I never yielded to your advances!'

'Is that what they call it in your set? Phew!'

'They call it that in the novels we used to read under the bedclothes at school. In our set – as you call it – in our set they still use cruder words.'

'Tell me.'

'After we are married.'

The crowd was getting thicker as they approached the horses. Clowance saw Valentine over the other side of the ring, with a young man in naval uniform, but they did not see her.

'Clowance.'

'Yes?'

'Let's run away?'

'When? Today?'

'Aye. I don't savour this fancy wedding that is being prepared.'

'No fancy wedding. I have promised.'

'But how much easier . . . We could slip away now when no one is looking, take those two nags we came on – ride away somewhere – where's the nearest port? Falmouth. Ride away to Falmouth, take a room; there'd be a little sour-pussed landlady with a yapping dog. We'd pay her two nights in advance, lock the door in her face. Then I'd have you. You couldn't taunt me, tease me any longer. I'd take all your clothes off, very slow, very careful . . .'

'Stephen, stop it!'

'What's the matter – scared?'

'I believe you're half serious.'

'More than half, I tell you!'

'Well, don't be. And pray change the subject.'

'Now, now, don't go prinkish on me or I shall slap you.'

'D'you think we shall fight a lot when we're married?'

'*No*. Two doves cooing, that'll be us. But if there *is* a fight, well ... loving, fighting, eating, drinking, breathing deep and living to the full, that's how folk are meant to be, isn't it? Life's short enough anyway; youth's shorter. I can't bear to sleep long of nights for fear of missing something!'

'Agreed,' said Clowance, taking a breath. 'Oh, I do agree with you on that!'

A hand was plucking at her sleeve.

'If ee plaise, miss. Yer leddyship. If ee plaise. Buy a purty necklace. Handsome stones, they be. Handsome, 'andsome, you. Very cheap. Very good. All made wi' special strong thread, so it shall not ever snap. Not ever, yer leddyship.'

A wizened child of uncertain age – perhaps ten, perhaps fourteen – a girl probably, held in her thin dirty hand two necklaces made of some sort of blue stone, which no doubt had been picked up round the coast and crudely polished. There were a half-dozen stones to each necklace, drilled, and threaded with coarse twine. Clowance did not know if the girl had attached herself to them recently or followed them from the gypsy camp.

'Get off!' said Stephen. 'Be off wi' ye!' And raised a hand to strike the child. She shrank away behind Clowance but did not retreat, keeping her glance first on the young lady for a sign of weakness, then on the young man for risk of attack.

Once, about a year ago, Demelza had told Clowance frankly of her first encounter with Ross, starving, cursing, ragged and bug-ridden, and although at the time Clowance's youthful imagination had not been quite up to the task of picturing her beautiful mother in such a scene, now, a year later, it occurred to her suddenly like a knife in the side, that this must have been – or might just have been – the way her mother had looked at Redruth Fair thirty years ago.

She glanced up protestingly at Stephen, who, for Heaven's sake and according to his own story, had been even worse circumstanced only twenty years since, and should by rights have all the sympathy in the world.

'How much are your necklaces, child?' she asked.

'Six shillun, miss. Six shillun. Or five to you, yer leddyship. Five shillun and the best stones ye could ever find. An' special strong thread that'll never snap.' The litany of praise went on, while Stephen glowered and Clowance considered.

''Tis rubbish,' said Stephen. 'Ye'd find as good in the attle of any mine! Come away, m'dear, and leave the little gypsy rat go back to her hole.'

'Three shillings?' said Clowance.

'Four.'

Clowance hesitated and seemed about to turn away.

'Nay, three,' said the child. 'I'll tak three.'

So the necklace was bought.

'Do not put it near your neck,' said Stephen. 'Else you'll get scrofula. Off wi' you! Go on now! Back to your den!'

The child took the coins, bit them and then thrust them into some pocket in the depths of her grimy tunic. Then she suddenly spat on the ground and made a mark in the spittle with her finger. She looked at Stephen with small red-rimmed eyes.

'Ye'll never live to be old, mister. I'm telling ee. Ye'll never live to be old.'

IV

They had picnicked and wined excellently in the wagonette, with a lot of chatter and laughter, much of it contributed by Augustus Bettesworth, who seemed even more than
usually boisterous, and by Jeremy who, released temporarily
from the glooms of his passion, sparkled in front of the
object of that gloom and made her laugh. Valentine Warleggan had come in second on *Larkspur* in the 2.45, and Jeremy
and Cuby had lost their wager to a dragoon from St Austell,
whose horse had won by a neck. About 3.15, with three
more races still to go, an auction of some of the winning
horses was held behind the first stand, and most of the
party, having no interest in the next race, drifted across to
watch the bidding.

. Although clouds were building up again in the west, the
sun was still brilliant and the heat that of high summer.

Jeremy said to Cuby: 'Do you want to buy a horse?'

'I don't think so.'

'Nor do I. Are you interested?'

'Oh yes. I love horses.'

'It will be very hot in the crowd. One will be jostled. Your
frock might be trodden on. And the mud is not yet dry.'

She lifted an eyebrow. 'Why are we all going, then?'

'*We* need not. We could just walk.'

She considered this. It was a challenge. 'Where to?'

'You know, I suppose, we are near the river here.'

'Fairly. But the ground must slope sharply. Here we are
on top of the hill.'

'Those woods lead down. About a mile perhaps. Even if
we didn't go so far, we could stroll. It would be pleasanter.'

'And muddier.'

'Oh no.'

'Not muddier?'

'The tracks will be soft, perhaps. Damp leaves, perhaps. But mud is here only because of the carts and the horses.'

Cuby glanced across at Augustus who was talking flirtatiously with Elizabeth Boscawen. Clemency was with Nicholas Carveth.

'Well,' she said, 'then let us go for a stroll.'

At the edge of the field a gate led into the wood. Jeremy unlatched the gate and they went in. The ground *was* damp and he glanced anxiously at his capture but she did not complain. His light-hearted approach of today had succeeded beyond all his expectations. Aware that this was a holiday occasion, and particularly aware that at the moment they had both drunk numerous glasses of canary wine, he was not at all sure that this apparent progress really was advancing his suit – not when it came down to the cold light of day. Yet merely to be with her gave him new life and hope. And, whatever the softening circumstances, it was very unlikely she would have agreed to come with him in this way if she did not find pleasure in it too.

She lowered her sunshade as they went further in and down. 'When is your sister to marry?'

'At the end of next month. Would you come to the wedding?'

'I think not. That would be too formal an acknowledgement that I was going against my brother's wishes. Jeremy—'

'I know. I'm sorry. I was breaking our agreement. Nothing serious shall henceforth be said.'

She stopped to examine one of her boots, pulled three large damp leaves off the heel. 'I wish nothing serious ever *had* to be said. How agreeable if we could just meet people in so unserious a manner!'

'Perhaps we can.'

'How?' she replied. 'It is impossible! In any event pleasantries would soon wear thin. It was beginning just then. Let us enjoy today.'

They walked on. There was an empty quiet in the wood, except for the thin rilling of water in a ditch. All the birds seemed to have fallen silent.

She said: 'Tell me about your experiments with the steam engine.'

'Oh, those. They are not prospering.' He spoke of his meeting with Trevithick, his semi-abandonment of the project.

'But you should not!' she said. 'If every inventor despaired when something went amiss, how little would ever be discovered.'

'I'm not an inventor. I am a user and perhaps developer of other people's inventions.'

'Even so.'

'Well, yes, I suppose you are right. I should continue. Of course recently I have lacked—'

'Go on.'

'You may guess what I have lacked, which proves again how right you are to say that pleasantries soon wear thin.'

There were giant cow parsnips here, flowered and gone to seed, a thicket of gaunt stalks holding up Japanese heads. She flicked at one and broke the stem with her parasol.

He said: 'Let me tell you of our new mine. It is open now and the engine I designed is working and working well. I have never told you of this?'

'No. Last year it was projected.'

'But you are interested?'

'Of course I am interested! Just because . . .'

He told her. After a while she began to chat of her own life, of Augustus's holiday with them from his work in London, of Clemency's misunderstanding with her music teacher, of a visit from her aunt and of the spaniel that nipped her ankle. Jeremy told her of Clowance and about Stephen. The most ordinary information, the lightest of communication between them, assumed instant importance.

They went down and down, unheeding. Then Cuby slipped on a fallen branch half buried in the ground and damp with lichen. He caught her arm and she steadied herself. She looked at the slanting light and said: 'Mercy, we must go back!'

'You can see the river from here.'

'I know, but we must turn back nevertheless. I would not wish John to join our party and find me wanting.'

They began to retrace their steps. Jeremy retained her arm in a light, un-familiar fashion and did not find himself rebuffed. They climbed back alongside the rill of water, pushing among sycamore saplings whose huge damp leaves glowed in the shafts of sun.

After a bit they paused for breath and Cuby leaned back against a tree behind her. He put a hand on her other arm, smiled at her cheerfully. They stood for some seconds before he kissed her, and then it seemed as if her mouth came up to meet his own. The heightened sensation of face to face and lip to lip created emotions that made the rest of the day trivial and without point.

After a pause to take in scant breath Jeremy allowed his fingers to stroke the curve of her cheek.

'That was,' he said, and swallowed and tried again; 'that

was not at all disagreeable. All things considered, it was –
not at all disagreeable.'

He stopped, aware of the flicker of surprise in her at the
lightness of his tone.

'D'ye know that poem?' he said. '"Then come kiss me,
sweet and twenty, youth's a stuff will not endure."'

Her face looked as if it was going to go dull on him, but
after a hesitation the sparkle came back, and she smiled –
though there was a hint of wryness in the smile.

'Jeremy, I have told you, it is time we went.'

'Of course it is time we went! We must hurry away. But
don't you agree that we are behaving according to the rules
we set ourselves today?'

'Well, I'm not sure.'

'Why are you not sure? We are not being serious, are
we?'

'It is not so much that . . .'

'Did you not ever play kissing games as a little girl?'

'Of course. But this—' She stopped, hoist with her own
petard.

He bent to kiss her again.

'Stop it!'

'But why?'

'You know why!'

'No, I do not.'

'Well . . .' She tried to move away from the tree. 'It is
time we were back.'

'Of course it is time we were back. Was I not just saying
so?'

Because she did not offer him her mouth, he kissed her
forehead, her hair, her eyes, her cheeks, the very edge of
her lips. She jerked her head away.

'Jeremy! I have told you!'

'What have you told me? Am I not behaving in an unserious manner?'

'You are behaving in an *unseemly* manner!'

'But is it not fun? Is it not what we came into the world for? Should we not seek happiness on this superficial level while we can?'

'Yes, yes, yes, yes, yes! There: now let us go!'

He gently edged away from her.

'So we shall go back now. I am at your service.'

She moved from the tree, brushing at a few green marks on her velvet frock. 'I shall have leaves all over me.'

'No, no. Just one or two.' Respectfully he picked them off her back and skirt.

She drew a deep breath. 'You really are quite ridiculous.'

'Of course,' he said. 'But you'll agree I am not allowing sincerity to break in.'

'I am coming to believe, Jeremy, that your only purpose in this world is to torment me!'

'My only purpose in the world is to *please* you! To accept and honour your wishes in everything.'

She considered him, the oval of her face in shadow but clear like a cameo against the darker frame of her hair.

'Then let us go.'

They proceeded a little way. Bracken, creeping every-where, clutched at them with fingernails as they passed. Two magpies began to chatter harshly, breaking the bird silence. Cuby bowed towards them.

'One for sorrow, two for mirth,' said Jeremy.

'I say, one for sorrow, two for joy.'

'Equally suitable.'

'You know I came with you,' said Cuby, ' – have come with you, just for the walk.'

'That is the agreement.'

'You having – me having – that embrace that you forced upon me – meant nothing more than . . .'

'Than an embrace. What could it mean? Were we not friends who had quarrelled? After a quarrel is it not proper for friends to kiss and make up?'

There was the sound of children shouting in the distance, but it was another world. The green damp wood still surrounded them in sunlit silence.

'Indeed,' said Jeremy, 'I am relieved that it is all over between us.'

'All over?'

'I mean the quarrel is over. Now we may meet as loving friends.'

'Well . . . yes.'

'Dear Cuby,' he said gently. 'Don't be doubtful. I am going to make no claims on you except—'

'But you do! You have done!'

'Except – let me finish – the claim to be considered your loving friend – right up to the time of your marriage. Even after your marriage, if your husband will permit.'

'I have no husband yet in view!'

'That is something I cannot comment on,' said Jeremy, continuing his double-edged remarks.

Laughter and annoyance seemed to be struggling with each other in her face. Eventually, to hide other emotions, she looked down at her parasol.

'Very well,' she said in a small voice. 'Let it be so.'

Chapter Five

I

Ross had bought a new pony for Isabella-Rose and he had his eye on a horse for himself which had won the second race of the day.

Few of the entries measured up to what would be considered a racehorse up-country. Most of them had been locally bred and, like their breeders, were a bit heavy in the beam for real speed. But Ross had been impressed by the way Bargrave — that was his strange name — had come back at the end of a mile and thrust his great hoofs into the soft and tiring turf and overhauled his rivals. There must be blood in him to do that. He was a four-year-old, so there was a good and honest life ahead. Pity if he had to be sold for a carriage horse, which would mean a further life of three more years at the outside. Ross had no ambition to burn up the countryside by taking fearsome gallops, but he liked and admired courage and willingness, and he thought Bargrave had both.

The bidding began at five guineas, rose quickly to fifteen, and there stuck.

'Now, gents,' said the auctioneer, 'this bain't good 'nough. Can we say seventeen? Will anyone give me seventeen?'

Ross raised his glove.

'Seventeen I'm bid, seventeen I'm bid, seventeen. Can I say twenty? Twenty I'm bid. Only twenty for this fine strong animal. Look at his fetlock joints. Look at his pasterns! Can I say twenty-two? Can I say—'

Ross raised his glove.

'Twenty-two. Thank *you*, sir. Twenty-two. Twenty-five. Can I say, twenty-seven? Twenty-seven. Can I say – thirty it is. Thirty. Thirty. Thirty-two. Thirty-two. Thirty-five. Thirty-five. Forty. Forty-five, can I say forty-five? Thank you. Forty-five it is. Can I say fifty?'

Ross peered across the ring to see who it was bidding against him. There was no one. It was someone almost behind him, just to his right. He turned his head. George Warleggan.

Beside him was a tall, very dark young woman. Major Trevanion was with them.

'Against you, sir,' said the auctioneer, pointing at Ross.

Ross raised his glove.

'Fifty,' said the auctioneer. 'Thank *you*, sir. And may I say? . . . Fifty-five. And fifty-five. *And* fifty-five. And sixty. And sixty. *And* sixty-five. And seventy. Seventy. Against you again, sir. All finished?' Ross raised his glove. '*And* seventy-five. Seventy-five. And eighty. And eighty-five. And eighty-five. *And* ninety. And ninety-five. And ninety-five. May I say a hundred, sir?' Ross shook his head. 'No, sir? All done at ninety-five? Ninety-five? Going at ninety-five.' Bang went the hammer. 'To you, sir. To you, Sir George,' the auctioneer added with an obsequious smile, and the clerk left his side to make for the Warleggans, while the stable boy began to lead Bargrave away.

'No,' said George, shaking his head, 'the horse is not mine. The other man's was the last bid.'

A look of anxiety came upon the auctioneer's face. 'Sir?'

George repeated what he had said. The auctioneer looked at Ross. Ross shook his head in turn.

'My last bid was ninety.'

'No,' said George. '*My* last bid was ninety. The horse is yours.'

The auctioneer came down from his rostrum and then, aware that by so doing he lost authority, climbed it again.

'Sir George, I was certainly of the opinion. I was watching *careful.* You was both close together, I know; but . . .' He consulted his clerk. 'Mr Holmes here say the same, begging your *pardon*, of course . . .'

'I was the underbidder,' said George. 'The horse has been bought by Captain Poldark.'

'Nay,' said a snarling voice behind them all. 'I seen Les Downs a-looking straight at ee, Sir George, when the last bid was given – I seen it wi' me own eyes!'

Old Tholly Tregirls, his ravaged, mischievously evil face serious for once, his hook high in the air to catch attention.

'Well,' said George, 'if I am to be subjected to the accusations of one of Captain Poldark's creatures . . .'

Ross said: 'Tregirls is not one of my creatures, and I did not know he was even at the races. Indeed, I'd be grateful if he did not intrude in matters which did not concern him. What's amiss, George, do you feel you have bid more for this horse than you can afford? If so, pray allow me to take it off your hands . . .'

'Indeed you may,' said George, flushing, 'as indeed you must, since it has in the first place been bought by you—'

The woman at his side moved. 'Captain Poldark.'

Ross turned unfriendly eyes on her.

'You are Captain Poldark?'

'Yes.'

'I am Harriet Warleggan.'

Ross bowed. They looked at each other.

'My husband was buying the horse for me, Captain Poldark, and I should consider it a little ungentlemanly in you to insist on taking him away from me, when I had hoped to be able to ride him tomorrow. This without regard to the matter of who made the last bid.'

There was a momentary pause. People were watching, gaping.

Ross said: 'I would never stand in the way of a lady. Pray consider the horse yours.'

'Thank you, Captain Poldark. George, I think we need not pursue this argument further. We have Bargrave, and I am happy.' She said to the auctioneer with quiet arrogance: 'We shall take the horse at ninety-five guineas. Please continue.'

George did not look at Ross. Pink spots remained in his cheeks. He tapped the ground with his cane. Harriet took his arm and steered him towards the enclosure. As Major Trevanion was moving to follow them he caught Ross's eye. They did not even nod to each other.

The auction went on but Ross did not bid again.

After a couple of minutes the hoarse voice of Tholly Tregirls broke through a sputtering cough to say: 'You was well out o' that, young Cap'n.'

'Tholly,' said Ross, 'I have no doubt you have my interests at heart, but when I need your help I'll ask for it. Until then champion whom you may, but not me.'

'Just as you say, young Cap'n. Just as you say. There was a time when you needed my 'elp, eh, and was not above taking it, eh? Not above taking it. Now if you want a bit of good 'orseflesh . . .'

'I don't, Tholly,' Ross said. 'Not the kind you can sell me.'

Tholly convulsed himself with another cough.

'All the same, you was well out o' that. Horse wasn't worth more'n forty guineas of anyone's money.'

Ross said: 'I know that.'

II

Stephen and Clowance had witnessed the argument from the other side of the ring.

'So that's Sir George Warleggan,' said Stephen. 'Reckon I shall know him again.'

'And his new wife. I met her last year.'

'Handsome woman. I reckon he'll have his work cut out bridling her.'

'Do you have to think of women as horses? Could you not perhaps turn me into a ship for a change?'

He squeezed her arm. 'Yes, we could talk about luffing.'

'Oh, what a horrid pun!'

'Serious though, I'd hardly suppose the horse was worth so much.'

Clowance said: 'The old rivalry dieth not.'

'What?'

'No matter. Have we lost any money today?'

'Three on the first race, five on the second; but we've made it up since then. Reckon we're about two guineas up.'

'Good.'

They turned away and a voice said: 'Clowance? It is Clowance? Yes, for sure it is. By the Lord, now, just imagine it!'

It was the young sailor whom Clowance had seen earlier in the company of Valentine.

He said: 'It is more than two years, and for a moment I could not be sure. How are you, Cousin?'

'Andrew! I saw you earlier in the day but thought I must be mistaken.'

'I should be in the Bay by now, but was held up a couple of days, so came here with Valentine Warleggan and Antony Trefusis and Ben Sampson and Percy Hill. How *are* you? How you've grown up!'

Clowance laughed. 'Oh, you have not met Stephen Carrington whom I am engaged to marry! Stephen, this is my cousin, Andrew Blamey, who lives in Flushing but is more often at sea!'

The two young men shook hands. Andrew was stocky built and sandy, with tight curly hair and thick eyebrows, and sidewhiskers which made him look a good deal older than his years. He was wearing the smart blue and gold uniform of a junior officer in His Majesty's Packet Service. Stephen, at once interested in anything to do with the sea, began to question him about the service, and Andrew was ready enough to explain; but after he had been speaking a few moments a look of frowning puzzlement came to his face, and he broke off what he was saying.

'But, Mr Carrington, haven't we met before?'

'Met?' Stephen stared. 'Nay, I have no recollection.'

'Surely . . . Let me see. Surely it was you.'

'I don't know what you're driving at. Though—'

'Four or five months ago. April, it was. In Plymouth. In the Ring o' Bells in Plymouth Dock. Don't you remember? You bought me a mug of ale. You were in fine fettle that night, offering drinks to strangers . . . That was before the press gang broke in . . .'

There was silence between them. 'What am I bid?' came

the auctioneer's voice. 'Eighteen guineas, eighteen guineas. Eighteen – has everybody done now? Going, going.' Bang. '*Sold* to the gent in the blue coat.'

'Ye've made a mistake, Mr Andrew Blamey,' Stephen said shortly. 'I never was in Plymouth in all me life.'

Andrew went red.

'You – were never in Plymouth?'

'No. Nor in this – what is it? – Ring o' Bells. Did ye suppose I wouldn't've remembered you?'

'Well . . . well, I'll be damned! Sorry, Cousin Clowance. And sorry to you, Mr Carrington. If it was not you it was your spitting living image! You were with a pale-faced dark fellow, who had a girl with him, and you led the singing. Or at least – crave your pardon – if twas not you then this fellow who was the spitting living image led the singing . . . Well, I have never been so confounded in my life by a similarity! Though I grant this fellow was none too well dressed and his hair was longer and – and of course he had been merrying himself with the drink – as of course so had I! . . .'

'Perhaps that helps to explain the mistake,' Stephen said more genially. 'I was never out of Cornwall all through April, was I, Clowance?'

After a moment Andrew said: 'Well, I suppose it's natural it should not have been you, engaged as you are to my cousin – though damn it, the uncanny resemblance still disturbs! I will tell you, Cousin, it was not at all a pretty night, that night, in the end. It was the merest chance I was there myself, the *Countess of Leicester* having been ordered direct to Plymouth with the Governor of Gibraltar aboard. Having disembarked him, we were setting sail for Falmouth by first light on the morrow, but, belay me, after a few days at sea I never can resist testing my land legs and my thirst at the same time! I was with Lieutenant Peter Dillon and we turned in at the Ring o' Bells because we heard the singing ... "A leaky ship with her anchor down, Hurrah, me boys, Hurrah!" They were all singing fit to raise the beams, and this big fair-haired feller was standing on a stool leading it all! ... However—'

'Why did the Governor not come back on a naval vessel?' Stephen tried to interrupt this flow.

'Eh? What? Oh, he had heard that his son was ill, and we were leaving that morning and have the legs of most things ... I tell you, Cousin, the singing was at its height when in burst a company from the Navy intent on pressing any able-bodied men they could find. Dillon and I, of course, were safe enough in our uniform, but this blond fellow and the dark thin one with him were not, and were being lined up with others for inspection when they made a dash for it, and in a moment all was pandemonium! Hang me if they didn't get away, leaving one of the sailors dying of stab wounds on the floor!' Andrew coughed behind his hand and looked apologetically at Stephen. 'Beg your pardon again, Mr Carrington, when I recognized you – *thought* I recognized you – I'd scarce remembered where the story was leading, so to say. You do right to be indignant at such a mistake, for it is generally acknowledged that it was the blond man who did the stabbing. Clowance, will you ever speak to me again? To think I confused your betrothed with someone who, whatever the justification, was really a common murderer! ... When is the wedding to be?'

'What happened to the girl?' asked Clowance.

'What girl?'

'The one that was with – those two young men.'

'Oh, stap me, I have no idea. I expect she looked after herself. She looked the type who could do ... The wedding?'

'Oh ... the twenty-fourth of October.'

'So soon! Alas, I shall be at sea.' There was an awkward pause, during which they all carefully watched the auction of a fine farm horse. 'Hr-mm! You were asking me about the packet service, Carrington.'

'Was I? Oh yes. About the discipline.'

'It is a good life. Discipline, like the uniform, is semi-naval, but of course none of this flogging nonsense. We've – what? – thirty-four, thirty-five vessels in service at present. We carry mail, passengers, goods to and from Lisbon, Corunna – only restarted this month, I may say – Gibraltar, Carolina, the West Indies, the Brazils, *and* New York till the Yankees declared war on us.'

'What size are your vessels?'

'One hundred and sixty tons to about two hundred and thirty tons burthen; crews of thirty-odd, all picked men; mostly three-masted full-rigged ships, and armed to defend themselves. Some of the packets are owned by groups of shareholders, some solely by the captain himself. They are hired by the Post Office at around eighteen hundred pounds per annum per ship.'

'And risk of capture?'

'Eh? Oh well, there's some risk of that, that's for sure. There's always the French. And now the American priva-teers, larger vessels, heavier manned and gunned. But we're pretty fleet, y'know. It takes a fast vessel to catch us.'

Conversation went on, but it was not quite easy, and Andrew took the first opportunity to escape.

'Well ... there's Valentine, I see. And Ben. I lost a pony

on Valentine's horse today. Thought he would romp home. Only faded in the last furlong. Still . . . I've just bought some tickets in Swift's Lottery. Maybe I'll furnish myself with a prize. Surely I need it! First two prizes are for twenty thousand pounds. Just think on it.'

'I'm thinking,' said Stephen.

'Well . . . I wish you all happiness, Cousin. Wish you *both* all happiness, and greatly regret I shall not be there to toast your health on the day! Though now maybe I should not have been invited even if I *were* ashore, seeing the insult my mistake has been to you . . .'

'Of course ye would,' said Stephen soothingly. 'Except that we plan a quiet wedding. I do not know what Mrs Poldark's plans exactly are, but if twere me own choice I should just have the ceremony over as quick as you like. I am from Bristol, ye know, and have few friends and relatives in the district, so whoever is invited to the church will be Clowance's side of the family. Isn't that so, me dear?'

'Yes,' said Clowance.

III

'George,' Harriet said, 'you must not sulk.'

Her husband glanced angrily at her and then away. His expression did not change.

'Sulkiness', said Harriet, 'is not becoming in a man of elegance and distinction. You should not suffer it to become so noticeable.'

'I suppose you realize,' he said, 'that you have made a fool of yourself. And me into the bargain!'

'Bargain?' she said and laughed in her throat. 'Certainly it was no bargain. But a few guineas is not the greatest disaster that can befall. A greater one is to have a disputation at the ringside like a farrier arguing the price of a shoe.'

He flushed now. He would never have stood such insults from Elizabeth, but this woman seemed unaware of the liberties she was taking. The most heinous offence of all was to compare him with a blacksmith, since his grandfather had been one; but either she had forgotten or did not care a damn.

George's life had been turned upside down since he married Harriet Carter. Although she had consented to become his wife, she seemed to lead a life both at Cardew and in Truro totally independent of his own. Even the social fact that she was Lady Harriet Warleggan and not just Lady Warleggan seemed to be a factor in establishing her separateness. She gave orders to the servants without consulting him. Of course Elizabeth had directed his house efficiently enough but in a gently firm way that was hardly perceptible; Harriet took major decisions, such as ordering a new carriage, such as discharging his cook, such as commanding his lake to be re-stocked with trout. And all with *his* money. She had brought little or nothing to him but a few pieces of good furniture, a few debts, a fair array of family jewellery, and a collection of damned animals.

These last were perhaps the greatest cross he had to bear. If she was extravagant with money he could swallow his chagrin and determine to make more. If she took too much on herself he generally if grudgingly admitted that she had effected an improvement. If she took liberties in her manner of talking to him sometimes, he had to remind himself that she was after all the sister of a duke. But the animals! His expectation before their marriage that the two boarhounds could be confined to the kitchens was quite disappointed in the outcome. They roamed everywhere, delicate, he had to admit, inside the house – except when one got a bee in his ear and upturned him – but frightening to the servants, demanding of the best places by the fires and capable of disgusting slobbering noises when they felt so disposed. There were few opinions George would have admitted to having in common with Jud Paynter; but they strongly shared the view that dogs were totally unnecessary and not infrequently obscene.

Still worse was the horrible little galago, which slept all day and only woke as dark fell; and climbed and swung and looked like a monkey – a very frightened, inquisitive, nervous monkey – discovered sometimes in Harriet's bedroom when George had other ideas, liable to startle one by being itself surprised in some extremely unlikely corner. Yet, in spite of its nervousness, George at times detected impudence in its saucer eyes. Sometimes when he shouted at it – when Harriet wasn't there – it would slide down the curtain as down a greasy pole and stare up at him as if to say, 'Lay a finger on me if you can.' Which he never could, for it was off like a flying squirrel swinging from chair to chair or scuttering behind a sideboard and instantly out of reach again.

So it had not infrequently occurred to George already that he had made a grave mistake in marrying again. The old life of solitary eminence, with no one daring to cross him and only mercantile problems to concern him, sometimes looked too alluring.

Yet, had he had the chance to return to his old ways, it is probable that he would not have taken it. Harriet was a dynamic woman and had all the faults of her qualities. But her very presence was a constant challenge to his pride and to his manhood. Elizabeth had been essentially a gentlewoman, in the sense of that word when it is made two, and could only be brought to vehemence when deeply stirred. Harriet was anything but gentle: she spat and swore and could be coarse in conversation. On the relatively rare occasions when she admitted him into her bedroom she had no passive thoughts at all, and he came away exhausted and stimulated, with wild passionate memories that kept recurring during the days that followed.

So far they had had arguments but never a downright quarrel. There had never been a test of strength. If there ever were, the probabilities suggested she would come out of it best, assuming she had the intelligence to choose her own ground. Being a woman, it seemed unlikely that she would ram her head against a wall she knew to be there.

'In any event,' she said on this occasion, 'I wanted the horse and we have bought the horse. Is there anything to complain of in that? I know you would have preferred to leave it with your old rival; but had you done so you would have been going back on your bid – which is not too admirable a thing to do – and Poldark would have had the horse, however expensive it might have been to him! We are well out of a vexing situation.'

George grunted.

'It is the first time,' Harriet said, 'that I have seen this gentleman. He has a certain sultry, sallow look which I admit give one curious sensations in the crotch; but I would not have thought him such an ogre as I had been led to believe. Trim his hair a little, give him a new cravat, and he would pass in a drawing-room as well as the next man. Indeed, were you not so daggers-drawn towards each other, I would favour his acquaintance.'

George grunted again like a bull being pricked with the finer end of the goad.

'Try inviting him,' he said. 'See what your response will be!'

'I might do precisely that! Anyway you permit his gangling son and his bonny daughter to frequent your house. Are we not all too near to each other to brangle like cocks on a dunghill?'

'They do *not* frequent my house! You have seen them there once, just once, at Easter, at Valentine's request . . .' George stopped and swallowed and carefully adjusted his hat. He fancied that Harriet enjoyed teasing him, and sometimes, when the subject was different, he quite enjoyed it. Not now. But he must not get fussed and angry. He must meet her on her own ground. 'My dear,' he said, 'however much you may fancy this gentleman, with all the unsavoury rumours that surround him, I regret that, now you have chosen me as your permanent companion, you cannot have him too. Ross and I . . . since the days we were at school together we have never found pleasure in each other's company. There is a saying, isn't there, about oil and water. We are oil and water. There are few things he and I agree on but I believe we would agree on this. However scornfully you may feel disposed to liken us to cocks on a dunghill, there is no way of avoiding the fact that – even if we no longer quarrel so openly – we *cannot* mix. You have to choose between us, and – and, as it seems, you have already chosen.'

Harriet's laugh was so deep as to be half buried, but lazily attractive for all that. George knew it too well. 'Then let us differ to agree. I have chosen. We have a new horse, Bargrave. I shall ride him tomorrow. You have an expensive wife, George, and pay the penalty. Captain Poldark must be forgot. Do I not see Major Trevanion bearing down upon us once again?'

She did. Trevanion arrived, looking flushed. Both he and George had heavily backed Valentine in the third race and had lost a good deal from the wagers. But a lucky bet on the fifth had restored Trevanion's fortunes. He was cheerful and sanguine and not a little drunk.

At that moment George's sharp eyes discerned Trevanion's sister Cuby returning, it seemed, to the racecourse, her eyes shining suspiciously, from the woodland which led to the river. With her was the young Poldark, streaky and thin and rather stooping. Quite clearly they had been walking together and not disliking the experience.

'Valentine,' said Trevanion expansively, as he came up. 'Where is Valentine?'

'He was down at the ring,' said George.

'Lud's my life, that was an excellent race he rode! Lud's my life; that other nag should never have overtook him! Had not Carapace fallen at the corner ... The course was damned badly planned. They should never have had such a slope at the corner. I believe Carapace's jockey is quite serious hurt.'

'I believe so,' said George. 'By the way—'

He was interrupted. 'When does Valentine leave for Cambridge?'

'Tomorrow.'

'Ah ... I had hoped one day next week he might come over. While Augustus is home, twould be suitable for him to call and see—'

'By the way,' said George, interrupting in his turn; 'have you noticed that Miss Cuby has been walking with Mr Jeremy Poldark? And from the look of them, they do not appear to have disliked their stroll.'

Major Trevanion's face wore a number of expressions as he turned his head and looked across the crowded field, moving from surprise to annoyance to self-satisfaction. They could all plainly see the wagonette to which Cuby and Jeremy were returning.

'That is a mere trifle,' said Trevanion heartily. 'Let them meet. We have a deep understanding, Cuby and I. She has promised me. She will not go back on her promise.'

'Promised you what?' Harriet asked.

'Ah, madam,' said Trevanion, 'that is a secret between her and me. But I have the greatest possible trust in her. See if I am not correct in my estimate of my dearest sister!'

Chapter Six

I

Situated near the winning post, between the two open stands, a marquee had been erected where the gentry – but only the gentry – might drink or eat a pie in seclusion and a degree of comfort. The pies were not a notable attraction, since most people had brought their own hampers. The drink was.

Shortly before the start of the last race Ross walked in with Isabella-Rose and Mrs Kemp. They would soon be leaving for home, but Isabella-Rose, who had eaten hugely of the food they had brought, was complaining of being hungry again, so he bought her a pork pie and sat her down at a small folding table with Mrs Kemp and two glasses of lemonade, and went back to the long trestle table to buy himself a last brandy.

Because the final race was imminent, the marquee was unusually empty, with less than a score of patrons. Among them were Lord and Lady Falmouth talking to Lord Devoran and his randy daughter Betty, and Dwight and Caroline in a larger group.

Ross, who knew how little Dwight cared to be in society, suspected the reason why he had become more social over the last couple of years: Dwight wished to see a mental hospital established in the county to stand beside the Cornwall General Infirmary which had been opened in Truro some thirteen years ago, and it was at gatherings where men of influence and affluence talked and drank together that such a project could be furthered. Indeed, there had been a public meeting in February of this year and a subscription list opened, with the Prince Regent donating five hundred guineas, Lord Falmouth two hundred, and Lord de Dunstanville, not to be outdone, three hundred; but while the war continued a beginning was in abeyance – no one had the necessary drive or initiative to take the next steps.

As Ross sipped his brandy, Lady Falmouth walked towards the door of the marquee with the Devorans, leaving Lord Falmouth temporarily alone. It seemed a matter of civility to join him.

'Ah, Captain Poldark,' the young man said, 'I had your letter last week. Thank you. You made your position perfectly plain.'

'Not discourteously so, I trust?'

'Not at all. Firm. Possibly a trifle misguided.'

'In what way, my lord?'

'There seem to be two distinct reasons why you do not wish to stand again in my interest. One, you are tired of the responsibility and wish to opt out of it. Two, you feel we shall quarrel over matters of principle.'

Ross considered. 'Yes ... I suppose that is true. Though ...'

'Though?'

'Well, I suppose it is the latter which concerns me most.'

'Yes. Yes, I see. But I trust I am correct in supposing the former also?'

'That I am tired of Parliament? I don't know, my lord. It has been known for a man to groan at some irksome responsibility and then to miss it when it is taken from him. Possibly when this has happened I shall not miss it at all.'

'Or you may.'

'Or I may. But only, I think, so far as the war is concerned. At the best, even as a member of Parliament, one is little more than a puppet activated by forces so much stronger than oneself. Can one *really* pretend that by sitting in that chamber one is at *all* able to influence history? One could be as well ploughing one's land or digging in the ground for tin.'

Falmouth ordered two more glasses of brandy. For the relatively small number of people in the marquee a lot of noise was being generated. Nobody was drunk, certainly not his Lordship, but everyone was at the end of a day in which an amount of liquor had been consumed.

'Do you yet know the exact date of the election?' Ross asked.

'Between the fourth and the eleventh of October. It's a good time – the harvest is in and the bustle of the Quarter Sessions will be over.'

'But in Truro itself.'

'The ninth. That will be the Friday.'

'There will be no contest?'

'Oh no.'

'Whom have you chosen in my place?'

'Colonel Lemon will retain his seat. In your place? There are one or two people I have in mind. One is Sir George Warrender.'

Ross took a gulp of brandy. 'Before God, I thought for a moment your Lordship was going to say Sir George Warleggan!'

They both laughed.

'No ... He is my brother-in-law. There is also another brother-in-law, John Bankes, who could be relied upon never to say a word out of turn.'

'As I could not.'

'As you could not.'

They drifted towards the opening in the marquee, where the rest were standing. The horses were lining up for the start.

'Mrs Poldark is well?'

'Thank you, yes. We are expecting our fifth child in December, and she does not care to come into company at this stage.'

'I had your daughter pointed out to me just now. The very blonde young lady.'

'Yes.'

'Outstanding fairness. Were your parents fair?'

'Not at all. Nor my wife's. Clowance is quite an exception.'

'Like you and your pro-Catholicism in a notably Protestant family.'

Ross smiled grimly.

'Very true, my lord. Though I do not see myself at all as pro-Catholic. On the contrary, I would that they were all Protestants. But since they do not wish to be, I think they should be allowed to worship as they will and not suffer material disadvantage for it.'

Lord Falmouth stared across at the horses, which would not get into line. 'Do you have a fancy for this race?'

'No.'

'Nor I . . . I suppose you know, Captain Poldark, that this Emancipation business is likely to be a dead issue in the next parliament.'

'No, I certainly do not.'

'Well . . . With Liverpool as First Minister you will see nothing under his government.'

'He left the issue to a free vote in the spring. And later

in the Lords, Mr Canning's motion was defeated by only one vote.'

'Maybe. But there is strong feeling in the country. And notably in this influential county. The heads of the Sidmouth party in Cornwall are being particularly careful, I notice, to choose candidates for their anti-Catholic views. I think you will find the new House when it assembles distinctly less friendly to Mr Canning's cause than the present one.'

Ross did not reply. In this respect he knew his Lordship was better informed than he was.

'So you see,' said Lord Falmouth with slight malice, 'you will be needed more than ever at Westminster to support so unpopular a cause.'

'Are you inviting me to change my mind?'

'Certainly not. It would be most improper.'

'It would certainly be improper to accept a seat from a patron and then to act directly contrary to his views.'

'Which is what you have said before, and I acknowledge the truth of it.'

'So?'

'So. You should not put any strain upon your conscience.'

'They're off!' someone shouted, and this was echoed by many voices.

Although Ross and the other man had no interest in any of the horses or in the outcome, they were drawn to the doorway to watch the contest by the magnetism that works in any horse race. The crowd cheered, the horses thudded their hoofs into the scattering mud, jockeys kneed themselves out of their saddles, crouching and urging and using the whip. Two horses came to the finishing post neck and neck, a black and a roan. In the soft going it had been strength and staying power that counted all day. In the end the roan won by a neck and the referee rang his bell to announce the winner. The rest of the group went out into the last sunshine as the losing horses galloped past. The two men remained standing in the doorway.

'Do you ever read the *West Briton*, my lord?'

'A radical periodical, with very little to recommend it. No.'

'The first editorial this week asks the question: "Shall we ever see a time when an election will really be An Appeal to the People?"'

Superior members of the public were now coming into the marquee for a final drink. Among them were Major Trevanion and Sir George and Lady Harriet Warleggan.

Ross went on: 'A friend of mine who as it happens is here today has also said: "When can we have an election like the Americans – no rowdiness or fighting or fuss and all seats contested on the same day?" You see, my lord, how unsuitable I am to continue to represent your interest when both of these must also be my long-term aims?'

Lord Falmouth nodded as he finished his brandy. 'Have a care for one thing, Captain Poldark. It is a mistake in life and especially in politics, to take so distant a view that one loses sight of the vital thing closest at hand.'

'Which is?'

'What you have mentioned yourself a few moments ago! To win the war.'

II

What might be described as the North Coast Convoy left to ride home as the twilight faded and a sliver of moon peered out behind the clouds. There were the two Enyses, four

Trenegloses, Paul and Daisy Kellow, the two Pope girls, five Poldarks, Stephen Carrington, Mrs Kemp, John Gimlett with the new pony, and two other grooms. Since the ways were not all that safe for the lonely traveller after dark – especially with so many gypsies and horse traders drawn together for the day – it was common sense to ride together. But inevitably, the tracks being so narrow, the convoy became a crocodile, there never being more room than for two or three.

Stephen said sulkily: 'There wasn't no other way – I've told you!'

'Except to tell him the truth.'

'It wouldn't have *done*!'

'I don't see. Of course if the sailor did die of his stab wounds . . .'

'That is not *true*, as I've said to you twice already! If the man died twas not from the pinpricks I gave him. If he did die – which I still doubt – then twas of some colic or other distemper he had picked up elsewhere, and they are trying to lay the blame on a slight wound so as to make it out it was a villainous act!'

Monuments of cloud had climbed up the sky again. The puny moon was obliterated, only the broken roots of one of the clouds being incandescent at the edges.

Stephen said: 'I ask you. Is there aught villainous in trying to escape being pressed? Everyone does it. Every able man who's right in the head! Would ye have wished me now at this moment to be a sailor, swinging athwart some lower mizzen tops'l yard and expecting the lash if I was not quick enough about me work? Would ye now? Just tell me that. Would ye?'

'Of *course* not!' said Clowance fiercely but unhappily.

'But you blame me,' he said. 'You blame me, don't you.'

'Stephen, *no*! That is not it at all!'

'Then what is it?'

'It is just that I am not sure . . .'

'Not sure of what?'

She said: 'That it would not have been better – the best *policy* even – to have told Andrew the truth. Lies . . . they may be useful sometimes – I cannot say anything about that . . . But *this* time . . . You see, Andrew is a *relative*, one of the family. Surely it would have been better to have taken him into your confidence, to have said, look, Andrew, it happened like this. (Just as you have just told me.) You *didn't* kill him, you say. Even if the stab wounds had something to do with it, they were unintentional. So what is wrong with that? It was – a nasty fight. You were fighting for your freedom. Anything could have happened. It all sounds worse than it really was. So, Andrew, you could have said, pray keep quiet about it. Nobody else has connected me with the fight. In all likelihood, no one else ever will. So if you keep quiet . . . After all, I am affianced to your cousin, Clowance, and she is shortly to marry me. For everybody's sake it is better if this recognition goes no further . . .'

'Go on,' said Stephen bitterly, 'it's a good story.'

'But *now* . . . Don't you think he'll go on wondering? Wondering if he really did make a mistake. Thinking it over. And . . . if he ever comes to Nampara – as well he could – and sees Paul Kellow, he'll *know* you were lying. Then who knows what he will do or say on the spur of the moment?' Clowance tightened her rein as they came to ford a stream. 'That's what I mean, Stephen. That's really all that worries me.'

They separated while they clattered and splashed among the water and the stones.

When they came together again Stephen said: 'That's

not really all that worries you, is it. You're disgusted with me, aren't you.'

'What d'you *mean*?'

'That you're in love with a man who happens to be able to stick up for himself in a fight, who values his freedom and doesn't act spineless when he's attacked. You talk about truth! Well, that's the truth of it, isn't it. You're disgusted with me.'

'If I were – disgusted, as you call it – d'you think I should be worrying so much about your safety?'

'But even so – you're disgusted. You're only saying I should've confessed everything to a man I'd not known two minutes! Why, if I'd told him what you say I should have told him, he would have had a hold over me for the rest of me life!'

'But Andrew's a—'

'Yes, I know – a relative. But he's a relative of yours, not mine. How do I know which way he would jump, who he'd talk to, tattle with? You could smell the liquor on him today! I remember him at the Ring o' Bells; he was well in his cups when him and his friend came in. When the drink's in a man, who's to say what he will let out!'

They rode on for a while not speaking. External to the noise of the riders, the creak of leather, the clop of horses, only the crickets in the bushes were noisy.

Clowance was more upset than she wanted to show. She longed to idolize everything about Stephen, to admire and love his good looks, his confident maturity, his dashing enterprising courage, his quick wits, the startling quality of his maleness which made most men seem anaemic by comparison. But today had posed two less attractive aspects of the picture. The thought of him killing a man in a tavern brawl was disturbing both as to the act and as to the possible consequences. But worse was the quick, abrupt, yet glib way he had lied to Andrew in front of her, knowing that she must know he was lying – and not caring – and even inviting her to support his lies by providing him with an alibi. To kill a man is primitive, hard, male, ruthless, aggressive; yet it can have a justification. It is the law of the jungle. The lion in the jungle. But to deny it in all sorts of different ways, first that it never happened, second that if it happened it was not your fault, third that if it was your fault it was excusable, fourth that if it was not excusable it must more than ever be denied . . . this was not so much the part of the lion as of the jackal.

As they rode on, Clowance knew in her heart, though she did not yet acknowledge it, that the argument, the discussion, the crisis between them would eventually be resolved. Whatever else had been killed, it would not kill her love; and because that could not be more than temporarily harmed she would soon begin to see the situation from his point of view. On this matter she would begin to reason and argue as he reasoned and argued.

Above all things she wanted the preservation of his safety; so that very soon they could be married and live happily together at the Gatehouse and make love under the autumnal moon.

III

Left behind on the racecourse as darkness fell were several hundred people milling around, some tidying up and working on the dismantling of the stands, many lying drunk, many more staggering about in the just mobile stages of drunkenness, young girls and lads screaming and shrieking at each other, beggars and gypsies sorting through the refuse left behind by their betters and often squabbling and fighting over it; stray dogs, pigeons, jackdaws, gulls, the occasional rat. Most of the marquees where drink was sold were still doing a roaring trade by the light of storm lanterns. Fights began to break out, involving only a few but like sparks showing where a real fire might begin.

One of the noisiest of the groups of young men was from Grambler and Sawle, and two of the noisiest of that group were the two younger of the Thomas brothers, Art and Music. Ardent Wesleyans, they had fallen today into the pit of sin and shame, the Holy Spirit had left them and their souls were empty of the pure water of salvation. The spirit that now animated them was not holy at all.

It was chiefly the fault of Moses Vigus, from Mellin, who worked at Nampara. Moses was not so wicked a man as his father had been; but he already closely resembled him: at thirty-odd he was completely bald and his round polished unlined face was as guileful as that of a perverted cherub. He it was who had asked to borrow a farm cart and horse from Ross and, when granted it, had cast about for likely companions who could afford to pay 1s. for the return trip. He had asked the Thomases last because, unlike some Wesleyans, they were strict non-drinkers. So when they got to the races he thought it time to start tempting them, and he had succeeded beyond his best hopes.

Art had been a lively subject for temptation. He was making no progress with the Widow Permewan, and the tannery business as well as its owner remained beyond his grasp. Furthermore Edie Permewan, who was thirty years his senior, was dry company. (She repeated herself so often that she was like an organ, he thought, with very few stops: you pulled one out and got a predictable result.) Whatever his intentions towards other women in the village once the marriage ceremony was over, he was compelled to be totally circumspect during the prolonged courtship lest any whisper killed his chances. And whatever his Chapel beliefs, prolonged abstinence from the flesh-pots bit deep.

As for Music, he was of altogether frailer stuff. By nature a happy, jolly, even silly young man, given to darting impulses which he followed with carefree abandon, he had always been a trial to Sam Carne, the Leader of the flock. Music was a gadfly, almost enjoying his part as village butt, though struggling at the moment in the deeper waters of his first ever love-sickness and trying intermittently, with Dr Enys's help and encouragement, to throw off his role of a comic relief and become as other men.

Brandy smelt good. It tasted better. It was dearer than ale but you didn't need so much.

Somehow this afternoon Music had come to possess a child's kettledrum. Somehow someone had been able to lend him a widow's bonnet. Moses had stolen an apron for him. So dressed, Music led a recruiting procession round the race track. What they were recruiting they were not quite sure. Nor indeed did the song they sang sound quite suitable. So far as one could tell above the din, Music was singing:

> 'Parson Croft, Parson Croft,
> A married life he led, sur,
> His missus she were round and soft,
> And round an' soft 'is bed, sur!
> Sing tally-o! Sing tally-o!
> Sing tally-o! Why zounds, sur!
> He mounts 'is wife to 'unt the fox,
> Sing tally-o, the 'ounds, sur!'

Walking on his toes 'like a fly', as Prudie had once said, bonnet aslant his grinning greasy face, swinging his elbows as he beat on the kettledrum, he was at the head of an increasing procession of lumpish young men and girls holding each other by the waist and screaming and laughing and trying to join in the song.

Half way round the ground Music saw that he was being watched by four young women. Of these two were grinning broadly, but two were not, and one of the two who were not was Katie Carter, the tall black-haired girl he had taken a yearning, wistful fancy to. At Place House he thought himself lucky if he got even a word with her, let alone a civil answer. It was not that she was rude by nature, and it was not that she had other men to choose from (her size and clumsiness and morose shyness put them off), it was rather that Music, being half saved, poor creature, was not really worth consideration. Sometimes, more recent like, he had thought he impressed Katie a little more than he used to. But now he was caught in his own iniquities, dressed like a woman, prancing on tiptoe, reinforcing all the old prejudices he had been trying to overcome. And tipsy.

His drum faltered, his figure drooped like a leek, he stopped singing; those behind barged into him, hard fingers dug his ribs, he was pushed on. And then drink came to his aid, giving him courage, even if it was of the wrong sort; he straightened up and began to sing again and led the way prancing up to the four young women and made a circle round them.

'Sing tally-o! Sing tally-o!
Sing tally-o! The 'ounds, sur!'

Two still laughed, the third grinned, but Katie continued to scowl. She enjoyed a joke now and then, but *all* the ringleaders of this group were from her district and behaving quite disgraceful in their drunkenness. It gave Sawle and Grambler a bad name, especially among fellow Methodists. (Half a dozen had already fallen by the wayside, rolling and shouting in the mud.) Also as a separate special thing, she very much disliked Moses Vigus, who was always sneering and poking fun, and who, on one occasion, had tried to put his hand up her skirts.

For a moment or two Music paused in front of her, trying to make her laugh, but didn't succeed. She had no idea that she was the object of his admiration, having accepted the general view that that sort of thing was not his style at all. He was about to become crestfallen again and creep away, but someone just then tugged the kettledrum out of his hand, almost dislocating his neck with the cord. It was the elder brother of the boy he'd taken it from, a bull-necked red-faced lad obviously looking for trouble. Music grinned sheepishly and turned to Art who was just behind him to ask if he should return the drum. So doing, he observed Moses Vigus reach forward and tip Katie's best hat over her eyes.

From good-tempered reluctance to tangle with some stranger over a toy that was rightly his, Music changed his mood and took a wild swipe at the astonished Moses, who collapsed into the crowd behind. In no time thirty or forty people were fighting, some of them women, and in the midst of it, like temporary survivors at the centre of a cyclone, Katie and Music found themselves staring at each other.

After a few moments, receiving a flying fist in her back,

Katie shouted: 'Ye sprawling gurt gale, you, ye overgrown lobba, git outer my way! Stinking great lazy lootal! Cease yer dwaling and go 'ome!'

Hat in hand she fought her way out of the struggling crowd and stalked off into the dark, followed eventually and with great difficulty by her three companions.

IV

Demelza was in bed when Ross got home.

'Are you not well?'

'Very well.'

'You wouldn't lie to me?'

'I was up at six. Supper is laid if you wish for it.'

'So I saw. Jeremy and Clowance and Stephen are tucking in already.'

'Did you buy Bella her pony?'

'Yes, she's still out in the stables. Can't leave him alone.'

'What is his name?'

'Horace. Short for Horatio, I think.'

'That's one name lost to us, then,' said Demelza. 'Anyway, I don't believe I fancy Horatio Poldark. It might encourage him to go to sea.'

Ross looked round the room, the familiar room with its familiar well-used furniture. He loosened his stock and looked at Demelza who was sitting propped up with a pillow, one arm behind her head, bare where the nightdress sleeve had fallen back. It was her right arm, and she was a very right-handed person, but there seemed to be no sign of muscle development other than was necessary to give it an elegant shape.

'What are you looking at?' she asked.

'You.'

She gave a half-smile. 'Well, if you don't mind my size it is not yet too late.'

'Oh yes, it is. There are risks we have to take and risks we need not.'

'Well, I'm sorry. And yet I'm glad.'

'Both?'

'Yes, both. Sorry because I'd like it too. Glad because you still fancy me.'

'I fancy you.'

'Hm.' She looked at him, head on one side. 'Yet sight is so large a part of desire. Isn't it? To be ungainly . . .'

'That's not ungainliness, that's natural. You're too sensitive about it.'

'Maybe.' She lowered her arm and drew the nightdress sleeve down. 'Go and have your supper, my lover.'

'I'm not hungry. I seem to have been eating scraps with Bella all day. What an appetite the child has! And what combinations of food she can stomach at the same time! Rabbit pie, with cream and bananas! Hard-boiled eggs with cake and strawberry jam—'

'Thank you, that's enough. No doubt she will be sick tonight.'

'Have you ever known her to be sick?'

'No. Not except when she had the whooping cough.'

Ross sat on the edge of the bed and yawned. Demelza said: 'Did you buy a horse for yourself?'

'No.' He told her why, then went on to give a brief description of the day. He mentioned his meeting with Lord Falmouth.

Demelza said: 'So it is still open for you.'

'Not exactly.'

'Why not? How did you part?'

'I said if I reconsidered my position I would write within the week.'

'Well, then . . . You say there'll be no contest?'

'Not at Truro. Lord Falmouth's nominees will be returned unopposed.'

'But you are still hesitating?'

There was a long silence.

Then he said: 'You really want me to take it, my dear?'

'Do I?'

'Haven't you said as much these last weeks?'

'Not exactly. I want you to do what you most want to do.'

'But your advice . . .'

'I want you to do what you most want to do.'

'And you think I want to take it?'

She hesitated. 'I think. Yes.'

'I wonder why you think that?'

She looked at him, her eyes reflecting the candlelight, which blurred their expression. 'Because you are as you were born – restless, wanting adventure . . . or if not adventure, some sort of action. If this meant more travel abroad I would be at a dead set against it. But to go on until the end of the war, it seems to me that is what in your heart you would most prefer to do. After all, as you have told me so often, a member of parliament *need* not leave his home for long periods. If you go up thrice yearly it should be enough. You certainly need not – must not – be absent from home for more than three months in twelve. In that way, you can feel you are still helping a little more towards the war and yet be able to be home with your family for three-quarters of the time. Did I not say once that you wear a hair shirt? You live with a sort of, a kind of self-criticism which never allows you any complacency. Is this not the best way of easing it, of keeping a check on it, of not allowing it to fret you too much?'

'So,' said Ross thoughtfully.

'So,' said Demelza.

Downstairs there was a sudden shouting. Isabella-Rose had returned from the stables. Mrs Kemp's voice could also be heard in open rebuke.

'Time someone took a belt to her,' said Ross.

'I know. Will you do it?'

'It is the mother's duty,' said Ross.

'What? In my condition?'

'Then it will have to wait,' said Ross. 'The most I have ever managed with her is a slap.'

'Which brought her galloping to me demanding that I should hit you back.'

'Did she now? Did she now? Well, well.'

They listened while the noise slowly subsided.

Ross said: 'Jeremy was with a girl today. I think it was that one. I saw them walking together.'

'I trust it is a good sign. Though if her brother is so determined against it, one cannot see much hope.'

'There's always hope if they are really in love with each other.'

'Jeremy is,' said Demelza.

V

When Ross had gone down to supper Demelza stretched her legs in bed to gain a more comfortable position. She had *not* felt well today. It had been a light fever but it was passing. She had been in bed since seven.

Having lived so long together, Ross and Demelza found it hard to deceive one another. Their ears were attuned to tiny nuances, and a hint of insincerity or mental reservation was usually detectable. But tonight she had brought it off in two respects. First she had deceived him about the unimportant matter of her indisposition. Not so unimportant from the point of view of her own morality was her deception about his retaining his seat in Parliament. What she had said to him was not literally untrue: she believed him a man who needed the stimulus, even the goad, the frustration, of such a position. But in so urging she had not been thinking of him, nor even of herself, but of Jeremy.

With a sympathetic but observant eye she was aware of how hard he was finding it to get Cuby Trevanion out of his blood. She also knew that as instigator of the reopening of Wheal Leisure he felt keenly the present failure of the mine to pay its way. Further, from conversation with him before he met Mr Trevithick, she understood what hopes he had been building on the development of his steam carriage.

Now all was bitterness and disappointment and failure; and she remembered the conversation they had had over the supper table in May. To drop all his failures behind him and to go and fight was a clear-cut solution. As a patriotic man Ross would not dissuade him. And how could she?

So in a delicate balance Demelza reasoned that she would rather lose Ross for periods of the year because she could lose him more safely. With Ross at home there was no real need for Jeremy to be on hand at Wheal Leisure; with Ross away an extra responsibility devolved on his son. Happily they got on well together now after the frayed relationship of a year or so ago; but Ross at Westminister left Jeremy the only male in the house.

This might not tip the scales, but it just could. Where preservation of her son from the hazards of war came in, Demelza was prepared to use any strategem that offered itself.

Chapter Seven

I

News was filtering in of bitter disasters to the Russian armies at a place called Borodino, with the French triumphant everywhere. General Kutusov, it was said, had evacuated Moscow and the French had already entered it.

Even in Spain things were not now so favourable. Following the triumphant entry into Madrid, with the populace welcoming the liberating armies in an ecstasy of joy, Wellington had been loaded with honours; but after the heady celebrations came the grim reality. Commanding 80,000 troops of four nationalities grouped in two armies divided by 150 miles of difficult terrain, Wellington still faced four French armies which outnumbered his own by three to one. And if Napoleon returned the victor from his war with Russia . . .

What had to be done must be done quickly, and Wellington had left Madrid as soon as he could and had marched with four of his divisions a distance of a hundred and sixty miles to invest Burgos. Since then little had been heard. It could be that any day a fast frigate would bring news of the fall of the fortress city and another great victory. But Burgos, people said, was a little like Badajoz, and Wellington was still without his siege trains.

Looking at his maps, with Jeremy and Dwight, and sometimes Stephen, Ross expressed his concern. Not only was Madrid, it seemed to him, in danger of being retaken –

which militarily did not matter so much – but Wellington's army was in some danger of being caught between Clausel to the north of him and Soult to the south.

The harvest in England was the best for years, and as the time of the election came on a comfortable glow lay over the farmlands of which England was still largely composed.

Not that prosperity or discontent made much difference to the election, for the days the *West Briton* dreamed of were not yet come. Lord Liverpool was likely to be supported in Parliament by a much more comfortable majority. There were several bitter contests in Cornwall, notably those at Penryn and Grampound, where the election in each case took three days. In Truro, where it occurred as forecast on Friday the 9th, it was all over in half an hour. The Burgesses assembled and elected Lord Falmouth's candidates *nemine contradicente*, as Mr Henry Prynne Andrew put it. They were Colonel Charles Lemon and Captain Ross Poldark.

George Canning had been persuaded out of his safe seat to contest Liverpool, one of the open boroughs with a more or less popular franchise; out of its 100,000 odd inhabitants about 3,000 had the vote, though the voting was not secret.

The contest, Canning wrote to Ross later, took eight days and brought him to the very edge of exhaustion, for each day the rival candidates had to attend the polling station and shake the hand of, and speak a few words to, every single voter as he turned up. Two men were killed in rioting between rival factions and a couple of hundred injured, but this was a quiet election for Liverpool.

When the seat was at last won he was carried through the streets for three hours. 'I am', he wrote, 'off to Manchester soon where I am to make a big speech, though it will not be to advocate the enfranchisement of that great city, much though they may expect it. As you know, my feeling is that it is better to risk a few injustices such as this than to consider a reform of the whole system, which could do irreparable harm to the balance of our constitution.'

Though neither could see into the future, Canning's becoming a member of the Liverpool constituency was to bring his friendship with Ross to breaking-point because of his advocacy of Liverpool metal interests. But that was far ahead.

'It gives me a feeling of distinction to represent so fine a city as Liverpool,' he ended his letter, 'and there has been a heady stimulus in this close contact with a living – and very lively! – electorate. I had many doubts at the beginning as to the wisdom of attempting it, but now I feel war-weary and triumphant. I could, indeed, have saved myself the tremendous wear and tear because I find I have also been elected both for Petersfield and for Sligo.

'But what good news that my old friend has not altogether cast us off and is returning to the battlefield! From the way you spoke and the way you wrote I had felt you an altogether lost cause. We are in for a strenuous session and I believe you will not regret this change of mind. We shall at least be together shoulder to shoulder in encouraging the firm prosecution of the War!'

II

October 9 was a day that came to be remembered by the Nampara household in ways other than for the re-election of its head to a seat at Westminster.

At eight Ben Carter and Jeremy had their usual half-hour discussion about the mine. The £10 a share call would take them to the end of the year. There was certainly no justification yet for the re-opening of the mine, certainly nothing to cover the initial outlay of the engine, but what was being brought up and sold was lengthening the time it could run.

Similarly there was no justification for building a whim engine, so the old Trevithick boiler continued to languish on its trestles in Harvey's Foundry, together with the other bits and pieces assembled there in more hopeful days. What Jeremy *had* obtained from the other venturers when they met last month was sanction to try to improve the water supply. Jeremy's catchment was clearly not going to be a great success in such a dry summer as this had been. What water fell tended to evaporate under the sun; so the supply of pure water almost since the mine was opened had had to be supplemented by mules carrying barrels from the Mellingey. It was wasteful and time-consuming.

In a survey of the land, Jeremy had come to the conclusion that there was a point at which the much utilized and ill-treated Mellingey stream was twenty or thirty feet higher than the rain catchment he had built beside the mine. This point was not far from Wheal Maiden before the stream began its plunge down towards Nampara. The distance from Wheal Leisure was about a mile as the crow flew but nearly two by any feasible route. It was hard to be sure of the degree of fall, but even ten feet would be enough, and he was fairly certain there was that. So it was technically not impossible to construct a leat, which in places would have to become an aqueduct, which would convey a portion of the water from the stream in a wide semi-circle to the mine. This morning Jeremy was going with Zacky Martin to work out the practical difficulties and the cost.

At eight-thirty, having seen Jeremy off, Ben made his

usual tour of the mine, talking to the workers where he came on them, seeing that nothing untoward was occurring. In the last six months of extensive exploration the mine had been tunnelled and re-tunnelled so that it was now quite possible to lose one's way in it, if a few basic principles were not known and observed.

Having been over it all, Ben climbed back to the east workings of the 30-fathom level where much of the most productive work was still going on. There were twelve miners working here and they glanced up at him as he passed, wondering why he had returned. He could not have told them himself. It was not a suspicion that anything had been missed or that anything new could be found. The miners of twenty years ago had taken the best of the copper ore and left the less good, so it still paid to clear up this residue, still paid sometimes to pick at an unproductive-looking heap of deads or to climb up the long-since-abandoned rubble of an overhand stope to see what might yet be found there. But most of this had now been done.

It was back thirty yards or more from where most of the miners were now working that Ben observed a little fall of rock. It was new and, ever mindful of safety, he upturned a box and stood on it, trying to see whether the timber of the roof – which was necessarily an old roof – was sound. It looked like beech and alder, which meant it had, like so much of the rest of the timber, been imported, probably from Dorset or Devon. This roof was known as a stull because it supported the attle from a stope – or series of deep steps cut overhead into the lode. As the miners climbed, the non-paying ground was piled up for them to use as a platform to work their way upwards. The ground being loose above this roof meant that the timber had a great weight to support. But it all looked sound.

He went back another ten yards and mounted the stope, climbing to the top. This was one of the first pieces of work to be examined and one of the first to be discarded, for the lode had been thoroughly worked and there was nothing more worth considering.

All the same he did examine the rock roof at the top, pulling at a piece of fairly solid-looking ground and finding rock and stones crumbling and rattling on his helmet. He lit another candle from his helmet candle and found a place for it on a slaty ledge. He took out the small pick he always carried in his belt and considered the matter. By rights there should have been another man with him; but he decided to chance it and gave a few sharp blows at the ground above him. He was at once engulfed in a cascade of falling stones which nearly knocked him over. He then perceived what looked like another tunnel or winze running above.

At first he thought he had climbed as far as the 20-fathom shaft, but then realized he could not have done. Cautiously but without great excitement he slithered down the rubble to the 30 shaft, found a short ladder, carried it up and again mounted. Presently he found himself in a considerable cavern about ten feet high and some thirty long. It was not really above the shaft he had climbed from, but seemed to be pointing north.

The air was very stale but breathable; his candle bobbed and dripped, lurching its insecure light into one hollow after another; grey walls, unmetalliferous; a broken spade, heaps of rubble, a drip or two of water from a greenish point in the roof. He picked at the wall here and there: rather slatier ground than usual, a few gleams of iron pyrites and copper pyrites. Ben coughed to clear his chest and moved towards the tunnel showing at the farther end. A little extra stirring of interest as he saw that this went deeply on and slightly down. Clearly this was a part of some old workings which had not been opened in recent years. Had there been an earlier mine? From memory he could not recall whether Captain Poldark had first started this mine in 1787 or *re*-started it.

Safety again suggested he should fetch one of the men up from below to go with him – it was the common precaution against a sudden fall or foul air. Since he made it a rule for the men to obey, he could hardly flout it himself. He turned back to the ladder to go for either Stevens or Kempthorne, and as he did so he picked up the handle of the spade to see if it would give him a clue as to its origin and age. As soon as he touched it, it crumbled into dust.

III

Florence Trelask, Mistress Trelask's daughter, now a thin bloodless spinster of thirty-nine, had called in the morning for a fitting of the wedding dress. Earlier Clowance had chosen the material and the design: it was to be a gown and petticoat of fine blue satin sprigged all over with white, and with white Ghent lace at the collar and cuffs. She and her mother and Miss Trelask had been closeted upstairs for an hour this morning. It almost fitted, it would almost do, but Miss Trelask, a perfectionist like her mother, had packed it all up again, wrapped it in innumerable folds of tissue paper and borne it away in a large white box which she tied to the saddle of her pony. It would be returned fully completed by the end of next week.

After she left, Demelza rode to Killewarren to take

dinner with Caroline, accompanied much against her will by Jane Gimlett to see that she was safe and did not tire herself. Demelza thought all this coddling nonsense. It was true that she felt unwell from time to time, and this was a complete change from previous pregnancies when, after the first three months, she had always felt most exceptionally healthy. But the symptoms were slight – a swelling of the hands, giddiness, a tendency to light fever – and might not even be connected with her condition at all. She hadn't told Dwight and had no intention of doing so unless it became worse. And certainly it was no malaise that the presence or absence of Jane Gimlett was likely to influence.

Clowance stayed behind to do some sewing, which was clearly the proper occupation for a young lady within two weeks of her wedding day. But although a much better sempstress than her mother, she had really little more taste for it, and would have preferred to be out riding or walking or picking wild flowers.

In fact the day had a melancholy and autumnal look. There were precious few trees in this district to change colour or to drop their leaves, but the sea can look autumnal in its own right. Low clouds drifted across a fitful sun, and groups of sea-birds – gulls, kittiwakes and terns – were mirrored like mourners in the damp sands, all facing the breeze.

When Ben Carter hesitantly opened the door into the parlour his eyes lighted at the sight of its only occupant. He came slowly in.

'Oh, beg pardon, Clowance. I was looking . . . is anyone else at home?'

'I think that could have been more elegantly said, Ben.'

She seldom teased him, for he had no defences against her, but this time she could not resist.

He flushed, and then smiled. 'Well, you d'know what I mean.'

'No,' she said, 'I don't. Except that it is not me you are looking for.'

'Well,' he said again, and narrowed his brows. 'No one is ever more *welcome* than you are . . . I mean, to find 'ere. It's just . . .'

'Just someone else you seek.'

'Twas Cap'n Poldark I wished t'ave word with if he should be about. But they tell me—'

'Papa is in Truro. And will not be back tonight, because he has to attend an election dinner. He will be home tomorrow complaining of the quality of the food he has been served and asking for one of my mother's special pies.'

Ben nervously fingered his jacket, which he was aware was not suitable for a social visit.

'Jeremy not back yet, is he?'

'No. I thought he was with you.'

'And – and Mrs Poldark?'

'Is out to dinner. There is only me, Ben. And Isabella-Rose. Which would you prefer?'

There was a pause while he glanced at her sewing and she put it down.

'Then I must wait till tomorrer, eh?'

'For what?'

'For what I have to tell.'

'If you wish to. I don't know what you have to tell.'

'Tisn't that I *wish* to . . . Clowance, I have made a discovery at Leisure, and I thought twas only right and proper to come over to Cap'n Poldark and see him about 'n.'

She sat up. 'What *sort* of a discovery? *Copper?*'

'Can't rightly say yet. I thought I'd best tell Jeremy or

your father so's we could look at this new thing together, like. I see no special signs of nothing as yet, but I have broke into old workings which I don't b'lieve have been opened for a 'undred years or more. Know for sure, do ee, whether or no your father opened Wheal Leisure as a *new* mine back in 1787?'

'There was something there before. Surely has not everybody from time to time spoken of the old Trevorgie workings? Jeremy said they have tried to link up with them at Wheal Grace.'

'Well, it seems to me then that I have come 'pon them – that or something of that sort. Tis a kind of small cavern; I climbed up into 'n, and there was a broken spade handle lying 'pon the ground and when I picked him up he fell abroad just as if twas made of sand.'

Clowance looked at him. They looked at each other. Clowance said: 'Is it a shallow level?'

''Bout twenty-five, I should reckon.'

She got up. 'All right. I'll come with you.'

'What? No!'

'What d'you mean, *no*! I am the only Poldark here and it is my duty—'

'I – I don't rightly know as tis all that *safe*! Anyhow, I could scarce permit . . .'

'What could you scarce permit? Wait here; I'll be no more than two minutes.'

'Clowance!'

But she was out of the door like a gust of wind, wafting a faint perfume in his face. He bit his dirty fingernail and waited.

In less than four minutes she was down, in a blue seaman's jersey, barragan trousers, heavy shoes, her hair caught in at the nape of the neck by a yellow ribbon.

Protesting, he was led back across the beach to the mine, but his protests grew less as he saw they were having no effect and as the pleasure of her company overcame his doubt. When they stood in the engine house preparing to go down he thought he had never seen anyone so heart-breakingly beautiful as she was just then, wearing a drab miner's jacket rather too big for her, her skin looking fresher in contrast, her brilliant fair hair flowering under the dirty miner's hat.

They climbed down to the 30 level, stepped off the ladder and splashed through the trickle of water escaping from the mouth of the tunnel, began to grope their way along in the direction of the east lode. Several times he held out a hand to help her over piles of attle, across supporting timbers, through narrowed channels where pil-lars of granite had been left to strengthen the pit props and the roof, but each time she waved him on with a smile. They reached the sloping rubble stretching up below the exhausted lode, and here, some of the ground still being loose, she accepted his hand to be helped up. When he came to the ladder he went first and she quickly followed.

They stood and looked around, holding their heads still so that their candles should not flicker. Ben lit two more candles he had brought and watched their flickering flames before he stuck them in convenient crevices. Clowance stooped to pick up the remnants of the spade.

'Does this continue?'

'Oh yes. Over there. I intended to 've went in but thought I should first acquaint Cap'n Poldark of it all.'

'Let us go. Lead the way.'

'Nay, Clowance, I think this be as far as you should go. Tomorrer . . .'

'Tomorrow they will all be here. Lead on.'

'But—'

'If you do not go, then I will go alone.'

With a sigh, Ben went ahead down the tunnel. They sometimes had to stoop almost double to avoid projections in the irregular roof. There were numerous cross-cuts and winzes, but it was not hard to distinguish them from the main tunnel, which was falling by perhaps an inch a yard all the while. They came to another larger cavern.

'See here!' said Ben. 'They've used fire-setting, I reckon! That'd be afore gunpowder.'

'What's that? What d'you mean?'

On one side of the cavern there was a pile of rock debris at the foot of the face: it looked like granular stuff, finely powdered quartz, as fine almost as sand.

'In the old days,' Ben said, 'they'd belong to start a fire of brushwood and logs against the rock face; then when the face was heated proper, they'd quench it wi' water, and the expansion caused by the heating followed wi' the contraction of the cooling would make cracks where the face were weakest, so the rock could be picked out by pick and wedge later on. Twas hard work, and the fire and smoke below ground must've made some awful smeech, but twas the only way they 'ad. You can see the ashes here and the way the cracks was made.'

'But this was *before* gunpowder?' said Clowance. 'How long has gunpowder been invented?'

'Gracious knows. Hundreds of years, I reckon.'

'But is there any *copper* here, Ben? Or other metals? Can you see any real signs?'

'Oh, aye, they've worked here proper. Though it look more like tin to me. See these holes, they be what is called a working-big.'

'I don't follow you.'

316

'A space two feet and a half wide be the room a man must 'ave to wield his pick in a lode without breaking any of what they d'call the non-orey strata. So they call it a working-big, meaning the lode was at least two and a half feet wide. Here and here and here. See.'

'But is any left?'

'Not so's I can see. You'd have to break up this face to be sure. We've a whole new lot o' workings to explore, that's for certain.'

'Let's go on a bit further.'

'The air's none too good. The further we d'go . . .'

'It's not *bad*. No worse than in the fifty level you're just opening.'

Ben hesitated and then obeyed. In fact he was just as excited as Clowance. The next piece of tunnel was more broken, with shafts and winzes running and climbing in different directions. It was becoming a honeycomb. Ben chipped now and then with his hand pick so that the glint of new-cut stone should be there to guide them back the way they had come. The temperature was high and humid; but the ground looked more promising, the walls having greenish tinges, which Ben said was probably iron sulphate. He stopped again and they bent together.

'Thur's still some better stuff here. I reckon we may yet find where they've finished working the lodes.' He looked up at the lowering, uneven roof, from which came the occasional drip of reddish water. 'We gone far 'nough now, Clowance. These here props is rotten.'

'If they've stayed up for centuries they're not likely to fall just this moment. See round this corner.'

But round the corner an underhand stope had been worked, and the ground fell away sharply, some of the steps looking slippery and damp.

'Tis far 'nough, Clowance. Without a rope I'd not go no farther myself, that I wouldn't.'

She stopped, peering down. She was in her element.

'Sure? You're not telling me—'

'No. *Sure*. There's water down thur.'

Her candle lurched as she stooped to pick a stone from among the rubble. She threw it down the stope. The stone rattled a couple of times and then there was a *plop*.

'All the way we've come,' said Ben, 'it has been draining this way.'

'Yes . . .' Clowance still peered down towards the unseen water, then she looked at the rubble she had disturbed. She knelt and ran her fingers over it.

'What's to do?' said Ben.

She stood up. 'This. This is not a stone, Ben.'

He stared at a circular brown thing she had in her hand. It was about the size of a ha'penny. He picked it out of her palm, stared at it.

'Some sort of a coin, I reckon.'

'Some sort of a coin,' said Clowance.

Heads together, they examined it by the light of two candlepower.

'Ha'penny? Penny? Tis not quite neither. You can see the head thur. But what head, that's what's a puzzle.'

'What's the metal?'

'Copper or bronze.' He scratched it with his nail. 'Tis more like bronze to me.'

'What is bronze, Ben? I never quite know.'

'Mixture of copper and tin, I s'pose, mainly.'

'Has there ever been bronze coinage in England? For many years, I mean? I doubt it. Look. You can see the letters round the head.' She rubbed the coin. 'A-N-T-O-N. Can you not see that?'

'Yes.'

'Perhaps it's foreign. French or Spanish.'

'May be.'

'Was there ever any king of England called Anton?'

'The lettering d'go on. Round the corner, see. But it don't do to get too excited, Clowance. You know how the tin comp'nies used oft-times to make their own coins. Most possibly tis one of they.'

'What is on the back? I can't make it out.'

'It d'look like a vase to me. Or a jug. And there are some letters. P.O.T., is it? But that would be a shortening of something. Be they sticks?'

'Or ears of wheat? Ben, have you seen coins that the tin companies struck?'

'A few.' Ben was cautious.

'Any ever like this?'

'I don't mind that they were.'

'Or of bronze?' She reversed the coin again, rubbed it with a corner of her jacket. 'Round the corner by the head it says – seems to say – INNS. Isn't that a religious abbreviation, put over the cross? Early Christian surely.'

'I dunno nothing 'bout that.'

'No, I'm *wrong.* That's INRI. Damn, I thought it might prove . . .'

'Seems me it be more like IUNS.'

'Or IUUS. Or INUS.' She clutched his arm. 'INUS. It could be INUS!'

'I don't see what *that* d'mean.'

She continued to hold his arm. 'Look, dear Ben. Look carefully. Hold *still,* dear Ben! Your head down a little more. Now see! Spell it out. Running up round the coin, you get what?'

'A-N-T-O-N. What we've said afore.'

319

'And going further round, down the other side? If that is I-N-U-S? What do we get *then*? Run them together, dear Ben, run them *together*.'

'Anton – inus,' he said, mispronouncing it.

'Antoninus!' she cried. 'There was a king of England called Antoninus – though they called him emperor then. A *Roman*, Ben, a Roman Emperor!'

Ben stared at the coin, much more disturbed by Clowance's warmth towards him than by the possible discovery. 'What do that mean?'

'It means that if this coin is really what it seems, that it dates from Roman times, from the time when Rome ruled Britain. Which was around the time of Christ. Which was one thousand eight hundred years ago! I don't know when Antoninus lived, but I've heard of him. It means these old Trevorgie workings may have been used, worked . . . Papa will be entranced! And Jeremy. Oh, Ben, what a wonderful discovery!'

They held hands there in the slimy dark, her face aglow, his reflecting her pleasure. Then they turned, still holding hands, began to make their way slowly out again, stopping every few yards to notice something new, things they had missed on the way in – a basket half full of broken ore-rubble bursting open at the side, a stone wedge, a piece of horn that had come probably from a pick. All these things seemed now to be of the greatest antiquity. It was as if they had gone in blindfold and the discovery of the coin had unbandaged their eyes.

They returned to the second cavern, which was the largest of those they had so far discovered, and Ben began to pick here and there at the rubble. He soon unearthed part of a wheel, but it was not a wheel from a cart. It lay

near a narrow pit running along one side of the cavern, and
was iron-bound at the sides.

'What's this?' Clowance asked, picking up the end of
something white. Suddenly she dropped it.

Ben squatted beside her. He fished at the thing and gradually drew it out from the rubble. Then he too dropped it.

'Well . . . could be an animal.'

'It doesn't look like it to me!'

'Dr Enys'll no doubt be able to tell us 'bout that.'

'It is like the bone of a man's forearm!' said Clowance.

'Maybe . . . Though tis some thin.'

'Well, they *are* thin. There's two aren't there, side by side.
Feel your own arm.'

They stared at the long slender bone. No doubt if they
dug further into the rubble they would come upon other
bones which would settle the question. After a few seconds
Ben stood up.

'Best go, my dear.'

Clowance continued kneeling. 'I wonder how long – who
it was – why he should be left here.'

'No one'll ever know that.'

Quietly they left the cavern, stooped and twisted through
the next tunnel and out into the first cavern, then down the
ladder to the 30 level, and more tunnels till they reached
the ladder leading up the main shaft to the daylight.

'Tis a proper mystery to me,' Ben said as they paused for
breath, for a cleaner breath at last. 'How that has all existed
all those years and no one has never found'n before. And
there's air – of a sort – bad but bearable. There must be an
outlet somewhere, two outlets more likely, probably part
blocked. I wonder . . .'

'What?'

'They d'say the blown sand have moved over all they 'undreds of years, have buried houses, villages. Maybe the old mine have been so buried.'

Clowance was thinking of the bone they had found. 'I wonder,' she said, 'if the Romans used slaves . . .'

They went on up the ladder.

Beside the engine house was a timber changing shed where the miners left and collected their gear. Squinting in the bright daylight, they went in and Clowance took off her hat and jacket. Ben relieved her of these and hung them up, took off his own hat.

'Cap'n Poldark'll not be back tonight?'

'No, but Mama will, also Jeremy. Ben, I think you should be there before I tell them. It is your find really. Why do you not come about six, and I'll wait till then? We'll tell them together.'

He flushed. 'That'd be proper. Thank ee. About six, then. And Clowance . . . thank ee for coming down.'

She smiled brilliantly. 'It was – wondrous. It *must* be good news – for us all.'

They came out of the shed. Stephen Carrington was standing there.

IV

He said: 'Where've you *been?*'

They stared at each other. His face was taut with anger.

Clowance said: 'Down the mine with Ben. Stephen, we've—'

'Didn't we *agree* to *meet* today, Clowance? Didn't I say I was taking time off and would call for you at eleven?'

'Oh, Stephen. I am *very* sorry. In the excitement I had

totally forgot. Yes, you did! But it slipped my mind when Ben came—'

'Oh, it did, did it?'

'It was thoughtless of me. But when you—'

'Just slipped your mind when this little *misbegot* came to call! When he came crawling out of the mine to see you—'

'Stephen, don't be stupid! What's got *into* you? Look what we've *found*! Ben's found—'

But it was too late. All Ben's frustrated, buttoned-down antagonism exploded. '*What* did ee call me?'

'I called ee what ee wur!' snarled Stephen, mimicking Ben's accent. 'A little misbegot from Wheal Leisure that's come crawling out of the mine intruding where he's not wanted—'

'Stephen!' Clowance shouted angrily.

Ben aimed a swinging round arm blow at Stephen, who half parried it, but it hit him on the side of the jaw. Stephen stepped back, fists bunched, his whole face blazing, then rushed at Ben, brushing Clowance aside as he did so. There was a flurry of blows, and in a few seconds they had each other round the throat; they swayed across the yard and barged into the changing shed so that the wood nearly cracked; then they fell and rolled upon the rubble floor, fighting each other with the pent-up hate and rivalry of snarling animals intent on the ugliest injury.

'*Stephen!*' screamed Clowance. '*Ben! Stop it! Stop it! Stop it!*' She rushed at them, clutching coat and hair and flailing fist, being hit herself in the process, her own sturdy body half involved. But hatred was too strong for her; so was the momentum of the clash.

Two men came out of the changing shed, Paul Daniel and one of the young Martins, startled by the crash against the side.

'Stop them!' Clowance turned, trying to get to her feet.

'Paul! Harry! Stop them! They're . . . They're . . .

Soon five were involved. Paul, though now in his fifties, still had great strength and he took Ben by the coat, began to drag him away. Harry was not heavy enough for Stephen, but Clowance lent the help of all her own strength and great anger.

Presently they were separated, began slowly getting to their feet, trying to shake off the clutch of restraining hands. When it was seen that they were making no new move towards each other, the hands let them be. It seemed likely that Stephen, being the heavier man, would in the end have got the better of the fight, but at the time of interruption there had been little in it. Stephen's coat sleeve was rent from shoulder to cuff; one eye was very red and would go black, his lip and his hand were bleeding. Ben's shirt was in ribbons and he had livid marks round his throat and a split eyebrow. What injuries they had done to each other's bodies was not perceivable.

Nobody spoke for a few seconds. Paul Daniel broke the shuffling, gasping pause.

'Couldn't think what that thur thump was,' he said. 'Shook the whole 'ut. Didn't it, young Harry? Maybe twas fortunate we was around!'

Ben's face was grey and sweaty, He coughed and swallowed. 'Sorry,' he said. 'Sorry it ever 'appened, Miss Clowance.' He turned and walked away.

'*Ben!*' Clowance commanded, and he stopped but without turning to face her.

'Stephen!' she said, trembling with anger, and near tears; 'in front of Paul and Harry you will both apologize to me for this – this the most *insulting* scene I have ever witnessed! And you will apologize to each other!'

Silence again fell on the scene. A few jackdaws were chakking around the engine house as if themselves disturbed, but no one else apparently had witnessed the fight.

'*Stephen!*' Clowance said.

He was taking deep breaths as if still trying to rid himself of his anger.

'Sorry,' Ben said. 'Sorry, Miss Clowance. Sorry, Mister Carrington,' and went on his way.

After a few seconds Stephen said harshly: 'Look, Clowance—'

'That's not what I want!'

Paul Daniel shuffled his feet. 'Well, come along, 'Arry. We're late enough as tis.'

They moved off just in time to hear Stephen say: 'I'm sorry, Clowance.'

She took another trembling breath: 'How *dare* you! How dare you make such a scene, say such utterly offensive things to Ben!'

With an anger growing in him again he tried to overbear her. 'Because I happen not to like you going down the mine on your own with him, see! And I happen not to like you forgetting my existence just because he came to call on you. I had promised to come to see you; but what did *that* matter? He calls in and you forget everything—'

'I forgot! Well, I forgot! It happens, for a very good reason—'

'*What* reason?'

'What does that matter now?' Clowance said bitterly.

'Well, ye forgot, didn't you. Forgot I was even alive! And you was down on your own together best part of an hour, for that long I've been waiting! An hour! And then coming up all flushed and secretive as if—'

'As if *what*?'

'Well, how am I to know? What am I to know? Treated like a lackey!'

'You've just behaved like a lackey!'

'Careful what you *say*, girl!'

'You treated him disgracefully! And then to fight like – like a scruffy dog . . .'

'*Two* dogs. He struck me *first*! Did you happen to notice that?'

'Stephen, he's my *friend*! I've known him since I was a child and—'

'And what am I supposed to be – not your friend?'

'Don't be utterly stupid!—'

'God damn it!' he shouted; 'd'you think all your friends have a right and entitlement to swing their fists at me just when they fancy? If so, you can think again!'

'I can think again about a lot of things,' said Clowance, hardly able to get her breath.

'Just tell your friends,' Stephen said, towering over her, 'just tell your damned friends to keep their jealousy and their hands and their fists to themselves in future, will you . . . By God, it was as well Daniel and that lad came between us when they did—'

'It was certainly as well, since you had no regard for me!'

'If we'd gone on like that much longer, him using his boots and nails, I'd have *killed* him!'

Clowance looked at him through her blurred vision. 'Yes,' she said. 'You'd have killed him, wouldn't you. Like that sailor in Plymouth. You only had to draw your knife!'

She turned and left him standing there before he could reply.

Chapter Eight

I

Friday, October the ninth.

After thirty years of searching, the old Trevorgie workings had been discovered at last – and dry enough in part for investigation without putting much extra work on the engine. A whole new area was opened up and pointed the way in which earlier lodes had been followed.

It was the day when Ross Poldark was re-elected for the corporation borough of Truro.

It was the day when Clowance Poldark broke off her engagement to marry Stephen Carrington.

It was the day when Ben Carter resigned as underground captain of Wheal Leisure mine.

The conflict, though at first mercifully private between the five of them, soon spread. Paul Daniel could be trusted to say nothing, but Harry Martin bubbled with the news until he burst. In any event the consequences were bound to make themselves known.

Ben did not return to Nampara at six as invited, so it was left to Clowance alone to break to her family the news of the discovery of the old workings. Jeremy was wildly excited about it and wanted at once to go to the mine to see for himself. Why was Ben not here? What sort of ore-bearing ground had he found? Was there a group already exploring the workings? Clowance, her round face gone curiously thin, had then to explain a little of what had happened when they came up, though she treated the quarrel as undramatically as possible. Ben had gone off – she did not know whither – and she had returned to the house, having had no further contact or conversation with Stephen. Demelza, observing her daughter's brimming face, said pacifically:

'There, there, my dear, it is not the first time two men have quarrelled over a girl; and this pot has been simmering for a while. Let us hope in a few days it will all cool off—'

'You don't need to suppose it'll do that,' said Clowance, annoyed with her mother for taking it too lightly. 'You don't know anything about it, do you!'

'Only what I have been told. Well . . . let us look at the good things that have come of it. Did you say you had found a coin?'

'Yes . . .' Clowance fumbled miserably in her pocket. 'Now where did I . . .? Oh, here it is.'

They found an old magnifying glass and peered through it.

'She's right, in faith,' said Jeremy excitedly. 'Antoninus in full, and then AUG, which means Augustus. Then PIUS; then it looks like P.P. whatever that may stand for. On the reverse side it – it seems to say TR. POT COS. III. SC. I've no idea what *any* of that can mean. But it is perfectly genuine! I thought – I was certain it was a coin minted by one of the tin or copper companies.'

'Ben thought that,' said Demelza. 'Didn't he?'

'Yes.'

'Lord's my life, I cannot *contain* myself to go down! Where *is* Ben? He must be somewhere around! I hope this quarrel is not going to bite too deep – just at the moment of this marvellous discovery! I'll walk across now, see if he's there. If he's not, would you come and show me, Clowance?'

Before she could reply, if she was going to, Demelza said:

'As it is so late, as it has been there so long undiscovered, would it not be more proper to wait for your father? If I know him he'll be back before noon tomorrow. Then we could all go down together.'

'*You* would come, Mama?'

'Indeed I shall.'

'But . . . in your present condition . . .'

'Clowance tells me it is just up a ladder.'

'Yes, but you have to climb all the way down first.'

'Exercise is good for one.'

'I do not think Father will like it.'

Demelza said: 'I shall persuade him.'

Jeremy said: 'I wonder when Antoninus lived. I'll go and see Uncle Dwight – he has an encyclopaedia. I can't sit still this evening. I have to do something with the time. Then I'll go and see if I can find Ben. But we'll not go down. You're right, Mama: it *is* a family concern. We ought to go together. Perhaps we can winch you down.'

Demelza said: 'I'll sit astride a kibble.'

II

Two days later, as the evening was falling, Clowance came upon Ben, who had been working near Jonas's Mill, digging over the site he had been engaged on before Wheal Leisure was opened.

As they stared at each other in the windy twilight she could just see the swollen eyebrow, the slow flush mounting to his face, colouring the sallow skin.

Without any preamble she said: 'Jeremy tells me you have resigned as underground captain of Wheal Leisure.'

'Yes . . .'

'Because of the fight you had with Stephen?'

'Yes, I suppose.'

'You don't suppose. You know.'

'Well . . . I was the first, the one to start it. I hit 'im first. That's no way to be'ave. Not wi' the man who's going to be your husband.'

'He insulted you!'

'Mebbe.'

'There's no maybe about it. Ben.'

'Yes?'

'I expect a lot from my friends. From Stephen as well as from you. Are you my friend?'

'You should know.'

'Are you my friend?'

'Yes.'

'Then I want you to return to Wheal Leisure.'

He shifted in the gusty half-dark, leaned on his spade.

'I cannot do that, Clowance.'

'Why not?'

'Twouldn't be right. Twouldn't be fitty. *Your* husband. *And* he's a shareholder.'

'He's not going to be my husband just yet.'

Ben looked up. 'Why not? Because of me?'

She pressed her hair back with her hand. 'Look, Ben. You – found the old Trevorgie workings. You came to Nampara and I was the only one there. I went back with you. Was that wrong?'

'Well, no.'

'Did you do anything wrong by telling me?'

'No.'

'Did you not try to dissuade me from going down?'

'Well, yes.'

'But I went down. I insisted. I went down with you. When we came up to grass Stephen was there and made those offensive remarks . . .'

She stopped, struggling with words which could not be spoken here. She could not explain that to behave that way towards her in front of Ben was the most odious insult Stephen could have shown her. Of course she was not in love with Ben; but knowing his feelings for her, it was enormously important to her that Stephen should behave with at least a show of decent manners, just *because* he was going to become her husband. If Ben couldn't admire him he could at least respect him. But the sheer nastiness of the insults he had levelled at Ben became that much nastier because Ben, although a lifelong friend, was not of their class, on a different level from them. That more than anything else made her unappeasably angry. The quarrel was totally degrading. It would not even have been so intolerable if Stephen quarrelled and fought with Jeremy.

'That fight,' she said.

'I'm *sorry*.'

'That two men could – could . . .'

'I'm sorry, Clowance, sorry.'

She brought her thoughts away from it to what she was about now. 'Ben, I want to ask you something.'

'Yes?'

'Was there anything neglectful of the mine in what you did?'

'Not of the mine, no.'

'Well, is it not from the mine you have resigned?'

'Aye, but you cann't just forget the folk involved—'

'In this you can. For they are two separate issues. If you – if you quarrel with the man I intend to – intended to marry, that is something between him and you and me. I may indeed be at fault for being between you. But it is *nothing whatever* to do with the mine. You have no *right* to resign on those grounds! Especially in the light of this new discovery you have made. Jeremy is relying on you to help him exploit it. My father is relying on you! You must go back!'

He rubbed his short black beard. She stood there so sturdy and yet so feminine, so honest and yet so – apparently – unable or unwilling to see that she was asking the impossible.

'Ben!'

'Yes, Clowance, I see what you d'mean, but tisn't as easy as that—'

'I didn't suppose it to be easy. But I ask you to do it.'

He struggled for words. 'Twouldn't work. Not any longer.'

'What wouldn't work?'

'The men. The women. They'll gossip 'nough as tis. Be'ind their hands. Me, underground cap'n, when I been in a fight wi' a shareholder.'

'Are you afraid of facing them out? I wouldn't believe *that* of you!'

'Well . . . coming down to it – if you forget the miners, there's me and him. Me and him. We could never pass the time o' day, never meet face to face, wi'out snarling . . . And him one of your family!'

'Not yet!'

The half-dark and the pressure of her urgent demands gave him courage he'd not had before, courage at least to try to say what was in his heart.

'Y'know, Clowance, y'know what I d'feel for you. Ever since you was ten or eleven – all these years. I tried – have tried never to think on it, on account of I know tis hopeless, and so I . . . haven't thought on it much. Not more'n I can help anyway. But then when this man come along . . . Tis not for me to say who you shall wed – or where or when. But neither is it for me to say what I can feel and cann't feel. It is not in me to master that. And if so be as I don't like Stephen Carrington, that d'make it fifty times worser for me than if he been someone I could b'lieve was good enough for you. There, I have said that! Follow me, do you?'

'Yes,' said Clowance.

'So then come this quarrel. Twas bound to be soon or late, for he was waiting for me and watching the opportunity. He's jealous because he d'know how I feel for you. He thinks I wish him ill. So how could it be that I could go on working at bal, and me knowing and him knowing of this hatred?'

Clowance said slowly: 'There's no *need* for hatred.'

'Nay, mebbe no. But you say . . . Did you say he's not going to be your husband just yet?'

'Yes.'

'But if you're doing this just because of this that happened yesterday—'

'I'm not. Well . . . not altogether. I think I have made a mistake. But what happened yesterday was important – the breaking-point. You see, the thing that I find impossible to accept . . . Do you mind if I speak to you in confidence, Ben?'

His throat swelled. 'Of course not.'

'I think I loved Stephen. Perhaps I still do in a way. Do you know how it is if someone comes near you and your mouth dries, your heart beats.'

'Do I not, just!'

She blinked. 'Well, yes. Well, that is what happens when I see him. That is what happens, Ben. I am sorry if I have to tell you this.'

He did not speak but gripped his spade the harder. A flock of crows flew creaking overhead, urging their rusty wings into the night.

She said: 'Perhaps that is enough. Perhaps it should be enough. But ever since we have been going together...' She stopped. 'Now I am being unfair to him ... I can only say that there is a level of our – our understanding where *nothing* meets. Perhaps I am as much to blame as he is. When – when he was visiting Violet Kellow I allowed myself to become jealous. Jealous of *her*. In what then am I better than he, who was jealous of you yesterday?'

Ben said: 'Tisn't quite the same.'

She choked and then coughed to hide her tears. 'Dear Ben. You would say that. But there are other things – things I cannot tell you about which have helped to build up, to make this break. I cannot tell you about them for I do not altogether understand them myself. I feel I am being drawn into a world where meanings are never so clear any longer, distinctions between this and that, colours are blurred, edges of plain speaking, candour maybe. Perhaps it's not his fault. Perhaps it is all part of the deceit of growing up, and I blame him for it!'

'My dear,' said Ben indistinctly, 'twould be error to blame yourself. Yet what can I say that don't sound like I were trying to make you take my opinion of him? He is *not* good 'nough for you, but if you d'love him maybe that's the way it must be.'

'Nothing *must* be,' said Clowance fiercely. 'Nothing yet *must* be.'

III

When she left him it was too dark to work, so Ben shouldered his spade and walked home. It was less than two miles across rough country to Grambler village where a few dispirited candles glimmered, past Sawle Church and down Sawle Combe with the tin stamps endlessly clanking and thumping, over the steep cobbles of Stippy Stappy Lane till one came to the small bow-windowed shop in which the Carter family lived. There were lights in here and the shop was still open. His mother was behind the counter weighing out a piece of hardbake for Music Thomas.

As soon as the bell pinged Music swung round sharply but his smile of welcome faded when he saw Ben.

'Aw, tis thee, Ben . . .'

'Who'd you expect?' Ben said irritably.

'Mind that spade, there's mud on it,' said Jinny Carter. 'An' your boots.'

Ben, who was normally careful enough but was too emotionally exhausted tonight to have given it much thought, went back to the door and began to scrape his boots on the iron grating outside. When he came in his mother gave him a smile of thanks.

'That's twopence,' she said to Music.

'Ais,' said Music, 'an' I'll 'ave a quarter-pound of they sweets.' He pointed.

'Music,' said Jinny to her son, 'be waiting for Katie, I reckon.'

'What for?' said Ben.

Music swallowed and grinned and looked embarrassed. 'I just came in fur they sweets,' he said.

'Well, you asked for her,' said Jinny. 'That's all I was thinking.'

'I come for the 'ardbake,' said Music, 'an' the sweets.'

'You've grown a proper sweet tooth this last few days,' said Jinny.

'Ais,' said Music.

'What for d'ye want to see Katie?' Ben demanded. 'Don't you have sight of her every day at Place 'Ouse?'

'Oh, ais. I d'see Katie every day.'

'Well, then.'

'I come for the 'ardbake,' said Music.

'Got a message for 'er, 'ave ee?'

'Naw. Tis just . . .' Tormented by Ben's questions, Music forced words out. 'I'd see Katie every day, like. I 'ave sight of 'er. But never a word d'pass . . . But I come in fur they sweets. Brother Art sends me. Says he d'want more of they sweets.'

'How many d'you say d'you want?' Jinny asked. 'Your father's in back, Ben. There'll be supper just so soon as we close.'

While the sweets were being weighed Ben went inside, nodded to his stepfather who was stirring the soup on the fire, put his spade in the outhouse and came back to hear his sister in the shop. He parted the curtain.

Tall and long-faced and untidy but not without looks if only men could see it, Katie was just untying her head shawl, shaking out her Spanish-black hair and staring at Music who was stuttering over something he was trying to say. It seemed, so far as Ben was able to understand it, that Music had been trying to get Katie alone for days, had failed completely at Place House, and now was reduced to waiting for her at her mother's shop and was blurting out what seemed like an apology – not just to her alone as no doubt he had hoped, and no doubt could have contrived if he had had the nous to wait outside the shop, but now semi-publicly, in front of Katie's mother, and her brother too. Something had happened, it seemed, at the Truro races that he was unhappy about, and he had been trying to explain. Drink – the drink had been in him. The Devil too – the Devil in some guise. He was concerned at the offence he had given. He did not quite understand the word apologize, but that was clearly what he had in mind. To apologize.

But why? There was a puzzled expression on Katie's face, reflecting the puzzlement on Ben's. If there were some horseplay, some ill-humoured buffoonery in a village, at a fair, on a Saint's day, however far it went it would never have occurred to anybody to say they were *sorry*. They wouldn't know how. It would have been outside the conception of normal behaviour. It was clearly outside the conception of Music's behaviour. *He* didn't know how. But he was *trying*.

A sort of explanation crossed Ben's mind very much at the same time as it occurred to the two women. He gave a guffaw. If his own feelings had not been so much at stretch this evening it would not have occurred to him to laugh. But this was a release from intolerable tension. Music shot him a look which in a less vacuous face would have been taken for anger.

Then Katie laughed too. That was the worst part for Music. She laughed and laughed. She dropped her scarf on the counter and laughed. Ben laughed. Mrs Jinny Scoble smiled. After a moment or two, Whitehead Scoble put his head round the curtain and said:

'Supper's ready. What's to do?'

Jinny said: ''Tis just a little private joke, m'dear. A joke twixt Katie and Music.'

'Katie and Music?' said Scoble, scratching his head. 'What've they got to do with each other.'

'That's it, Fathur,' Katie said. 'That's just it!' And laughed again.

Music stared from one to the other, then turned and ran out of the shop. You could hear his hob-nailed boots striking sparks on the cobbles as he ran up the hill.

'Dear life,' said Jinny, sobering a little, 'he's gone and left 'is sweets be'ind.'

But Ben, pursued by devils of his own, was already on his way upstairs.

IV

Two days later, at about the same time of the evening when Ross was riding home from a brief visit to Killewarren, a figure stepped out of the hedge and said:

'Could I have word with ye, Cap'n Poldark?'

Stephen Carrington's coat collar was turned up, his mass of yellow hair subdued by the drizzle.

'Of course. Why don't you come to the house?'

'I'd rather not. Thank you all the same. It will not take more than five minutes.'

Ross hesitated, and then dismounted. To be five feet above the other man put him at a disadvantage.

'Yes?'

'You'll be likely to have heard that Clowance and me have split up.'

'I have.'

'Did she say definite that the wedding was off?'

'She did.'

'I doubt you'll have heard all the rights and wrongs of our quarrel.'

'Only the barest details. Clowance has said very little. I don't know that I specially want to hear more.'

'You mean you're content with the way things have turned out.'

'I did not say that. But – unless it directly concerns us as parties to the quarrel ... Of course we'll listen if we are told; and of course we are vitally concerned for Clowance's happiness. But as you know, we have always tried to allow Clowance freedom to make up her own mind.'

'Yes. Yes, I do know that.' Stephen's bruised face was grim, the lines drawn fine about his mouth. 'What I take leave to doubt is whether she *knows* her own mind at this moment.'

Ross said: 'You were content that she knew her own mind when she promised to marry you; so I think you must equally accept her decision now.'

'Over a lovers' tiff?'

'Is it that?'

'Little more.'

'Then I imagine time will show.'

Ross's horse was restive so he began to walk the animal in the direction of home. Stephen walked with him.

'Time,' said Stephen. 'That's of it. I'm prepared to wait. With your permission.'

'Why do you need my permission to wait?'

'When we were to be wed you gave us the Gatehouse. This summer I've spent much time and some money putting it to rights. But it is still your property. If Clowance is not to have it you may want to take it back.'

'Ah,' said Ross. 'Yes, I see.'

They were coming into the shelter of the hawthorns and nut trees that bordered the lane. Here the misting rain was less thick but the drops when they came were heavier. In returning to Nampara, even if he had only been a few miles, this was the part that Ross loved best. He knew himself to be on his own land; Wheal Grace flickered and steamed on his right, the stream must soon be forded, and then he would be at Nampara, where supper waited, and, in spite of any family problems which might present themselves, he was home. He looked at the heavy young man beside him.

'Do you intend to stay in this area whether or no?'

'Yes. At least for a while. Oh yes.'

'And still work at Jonas's?'

'It's a living of a sort.'

'You feel that Clowance will once again change her mind?'

'Yes, I do.'

'I don't think you should take that for granted. I'm slightly in a dilemma here, Stephen.'

'What dilemma?'

'Clowance may feel strongly that she may wish you at a greater distance.'

'Maybe.'

'As for myself, I'm trying to be fair. I want Clowance to be under no duress. Nor do I wish to deal unjustly in this matter with you. So may I make a bargain?'

'What is it?'

'Stay at the Gatehouse for three months. At the end of that time come and see me again. The bargain is that in that time you will undertake not to see more of Clowance than chance dictates. Not to call on her specially. Not to write to her. Not to deny her her freedom to live her own life and to make up or remake her own mind as she wishes. More than anything I want her to be happy. *Do you?*'

The question at the end came like the sudden production of a pistol after a rational argument. Stephen halted and rubbed the moisture off his face.

'I think she will find her best happiness with me.'

'I'm sure you think so. But if she finally decided not to marry you, would you agree that she had full freedom to choose to marry someone else and seek her happiness elsewhere – without any interference?'

He was silent again. 'I couldn't do any other, could I.'

'And go away then?'

'Yes, I suppose.'

'I do not know whether Clowance will be content with the terms I suggest. But first of all they are there for you to accept or refuse.'

'And if I refuse 'em?'

'I shall want the Gatehouse back. Though I shall certainly pay you for any expenses you have incurred in putting it to rights.'

They walked a few more paces, their boots squelching in the mud. A bell rang at Wheal Grace. A cricket rubbed his wing covers together in the hedgerow.

'I accept,' said Stephen.

BOOK THREE

Chapter One

I

In Trevorgie Mine they found eleven complete 'rooms' of various sizes, from which the ore had been worked in a regular manner, pillars of killas and granite being left and the walls squared off. One wondered if anyone had actually *lived* here, and how long ago. One complete skeleton was found and part of another. No other coin was discovered, but a number of tools and buckets and baskets of which the wooden parts again crumbled to dust when touched. Of course the workings as a whole did not date so far back as Ben and Clowance had supposed: most of them were probably seventeenth-century – or at the earliest Tudor – style of tool, character of excavation showed that; but these themselves were clearly a development and enlargement of much earlier tunnelling, the development largely obscuring what the earlier tunnelling had amounted to.

The question mark – and the coin – remained. Dwight's encyclopaedia informed them that Antoninus Pius Titus Aurelius Fulvus had been Emperor of Rome from 138 to 161 AD and had been in Britain about the year 140. He had generally been a just and benign ruler. Who, representing him, what primipilus or centurion had first ordered this mine to be worked – or re-worked? – and who had laboured in it?

For the Poldarks, however fascinated they might be by the extreme antiquity of the mine, another consideration took precedence. Indeed, Ross put out a request that no one should mention the great age of the discovery because he did not want antiquarians arriving from Truro or Exeter and holding up work. He also issued instructions that an area round the bend in the tunnel where the coin had been found should not be developed or interfered with.

In all probability the original metal mined had been tin; copper a fairly late quest. With all the branches and tunnels leading off the 'rooms' and the less developed caves, it would take a month or more to explore the find. Three pairs of tributers at once accepted pitches where a modest amount of copper was indicated. In the shaft that Ben and Clowance had first explored, the tunnels had followed the lode down and water barred their way.

It looked, from the remains there were of wheels and pipes and rods, as if there had been an attempt to drain it; but those levels had now filled up and offered a daunting prospect to unwater. Just for the moment Ross let this problem lie on the table – with a few others. Wheal Grace was losing money now. Unless some last-minute find reprieved her, she must close within a year.

Parliament was to reassemble on December the first, but it would have to do without Ross. Demelza was up and down in health – mopish, she called herself – but pooh-poohed it in front of him. Eventually she agreed to see Dwight officially, who prescribed some medicines for her without any great confidence that in so doing he was getting to the root of the trouble. 'It is a disorder of the blood,' he said to Ross. 'And possibly some infection of the kidneys. That will give rise to these mild fevers. The fashionable treatment for this is still leeching, but my practice is to try to build up the patient's strength rather than to lessen it. After all, she has two lives to sustain.'

'This swelling of the hands and of the face.'

'She's certainly very much out of sorts.'

'And she drinks too much port.'

Dwight smiled. 'I hope that doesn't give you cause for alarm.'

'Not as such. But . . .'

'She asked me about the port. She complains of giddiness, of faintness. Has she told you?'

'No, not that . . . And what did you say?'

'It is not carried to excess, is it?'

Ross rubbed at his scar. 'She's never drunk, if that's what you mean. She sometimes becomes a little merry.'

'Let it be for the time. It is only about eight weeks now. I think the wine will be a useful stimulant.'

In late October Ross saw an advertisement in one of the local newspapers for 'a fine toned grand Pianoforte, lately the property of a nobleman. Twenty-five guineas.' It was an address in Truro, so the next time he was in he bought it and left it to be delivered when he sent the word.

The same newspaper contained more details of the fall of Moscow, which had only just been announced to the Russian people by the Czar. After General Kutusov had abandoned Moscow the Governor, a man called Rostopchin, had ordered the city to be set ablaze and had taken away all the fire-engines. The city had burned for three days and then a great wind – the first violent gale of winter – had arisen and the city had lit up again with even more ghastly fervour. A thousand palaces had been destroyed, it was said, one thousand six hundred churches, thirty thousand sick and wounded burned to death. And with them had gone all the food and victuals to see the province through the winter. Nobles and commoners alike were ruined, as indeed was Russia. Apparently a hundred of the ruffians who fired the city had been captured and shot; the universally execrated Governor Rostopchin had fled. Some thought him in the pay of the French.

Jeremy wrote to Cuby but did not receive a reply.

Stephen, breaking his agreement with Ross, wrote to Clowance but did not receive a reply.

Demelza, taking things easier than usual, wrote to Geoffrey Charles but did not receive a reply.

Ben, in spite of Clowance's requests, did not return to Wheal Leisure as underground captain. Clowance – and Jeremy – were concerned that Ben and Stephen were living too close to each other and that a chance encounter might lead them to conclude their unfinished business.

Demelza, seeing her daughter's unease and unhappiness, said to her one day:

'Clowance, I have told you from the beginning I'd better prefer that you and Jeremy should be elsewhere when the baby is born, just as you were ten years ago. Why do you bother to wait until next month? I can write to Aunt Verity and ask that you may go on a visit to her next week. You could stay until nearly Christmas.'

Clowance went on stroking the cat.

Demelza said: 'To speak the truth of it, you have twice before gone away to – to distance yourself, to make up your mind about Stephen. This would be different, for now it seems you have *made* up your mind. But while he stays so close it must be a sort of embarrassment . . .'

'It is an embarrassment,' Clowance said. 'Of course Papa was trying to be fair, but I *wish* he had turned Stephen out of the Gatehouse. I wish he could go away so that I shall never see him again.'

'Well, the next best thing is that you should go instead. And you'll not be too far away. Half a day's ride . . .'

'But if you have to take things more easy . . .'

'This is all coddling nonsense, my lover. Where I came from when I was young, bal maidens would work at the mine until the day before a baby was born, and not uncommonly were at work again the day after.'

'All the same, that does not follow . . .' Clowance was about to ask another question but restrained herself. She asked it the next day of Caroline, who had called and found herself cross-examined when she was leaving and waiting for her horse.

'Your grandmother? Your mother's mother? I don't know. She was very young: twenty-five or twenty-six. Why do you ask?'

'I think she died in childbirth – when Uncle Drake was born. I think Mama told me once.'

'Maybe. Why do you – oh, Clowance, how silly! You mustn't think such stupid things!'

'Why are they stupid?'

'*Well* . . . there is nothing wrong with your mother; nothing serious, that is.'

'Does Uncle Dwight say so?'

Caroline glanced uneasily round to be sure Demelza was still out of earshot. 'He thinks she should take care. Just as a precaution – nothing more. In any event, there is no similarity – no comparison. From what your mother has told me, *her* mother lived in poverty and great squalor and had a drunken husband. You could hardly call the circumstances the same!'

'No, but—'

'And she had seven children in about eight years.'

'This is Mama's fifth. It is not, I suppose—'

'Over about twenty-five years. Besides, do you not have a greater faith than that in your dear Dr Enys?'

'I know he has pulled me through some grave times,' said Clowance. 'At least two stomach aches ... Well, yes, I suppose it is all silly. But this scheme that is now being hatched to ship me away to Falmouth for a month ...'

'We can send over at the least thing.'

'But *will* you? Will you promise, Caroline, personally, to send over – not to be swayed by them, to send over at the least thing?'

'If Dwight thinks so, I'll send right away.'

'Even so,' said Clowance decisively, 'it is too soon. Mama will do things if I am not here that she would not do if I were. Do you know, after all this time she has never become used to servants in the way you are, even in the way I am? If she is short of a needle and thread she might ask me to run up to her room for it, if I were immediately about, but she would never, never, never think of ringing for Ena or Betsy Maria.'

Caroline laughed. 'Some women are born with great energy. Your mother is one. To her it is easier to move than to wait.'

'That's why I think I should stay home a little longer.'

'I do not think Dwight supposes she should do *nothing* for the next month – only that she should be careful. Do you think your personal supervision will make her more careful?'

'It will make her more irritable,' said Clowance, and they both laughed.

II

On November 21 the newspapers carried the announcement that Napoleon had left Moscow. Information as to his reasons was scanty. But having occupied a burnt-out Moscow for five weeks, it seemed likely that his army had become short of provisions. The Russians had made no attempt to re-take their largest city, nor apparently had made any move at all. But neither had the expected surrender come in. There were reports that the French were now making south for Kaluga, no doubt towards warmer climates before the winter set in.

On the day that this news arrived Clowance had an encounter with Stephen.

It was almost inevitable sooner or later in so small a community. Rosina Carne, Demelza's sister-in-law, had been over with some baby clothes she had been making and had stayed for dinner. About three she left for home, and Clowance, feeling the need of exercise, said she would go with her. From Nampara to Pally's Shop was about four miles and by the time they reached there, there was less than an hour's daylight left. Clowance refused tea and said she would turn around and start back at once.

'Sam'll be in any minute,' said Rosina. 'He'll be glad to walk you back so far as his Meeting House.'

'No, thank you. I shall be fine. And his meeting is not till six, is it?'

'Or you could borrow the little pony. Bring him back tomorrer.'

'No, really. I shall enjoy the walk. This month I have been very lazy.'

'Then just let me wrap you up these cakes. I should have brought them except that my hands were full!'

Rosina began to wrap the cakes. As she did so there was a tap on the door. She opened it and Stephen stood there.

'D'ye do, Mrs Carne. Is Clowance there?'

'Well – er – I'm not quite sure—'

'Of course you're sure, Mrs Carne. I saw you both just come in. You'll give me leave to enter? How d'ye do, Clowance. You going home?'

Clowance found her throat was tight. 'Presently.'

'Then I'll wait.'

It was Saturday, and he was not in his working clothes. In the tiny room he looked too big, as if he could push the walls down. His lip still looked swollen; yet it could hardly be so after all these weeks.

'How've you been?' he asked.

She felt the colour mounting as he looked her over. 'Well, thank you.'

'Ah . . . You be home for Christmas?'

Rosina said nervously: 'If you want me to leave you alone, Clowance . . . Or I'll stay if you want me to stay.'

'Leave us alone,' Stephen said. 'Eh? Five minutes. That fair? Go wrap your cakes.'

Rosina looked at Clowance, who made no sort of sign. She might have been a graven image. After hesitation Rosina said: 'I shall be in the kitchen if you want me.'

'I want you now,' said Clowance. 'Here.'

'Oh,' said Stephen. 'So that's how the land lies, is it?'

'That's how the land lies.'

'You too stiff scared to speak to me alone?'

'What is there to say?'

'What is there to say? That the sun rises and the sun sets. And you belong to me.'

'I belong to nobody!' she said passionately.

'Oh no? You'll find you do. In the end you'll find you do.'

'Well, the end isn't yet, is it.'

'No, the end isn't yet. You've got to learn a lesson first.'

'I've already learned it, Stephen,' she said.

'May be we're not talking about the same one. Allow me to tell you—'

'I don't want to listen,' she said swiftly. And to Rosina: 'Isn't that Sam?'

'Yes . . . I think he's just stabling his pony.'

Stephen stooped to look out through the window. 'She don't want to listen, Mrs Carne. That's what she says. Isn't that strange?'

Rosina did not reply.

'How'd it be,' Stephen said, 'If I told you and then you could tell her?'

'Mr Carrington . . .'

'Mrs Carne. Tell her I'm off in the New Year. Tell her I'm going back to sea – most likely from Bristol. That'll be the end of it then. It'll be all over then betwixt her and me. Six or seven weeks and I shall be gone. Till then I'll be at the Gatehouse. If she want me, tell her to send a note. I'll come if she want me, Mrs Carne, to talk – no more. I'll not be coming asking any favours. It's not in me nature, see.' He turned. 'You know that, don't you, Clowance.'

Sam Carne walked into the house, stooping to come through the door. 'Ah, my dear . . . Oh, good day to you, Clowance. And you, friend.' He smiled his welcoming, forbearing smile. 'God be with you. Have you taken tea?'

'Never one to ask favours, Clowance,' Stephen said. 'I'll wed you tomorrow, if need be, but not as a favour. You'll be my wife or nothing . . .' There was the semblance of a threat in his tone, and he swallowed it down. 'Afternoon to you, preacher. No, I've not taken tea for I've not been asked. Not everyone in this room is as full of the Holy Ghost as you are; so I'm just off. Shall I walk you home, Clowance?'

'Thank you,' said Clowance, 'I'll wait for Sam.'

Stephen looked at her with a frown almost of disbelief, loosened his collar.

'Remember, Mrs Carne, to tell her what I said, won't you. Tell it her just as I said it, Mrs Carne.'

'I don't understand ee,' said Sam, looking from one to the other.

'No, tis not in the Prayer Book,' said Stephen. 'Nor yet in the Hymn Book. But it's God's truth just the same.'

He went out, shutting the door behind him with a wall-shaking clack.

He left silence behind. Then Rosina to try to break the tension began again to wrap up the cakes. Clowance sat down, her knees weak.

Sam said: 'I do not know what was abroad, but perhaps tis as well I came. What did he mean, Rosina?'

'It was as well you came, Sam,' Clowance said. 'It was nothing to do with Rosina at all – only with me, as you might have guessed. Rosina, I think – I will – take tea with you – after all.'

Chapter Two

I

A week later Clowance, receiving further reassurances from her mother and upset by the encounter with Stephen, left for Flushing. The morning after she left Demelza fainted in the kitchen and was carried upstairs by John and Jane Gimlett, who were the only people in the house. Dwight was summoned and arrived at the same time as Ross, who had been over at Wheal Grace. Dwight made a thorough examination and came swiftly down.

'She seems quite restored now and is asking for you. The baby is alive and – kicking. There has been no haemorrhage or discharge of waters. I don't believe the child is quite due yet. It seems simply a passing faintness, a fainting fit. Fortunately she fell lightly and only bruised her arm.'

'But what is amiss with her, Dwight? What has gone wrong?'

Dwight hesitated. 'If medical science were further advanced perhaps I could tell you. There is a toxic condition in the blood which I believe is at the root of all these disquieting symptoms. But the cause of the toxicity and the cure for it are quite unknown to me.' He looked at Ross, who was scowling and tapping his boot. 'I think you have to remember that until now Demelza has been the perfect mother. All the children have been born very easily, very quickly, and after the first month or so of pregnancy she has been in the finest health all through. Often she has joked with me and said that it is because she comes of peasant stock. This time – well, generally the more children women have the easier they produce them – except that as they themselves grow older it weighs a little more heavily upon their own constitution. It may be the case here – just that, no more. She is ten years older, and therefore there is just that little more strain on her. God forbid that I should be complacent; but neither should one allow this to become magnified out of its true proportion. Just now, when I left her, she was joking with me as if she had not a care in the world. And wanting to get up.'

'Wanting to get up!'

'All the same, I do not think you should discourage her from all exercise, so that it be light. A little walking. She certainly intends to get up to supper.'

'Do you know what I think of?' Ross said.

'No?'

'Elizabeth.'

Dwight let out a breath. 'Forget it. Forget Elizabeth. That was quite different.'

'How different?'

'It – was. She died . . . well, you know how she died.'

'I can never forget it. Not as long as I live. So . . .'

'Yes, but there can never be any similarity between the two conditions.'

'Why not?'

They stared at each other.

Dwight said: 'Take my word for it, Ross.'

'But I want to know why.'

'I can't tell you.'

'Because you don't know or because what you know may not be repeated?'

Dwight lowered his eyes. 'Look, old friend; forget Elizabeth and accept my assurance that there can be *no* similarity. What do you wish me to do here? Call in Dr Behenna for a second opinion?'

'God forbid that too!'

'Or there is a new man in Redruth who has taken Dr Pryce's place. They say he worked in one of the Plymouth lying-in hospitals and has a good reputation.'

Ross made a dismissive gesture. 'There is no one in Cornwall and few in England who know more about these things than you do. Do you suppose I'd rather trust her to some self-opinionated surgeon who subordinates all his clinical observations to a pet *theory*? Who would put her on some outlandish diet of raw meat and snail water . . .'

'These would not be such ill ideas,' said Dwight. 'She needs iron.'

Two days later when Dwight called Demelza was out. He strolled about the house for a few minutes, and then met Ross who had been busy in the library.

'How is she this morning?' Dwight asked.

'Should I not be asking you that?'

'You should if I could find her.'

'Well, where in Heaven—'

'Apparently she told Jane that she would be taking a short walk.'

'With Jane?'

'No, no, on her own, I think.'

'Damn the woman! She ought to know better.'

'How was she yesterday after I left?'

'Oh, better than Wednesday. Better spirits. And this morning when she woke.'

'A little walking will do no harm, provided she feels up to it.'

'Jeremy!' Ross called to his son, who was just about to go on the beach with Farquahar at his heels.

Jeremy came back. 'Hullo, Uncle Dwight. I have a couple of books I must return to you.'

'Dwight has come to see your mother,' Ross said, 'and no one knows where she is.'

'I think she was going over to see Jud and Prudie.'

'Oh, God in Heaven!' Ross exploded. 'Has she no sense? Did you not try to dissuade her?'

'Yes, I did. I said "that bug-ridden place". But you know what Mama is when she takes an idea into her head.'

'It is much too *far*,' said Ross. 'Is it not too far, Dwight?'

'Yes,' said Dwight. 'Of course had I come direct from home I would have seen her.'

'Would you like me to go after her?' Jeremy said. 'I was off to the mine but that can wait.'

'Thank you. I think it would be – very acceptable to me. Bring her back.'

Jeremy wrinkled one eyebrow. 'Only you could be certain to do that, Father. But I'll use my wiliest persuasions.'

Ross watched him run off whistling up the valley, the spaniel gambolling close behind. He said to Dwight: 'He'll do it more tactfully than I could. She gets strangely irritable with me at this time. It has always been a matter of pride between us that we do not get irritable with each other. Her – her personality seems to be changing.'

'That will pass,' said Dwight. 'That at least I can promise you.'

II

The object of their joint anxieties had got very little further than the crest of the rise beyond Wheal Maiden where the land began to fall away in a moorland scrub towards the village of Sawle. There she met Emma Hartnell, who had been to see her father, old Tholly Tregirls, who was recuperating after a vicious bout of asthma.

As Emma Tregirls, tall, dark, handsome and pale, and as noisy and as brash as they come, she had worked as a parlour-maid at Fernmore when the Choakes were there, and there had fascinated Sam Carne, Demelza's deeply committed Wesleyan brother. The chaste affair had run its course with Sam as much devoted to saving her soul as to possessing her in carnal love, and she apparently in love with him but all too aware of her reputation and the effect such a marriage would have on Sam's painstakingly collected flock. After much stress on both sides Emma had come to see Demelza one late summer afternoon when she and Jeremy and Clowance were picking blackberries and had asked for advice.

Shortly after, Demelza had been able to get Emma a new position at Tehidy House, ten miles or more away, and had proposed that she and Sam should separate for a year and then meet again and see if they could come to a more definite decision. Within the year Emma had married Ned Hartnell, the second footman.

Since then Demelza had had a conscience about her own part in the affair. In her youth and in the ebullience of her own love for Ross, she had wanted everyone to marry and be happy, and she felt that her advice on this occasion had been over-staid, over-cautious. Who was to say that these two people should not have come to live in amity with themselves and with the outside world, and let bad reputation and religious conscience go hang?

Emma was wearing the same style of dress as that day in the Long Field fifteen years ago; a white straw hat perched on her gypsy-black hair, a white dimity frock, black boots and a long scarlet cloak. Innkeeper, housewife, mother of two children, prosperous now in a small way, she seemed little different in herself except perhaps a little more ordinary. Some of the startling bloom had gone.

Demelza asked how her father was.

'Oh, some slight. You wonder how a man d'come to fight for breath so long.'

'There's little choice, I conceit.'

Emma looked her over. 'How long be it now, Mrs Poldark?'

'A few days. Maybe a week.'

'Do you want for a girl or for a boy?'

'Oh, it does not matter. I believe my husband has a fancy for a boy. But either will be a joy to us.'

'Aye indeed.' Emma held her hat against the wind. 'But don't some folk act strange, unnatural . . .'

'What is that?'

'The way my father behaved to we when we was little. Twas unnatural like, to leave my mother with her brood, to care nothing, not the toss of a button for we. Ned and me, why we cann't do 'nough for our two lads! Tis a rare pleasure to *care* for 'n.'

Demelza watched a shower skating across the sea. With luck it would miss them. 'You have settled down at the Bounders' Arms?'

'Oh yes, mistress. I reckon we'll never make a fortune there, but twill serve.' Emma laughed.

'Do you see – do you ever see Sam?'

'Once or twice we've spoke. He be just the same as ever, edn ee. Dear of 'im. But . . . he've got a good wife. Maybe twas all for the best.'

'I hope so.'

'Fair gone on him I was. Didn't seem natural to me then, feeling like that. Never felt like that afore; nor never since. Ned . . . he's a pretty husband. We fight but rarely. I reckon I'm well pleased wi' what I got!'

Demelza glanced at the handsome young woman, some of whose black hair, uncontained by the hat, stranded across her face as she spoke. Was there a hint of an attempt at self-conviction?

'That advice you give me that day . . .' Emma laughed again. 'I reckon all told twas the best advice I could've had. *We* could've had. We was in a cleft stick, Sam and me.' She shrugged her cloak around her. 'Anyway, tis all over and past . . . We see a fair measure of Mr Jeremy these days. Comes in two, three times a week. Along of Mr Carrington and Mr Kellow.'

'Yes, he tells me.'

'I think tis more my line, bearing the ale in for Ned Hartnell than reading the prayers for Sam!'

Demelza smiled back at her and moved to go on. Standing made her dizzy these days.

'They reckon there's some big vict'ry,' said Emma.

'Oh? Where?'

'Stephen Carrington put his head round the door this morning. Forgot about it till mentioning his name. War and peace: it don't mean much to me, so I don't bring to mind the names or the notions.'

'In Spain, you mean?'

'No, twas Russia or Poland.'

'Stephen told you?'

'Yes. He've heard it from some ship's captain just put in at Penryn from some place I can't mind the name of. But tis rumour on rumour these days. Ned never said there was naught in the paper last Sat'day.'

Demelza glanced back the way she had come and saw Jeremy taking long lanky strides up the valley in her direction. She sensed that he was coming for her.

'Well, goodbye, Emma.'

'Goodbye, Mrs Poldark.'

Demelza began to walk down the hill, and for a few paces Emma continued with her.

'Stephen Carrington be much upset because of him not being able to wed Miss Clowance, Mrs Poldark.'

'I think she is upset too.'

'He's a matter of a wild man. Twould not be for a quiet life that anyone would wed him.'

Demelza said: 'I don't suppose Miss Clowance had those thoughts in her head when she broke off the engagement.'

'Oh no. Oh no. Maybe she was lucky to draw back in time. Like me! Only all the other way round, like!'

Jeremy was gaining on them. Demelza had some wandering pains which she carefully ignored.

'When they come in the Arms,' said Emma, 'they always go in the private room. Mr Jeremy, Mr Paul and Stephen Carrington. I come on them sometimes all talking serious – just like they was planning a war of their own . . .'

Farquahar caught them up, leaping round Demelza, licking her hands, gambolling about her skirt.

'Planning a war of their own?' she said. 'How very strange.'

'Oh, twas just a figure of speech, Mrs. I expect they'm

really setting the world to rights, the way young men belong to do.'

When Jeremy reached his mother Emma was bobbing off in the direction of the Bounders' Arms, one hand to her hat as the wind tried to snatch it away.

Jeremy said: 'What man of you, having an hundred sheep, if he lose one of them, doth not leave the ninety and nine and go after that which is lost, until he find it? And when he hath found it he layeth it on his shoulders and beareth it home rejoicing.'

'I should be a thought heavy for you,' said Demelza 'considering what I bear too. Did your father send you?'

'Concern for your well-being, woman, is not confined to one man. The whole family shares it. Think if you were taken queer at Jud's. I wouldn't wish a brother or sister of mine reared among Prudie's ducklings!'

He had taken her arm and they had stopped.

Demelza looked up at him. 'The Devil can cite scripture for his own purpose. I never imagined you were so well read.'

'Ah, another mother who doesn't know her own son!'

'I thought it was all to do with engines.'

'Nearly all, yes.'

Demelza found herself facing the way she had come. 'I still have a sense of direction,' she said.

'All the same . . .'

'All the same I want to see Prudie. I gave her no money last week.'

'I'll take it. This very afternoon, I swear to you. Let me tell you about my engines. Let us stroll back in genteel style and I will tell you about this whim engine I am now going to build for Wheal Leisure.'

'This is why you were at Harvey's last week?'

'Yes, the preliminary design has been agreed.'

'All right, then tell me about it.'

'Instead of the horse whim to draw up our ore, such as we now have both there and at Wheal Grace, we shall do it all by steam. We shall build the engine round the Trevithick boiler that I intended to have used for a road vehicle. It will – the boiler will now of course have to be bolted down to the floor. The crankshaft will be sited under the cylinder end of the boiler in much the same way as in the steam carriage. The fly wheel will run in a semi-circular slot let into the floor. We intend to put up a separate small house to contain it, with the drum behind on which the cable winds, and another chimney – oh, of brick probably – twenty-five or thirty feet high. Do you follow me?'

'More or less.'

'Now that the Trevorgie workings have been uncovered it is worth the extra expense to have the kibbles drawn up by mechanical power. I am going again tomorrow when William West is at Hayle. The Harveys have invited me to stay the night, so . . .'

'Why do you not make it two?'

'Oh, as near as that, is it?'

'I did not say so.'

'Well, a nod is as good as a wink. I know when I'm not wanted. Though I shall not be at all happy to be away from it all.'

'It is a horse whim of mine,' said Demelza.

'Oh, my dear Mama, now I know you are not feeling well!'

They had returned to where a few scattered stone walls marked all that was now left of Wheal Maiden. A shaft of sunlight – the first visible that day – provoked a rainbow to emerge briefly in the wake of the passing shower. A single giant black-backed gull hovered overhead: it looked as big as a goose. Demelza perched herself on a wall.

'Do you see just so much as ever of Stephen, Jeremy?'

'A modest amount. Has *she* been telling you?'

'It only came out in talk. Does he say much of his plans?'

'Only that he will not stay here after the end of the three months – that is, when he leaves the Gatehouse. That is, of course if . . .'

'If Clowance does not forgive him.'

'It is not forgiveness, Mama, as you know. Clowance is not so pious as to see it in those terms. She said to me it was that in some respects they did not seem to mean the same things when they used the same words. With her I think it has been cumulative, over the months, a slow realization that his ways are not, and never will be, her ways. She has rejected something just before it became too big for her. Something was wrong. The fight – the quarrel over Ben only brought it to a head . . . Of course, Stephen is furious.'

'Furious?'

'Yes. You see, to him the causes of the break were at the best flimsy. He had got into a temper waiting an hour at the mine, and had had a rough and tumble with poor Ben. That was all. He has written to her a sort of apology and now is furious that she has not accepted it. You see, dear Mama, *he* has his pride, *he* has his dignity. His pride is not in what he possesses, not his name or his reputation or his manners, but in himself as a man. He knows his own worth as a man. He knows how other women look at him. He's old enough and experienced enough to know what they see in him. He loves Clowance – I believe he loves Clowance dearly. And he knows that he would be marrying above his station. But he has a very distinct awareness of – of the value of himself, so to say. This is what he would bring to the wedding: good looks, good health, strength, experience, manliness – out-manning most people around here. He's – he's a frigate, armed to the teeth, well-found, in perfect condition, wishing to board the beautiful white schooner. But – but, now they have exchanged gunfire, he is no more prepared to strike his colours than she is.'

Demelza said: 'So it will not come easy to either of them.'

'No.'

'Perhaps it will give them both time.'

'Did you ever want it to happen?'

'Did you?'

'I don't know. I see exactly what Clowance means. Yet all the time I find Stephen's company a stimulus, a goad . . .'

'I only want her to be happy.'

'So do we all. Except Stephen. Who wants her in an altogether different way.'

Demelza slipped off the wall. Except for resting her feet, the position had not been comfortable. *He – she –* had not liked it at all.

'And Cuby?'

'You know I met her at the races?'

'Yes, yes.'

'Well, not since then, but that meeting greatly helped. It was – frivolous. We had both wined well and the sun was out, but I can't believe . . .'

'Good. I'm that glad . . . I *wish* I could meet her.'

'So you shall . . . if my suit prospers a little more.'

They began to walk down towards Nampara. Again he linked her arm.

Demelza said: 'When a family is close-knit, such as ours, it is terrible vulnerable. Whoever comes from outside to marry into it *must* be welcomed, must be made to feel a part. But the risk is . . .'

'The risk is?'

'That he or she who comes from outside is interested only in the one person they wish to marry and resentful of everything that happened before they met. *Really* resentful, to the extent they wish to blot it out. All, all those distasteful faces around their loved one belong to another age, which is past. They want to take their husband or wife and walk with him alone into the future.'

'How do you think these things?' Jeremy asked. 'Seeing that it could never have happened to you?'

'It never happened to me,' Demelza said. 'But I have seen it happen.'

'Seriously,' Jeremy said, 'I would rather see Clowance married to Stephen than to some vapid, goody-goody young man whose only thought was to please her. Yet, like a responsible brother, I had anxious thoughts about the marriage. Maybe this way will do no harm – give them a little more time.'

Demelza watched something stirring in the tangled undergrowth beside the wall. 'By the way, Emma tells me she heard there had been a victory, a big victory – by the Russians over Napoleon. I don't know if it's true. She said Stephen had told her.'

'It would be amazing if one of our allies could do something useful at last! I was reading the other day about the subsidies England was paying to every country in Europe which will fight Napoleon. It is costing us millions every year – and we so small a country! Precious little so far we have had in return.'

'I was a thought dismayed at Geoffrey Charles's letter

yesterday. It looks as if they are back where they began, and all's to do again.'

'I hope it is not as bad as that,' said Jeremy. 'But I still wonder from time to time . . .'

'What?'

'You know. Whether I should not be with him.'

Demelza thought perhaps she should not have spoken. Yet was this not all better out in the open?

'I suppose your father will be leaving for London early in the new year.'

'Yes . . . Sometimes there are two duties, aren't there. It depends which comes uppermost . . .' Jeremy kicked at a stone. 'I wish Ben were not such a fool. I wish he would come back, as we all want. He's so stiff-backed, so pig-headed . . . He knows enough about the mines to *run* them. And Carnow and Nanfan can tend the engines just as well as I.'

'And – the new whim engine?'

'Can be operating by March or April. It is really quite straightforward, once one has accepted the basic design – it should present no problems. But to be truthful . . .'

'Yes?'

'I confess I have no towering ambition to become a soldier. It is not in my nature to fancy winning death or glory. Even the discipline would, I believe, greatly irk . . . And of course I can make the excuse to myself that the mine engine at Leisure is still young, has to prove herself over a longer period of time. And while I have this sort-of friendship with Cuby . . . If I went away now I should be abandoning what chance I have of making something of that . . . Cowardice, you see, can find many reasons . . .'

'What has cowardice to do with it? Is it not a choice you are free to make? You know well, Jeremy, that if – if it was really your wish to become a soldier neither your father nor

368

I would stand in your way. But if it is not particularly your wish, then the fear of being thought afraid should not enter into your mind. It does not appear to have occurred to Stephen Carrington that he must join the Navy – indeed, according to Clowance, he fought hard to stay out! So did your other friend, Paul Kellow. Horrie Treneglos has not bestirred himself. Nor has – well, I could name a dozen other young men of your age – and so could you.'

'Yes,' said Jeremy. 'Oh yes. Perhaps they do not have a soldier for a father.'

'That's not clever,' said Demelza, 'that's proper stupid. Your father was in the army only for four or five years. He is known – at least in Cornwall – as Captain Poldark more because he owns a mine than because he served in the American war. If your father is to be the example, you could as well put up for Parliament!'

Jeremy laughed. 'Along with Valentine.'

'Emma tells me,' Demelza said, moving herself uncomfortably, 'Emma tells me that you and Paul and Stephen sit in the Bounders' Arms together as if you were having a council of war.'

'Does she now?'

'Yes, she does.'

Jeremy laughed again, but more grimly this time. 'Believe me, Mama, it is not that sort of war we discuss. And anyway the greatest part of it all is hot air.'

'I hope so.' They began to walk down the valley. Demelza swayed.

'Mama, are you ill?'

'*No!*' she said, 'of course I'm not ill. But I believe this baby must be a little lop-sided within me and weighs me over from time to time. Small wonder with such a family possing around him.'

'I shall be jealous if it's another boy,' Jeremy said. 'He'll want those wooden toys I have. Those that I would not let Clowance and Bella get their grubby hands on.'

'I see Dwight now,' said Demelza, 'and your father. How anxious they are looking! Do they not look like two mother hens, Jeremy? Do they not now?'

She was sweating slightly, aware that the fever had come back.

III

Geoffrey Charles had written:

Well, it was to have been a great triumph. To have
ended the year on such a note of victory as
Salamanca sounded. But in the end all went wrong
before the fortress of Burgos. I do not know if his
Lordship over-reached himself, for I was not there;
but it is clear we have many more battles still to fight
before we have the Frenchies out of Spain.

The Light stayed behind with Hill in Madrid, to
their great disgust, and, abandoning the capital six
weeks later and marching northwest, we rendez-
voused with Wellington and his retreating
troops on I believe the 8th November on the River
Tormes, by which time his First Division was in a very
poor state, thousands of them having drunk
themselves into Insensibility in the wine vats of
Torquemada and been picked up by the French, who
were following close behind.

Even so all would have been well but for this
unprintable fool Gordon – Colonel Gordon. Our

part of the army – Hill's army – was in good Fettle.
Wellington's – when we joined it – was losing
discipline but would have stood and fought well
enough if the French had come too near. But
Gordon, our quarter-master-general, misdirected our
food supplies by twenty miles, so that after short
rations for the first week we then marched the last
four days of the retreat with *no food* at all, except for
the wild nuts in the fields and anything that could be
culled or stolen. So we became a broken rabble, rain-
drenched, fever-ridden, sinking ankle deep in mud,
quarrelling, fighting and dying by the thousand.
When at last we reached Ciudad Rodrigo it was as if
we had suffered a Crippling Defeat at the hands of
the French, instead of there only having been a few
skirmishes and *no battle* at all!

Old Douro looks Beside himself with anger and
frustration.

However, to end this wailing missive on a happier
note, I have now with Hamilton – did you ever meet
him? – I have now with David Hamilton for the last
two weeks been billeted on a charming Spanish
family in Ciudad. Señor Amador de Bertendona is a
member of the Cortes and normally lives in Madrid;
but when Wellington left Madrid he decided to leave
also and came to his country house in Ciudad with
his wife and family. He has been an outspoken critic
and opponent of the French, and he feared reprisals.

Señora de Bertendona, who is Portuguese, and
her three children, are quite charming. The two
boys, of eighteen and twelve, are called Martin and
Leon, the daughter, aged about nineteen, is
Amadora and is considered a Beauty. I would not

quarrel with that estimate. All are graciousness itself; and that under stress; for not only do we two English officers share their home but a priest and seven Spanish guerrillas, all for their various reasons fugitives at this time! Fortunately I now speak Portuguese fluently and Spanish a modest second; but all of the Bertendonas except the Señora have a little English.

Although in the Army the death toll from sickness still runs at about 500 a week, those who survive are quickly recovering their spirits and their ardour. Tobacco and such luxuries are cheap, and Señor de Bertendona's port wine is beyond *Praise*! Soon we shall be fox-hunting and beagling to regain our health and our address, and of course to pass the winter away. I only hope I shall be permitted to stay in my present quarters!

As always, please pass on my love and respects in whatever measure you deem fit to all who know me.

I have a feeling that I shall visit Trenwith soon!

Love to you both,

Geoffrey Charles.

Chapter Three

I

Being an honest girl – honest with herself as well as with other people – Clowance did not pretend to herself that she was happy or contented during her visit to Verity. But she put on a show and partly deceived the lady who, though actually her father's cousin, had always been regarded as an aunt. And after that last encounter with Stephen, Clowance was specially grateful for the move. Her love for him, which had often warred with her cooler judgments, was now turned inside out and become a sense of self-disgust which for the first time allied itself to reason. This made it no easier to live with. But that the object of so much of her thoughts and wayward sentiments should not be liable to turn up round any unexpected corner like an ogre or a handsome hobgoblin made life more endurable.

After the break-up it seemed she had not slept for a week. Over and over again, in endless repetitive procession, came the events of that day, what he had said, what she had said, what Ben had said, the hideous fight, which perhaps in all could only have lasted three minutes but which spoke for ever of male violence, hatred, rivalry and the utter determination to inflict serious injury. She could still hear the thumps, the muttered curses, the grunting breaths, the scuffling feet, the crash of bodies. In an earlier time she supposed she would have been expected to feel flattered at two men fighting over her. But at least then there would have been an element of chivalry. This encounter was devoid of any such element; it had been vile, sordid, and shocking. In a fairly rough society in a fairly rough age, she had never seen men fight like dogs before.

Over and over again, what he had said, what she had said, what Ben had said, in endless procession; but it was the same sheep over the same gate, and counting them did not send her to sleep, they made sleep impossible.

It was a fine December, the occasional damp day interspersed with days of slanted sunshine and gentle autumnal airs. The sun lay white upon the front of the Blameys' house, which drowsed like a square-jawed cat. The river glimmered, and blue shadows and stained-glass reflections were broken only by the passage of a fishing boat on the way to Penryn, a coracle conveying someone across the creek, or a group of swans paddling with the tide. On the other side of the pool Falmouth climbed the hill, grey and hunch-backed and smoking, but at night it looked like a fairy castle lit with lanterns.

Clowance always enjoyed pottering with a boat, though on the north coast the constant surf made launching hazardous. Here one simply walked down to the quay, untied the painter and cast off. So in spite of the month she spent two or three hours most days exploring the Penryn River, or sometimes sailing the other way round Trefusis Point and into Carrick Roads and the Fal. There were seldom less than a dozen packet boats moored in the area, and Andrew Blamey senior took her with him to visit old friends. There they would climb down into the little cabins and exchange reminiscences and latest news and drink wine. The captains were ever courteous to her – all except one old man, who was afraid that because she was a woman she would bring him ill luck.

So she listened to talk of the swift four-day passages from Lisbon; the narrow escapes of this and that packet; the running fights; the constant double qui-vive against storm and privateer. She listened to a Captain Erskine telling of the loss of his sister ship, the *Princess Amelia*, homeward bound from St Thomas's, taken by the American privateer *Rossi* after an action of two hours, in which the captain, the master and three others were killed and nine wounded, and the loss of the mails. (*Rossi* had put the wounded ashore in Gibraltar, and they were just home.)

A week later – the day before Valentine called – another captain, Morrison, came to the house to tell of the capture of a 36-gun naval frigate, HMS *Macedonian*, Captain Carder, with thirty-six killed and seventy wounded, by an American frigate, the *United States*. 'A pretty pass,' said Morrison. '*Macedonian* was much out-gunned and did not strike until a mere wreck; but I question what our own navy is about! This *United States* had the scantlings of a 74-gun ship; crew of near on 500 and none pressed; 30 long 24-pounders, howitzer guns in her tops and a travelling carronade on her upper deck. She's been well designed. It is doubtful if those who could kill her could catch her or those who could catch her could kill her.'

'It has been a problem in naval warfare,' said Andrew Blamey senior, 'ever since the Armada.'

'Nelson solved it,' said Morrison.

'Oh yes. And always would. But you cannot stop the solitary marauder. And you have to admit it: Yankees make fine seamen.'

For the most part Clowance was alone with her uncle and aunt. The days were too short and passed swiftly, the nights, by candlelight sitting round the fire, too long. So as dusk was falling on the Tuesday, the clatter of horses on the cobbled street was not an unwelcome sound to her. Janet showed two young men into the withdrawing-room.

Verity said: 'I cannot come for a few minutes. Go and greet them for me, will you?'

Valentine was standing with his back to the fire warming his coat-tails. His dark narrow face lit up at the sight of her.

'Cousin Clowance, by the Lord God! This is standing the world on its head! But what a delightful *bouleversement*! I thought you were wed by now! Or are you passing by after your honeymoon?'

'No,' said Clowance.

He bent over her hand and then kissed her on the mouth, allowing his lips to linger.

'Have you met Tom Guildford?'

'No, I haven't.'

'This is my cousin, Clowance Poldark. Tom is a nephew of old Lord Devoran and has come down to spend Christmas in Cornwall. We only arrived yesterday. Tom, may I present you to my cousin, Miss Clowance Poldark. Or Mrs Stephen Carrington. Which am I to say?'

'Miss,' said Clowance, 'as yet.'

The young man was shorter than Valentine, but rather the same colouring, sallow, dark. In spite of being thin he was strongly built. Not good-looking but a sweet smile. He bent over her hand.

'So, Miss,' said Valentine, 'pray explain yourself, Miss. Is Stephen here?'

'No.'

'Put off? Postponed? Cancelled?'

'All,' said Clowance, smiling at last.

'"And now their honey-moon that late was clear, Doth pale, obscure and tenebrous appear." How droll! I do take the most outrageous pleasure in inquiring into other people's affairs. Tom, my beautiful cousin was sworn and betrothed to a handsome sailor lad called Carrington; but while I have been away tediously drinking myself into an early grave in Cambridge all has changed! A single term! When I was riding that nag at the races in September, you were there with him, Clowance, and all was well. Now – a bare two months later! But tell me, have all the Blameys fallen into Gwennap Pit? Janet I recognize, but . . .'

'My aunt will be down in a moment. My uncle is in Falmouth but should be home within the hour.'

'And Andrew?'

'Still at sea. I believe his vessel is due in on Friday or Saturday.'

'Ah, it was him we called to see, hoping he would be free to play backgammon tonight.'

'What a disappointment for you,' said Clowance.

'On the contrary! Not that I would ask you to game with us. But you must come to Cardew tomorrow! We are giving a party to celebrate the Russian victories.'

'Have there been some?'

'Oh, my little cousin, have there not! Not that anyone is quite sure of the extent as yet. But the country is *rife* with semi-official rumour! In any event, I am seeking an excuse to celebrate something. Could there be a better excuse? I have even prevailed upon Smelter George.'

They went on talking, chattering, with Valentine occupying eighty per cent of the floor. Clowance's common sense remained mildly critical of his flamboyance; but her injured soul leapt in response to such light-hearted chatter. It was the first time she had really laughed for weeks.

Presently Verity came in, and they drank wine and joked and made the evening noisy. They refused an invitation to sup, but before leaving they extracted a promise from

Clowance to go to Cardew tomorrow and spend the night. Because the elder Andrew disapproved of Valentine's influence on the younger Andrew, it was perhaps fortunate that he was late home and missed them.

As the three of them later sat down to a quiet supper, Clowance thought to herself that young Tom Guildford had hardly addressed a word to her.

But he had looked a lot.

II

Sir George Warleggan – who would have skinned his son if he had heard his insulting appellation – never intended a large or such an improvised and extended party. His entertaining, like most of his other activities, was usually conducted with the utmost prudence and purpose.

But Lady Harriet, who had not been seen much during the last two months except on the hunting field, or arriving bedraggled and muddy each night at the supper table, emerged now suddenly from the stables to side with her stepson, and before George quite knew it the thing was out of hand. Musicians who sometimes played at the Assembly Rooms were hired from Truro. Grooms and even stable boys were sent flying over a ten-mile radius with invitations for suitable – and in George's view unsuitable – people, and huge amounts of food were hurriedly got in and cooked and laid out on platters and dishes.

People began to assemble about five, just as it was going dusk, and soon a concourse was moving about the public rooms. Music was already being played in the large drawing-room and a few were dancing. Because it was all such an *ad hoc* affair there were wide variations in dress from the formal to the casual. Viewing the whole party with an uneasy disfavour, which he did not make a show of because he did not wish to displease Harriet, George felt that the evening would cost him at least as much as a full-scale Ball, and that entertaining the best of the county.

Yet adding to everyone's delight and underscoring the rumours of the last few days, special editions of the newspapers were circulating this evening giving factual details of Napoleon's defeat. That he had lost 40,000 men between Moscow and Smolensk. That afterwards the Russians had attacked in a bitter snowstorm near Krasnoi and vast numbers of the enemy had been killed and taken prisoner. 200 guns captured. The pick of what was left of the French cavalry and the Imperial Guard were fighting a rearguard action to prevent total destruction.

It was too much to believe, but it was there in black and white. The dispatches were three weeks – four weeks old, but they were official communiqués not hearsay or rumour any more. Napoleon defeated in battle. Not one of his generals. Napoleon himself: the great marshal, the military genius, the colossus who had bestridden Europe for two decades, the bogey man of children, the hero of the die-hard Whigs, the statesman whose word made nations tremble, was fighting a rear-guard action with his decimated and typhus-ridden troops among the driving snows of Russia!

As the evening proceeded the party caught fire: drink had been circulating from the outset, and even those normally circumspect had tossed back an extra glass or two for such a celebration; conversation was overborne by laughter.

Many of the guests Clowance knew, either well or by sight. Major Trevanion, like many others in hunting pink, and Clemency and Cuby Trevanion; old Lady Whitworth with her frost-encrusted face and porker-like grandson; Mr and Mrs Clement Pope – she in ravishing green – with their two pretty but insipid daughters; Paul and Daisy Kellow; John and Ruth Treneglos with their son Horrie and their problem daughter Agneta; Lord Devoran with his lickerish but now somewhat elderly daughter Betty. (Nobody had seen Lady Devoran for years: even when they called at her house she hid in corners.) There was Eric Tweedy, son of a wealthy Falmouth solicitor. And young Robert Fox, the Quaker. And, of course, Mr Tom Guildford.

Many she did not know, and assumed they came mainly from Falmouth and from the handsome small manor houses which sheltered in verdant valleys between the Fal and Helford rivers. The company came to number about sixty, and outside a low moon helped the lanterns to light the big gravel courtyard which was full of carriages and horses and gossiping grooms.

Tom Guildford said: 'Miss Poldark, would you add to my joy on such a joyous evening?'

Their faces were almost on a level. His eyes were serious.

'Gladly, Mr Guildford, if it is in my power.'

'Would you dance with me?'

She smiled at him. 'Of course I will dance if you will tell me what it is! It is not the dancers but the band which has lost its step! I believe Valentine has been filling their beakers.'

'He told me he would. But again, does it matter? Cannot we improvise? See – a little step here and a little step there, then one turns and bows and – and . . .'

'What happens next?'

He had been making the movements as he spoke. Now he stopped and laughed. 'Let us try.'

'Yes,' she said, 'let's.'

They proceeded round the floor, laughing as they danced. Luckily at the last moment before leaving Nampara Clowance had packed the scarlet brocade frock she had worn at Bowood, so she was better and more elegantly dressed than most on the floor here tonight. Mr Guildford was in a blue silk coat buttoned to the chin, kerseymere knee-breeches, white stockings and patent shoes. Sir George, on his way to find Major Trevanion with whom he hoped to conclude some business, paused a moment to watch them. He had not known Clowance Poldark would be here tonight; thank God her impudent brother had not turned up. But this woman, this girl, whom he had first encountered stealing foxgloves on his property on the north coast a couple of years ago, continued to trouble him with her looks: the brilliance of her fairness, the frankness and innocence of expression, the freshness of skin. The fact that she was slightly less than slim gave her the look of a ripe peach, slender and yet full, ready for picking. That was Devoran's nephew with her. Surely the damned girl was engaged or married; if not, she ought to be, take her off the market, out of circulation; was she *really* as innocent as she looked, dancing like that?

Troubled, he moved away. A hand clawed his arm. 'Uncle George!'

It was Conan Whitworth, that tall, heavy boy with the beady eyes and the mouse-cropped hair.

'Yes?' He hated being addressed as uncle by this youth of sixteen who had no claim so to call him. Conan was dressed in brown corduroy with a shirt of heavy yellow lace and a flowing brown neckcloth. Was he too going to turn into a dude like his father? His present looks did not suggest he would succeed.

'Grandmother says we may not sup till nine. But we cut our dinner short in order to be here in time and these biscuits are poor sustenance.'

'Live on your hump, boy,' George snapped. 'It is but an hour to wait. Take some healthy exercise to entertain your mind.' He passed on.

Conan picked at a pimple on his face and gazed at George's retreating back. A voice behind him mocked:

'Live on your hump, boy.'

It was little Ursula Warleggan – not so little now, but humpy herself, in dark green velvet.

'What do *you* want?'

'You heard what Papa said! Take some healthy exercise to entertain your mind!'

'I'd like to take some healthy exercise and beat you with a stick,' said Conan.

'You dare,' said Ursula. 'You dare lay a finger and I'd scream to stop the band. Go on, I dare you! Lay a finger.'

Conan extended one stubby forefinger. Ursula opened her mouth to scream. 'I'm not touching you,' said Conan, grinning. 'It's free air. Look, I can put it quite close to your nose!'

Ursula struck at the finger, but Conan was too quick for her and snatched his hand away.

'Big fat toad!' said Ursula.

'Little fat toad,' said Conan, not to be outdone.

'If you're not careful I'll get Mama to set the dogs on you.' She ran off.

'She's not your mama,' he called, but she did not seem to hear.

He watched her until she had left the room, hesitated whether to follow, then changed his mind and sauntered after Sir George . . .

Tom Guildford said: 'How long shall you be staying with Mrs Blamey?'

'Oh, I may return home any day now,' Clowance said. 'It was an arrangement.'

'But Valentine says your home is not far beyond St Ann's on the north coast.'

'That is true.'

'May I call, then?'

They tried to take some extra steps in keeping with the beat of the band, and stumbled and laughed.

'May I call, then?'

'I expect Valentine will be coming to see us.'

'But may *I* call, Miss Poldark, with or without Valentine?'

'My mother ... Oh, this music! What will they be like after supper?'

'Your mother?'

'She is expecting her fifth child any day. Our household is likely to be a trifle disorganized.'

'I shall not be calling to see your household.'

'No, you will not, will you? Then pray come. Always assuming ... that all is well with my mother.'

'Should it not be?'

'She has been ailing, and that most unusual in her ... You may think it strange that I am not with her; but it is an order of hers ... she prefers me out of the way, and my brother also.'

'Would you prefer me to write first, then?'

'It may not be necessary. I shall know most likely before my return.'

III

Supper had come and gone – literally gone. Harriet had doubled George's original orders, and she looked with amusement now at the empty dishes, the piles of plates, the occasional corner of a pie left on a platter, the regiments of empty bottles waiting conveyance back to barracks. George made an ill-tempered remark to her and she laughed at him.

'Breaking eggs, George, breaking eggs. It is the only way to make an omelette. And was there ever a better occasion for an – an omelette than this?'

He didn't know what she was talking about and doubted very much if *she* did. He disliked seeing women the worse for drink, and particularly his wife. It could never have happened with Elizabeth. There was not much to show in Harriet's demeanour; her deep drawling voice had become a little gravelly, her magnificent eyes antic-bound as they sometimes were when she was ready for sex. But there was no opportunity for any such indulgence even had he wished, with the house full of semi-riotous people and likely to remain so far into the night.

Just before supper the band played 'God Save the King' and again after, when everyone in every room joined in, with dubious musical effect but to everyone's total satisfaction. Some of the ladies were in tears. The whole house was full of stupid, sentimental, emotional patriotism, as if it was the British who had gained the victory and not the Russians – as if it were really the end of the war. George very much doubted this: Buonaparte and the French had enormous powers of recuperation; and *was* this victory so complete as it sounded? Neither the Russians nor the Germans nor the Poles nor the Austrians nor the Spanish had *ever* done *anything* worth while before.

From eyeing with resentment the crowds about him, George began to have other thoughts: if by any remote chance it did mean the end of the war, he now stood to gain nothing. How much better to have hung on to his heavy and speculative investments in the North instead of realizing them at a dead loss last year!

At least his business with Trevanion was now complete. All details signed, sealed and settled. It had cost him or would cost him a pretty penny; yet it was a splendid arrangement. The two young people most concerned should be told soon.

Clowance had exchanged a few words with Cuby Trevanion at supper. On principle she detested the girl for making her brother so unhappy, above all for apparently falling in with *her* brother's attempts to marry her off to a rich man. If she did not care for Jeremy – and Clowance could not imagine how any girl could not – that was a black mark in the first place. But having, according to Jeremy, some feeling for him – certainty led him to believe she had some feeling for him – then cold-bloodedly to turn him down because he hadn't the money, was unforgivable, insufferable. But since the races there had been some sort of a reconciliation, however tenuous, however uncertainly based, and Clowance now wanted to do her best to help.

So they smiled at each other and talked about the warmth of the evening and the amazing news. She *was* pretty, Clowance realized, much more so than she had thought at Easter; she lit up when she was speaking, the sulkiness was gone like a cloud breaking into sunshine, and of course because of the cloud the sun seemed the brighter.

Presently she said quite casually, as if it were the last thing that occurred to her, that she had not seen Jeremy here tonight. No, Clowance agreed, perhaps they had not sent him word. Of course I sent him word, said Valentine, who was beside them helping Mrs Selina Pope to ice-cream, but he was away, in Hayle or somewhere. Hayle? said Clowance. The groom said no more, said Valentine; Mrs Pope, I declare you have become even more slender than your daughters, pray allow me to put this on your plate: waste it if you will, waste it if you will. Can I take something to Mr Pope?

Mr Pope's decision to come tonight had been a big surprise and a big mistake. It was his first appearance in company for several months; but being in better health than for some time he had decided to accept the invitation for the whole family, supposing, since he knew Sir George as a dignified and sober figure, and one who only mixed in the best company he could find, that this event would be an elegant evening worthy of his attendance. He had reckoned without George's new wife. He was sitting now in an ante-room, high-collared, black-coated, stiff-necked, looking more than ever like Robespierre, a glass of port untouched at his side and on his face an expression of costive goodwill that was intended to hide the annoyance he was feeling. One or other of his daughters, or his wife, would pop in for a few minutes in turn to keep him company.

In a corner Betty Devoran was making a set at a tall young Welsh officer of the Brecon militia, disfigured by a birthmark on his forehead and cheek. Betty was not deterred by a little thing like that. She had never married and now probably never would, though it was said on good authority that she had at least three illegitimate children farmed out around the county. She was known never to resist a pair of trousers, but it was all done with such laughing good humour and such obvious enjoyment that polite society turned a blind eye. Everyone knew Betty.

In another corner Horrie Treneglos was laying siege to a dowdy girl called Angela Nankivell, only daughter of Arthur Nankivell, who by his marrying a Scobell had become a rich man. Horrie, aged twenty-four, had a curious fancy for dowdy girls. He had bedded many of them but, except for a couple of paternity suits on which payment was made quarterly to abandoned servant girls, he had so far come out unscathed and unattached. On this particular pursuit on this particular evening, John and Ruth Treneglos watched him from the other side of the room with the very greatest benevolence. He was unlikely to get Angela without marrying her, and even if he did, subsequent marriage would be all they could desire. The Tranegloses were of ancient lineage and landed possession, but never had any – or scarcely any – of that curious thing called money. They never lacked any of the amenities of life but they were always short of coin. Arthur Nankivell, and by association his daughter, was never short of coin.

After supper Tom Guildford danced with Clowance several times more. She told him about herself. He told her that except for his uncle there never was a trace of a title in his family, in spite of the name, but that he was of Cornish descent and related to the Killigrews, now extinct, through a Thomas Guildford Killigrew; and that he often stayed with Lord Devoran, whose estate was near Kea in the neighbourhood of Truro. This was such a free and easy occasion, such a sturdily Bohemian occasion, that it seemed not at all out of line that they should dance together just as often as they wished without regard to propriety. Tom Guildford was very ardent and Clowance could not, or did not, resist him.

As the clocks were striking twelve Betty Devoran performed a solo dance which owed nothing to preparation but much to drunken inspiration. The noise she made and the band made and the watchers made roused the boar hounds, who had suffered so far in silence, and their baying and barking almost stopped the clock. But after it the dancing became ever more frenzied until one a.m., when George passed sternly among the sagging band telling them enough was enough. On this came a footman looking for Miss Clowance Poldark. Hot and dishevelled and glowing, she came forward to receive a letter from her father, which Verity had sent on to her in haste.

Dear Clowance [it ran],

You have a brother – another brother – whom we have yet forborne to name. He came at six of the clock this evening, and praise be to God, caused little trouble in his arrival. He seems well and is at this present sleeping peacefully. Your mother has survived but is very weak. We cannot quite understand why she is so ill, but your Uncle Dwight, who has taken a troubled view of her for the last three months, is now more hopeful. Indeed, he is optimistic – which as you know is not the commonest condition in which he passes his days.

So I can tell you I live hopefully – not optimistically, for that would be foreign for me too – but hopefully, that our Christmas will be a happy one after all. Come home soon. We do not need you but we want you. Tear yourself away from Verity and rejoin us.

As ever your loving Father.

'News?' said Tom Guildford. 'Not bad news, I pray?' Looking at her eyes brimming with tears.

'No, Tom, thank you. The best! The best!'

'Then why do you weep?' His face was close to hers.

'Pleasure. Happiness. *Relief!* I could not have borne it!'

'What could you not have borne, my angel?'

'What might have happened. What I feared was going to happen!' She waved the letter at him. 'Oh, I had the strangest premonitions! Now they have *gone!* What a perfect way to end the night!'

With a light hand on her shoulder he kissed her. Her mouth was like half-open petals. The crowd was standing all around them on the ballroom floor but no one seemed to notice. The band had given up. She dabbed her eyes with a handkerchief. He kissed her hand and then her mouth again.

Somebody shouted something, and two or three others took up the cry.

'The Miller's Dance!'

People were calling to the band: 'The Miller's Dance! The Miller's Dance!'

'It is a perfect way to end the night for *me*,' said Tom quite emotionally, but not talking of the dance. 'But must it end yet? If you are tired, let us go and sit out somewhere. There's wine and food still available in the library, Valentine tells me.'

'The Miller's Dance!' they were shouting.

'Oh, I am not *tired!*' said Clowance. 'Why ever should I be tired? I'm come alive! . . . what are they calling for?'

'It is an old farmhouse dance,' said Paul Kellow, coming up beside them. 'D'you not know it, Clowance? It is just an excuse for a noisy lark. "There was an old miller who lived by himself, He ground his corn and taxed the sun." Come on, let us make a circle, two by two, holding hands. Valentine! Valentine!' he shouted, 'you go in the middle to start it off!'

The violinist, a rotund little man with a purple face and a white wig, was talking to his two companions. Presently he swung his bow a couple of times and then drew it long and resonantly down across the strings, creating a deep echoing note such as is heard before a Scottish reel. Then he was off and away.

Of the twenty-odd people on the floor not a dozen knew what to do, but eventually the dance began to organize itself, although one of the features of it was that it was at best a mêlée. Two by two the dancers proceeded in a circle round a solitary man, who was kneeling on, supposedly, a sheaf of corn. In this case it was a cushion. The others danced side on to him, tripping in a courtly style but faster, and while they tripped to the music they sang:

> 'There was an old miller who lived by himself,
> He ground his corn and taxed the sun.
> The money he made he put on a shelf,
> But when he came to count his wealth:
> One ... two ... three ... it was *gone*!'

At the word *gone* everyone had to change partners, and the miller in the middle was expected to seize a temporarily spare lady if he could before she was grabbed by someone else. If the same man remained in the middle three times he was pelted with anything to hand, bottle corks, decorations off the cakes, paper balls, even an occasional shoe if someone had lost one and could not reclaim it in time.

It was, as Paul said, an excuse for a noisy lark, but the heavy beat of the music and its peculiarly melancholy rhythm had the same effect as some of the other old Cornish tunes, building an emotion by its endless repetition and conjuring up superstitions and practices which could not so easily survive the light. One wondered if at some time in the past the miller, or whoever occupied the sacrificial centre, had been stoned.

But tonight all was the most strident jollity; young people and older pushing and thrusting and grabbing and shouting with laughter, then, when they had all paired off again, prancing and tripping and hopping and skipping to the catchy, thumping, echoing, ghostly, melancholy tune.

Clowance was caught and released, grabbed and linked, hot hands clutching. (Different from Bowood, she thought!) Her partners were Valentine and Paul and Tom and Horrie and old Lord Devoran, puffing and grunting, and Tom and the militia officer and two men she didn't know and Tom and Valentine and Tom.

When it was nearly over and one or two were falling by the wayside out of exhaustion Clowance had a strange sudden sensation, as if the music had been communicating something to her which had been taken in by her psychic self rather than consciously through her ears. This was the Miller's Dance. The Miller's Dance. And the Miller, *her* miller, was somehow here among them, like an unshriven spirit. A vigorous, brash, fascinating man, a man of hair and muscle and sinew, reared to fight and always ready to fight, to grab, to claim, to lie, to steal if necessary, to demand what he thought to be his, charming, dominating, ruthless.

He was there somewhere among it all; he was by her side. And she knew, almost with a sensation of dread, that he always would be. It was like being in a period of health – almost having forgotten one's ill health – and then suddenly recognizing a stirring of pain again, a pain which one knew to be incurable, deep down, reminding one in the midst of happiness that for some complaints there is no cure.

Chapter Four

I

Jeremy spent two nights with the Harveys, a third with Andrew Vivian. Over the last few months the Harvey Foundry had run into serious difficulties, being the subject of a lawsuit in the Chancery Court in London. In September the Lord Chancellor had ordered the closing of the works until his judgment was made known, and this closure had endured until early December when the court had at last found in favour of Mr Henry Harvey. Though the suit had been the result of a split between partners, Mr Harvey was very bitter against the Cornish Copper Company, their obnoxious rivals, for having played a leading part in stirring up the brew. Sir George Warleggan was now a partner in the Cornish Copper Company.

For three months the coal yard, the granary, the forges, the ancillary shops and both sea-going vessels had been idle, and Mr Harvey was now struggling with many debts and intense shortage of capital. He therefore more than welcomed an advance payment of half the cost of the whim engine, an offer which Jeremy brought with him. (It would also, Jeremy thought, make his order come in for the highest priority.)

Though Mr Harvey lived with his sister, Foundry House was abounding with children, orphans of Henry's sister Anne and her husband, both of whom had died a few years back; and Jeremy found his social time full. He was disappointed not to meet Mr Trevithick, and the night he spent with Andrew Vivian he remarked on his disappointment.

'They may be close tied by marriage but they seldom see eye to eye,' said Vivian. 'It is not at all that they mislike each other; it is a question of temperament. Henry is careful, conscientious, businesslike, a true mercantile adventurer who is never afraid to take a risk if it can be justified in his own logical mind. Richard is a great innovator, a genius in the true sense of the word, a man whose mind takes wings and does not think kindly of being told that a brilliant idea must be pursued cautiously and painstakingly to its last decimal point. I am rather coming to the belief that Henry will in the end find more in common with Arthur Woolf who, though not the genius he thinks he is, has a splendidly inventive brain.'

All the same, Jeremy used his time well, having further meetings with William Sims and William West. Then Andrew Vivian took him to meet a Captain Joel Lean, who had just accepted a new position funded by various mines to issue yearly tables on the amount of work done and the efficiency of the mining engines of Cornwall. This showing up of the capabilities and work of the engines would be bound to settle many arguments and also to set the engineers themselves on their mettle.

One half-day Jeremy spent with his steam carriage; but, until he could devise and have built an entirely new boiler on the lines laid down by Mr Trevithick at their last meeting, it was hardly worth continuing to work on the rest.

It had not been at all absent from Jeremy's mind during all this technical talk that events might – and almost surely were – occurring at home; and when he finally left Hayle he would have wished to ride back by the shortest route. But during the days before he left Nampara he had managed to get a wisp of Clowance's hair, a curl of Isabella-Rose's, and, with no difficulty at all, a sample of his own. These he had taken in to Truro to Solomon, the silversmith, and had bought a silver locket for £8 and had asked the old man to fit these pieces of hair into the inner compartment of the locket, leaving room at a later stage for a fourth sample. He hadn't quite known what to buy his mother at this time.

So he made a detour by way of Truro to pick it up, and had to admit that it was worth while. Solomon had done the work with elegance and taste, thinning the original samples by about half but leaving enough of them to be clearly definable: Jeremy's own a sort of coppery dark not unlike his father's, Clowance's glowingly fair, and Bella's as black as a gypsy's; much more unredeemably black than her mother's, which often caught lights and seemed to reflect the company it was in.

Solomon's little shop was in St Austell Street, and immediately opposite it was Blight's Coffee House. Knowing he would be too late for dinner at home, he went in there and ordered pigeon pie.

It was a partitioned place, so that customers could be quite private one from another. Jeremy ate and at the same time read the special editions of the newspapers available there. He had heard something of the Russian victories but not seen it in black and white. It was overwhelming. Could it be the beginning of the end? US privateers, he read, were active in the narrow seas . . .

'Good day to you, Jeremy Poldark,' someone said, and thumped into the seat opposite.

It was Conan Whitworth.

Since the musical evening at Caerhays last year Jeremy had identified this boy, whom he had not been sure of then.

'Ah, Conan . . . Good day to you,' Jeremy said, trying to be polite.

The boy solidly occupied the other side of the table watching him. After a few moments Jeremy went on with his meal. The waiter came.

'That's good?' Conan asked, pointing at Jeremy's plate.

'Very good.'

'I'll have that then. And quick about it.' When the waiter had gone Conan said: 'My grandmother's at Miss Agar's. She sent me out, but not for food. I need a snack, though.'

'Oh,' said Jeremy. He turned a page of the newspaper.

'I get pimples.' said Conan.

'What?'

'I get pimples, See them? Discharging too.'

Jeremy stared at the boy's blotched face. His skin was pallid and looked as thick as peel, as if it would be hard to puncture. But yes, one could count pustules enough . . .

'There is a deal of smallpox in Truro,' Conan volunteered, making a fuss of his spectacles, taking them off, rubbing them, putting them back. 'A lot of it down by the river.'

'I suppose it's the season.'

'Grandmother says it is because the lower orders won't be vaccinated and get inoculated instead. Grandmother says this is spreading the disease, not stopping it.'

'That may well be.'

Jeremy took a last mouthful of pie.

'Wish that waiter would hurry,' said Conan. He opened his mouth as if to laugh, but no sound emerged. 'I made a mistake.'

'What?' Jeremy said irritably, as his reading was interrupted again.

'Made a mistake. Grandmother sent me out for a lotion.

"Solomon's Abstergent Lotion for Eruptions of the Skin."
Four shillings and sixpence a bottle. She gave me a half-
sovereign. I thought I'd take this snack and tell her the
price of the lotion had advanced to five and six. See?'

'So what of that?'

'Well, I went into Solomon's opposite. Solomon's Lotion;
Solomon's shop. You'd think so, wouldn't you? Solomon's
Lotion; Solomon's shop. But he's a silversmith. It was round
the corner in St Clement's Street – at Harry's – where they
sold it! The apothecary's!' Conan laughed again, and as
silently.

'The best quality wheat on Truro market is selling for
38/- to 40/- a bushel,' Jeremy read. 'But millers are asking
50/- to 52/-. This is gross profiteering and the Ministers of
the Crown should intervene to prevent it.'

'D'you think that's true?' Conan asked.

'What?

'About the defeat of the French. Everybody believes it,
don't they.'

'Yes, I think it's true.' This boy's mother had been
Geoffrey Charles's governess, and Jeremy remembered her
as a shy, gentle, withdrawn creature to whom his cousin had
become much attached and with whom his Uncle Drake
had fallen irretrievably in love. How could she have bred
such a boy?

The waiter brought a slice of pigeon pie. Conan took his
spectacles off to see the better and fell upon it with the
anxiety of a starving man. Jeremy paid his score and began
to roll the newspaper.

Conan said something with his mouth full that Jeremy
could not catch.

'What?'

'Big party at Cardew. Tuesday night. Went on near all

night. Everyone was decks awash. Uncle George was mad. Wasn't he mad!'

'What do you mean? What are you talking about?'

Conan looked across at Jeremy as he chewed. It was being borne in upon him that his company was not appreciated. It was not an uncommon experience for him but he still resented it.

'Valentine came home from Cambridge on Sunday. Wanted an excuse for a party. This defeat of the French. Uncle George was persuaded by Lady Harriet. Valentine sent out invitations everywhere. A crowd. Seventy or more. Wonder you weren't there.'

'I've been away.'

'Your sister was there.'

'Clowance? Oh, she's been staying in Flushing.'

'So was Mr John Trevanion there. So was Miss Trevanion. *And* her sister, Miss Cuby.'

Jeremy put the newspaper back in the rack. On the other side of the aisle two shepherds were sitting opposite each other wolfing pies and swilling them down with ale. They both wore hats, maybe to keep their hair out of their food, for they ate with their fingers, disdaining the knives provided, noses close to table like animals at a trough. Conan was in good company.

'Mr John Trevanion,' the boy said slyly. 'He's skinned for money, isn't he.'

'I have no idea.'

'Gambles his money away, they say. Gambles on his horses.'

'Well, that is his own business, isn't it.'

Conan again mumbled something through the pastry.

'*What?*'

'They say he should never have changed his name, don't they. They say he shouldn't ever have changed his name from Bettesworth to Trevanion, don't they.'

'I have no idea what you are on about.'

'Well . . . Bettesworth. He bet his worth. See? That's what they say. He *bet his worth.*' A mass of partly chewed food showed as Conan opened his mouth to laugh.

Jeremy got up. 'Well, I'm glad you enjoyed yourself at this party.'

'Oh, I did, I did. At two o'clock Valentine danced on one of the tables. Fell off and we thought he'd broke his neck. But not at all. All he did was sit up and shout for more wine.'

'I wonder you were invited, being so young.'

'Oh, not so young, Jeremy Poldark. Seventeen next birthday. Anyway I go anywhere my grandmother goes.'

'Was *she* invited?' Jeremy asked pointedly.

Conan stuffed in another piece of pie.

'I found something out. It'll interest you.'

'Tell me next time we meet.'

'Uncle George never misses a chance to do business, does he. Even when it is a jolly party and most people are decks awash.'

'I've no idea.'

'It may interest you,' said Conan, munching; 'what I have to say may interest you, if you are still heartsmitten on Miss Cuby.'

Jeremy stood there resisting a temptation to seize the boy by the scruff of the neck and shake him till he choked on the crumbs.

'Who says I am?'

'Well . . .' Conan pushed his spectacles along the table. 'I just thought. Seeing you at the musical evening. I just thought. And then at the races. And there's been talk here and there.'

'There's always talk. Goodbye, Conan. Commend me to your grandmother.'

'So it can't matter, then?'

'What can't matter?'

'I mean it can't matter to you that Miss Cuby is going to marry Valentine Warleggan.'

II

Jeremy reached Nampara soon after four. Although mid-December it was still full daylight. The setting sun had edged its way behind an escarpment of cloud, and the upper sky was ethereal, a thousand miles high, as if you were looking up at Heaven. In the distance gulls were wheeling and screaming, wings shadowed and glinting as they performed their lonely rituals. Smoke rose straight, and there was a hint of frost.

He didn't bother riding round to the stables but hitched Colley over the old lilac tree and tiptoed in. Jane Gimlett was just about to carry a candelabra of lighted candles upstairs.

'Oh, Mr Jeremy! You give me a fright!'

'Where ... How is ...?'

'The master and Miss Clowance are in the library. The mistress is better today, and—'

'What has happened?'

'Oh, you haven't *heard*! We have a *boy*!'

'God's my life! ... And are they both *well*?'

'Yes, well. Mistress has been some slight but is feeling better today.'

'Thank *Heaven*! That's *good* news! Is she awake?'

'Mistress? Yes, yes, she's just asked for these.'

'And – the baby?'

'Sleeping, I b'lave.'

'Go up. Tell her I'll follow.'

When he went in Demelza was sitting up hastily brushing her hair. She looked very thin but her eyes were brilliant.

'Well, my son.'

He bent and kissed her. 'Not the only one now.'

'Your rival is over there.'

'Bother him. How are you?'

'Brave.'

'The fever has gone?'

'Yes.'

'Let me feel your pulse.'

She hid her wrists. He picked up the brush she had dropped.

'Were you expecting visitors?'

'Only you. When Jane told me . . .'

'You decided you must put on your best bib and tucker, eh? For a visitor of such importance. What a strange woman you are!'

'Oh, I know,' she agreed. 'And getting stranger.'

His eyes roved to the cot and then came back. 'You don't look like a matriarch.'

'Why not?'

'Not fierce enough. Not *old* enough.'

'Just at the moment,' Demelza said, 'I feel very *young*.'

'You look it.' She did look exhilaratingly young, but frail, as if she were recovering from a grave illness.

'Where are Papa and Clowance?'

'In the library, I'm told. Moving furniture, I conject. Though for what purpose I have no idea.'

'Maybe turning it into a playroom. Bella will like that.'

'I do not think Bella is altogether taken with her new brother. She wrinkles her nose at him.'

'Who wouldn't when she's been so spoiled?'

'Spoiled?'

'Well, haven't we all been? What are you going to call him, by the way?'

'We . . . D'you know, Jeremy, we haven't decided!'

'When is he to be christened?'

'Christmas Eve, we think.'

'Well, that'll give us a few days to put our heads together. Would suggestions be welcomed?'

'Of course! Dwight has told me I must spend another three or four days in bed, but I'm not at all certain sure I shall obey him, so when I come down—'

'He is satisfied with you?'

'When was Dwight ever satisfied? I believe he is quite pleased. Caroline came this morning and said he was quite pleased, so I take that to be true.'

Jeremy went and peered in at the cot. A small round head, a wisp of dark hair, and a single fist like a pink walnut were to be seen.

'Stap me,' he said, 'I'm old enough to be his father!'

'Stap me, so you are. Now tell me of your visit to Hayle. Was it fruitful?'

'Oh, unimportant.'

'Never mind, I want to know.'

He told her. For the first time since he entered, his effortful concentration lapsed and she said:

'Was it not all to your liking?'

'Of course. All is going forward splendidly.'

'I did not think you sounded so full of enthusiasm.'

'Oh ... possibly I allowed my mind to dwell on something else – the fact that the steam carriage has got no further.'

'Perhaps it soon will. And the war ...'

'Wonderful news. Papa is pleased?'

'We are all pleased! And relieved.'

'Mama,' he said, 'I have bought you a little present.'

She blinked. 'My dear life. But why?'

'Should I not? You have just most notably added another Poldark to the world's population. Isn't that a cause for celebration?'

'I'm not at all sure! But ...'

Jeremy fumbled in his pocket and took out the silver locket. She accepted it and unwrapped it from its tissue paper. She turned it over and presently pressed the catch.

'My dear life,' she said again. 'Jeremy, my lover, it's so *kind* ... I don't know what to say ...'

'Say thank you,' he suggested.

'That I'll do double-fold. Jeremy, I can't just at this very moment ... think of more ...'

She reached up and he kissed her. 'I was hoping the new boy would be a redhead,' he said. 'Add to the colour in the locket. For a change, don't you think.'

Her vision was blurred. 'I don't *want* a change, Jeremy. Thank you. It was so thoughtful. Did both girls consent that you should take a clipping?

'Only Clowance. I robbed Bella while she slept.'

Demelza laughed, her voice husky. 'I believe I have children's hair from when you were all babies; but I better prefer what you have put in. I'll keep it near my heart.'

'That's of it,' said Jeremy in his Cornish voice. 'Proper job.'

They talked for a few more minutes; then he snuffed the candles, put coal on the fire, took a further peek at his tiny brother, grinned cheerfully at his mother and left.

III

He went straight across to his own bedroom but did not bother to take a light. He slumped down in the one easy chair before the undrawn curtains of the window, stared out. There were a few waifs of light left in the sky defying the encroachment of the December evening. It was cold in here after the warmth of the other bedroom.

Conan Whitworth's account was spiteful but convincing. He could not have invented it. And it was almost too circumstantial to be exaggerated.

It seemed that he had approached Sir George Warleggan before the break for supper, and Sir George had rudely rebuffed him, and immediately afterwards had gone upstairs to his study on the first floor in company with Major Trevanion. Conan had opted to sneak after them. They had shut the door of the study behind them and Conan had decided to see what he could hear through the keyhole. 'It's always fun,' he explained to Jeremy, 'hearing what you're not supposed to hear.' Unfortunately Sir George's voice was too low, but Major Trevanion's was always loud and what he said came clearly. And from this it seemed they were discussing some document which referred to Valentine Warleggan and Cuby Trevanion. There was to be a sum of money paid on certain conditions; but an argument developed as to the conditions and the date of payment. Then

Major Trevanion had made some remark about 'sharpening this damned pen'. Whereupon Conan had applied his eye to the keyhole and observed Major Trevanion doing just that. There was further murmuring and conversation and the clink of a bottle. Conan had just dodged away from the door in time as they came out and went downstairs. Major Trevanion had been stuffing some papers into his inside pocket.

At this stage Jeremy was still half for ignoring the boy and leaving, but he could see that Conan had more to tell, and he could not make the decisive move to tear himself away.

Conan had gone into the study. By the light of the single candle they had left burning he had lifted the lid of Sir George's desk and found a document lying open inside. 'It makes it more exciting,' he said to Jeremy. 'I often read other people's letters.'

This appeared to be a sort of marriage arrangement. Settlement? said Jeremy. Settlement, yes, Conan said, a settlement; a sort of agreement, all done legally and proper, with Sir George undertaking to pay Major Trevanion the sum of £20,000. £2,000, if Conan remembered rightly, within six months of the signature of the document, and the rest – the £18,000, on the day of the marriage of Valentine Warleggan and Cuby Trevanion.

There didn't seem to be any mention of the wedding day, Conan said, eyeing Jeremy slyly for signs of shock; maybe it had not yet been appointed. And signed that evening in the middle of a party? Jeremy asked. No, no, said Conan, all done a week or two ago, sometime in early December, couldn't recall the exact date, and witnessed: Trembath was the name of one witness, he thought; the other, Blencowe. Arthur Something Blencowe, clerk, of 21,

River Street. What about that for a good memory? He was always good at school at memory games. Remembering things on a tray – you know – twenty seconds to look and two minutes to write 'em down. Always won, especially if it was food.

But you said you thought they were signing something then. Ah, said Conan, stuffing in the last mouthful, that was something different, something arranged that evening, lying there freshly sanded; a further letter of agreement, so to say. Or that's what it looked like to him. It was marked *copy*, he remembered. No doubt Major Trevanion had the original.

Another sort of letter of agreement, Conan said. It stated that Major Trevanion was to receive a further £1,000 immediately in return for the undertaking that he would personally vacate Caerhays Castle within one year of the marriage. It sounded all right, said Conan, didn't it, it promised well for Master Valentine and Miss Cuby after they were wed.

The story all came out with relish. Conan might have learned it. No doubt he had repeated the details over and over again in the depths of his devious mind before spilling them out with a peculiar sort of pleased rancour in the shadowed cubicle of Blight's Coffee House over the greasy table and the crumbs of the pigeon pie.

But rancour towards whom? Sir George, who no doubt often rebuffed him? To Jeremy himself who probably had not disguised his dislike? Or perhaps it was a kind of spite directed at all mankind.

On the ride home and now in the privacy of his bedroom Jeremy went over the details again and again. It all fitted. Conan Whitworth might be a repulsive youth but his memory was not in question. It all *suddenly* fitted. George

Warleggan's ambition for his son, which fed his own ambition. For twenty thousand pounds he established his son as the husband of a girl of ancient family and put him in possession of one of the noblest houses in Cornwall. For a last extra thousand (Trevanion must really be on the edge) he ensured that Valentine should be sole master of that house.

It seemed likely that the wedding was not to be just yet. Valentine would probably complete his studies at Cambridge. They might marry towards the end of next year or early in 1814. In the meantime John Trevanion received enough to enable him to keep his head above water, and by next May or June a larger sum to see him safely to land.

Did either of the principals know? Were they party to this agreement? It seemed improbable, at least as recently as September: he could *not* believe Cuby would have accepted his light-hearted embraces so light-heartedly in return if she had known this then. Whatever her faults, duplicity in that degree was not among them. Did it matter? Did it matter if either of them knew? For each would dance when the strings were pulled. Cuby had already told him so to his face last Easter, and Valentine would always give way to his father where an arrangement of such importance was involved.

In any case, why *should* Valentine object? Jeremy's stomach turned sick. At that music party last year, had not Valentine made some salacious references to Cuby? – how he would like to untie the bow of her bodice. 'Watch the way she breathes – doesn't it give one pretty fancies?'

Well, might Valentine roast in hell! He was going to get his fancies gratified – and a castle to live in too! Object! Object, in God's name! What was there to object to?

Might all the Warleggans roast in hell! Had there not

been some rumour last year of George Warleggan and his bank being in trouble? He had heard some passing reference to it between his mother and father but had been too preoccupied with other things to take much notice at the time. And had there not been some suggestion of the Cornish Bank, in which his father was a partner, considering whether to exert pressure to bring the Warleggans down? God in hell! if that had happened Sir George would likely have had no money to contrive his vile stinking schemes.

His father, Ross, had tried to comfort him last year by saying that, much as Major Trevanion might hope for a wealthy marriage for Cuby, and willing as Cuby might be to further this ambition, there were precious few rich men about – though plenty looking for an heiress. And any rich man who *was* about would be very unlikely to advance huge sums of money to save his brother-in-law from bankruptcy.

Well, that was true. Broadly that was true. But both of them had overlooked the Warleggans. This evil family had lain like a blight across his father's and mother's life; now it was blighting his too. And there was nothing to be *done*.

Nothing. Nothing. *Nothing*. To confront Cuby. To confront Valentine. To confront Valentine's father. Cuby would be upset but dedicated to her promise. Valentine would joke it off, saying, dear boy, what can *I* do? Sir George would be grim and coldly polite, but all the time quietly rejoicing that in furthering his own aims and his son's advancement he had accidentally dealt a mortal wound to the son of his old rival.

For more than an hour Jeremy sat in the dark. Sometimes his feelings induced a claustrophobia which made him want to burst open the lattice window, shattering the glass into the yard below. He wanted to shout to get out. But it was not the house he wanted to flee from, it was himself.

However far he ran over the cliffs or across the beach, his own mind, his knowledge of what was going to happen, his own feelings about it, would dog his footsteps as inescapably as a moon shadow. There was no repeal, no avoidance, no hope.

The rattle of feet in the passage and the door shivered open. Isabella-Rose.

'Jeremy! I wondered where you was! Why're you sitting in the dark?'

'I was counting the moths,' Jeremy said.

'Oh, stupid! Here, you stole my *hair*! Mama's just shown me. You long-leggety beastie! Stealing my *hair*!'

'You've got plenty more. Look, what's all this? And all this? Enough to make a beard for a beggar!'

She squeaked and slid away from him. 'Supper's almost ready! What d'you think of the baby? Isn't he *ugly*? Uglier even than *you*. What are we going to christen him?'

'I'd call him Bellamy,' said Jeremy. 'Bella and Bellamy would go well together.'

'Then I'd call him Gerald. Gerald and Jeremy.'

'Or Clarence to go with Clowance. Doesn't Mama really know?'

'If she knows she's not telling. Come along, I was sent to fetch you.'

Jeremy allowed himself to be towed out into the light and jollity of the rooms downstairs.

Chapter Five

I

They called him Henry, after an uncle of Demelza's. And Vennor, after Ross – and Ross's mother who had been a Vennor. A tiny baby, five pounds at birth and less than six at the christening. If Henry was tiny Demelza was a waif and reminded Ross, he told her, of the day he had given her a lift back from Redruth Fair.

She smiled at him. 'I'm not as scared of you now.'

'More's the pity. You'd recover your health more quickly if you obeyed me.'

'By eating more? Ross, I'm eating like a horse!'

'More like a bony mare.'

'A bony pony.' She giggled at her own joke.

He said: 'But serious. You *do* remind me.'

'I wish it was that again. I'd wish for *all* my life over again from the moment you brought me home here as a dirty urchin!'

'Like to be swilled under the pump?'

'That water was *cold*. I mind it was cold.'

'Well, you'd have to take the rough with the smooth.'

'Yes, yes. And find Jud scratching his bald head and predicting doom. And Prudie and her feet. And my father coming to take me home ... But there was lots of smooth too, wasn't there. You must admit there was lots of *smooth*, Ross.' She drawled the word.

She was in one of her provocative moods this afternoon.

She looked about twenty-five and interested in men. It boded ill for their own relationship, if their intention was to keep that relationship chaste.

He said abruptly: 'It's time I went away.'

'Are you tired of us?'

'Of course. Cannot endure you any longer.'

'Seriously?'

'Seriously, my reasons are more self-sacrificing.'

'That would be a sad mistake, now that I am coming brave.'

'You must be left alone to come brave.'

'Who said so?'

'I say so. Look at you now, like a skittish colt! By all rights you should be *fat* and sitting in a big armchair in front of the fire with a shawl round your shoulders, smelling of milk and babies' clouts.'

'Would you like me like that?'

'Never mind what I would like. It would be a safer situation. Safer for you.'

She stared out at the slanting sunshine falling across her garden. It was in fairly good trim, but small things had been neglected during the last two months when she had felt too listless to work in it herself. Even the withered brown relics of the lilac flowers on the old tree by the parlour window had not been cut off.

She said: 'You don't live to be *safe*, Ross. You live to be alive, to take a deep breath of the air and to know your heart is beating! After Isabella-Rose was born I did not conceive for nearly ten years. There is no reason why I should conceive again for another ten years; and by then twill be too late.'

'Come along,' he said roughly. 'The others are waiting.'

'If you desert me now,' she said, 'for some fancy guinea-hen in London I shall think very hard on you.'

'Damn you,' he said. 'In another two weeks I will ask Dwight—'

'Oh, fiddle to Dwight. It is not any business of his.'

He put his hand on her shoulder. 'Well, maybe I will consider you suitable when I can no longer discern that bone so plain.'

'D'you think I'm a goose hanging in a poulterer's?' she said. 'Because if I were ever to buy a goose, *that's* not the part I would feel.'

His sudden explosion of laughter brought the children hurrying in, but neither of the elders would explain what the fun was about. A few minutes later they were all riding decorously off to church.

II

The church and churchyard were crowded. Everyone, it seemed, in the district of Sawle and Grambler and Mellin and Marasanvose had heard of the birth of a second son to the Poldarks and everyone wished to be there for the christening. There was simply no room for all who wanted to get into the church, and to make things worse Jud Paynter arrived at the last moment on a sort of throne-litter borne by four of his young neighbours, the two in the van being Art and Music Thomas. It was a lark, of course, but they had promised there should be no fooling, and Prudie followed behind them carrying a stick to crack over their heads if they did not behave. Jud sat on the top of it all like a careworn and unspiritual Buddha, staring gloomily at the too-distant ground and trying to keep his old felt hat in place. Everything about him looked rusty, from his eyes and his nose to the blanket stained with iron-mould that some-one at the last minute had thrown over his shoulders.

'Could as well be carred to me buryin',' he said. ''Twill be me next journey this way, and good shut to the world, I d'say. Poor little meader up thur,' he added in a loud voice, as soon as he got in church, pointing towards the font, '*'e* don't know what 'e's in fur, that'e don't, else 'e'd be turning tail and going backsyfore the way 'e come. To save his self from the fires of 'Ell and damnation, like all you folk 'ere. 'Ell and damnation to all of ye what 'aven't repented!'

'Hist your noise!' whispered Prudie. 'Ye promised ye'd be quiet, ye old gale.'

'Gale yerself!' said Jud. '*Hey up*, men! Load me if I didn't think ye was a-going to drop me like a basket of eggs! *Easy thur!*'

He was slowly brought to ground, his carriers, sweating freely, having apologized for stepping on the toes of, and elbowing, the people around them. Prudie, to his intense annoyance, whipped off his hat.

A degree of silence settled in the church while the Reverend Clarence Odgers was led in by his wife. There was nothing wrong with Mr Odgers's eyesight or his legs, it was only that his memory took in things like messages breathed on glass. It had even gone downhill since the opening of the mine: now, if not watched closely, he was as liable to marry Henry Poldark to his godmother, Caroline Enys, or indeed begin the words of committal on Jud – 'earth to earth, ashes to ashes' – which some possibly would have considered a sign of wishful thinking on the vicar's part. Jud had been a thorn in his side far too long.

'Thou shalt not move thy neighbour's landmark!' Jud said suddenly. 'That's what the Good Book d'say, an' mark my words and no missment, if ye don't obey the Good Book ye'll be cast into the burnin' fiery furnace along wi' Shamrock, Mishap and Abendego. But ye'll not come out like *they* come out – *Aah!*'

Prudie, not having needed the stick for his bearers, now rapped him on his bald head for silence. He turned like an empurpled frog, only to see the stick raised again, and he was constrained to swallow his fury, the noise of the fury reverberating in his windpipe like a pumping engine sucking up mud instead of water.

Thereafter the baptism would have proceeded uninterrupted had Mr Odgers not got it into his head that Henry was to be christened Charles. Three times he dipped his fingers in the water and began: 'Charles Vennor I baptize thee . . .' and it was only at the fourth attempt he got it right, by which time Henry Vennor was crying the church down and Bella had got a fit of the giggles.

The brief ceremony over, Jud's four bearers hurried to get him out of church and by the church door in time to receive the piece of christening cake that was traditionally presented by the parents to the first person they met coming out of the church.

'Blessed be the man that hath not walked in the counsels of the ungodly,' called Jud as he was borne out like a sinking lugger in a rough sea, 'nor stood in the way of sinners – Gor damme, what're ee about – tossing me 'ere and thur wi' no more consarn 'n if you was bearing a sack o' taties!'

But he was sitting quietly, a smirk on his face, all ready to take the cake that Demelza handed him, and he held tight to it with his big grubby hand and would not allow Prudie a sight of it.

The only notable absentee from the church was Stephen Carrington.

III

It was altogether a noisy Christmas for the Poldarks. By a piece of unpremeditated timing, while everyone was out at the christening, a large bullock cart drew up at the stream, and after some manoeuvring managed to cross it and arrived at the front door of Nampara, where the two drivers alighted and, finding no answer to the bell, scuffed their feet and blew on their fists until a great crocodile of people appeared wending its way on horse, on pony, and on foot down the valley. The bullock cart contained the grand piano Ross had bought earlier in the month.

Room had been made for it in the library, but edging it, even bereft of its legs, through the narrow door was a tricky job. Men struggled and spat on their hands and heaved and called advice to each other all through the early part of the christening tea, and it was late in the evening, when everyone who was going had at last gone, before Demelza had a chance of trying it. With great difficulty Isabella-Rose was persuaded that until she grew up the spinet in the parlour was good enough for her, except for the special occasion. Demelza played a dozen pieces that evening, and most of her family tried to put her off by singing out of tune.

On Christmas Day the Enyses came to dinner with their two little girls, and Sam and Rosina Carne; and on St Stephen's Day the Trenegloses came over, and Paul and Daisy Kellow.

The Kellows brought the Friday newspaper with them carrying the headline '*Total Defeat of the French Army!*' This dispatch confirmed that of the 17th but went even further.

Davoust's Corps had been completely destroyed. What remained of the French army had been confronted by two Russian armies barring their way on the Beresina. Led by the Emperor himself, the French had broken through, but had left 12,000 drowned in the river and 20,000 more as prisoners. Of all his great army of half a million men, it was said Napoleon had now only 10,000 left. At Warsaw he had taken coach for Paris and abandoned these remnants to their fate.

It was a time for dancing again on tables, and if the Poldarks could not quite achieve that, they did their best most ways. The piano, like a new and handsome toy, came in for much use, with ever more singing. Demelza played any number of old Cornish songs as well as all the favourite carols.

Since her return from Flushing Clowance had caught sight of Stephen twice, but had not been trapped into a direct confrontation as at Pally's Shop. Ferocious rumours of his doings sometimes reached her. But on the 27th a young man called Tom Guildford appeared just as they were sitting down to dinner and gratefully accepted an invitation to stay. It seemed that he had much of a taking for their elder daughter, and made no secret of the fact.

'That's better,' said Ross in an aside to Demelza after.

'D'you like him, then?'

'So far as I can tell. But I am not so much comparing him favourably with Stephen as welcoming *another* young man just for comparison. She became committed too soon.'

Demelza remembered a conversation she had had with Caroline Enys on this particular subject a couple of years ago. It was certainly better to see many, but in the end did it matter how many one saw?

All through Christmas Jeremy was in the highest spirits.

He flirted outrageously with Daisy, made puns and ludicrous jokes at the dinner table, got drunk and had to be helped to bed. He was absent on the evening of the 28th and Clowance, by chance encountering him as he was tiptoeing in very late, was certain he had had a woman. Her sharp nose picked up a whiff of cheap scent. There was not much open prostitution in this district, the nearest being in Truro; but no doubt there would be not a few in the villages willing to oblige the future master of Nampara. Clowance hoped he did not get landed with a paternity suit. She did speculate for a moment about Daisy, but she knew the next time they met that it had not been so.

The only trouble was there seemed no overt reason for Jeremy's explosive good spirits. Sometimes it was more like rage than laughter.

On Tom Guildford's second visit he said he had ridden most of the way with Valentine, who had branched off to pay his respects to the Pope family at Trevaunance and would be coming on to Nampara within the hour. After some lively chatter Jeremy went off to the mine, claiming a crisis there, and was not seen again until bedtime, by which the two young men had left. To Demelza's indignant complaint that he had missed both his dinner and his supper, Jeremy replied that he would raid the larder right away and make up for lost opportunities. Remembering what had happened to Francis, Demelza was never easy when one of her family was out on mining business and did not return when expected, so she had discreetly sent Matthew Mark Martin off to Wheal Leisure about seven to make inquiries. The information was that Jeremy had left the mine at six with Paul Kellow. When he eventually returned home he offered no explanation as to his whereabouts and no one asked.

The only one to comment earlier was Tom Guildford, who, having persuaded Clowance to go for a walk with him along the beach, said:

'I trust I'm mistaken, Miss Clowance, but it seems that your brother may not like me.'

'Oh, I don't think that at all!'

'Well, I had only been with you a short time and it seemed to me his face changed, and soon after that he left. I know of nothing I said that could have offended him.'

Clowance decided to be as direct. 'I think what you said that offended him was to tell us Valentine Warleggan was on his way to see us. I have no reason at all to suggest to you as to *why* he should not care to meet Valentine – they were friendly enough earlier in the year – but twice since Christmas when I have suggested we should call on him Jeremy has refused – and brusquely, as if the suggestion should never have been made. I'm sorry if that is so, for Valentine is very amusing. But Jeremy is not always easy to understand.'

Surf was thundering at them in the distance. So resonant was it that the beach might have been hollow like the stretched parchment of a bass drum.

'Well,' Tom said, 'if that is all, I am happy it is not I of whom he disapproves. For, wishing to stand so well with one of the Poldarks, I should be very unhappy to stand ill with any of them.'

'Certainly Isabella-Rose has a taking for you.'

'That is not kind.'

'Oh? It was not meant unkind.'

'In some circumstances the merest pinprick can stab deep.'

'Oh, Tom,' Clowance said, smiling, 'you must not play the ardent suitor quite so soon. We have met three times, is it, and have been comfortable in each other's company. That is all.'

'It is not all with me, I assure you. I swear to you I came to spend time at my uncle's house this Christmas quite heart free and fancy free, and looking for nothing but a pleasant relaxation; some gambling, some shooting, some drinking perhaps – but never this. An arrow has gone through my heart. If you cannot understand me you can at least pity me.'

Wheal Leisure had just been coaled and was sending up smoke from its chimney like curls escaping from a full-bottomed wig.

'Perhaps you know,' Clowance said, 'that I was until recently engaged to be married.'

'Valentine said something. I trust I am not...' He paused.

'No, you are not. At least...'

'What unfortunate creature can have been so careless as to let you slip away? I am sorry for him.'

'But not for me?'

'I cannot suppose you really loved the fellow, or I believe you would have stuck to him through thick and thin.'

'Oh, Tom, that makes me feel very uncomfortable!'

'It was not meant to, God help me. What minefield am I straying through?'

She laughed. 'Perhaps we should change the subject. It is a very difficult one to consider rationally, even for me – as yet. I only wanted you to know – to be aware – that...'

'A burnt child dreads the fire?'

'I was not going to say that, but I think you are right.'

'Fire can be warming as well as hurtful. However ... let us not press the point. Do you want to know anything about me?'

She looked at his sturdy darkness – not a very good skin for a young man, but healthy. His teeth showed uneven when he smiled, but the quality of the smile was not affected. Physically attractive, if not with the dangerous animal maleness of Stephen. She thought he would have more humour in his disposition than any of her previous suitors. Even when he was at his most passionate she suspected there would be a hint of self-deprecating irony at the root of his behaviour.

'Clearly you do not,' he said, after waiting. 'But I will tell you all the same, even though in the briefest way. I am twenty-three and in my last year at Jesus. I have one brother – older – and three sisters – younger. My family is not rich, neither is it poor. My parents live in Hampshire, but have property in Falmouth, also in Penzance. I am already reading law because I expect to go into that profession. But my ultimate aim is to live in Cornwall and possibly become agent for one or more of the big estates . . .' He broke off. 'Of course I should be saying all this to your father – and will in due course, with the slightest encouragement from you. But if I judge your family aright, their daughter is given exceptional liberty and freedom of choice; and what you personally decide will overcome everything else.'

They walked on. Two groups of birds, disturbed by their approach, stirred, moving reluctantly out of their path.

'What are those?' asked Tom.

'What? The birds? Those are sanderlings.'

'Sanderlings?'

'Mixed with a few plovers. They often come at this time of year. The other group, those keeping their own company, are scoter ducks.'

'And that is your mine we have passed on the cliffs?'

'Yes.'

'Isabella-Rose was telling me about it.'

They walked on in silence.

'And me?' said Clowance presently.

'What?'

'What do you want to know about me?'

He scrutinized her until she became restive under his glance.

'You?' he said. 'I want to know everything. But need to know nothing.'

IV

Jeremy had gone with Paul to the Bounders' Arms. After a while they were joined by Stephen. There the three young men sat talking and drinking and expressing their personal views of the world. None of them realized what a watershed in their lives the evening was to be.

'It looks now as if the end of the war may come soon,' Jeremy said. 'There must be an end somewhere to Buonaparte's manpower.'

'However early it comes it's not likely to come early enough to save our firm,' said Paul.

Stephen said: 'I'm going away in a couple of weeks. I'm going back to Bristol, see if I can find a ship that suits me. I'll throw me Leisure shares on the market – they may fetch what I put in. Twill be small enough capital; but it is only while the war lasts that a privateer can operate.'

'Even if the French collapse,' Paul said, 'which I doubt, we've still got the United States to fight.'

Emma came in with three fresh tankards. 'I didn't wait to be asked,' she said. 'I know now with you bonny swells that you keep time with the clock! Just regular, eh?'

'Where's Ned?' Stephen said in a stage whisper. 'Out of sight? Time to give me a kiss, have you?'

She pulled her skirt out of his hands and laughed. 'Don't you make free. He's a hard man when he's roused!'

'*I'll* wager,' said Stephen significantly. '*I'll* wager.'

She left the room to more laughter, but they sobered when the latch clicked. There was little to cause any of them amusement. Stephen and he, Jeremy thought, were in like condition now: equally deprived, equally cheated, equally putting on the clown's mask. Of course there were vast differences in their circumstances, vast differences in their chance of yet getting what they most wanted. Stephen, he knew, was still more than half convinced that Clowance would come round in the end. He had rehearsed to Jeremy – who absolutely refused to be drawn as to his own opinion – the many things he might say to her when she called at the Gatehouse or accidentally contrived a meeting. Absence would eventually make the heart grow fonder. Although he did not say so openly, Jeremy could tell, by reading the hints and the silences, that Stephen cursed himself for having been such a fool as to have accepted the sexual half-measures Clowance had imposed upon him. He should, he believed now, have over-ridden them, taken her by semi-force if necessary. Women never fundamentally disliked a little rough treatment. (More than one had told him it was their secret dream.) Clowance might be different but she was not *that* different. And, once he had taken her, marriage would have swiftly followed. And, once they were married, quarrels took place *within* the marriage. They might shout at each other, even come to blows; but they would have been bound then, living together; her mettlesome independence would have been forfeit.

Since October Stephen's name had been linked with one girl after another, but mainly with Lottie Kempthorne, the lanky daughter of Charlie Kempthorne who had come to a bad end a good many years ago by betraying the local smugglers. His two scrawny little daughters had been taken in by an aunt in St Ann's and brought up with her own children. May had married a patten-maker and gone to live away; but Lottie at twenty-five or six was still unmarried and a year ago had been turned out of her aunt's cottage for her loose behaviour. More recently she had been reluctantly allowed in again, but her reputation remained unredeemed. She was pretty in a rather limp way, and there were rumours that she had been seen coming out of the Gatehouse during the recent moonlit nights, an occurrence which would not commend itself to the Poldarks generally if it were ever confirmed.

Stephen still worked part time for Wilf Jonas. They had come to an arrangement whereby he could take a day off when he chose. So long as Stephen had any expectations of regaining Clowance he could count on some consideration from Wilf, and he'd agreed a cut in wages to ease the way.

Privately Jeremy could see Clowance's point of view and could have spent some time explaining it to Stephen; but what was happening in Clowance's heart he had no idea at all, and he was pretty sure that that would decide it in the end. The intervention of a third party, with whatever good intentions, would be a useless exercise and make him unpopular with both.

So they were two of a kind, he and Stephen – except that *he* had no hope at all. Two of a kind. Restless, deprived, unable to come to terms with what had happened to them.

Stephen began talking about the captured vessels that were for sale again in Plymouth and at other, smaller, ports around the coasts: a beautiful American brig, for instance; a fine fir-built French cutter; vessels of that sort could well be bought at knock-down prices; they were ready for sea, could be victualled and crewed within a matter of weeks and soon enough be cruising off the French or Irish coasts looking for the sort of prizes they had recently become. Did one have the money. Did one but have the money!

Paul yawned. 'You are becoming a thought tedious on the subject, Miller. You bring it up not less than once a week, I'll wager, and all to no end. If wishes were butter-cakes, beggars might bite.'

'Well,' Stephen said sardonically, 'there is another proverb: nothing stake, nothing draw. I am still the richer by not a few guineas – as you should be – from the Penzance lifeboat.'

'And observe by what a narrow margin we survived that!' exclaimed Paul. 'I would still be reluctant to exhibit my face in Plymouth even now.'

'I would exhibit me face in Plymouth tomorrow,' Stephen said, 'if twould profit me. But to buy one of those vessels you'd need maybe four or five hundred pounds; then there'd be the expense of fitting her out and getting her to sea. You'd need seven hundred to be on the safe side.' He took a gulp of beer. 'Lot of use me Leisure shares would be to meet that. No ... twill mean me trying me luck in Bristol once more – going as a paid hand but with a small share. God's wounds, I don't want a small share, I want the lion's share, so's I can go where I like, do what I like! Once you get started on your own, once you get launched ... And as soon as this war's over the opportunity's lost!'

Paul fumbled in his pocket. 'I came upon a mystery the

other day. Travellers leave all sorts of things in coaches – gloves, canes, parasols, mittens, shoes, purses, reticules, newspapers, books, monthly magazines. As often as not they come back for them or send a servant. But they scarcely ever return for newspapers or magazines. Last month I was going through these – in time you get a pile and you can sell 'em for a few pence; people down here don't mind their being out of date. Well, I was going through these, and one was *The Morning Post* for Monday, 23rd November.'

'What's that?' asked Stephen. 'Newspaper?'

'Yes. A London daily newspaper.'

Stephen grunted and wiped his mouth on the back of his hand. 'So.'

'So it had a news item in it. Thought it might entertain you both, considering some of the wildcat discussions we've had together.'

He brought out a wrinkled quarter-page of a newspaper, unfolded it. He studied it himself for a few moments, smoothing it with his hand, glanced at the others, hesitating whether to read it aloud, then pushed it towards them, between the beer tankards. They put their heads together and read it at the same time.

It was headed: 'Startling Robbery.'

It has been the custom for several years for Messrs Coutts Bank to despatch money to their branch in Brighton by 'The Blue Belle', a coach run by the well-known and long established carriers, Bouverie, Cartwright & Baynes, who have their head offices in St Mary-le-bone. 'The Blue Belle' leaves the Star & Garter Hotel in Pall Mall each weekday at nine a.m.

On Monday last the 16th inst. the coach left as usual, with the cash-boxes in the padlocked compartment beneath the coachman's seat. All six seats inside the coach were booked. Of these only two, a Mr and Mrs Pressby, arrived to take their seats at the point of departure. At Streatham a Mr Coningsby and a Mr Browne joined the coach as arranged, but the remaining two inside passengers failed to put in an appearance. When the coach stopped at the posting inn in Sutton Mrs Pressby was of a sudden taken ill and could proceed no farther. She and her husband were given accommodation at the inn and an apothecary summoned. The coach then proceeded on its way with eight outside passengers and two inside.

At Reigate, however, the two inside gentlemen alighted from the coach to rendezvous with a friend whom they had arranged to meet there. At the inn they discovered they had missed him, and, instead of accompanying them to Brighton, as planned, he had boarded a coach for London. Seeing no point in therefore continuing to Brighton, they remained behind at Reigate and resolved to wait for the next coach to take them home.

On arrival at the Old Ship in Brighton, after the passengers had alighted, the coachman's seat was unpadlocked in the presence of the Bank's messengers, whereupon both bank boxes were found to have been broken open and the cash extracted.

An attempt is being made to trace all the passengers who travelled on the coach that day. £300 reward is offered for the recovery of the notes and/or the arrest of the miscreants. The value of the cash stolen is between £3,000 and £4,000. Similar notes are being withdrawn and changed.

There was a long pause. Stephen eventually shoved the newspaper across the table at Paul.

'There's a Chinese puzzle for you.'

'My own feelings exact,' said Paul. 'But Chinese puzzles are meant to be solved. What do you think, Jeremy?'

Jeremy shook his head.

Paul said: 'I conjected it might appeal to you both.'

'*Appeal!*'

Emma came in. 'All dry, are ee? There now. Sorry. I been busy in the taproom.' She swept up their tankards with a clatter and went out.

Paul smoothed his sleek hair. 'I won't deny I have given the matter some thought since I read the piece. Money like that would not come amiss to any of us. I only wish I had the magic secret.'

'We talked of all this once before,' Stephen said brusquely. 'In May. It got us nowhere. Nor will it now.'

'Things have changed a little since May,' said Jeremy.

'Oh yes. Oh yes. For me? For you? For us. Maybe for all of us. But it don't – this newspaper story is a *fairy tale* – it don't offer us any help.'

'Oh, I agree,' said Paul. 'All the same I'd dearly like to know how it was done. I've thought. It must have been those early passengers – somehow.'

'Why?'

'Well, could you imagine a lamer excuse than those two men – what was it? – Coningsby and Browne. They had arranged to meet someone at Reigate – wherever that may be: he isn't there, so they return to London, even though they were originally booked for Brighton. It's a palpable lie, the feeblest excuse.'

'And the padlocked seat, with the coachmen seated upon it. There's always two of them. How did they manage that? You see it says . . .'

Emma came back, glanced at their preoccupied faces. 'I

can see how you all want to talk to me. Never mind. I'll go flirt with the sumpmen again.' She put the ale down and left.

Stephen said: 'You see it says the bank boxes were broken open. Not stolen. Broken open. How could that be?'

'The coachmen were either in it, or blind drunk,' said Paul. 'I've told you before, I know these men. They take a tot at every stage; by the time they're half home they almost leave it to the horses to find their own way.'

'It couldn't be that,' said Stephen. 'It's not just drink. Otherwise the seat padlock would've been forced too. You can see that. Now supposing the two coachmen go in for a drink and someone – inside or outside – climbs up with a crowbar, wrenches open the seat, wrenches open the boxes, grabs the cash, smooths over the damage to the padlock, puts the money in their own valises, and slips away.'

'The coach', said Jeremy patiently, 'is only left in the yard for a few minutes *anywhere*, and people are always bustling about. I doubt if it is left unobserved for sixty seconds. What would you say, Paul? You ought to know.'

'Well, you're right about the length of time a coach is left unattended. Once it leaves its starting-point . . . And it was daylight.'

'And the seat padlock was *not* forced.'

Stephen put his little finger into the gap of his broken eye-tooth, picked it abstractedly. 'One at least of the coachmen was in it. Must have been. Slipped his accomplice the key while he went for his drink.'

'Someone still had to break open the cash-boxes,' said Jeremy. 'In front of every one.'

One of the candles was guttering, sending up wispy smoke and making little shadows jump and dart. Even though it was the fag end of the year, a few moths were fluttering against the window-panes.

'Well,' said Paul, 'you've helped me to think a small amount more clearly. If, as I think, the coachmen were in it, then they had an arrangement with the two men, so that when they stopped at Reigate the keys should be slipped to the men. In order to make it seem like an outside theft, the bank boxes were forced.'

'If they'd wanted to do that, why was the seat-padlock not forced too, eh? That would have been much more conclusive, like, that the coachmen were not involved.'

They all took a drink.

'But how,' said Jeremy, 'could they count on the lady being taken ill at Sutton?'

'Well, it means they were all in it – all the original passengers.'

'Or none of 'em,' said Stephen.

'Why d'you say that?'

'The coachmen could've just arranged it betwixt themselves. Surely. Easy as easy. They stop at one of the main posting-houses. All the passengers get out. One of the coachmen goes in for a drink. The other does the job.'

'While the horses are being changed?'

'Well, in between. They could count a minute here and there. Twould add up in the end.'

'And what do they do with the money?'

'Pass it to some accomplice waiting at the next stage. I reckon that's why they broke open the bank boxes instead of stealing 'em. Much easier to carry.'

Paul folded the cutting from the newspaper again and again, as if trying to eradicate the questions in his mind.

Jeremy said: 'But weren't those boxes padlocked too? Weren't those padlocked you saw in Plymouth, Paul?'

'Oh yes.'

'How long do you suppose it would take, then, to break those boxes open, after the seat-padlock had been opened with a key? How *long* would it take? More, surely, far more than the three or four minutes you might expect at the *most* when a coach is stopped and the horses are being changed. It would not be *possible*.'

Stephen took a very long drink. 'God's eyes, what do it matter? You – you read a fairy story in a London news sheet, Paul, and you bring it to show us, and then we rack our wits like apprentices with a brain-twister their master has give 'em. We know we can never solve it nor answer it. We don't even know if the question be right all ways, because something may have been put in or left out. But whatever, twill do us no manner of good to rack our wits to answer it; for if we did answer it we should never have it just the same way as it was in the first place in London – the facts would never, never be the same – and so it is a sheer waste of time and energy thinking about it at all! Forget it! Let's think about what we can do down here – not what they did, or are supposed to have done, on the Brighton coach!'

Jeremy was staring at the smeeching candle, eyes blind with preoccupation. There was a roar of laughter from the taproom. Emma was entertaining the sumpmen.

Paul said: 'Two months from now my father will be in prison, my mother and Daisy turned out of doors. Then I'll have to find work to keep them somehow. I'm not trained, you know, not the way I should be, not in law or accountantship, nor even in office work, save what I've picked up in day to day business. It is not a pretty prospect . . .' He got up and kicked at the fire to make it blaze. 'All the same, I shall not risk my neck holding up a coach at pistol-point behind a black mask or a kerchief. I don't have the stomach for that sort of violence, nor the nerve to carry it through. Maybe you do, Miller, being bred to piracy.'

'I've never been a pirate,' said Stephen, 'nor ever intend to be – as you well know. A privateer, you little runt, is all the difference in the world, as I've also explained to you before. You get letters of marque. You're operating legally in times of war. You fight the enemy, but for private profit. That's why I'm anxious to get to sea again afore the war is over.' He banged on the table for Emma. 'Nay, I have no fancy for the black mask – little more than you, Paul – though I'm willing to stand me chance and fight me way out of most things. I carry scars enough to show it! But other folk carry more.'

'Like that sailor in the press gang,' said Paul.

'Aye. Like him.'

'And Ben Carter?'

'We'll leave that be,' said Stephen. 'Just for the time being. If you please.'

Paul came back but did not sit down. 'All the same . . .'

'What?'

'I'd dearly love to know how that money disappeared from the Brighton coach. If it was easy – or clever – or none too risky – I'd take a chance on *that*.'

'You can't never know,' said Stephen. 'It's a fairy story! Nobody'll know how it happened.'

'I'm not so sure,' said Jeremy.

They both stared at him. 'What d'you mean?'

'These coaches here, Paul. Those that ply around Cornwall. Do they all have two coachmen?'

'Yes. And some a guard as well. When there's money aboard there's usually a guard.'

'And passengers inside?'

'Four, not six. We haven't the turnpike roads to take the extra width.'

'That's the sort of coach that runs from Plymouth? The sort you travelled in after your fight with the press gang?'

'Yes. They're all very much the same as to size. Two coachmen, four horses, maybe a guard, four passengers in, eight to ten out.'

'I see.'

They waited. Stephen said: 'What d'you mean, you're not so sure. Sure of what?'

'Sure I don't know how it happened.'

'Get along!'

'Well,' said Jeremy, 'of course I'm not *sure*. I can't tell you how it *did* happen, of course, no one can. No one probably ever will. But I think I can tell you how it *could* happen. I think I've got a pretty good notion how it could be worked.'

Chapter Six

Relations between Sir George and his son were strained all through that far too long Christmas vacation. Valentine was a gregarious young man who never really liked to be alone, and since Cardew was much larger than the houses in which most of his friends lived, he thought it easier to entertain than to be entertained.

So a day scarcely passed when some few other young men or women were not seated at his supper table eating his victuals and consuming his candles and coals until far into the night. Sometimes they danced to a local fiddler who lived near by at Perranarworthal, sometimes they played backgammon, sometimes noisier games. George would have found it all much more acceptable if these visitors had been the sons and daughters of the noble houses of central and western Cornwall; instead in the main they came of genteel but not particularly distinguished or moneyed stock on whom, as George saw it, he was conferring a favour rather than that a favour was being conferred.

Indeed after the disgraceful scenes that took place at Cardew on the night of The Miller's Dance, when Valentine had scarred the top of one of his best tables with his boots, George would have put the house in quarantine for the rest of the holidays: the whole evening had been quite outrageous and should have been brought to an abrupt close before it got out of hand: unfortunately, more than ever this

433

holiday, Valentine had found a firm ally in Harriet. They hunted together, and when it was too dark to see the foxes they brought home noisy and muddy young people who turned night into day. She also stood up for Valentine in private conversations with George and lent her stepson money when he ran short. It was all very frustrating. Nor was George altogether proof against a stab of jealousy from time to time.

It was his intention to tell Valentine of the plans he had made for his future; but the occasion just did not arise. Each of the last three nights before he left for Cambridge Valentine was out visiting – for a change – and returned very late. And although George's character did not run to finesse, he was reluctant to call his son into his study and announce that plans had been drawn up for his future marriage rather in the same manner as if he were telling him of a change in his monthly allowance. The ideal time would be after dinner, preferably when Harriet was not there, over the port when a mellowing influence would be at work. Not that George supposed Valentine would need much mellowing to accept the idea; Cuby, as Major Trevanion had repeatedly pointed out, was a pretty girl, healthy, young, amenable, accomplished, and of one of the oldest and most distinguished county families. Their home would be in the only modern castle in Cornwall, surrounded by five hundred acres of garden and farm land sweeping down to the sea. George was more interested in joint stock companies and the discounting of bills, but even he had been impressed by his first sight of Caerhays. When the bluebells and the young beeches were out it was something conjured from a dream. No young man in his right senses would even hesitate.

It would cost more than the original agreement in the

end, for the two young people would have to be subsidized in order to live. But George had ideas about that too. Thanks to the advice of Sir Christopher Hawkins and with the backing of his new banking associate Sir Humphrey Willyams, he was feeling his way into a relatively new industry which was extracting clay and china stone from the hillsides and out of the ground in the districts of St Dennis and Carloggas. In two or three years, if all went well, he would have gained control of one of the companies working there and would put Valentine in charge. By then Valentine would be living quite near, and it would depend upon his own energy and acumen whether he could develop it into something suitable to his station. (A gradual withdrawal of the subsidies being paid out would be a useful spur to his industry; but of course he would not be told that yet.)

On the strength of their few conversations together, George had come to the conclusion that Cuby was a young woman of strong character, little like either of her brothers; and her influence, plus the accession of property and responsibility, might help to sober Valentine and enable him to become the sort of influence in the county he ought to be. In the meantime, therefore, George tried to overlook his present extravagances of behaviour and of purse, determined if possible to keep on modestly good terms with the lad, so that when the time came to announce his plans he could do so in friendly fashion, offering it as the generous reward of a loving father rather than as the coldly arranged dictates of convenience.

It occurred to him to discuss his plans with Harriet, but the thought never came to anything. In the old days he would certainly have told Elizabeth everything, but this marriage, though not as stormy, was not as close. George had been more unguarded with Elizabeth than with any other person in his life. Besides, Harriet's reactions were predictably unpredictable. You could not begin to guess how her views would jump. And her growing alliance with Valentine made her judgements more than ever suspect. Once the announcement was about to be made, then she could be told.

George had not yet begun to make any plans for little Ursula, who had only just celebrated her thirteenth birthday, but once or twice, observing suitably titled or landed parents with sons of a suitable age, he could not prevent the occasional speculation. Ursula was really the apple of his eye, though sometimes he wished she were a prettier apple. If Valentine was as unlike the Warleggans as well could be, Ursula seemed to resemble them all. She had a strong, thick body, a slight stoop, big features and big hands. Her movements were rather slow, but her eyes, though small and round like polished walnuts, were very quick and penetrating. She had been greatly spoiled by her grandmother, who could deny her nothing, and not a little by her father who saw and admired in her his own blood in a way that circumstances had prevented him from ever doing with Valentine.

Naturally enough she was precocious and grown-up before her time. Harriet tended to sit on her, so that an initial prejudice on Ursula's part against the newcomer had quickly been confirmed. This was a pity from George's point of view, who wanted his new wife to be popular with everyone at Cardew and saw the purpose, in theory, of Harriet's aims. (Yet by blood and by instinct he found himself, in practice, almost always taking Ursula's side in petty disagreements.) But he still felt it would become more comfortable between them when they came to understand each other better; and the fact that all Harriet's animals adored Ursula – and vice versa – was bound to be a reconciling factor in the end.

One thing that delighted him was that the little girl was outstandingly quick at figures. When she was seven she had opened a sweet shop for her dolls, and had kept an account in large childish figures recording how much each spent per week. At twelve George had bought her a model tin mine built by a crippled miner at Wheal Spinster. Erected on three-foot stilts in her playroom, everything worked except that the engine sucking up real water had to be animated by a manually operated handle. There were little miners underground, bending in tunnels and picking in caverns, waterwheels and tin stamps, washing floors, air adits, even imitation coal. A few months after it was installed George was particularly gratified to find that Ursula had opened a cost book and was drawing up her own make-believe accounts, striking bargains with the miners and paying out dividends.

Ursula was annoyed that Harriet wouldn't be a share-holder.

'She should go to *school*, George,' Harriet said one day when they left the nursery. 'Lord's my life, I have little room for the genteelisms that are taught as standard at most of these Schools for Young Ladies; but she needs more company of her own age, more *competition*, a certain levity of manner that comes from mixing with frivolous girls. Also a smattering of French would do her no harm. But most of all, to get out is the important thing.'

'She is often out,' George said stiffly. 'And she has one or two young friends. I don't believe she will be that much the better for mixing with the daughters of tradesmen.'

'Send her to Mrs Hemple's,' said Harriet. 'She opened a select school in Truro last July. I do not suppose that the girls she meets there will do her any social harm.'

In Harriet's view, Ursula badly needed to be jolted out

of herself. Apart from riding, which she did frequently but badly, she had none of the cheerful feckless pastimes common to girls of thirteen. Harriet had once been tempted to suggest sardonically to George that a suitable marriage might be arranged for Ursula by pairing her off with that stout sweaty spectacled schoolboy called Conan Whitworth, but consideration for the safety of her own marriage had prevented her.

It was January 12 when Valentine left for the Lent term at St John's, which began on the seventeenth. He had to make a very early start and came to take leave of his parents while they were still abed. He was in very good spirits and kissed his stepmother with his usual familiarity, resting fingertips gently on her bare shoulder as he did so.

'You look tired to begin the day,' said Harriet.

'It is an ungodly hour, ma'am, and I was up until an ungodly hour last eve. Tired but happy, I might say.'

Harriet raised an ironical eyebrow. 'Not happy to be gone, I trust?'

'That was not what I meant.'

'No, it was not what I thought you meant.'

Valentine said: '"Did you ever hear of Colonel Wattle? He was all for love and little for the bottle?" A noble song, that. I give you good morning, stepmother mine.'

She uttered her low chuckling laugh as he left the room.

Sir George was sitting in his dressing-gown. Valentine greeted him cheerfully. One thing about the boy: he never was sulky.

'Well, Papa, I leave you to take a little rest and peace after the noise and turmoil I have brought to the house.'

'You certainly have been a disturbing influence,' George said candidly. 'But it is no doubt good to be high-spirited in youth. And I think you have given pleasure to Lady Harriet.'

'Among others,' said Valentine. 'Among others. And thank you, Father, I have taken much pleasure myself.'

'It remains for you now, then,' said George, 'to pursue your studies at Cambridge with some diligence. Though I am not sure that the subjects you are studying . . .'

'Various things are obligatory if one wishes to read Classics later.'

'Ah well, it is all something of a mystery to me. But the dead languages offer, or seem to me to offer, little opportunity to pursue the subjects which will best serve you when you come down.'

'I think perhaps I should have been sent somewhere else to learn bookkeeping.'

George looked at him suspiciously, but Valentine's manner was so cheerful that he concluded no sarcasm was intended.

'Well, goodbye, Papa. I will endeavour to live beyond my means, but dodge the creditors so skilfully that you will not be troubled.'

They shook hands, and Valentine left. George reflected that there might have been time even this morning to hint at some of the plans he had for his son; but concluded it was better not. Next time when he came home it would be Easter; there would not be the same excuse for endless parties and most of the damned hunting would be over. They would be sure to get an evening together.

In fact George need not have concerned himself in the matter of choosing a right time, for Valentine already knew of the arrangement proposed for him. Conan Whitworth had taken the first opportunity to inform him.

Chapter Seven

The *Self-Defence* – Elegant Light Post Coach, as it described itself – left the Royal Hotel, Plymouth, each weekday at 8 a.m., reaching the New Hotel, Falmouth, the same evening at 8.30 p.m. On the way it called at the London Inn, Torpoint, the King's Arms, Liskeard, the Talbot Inn, Lostwithiel, the White Hart, St Austell, and Pearce's Hotel in Truro. It travelled with two coachmen and an armed guard, had accommodation for four travellers inside and eight outside. In view of the hard times such enterprises were enduring (though it did not say this in the advertisements) the price of the journey was reduced to £1.10s. inside and £1 outside, with lesser distances proportionate. No more than two pieces of hand baggage were permitted per person.

On Monday, January 25, everything was as usual. The coachmen were called Marshall and Stevens, the guard Blight. All four places were reserved: two were to join in Plymouth, the Reverend Arthur May and Mrs May, two in Torpoint, Lieutenant Morgan Lean, RN and a Mr George Jewell. The Revd and Mrs May were booked right through to Falmouth, Lieutenant Lean to St Austell, Mr Jewell to Truro.

It was a bright sunny day when the vehicle set off, a cobalt sky and a north-westerly breeze edging a few clouds before it. The gold-painted coach looked very smart, as did the coachmen and the guard in their scarlet coats and high black hats with gold hatbands. They rattled over the cobbles through the narrow, already busy streets of the town, the long horn blown shrilly to announce their coming. People were reluctant to edge out of their way: milkmaids, girls with baskets of shrimps, slatternly women dragging ragged children, an old man with a herd of goats, a one-legged beggar in a sailor hat, red-coated soldiers leaning and yawning, dogs fighting, and down an alley a donkey braying, stout townsmen in dark suits, then more and more sailors as they neared the docks; in the wind a smell of putrid fish.

There was already a slight blemish on the day in that, even as she left the inn, it was clear that the clergyman's wife was feeling unwell. She clung to her husband's arm and held a handkerchief to her mouth. The Reverend Mr May implied that she was suffering in the early stages of pregnancy and asked, if it should become necessary, that they might be permitted to draw up the blinds of the coach. This was readily acceded to, for it was not an uncommon custom to do this in foul weather or over bad roads where flying stones might shatter the glass. The Revd Arthur May was a tall thin man of perhaps forty, with a fresh complexion but greying hair, and heavy steel-rimmed spectacles. His sight was clearly not of the best, for he stumbled in getting into the coach. His wife was also quite tall, with pronounced dark features under a transparent white veil. She was very gracious to the coachman who handed her in.

The ferry carrying the coach crossed the Hamoaze, threading its way through a forest of masts: brigs, frigates, cutters, ketches, intermingled with great battleships of the line; two first-raters being re-fitted, a half-dozen double-deckers of different size and rating. The masts and rigging were like trellis, intermingling and glittering in the winter sun. Plymouth Dock was one of the main arsenals of British sea power. From here and from a half-dozen other such ports Britannia ruled the waves. Everyone except Mrs May got down to point out and admire.

Presently they were across and drawing up at the London Inn. Here the four outside passengers were joined by three others, and Lieutenant Morgan Lean arrived, a youngish powerful-looking naval officer with a white wig and heavy black eyebrows; but Mr Stevenitt, the landlord of the inn, had had a message from Mr Jewell that he would not be joining the coach until Dobwalls or Liskeard. Until then they must retain his seat.

So, a little before nine, the coach set off on its first substantial stage. This was the longest stretch of all, and with some of the steepest hills to be negotiated. Mrs May had not alighted from the coach at Torpoint, but a glass of brandy had been taken in to her. After a few miles the mahogany panels were drawn up to shut out the light and the view. It seemed a pity on such a fine day, for they were jogging and jolting among the lovely tidal creeks round Antony and Sheviock.

As soon as the blinds were up the Revd Arthur May looped off his spectacles.

'By God, I can scarcely see! I should have borrowed something with weaker lenses.'

'Did everything go to plan?' asked Lieutenant Lean.

'Seems so. And you?'

'Aye. I suppose you saw the cash-boxes loaded?'

Mrs May nodded. 'Two, as you said. So far so good. When do we start?'

They both looked at the sham clergyman. Because it was Jeremy's plan, he had come to lead it.

'Another few minutes,' he said. 'I believe they stop at Polbathic, don't they?'

They waited, unspeaking. Paul was wearing a frock of his dead sister Violet. Although he was taller than she had been they had been able to let out the hem and loosen the gown at the waist, so giving it extra length. They had all bought wigs, though at different times and in different towns. Second-hand wigs were plentiful, and Jeremy had bought one of horsehair, such as the Revd Mr Odgers always wore, much lighter in colour than his own hair; Paul, a full female wig of black curls; Stephen had cut his own hair much shorter in order to accommodate the naval wig. Stephen had complained that of the three of them he wore the least disguise; but Jeremy and Paul had both spent the night at the Royal, which he had not had to do, and Jeremy was probably right in saying that no one ever looked closely at a person's features – it was the distinguishing signs people would remember: a tall near-sighted clergyman with heavy spectacles, a thin dark pregnant young woman in a veil, a big naval officer in a smart new uniform with a white wig.

The coach stopped. The blind was made of very thin mahogany which was raised and lowered from inside the door exactly in the same way as the glass it protected, and Jeremy, with the window down and his thumb against the shutter, was just able to see a slit of the road outside.

'Look to yourselves,' he snapped, and sat back in his seat.

There was a respectful tap at the door, and after an appropriate interval, Jeremy allowed the blind to sink into its socket.

'We're stopping here, sur,' said one of the coachmen. 'Five minutes. Wondered if the lady'd like another glass o' brandy.'

Paul, still holding a handkerchief to his mouth under the veil, shook his head.

'Very good, sur.'

'I'll take a tot,' said Stephen. 'Nay, nay, I'll come for it.' He excused himself to his two companions and followed the coachman into the inn.

'Doubt if that's wise,' said Paul under his breath.

'The nearer normal we seem the better. Thank God it's a fine day. Otherwise, who knows . . .?'

Presently they were off again. Jeremy continued to watch things through the thin gap he was forcing in the blind. This slit, apart from guarding against surprise, allowed a little more light in for what they had to do.

'Right,' said Jeremy.

He was seated on the edge of the seat with his back to the horses. Stephen now pulled the cushioned seat away, and put it behind him. The lining of the coach behind the seat was of thick carpet-like red felt, stiff material which had been cut to fit the arch of the interior. It was sturdy enough to stay in position on its own, and only two screws secured it to the woodwork behind. Stephen took out a screwdriver, eased out the screws, bent the lining back into the coach, exposing the wood.

Paul felt under his skirts and untied a suspended parcel of linen, putting it on the seat beside him. From the parcel he unwrapped a brace and bit. In the meantime Stephen had taken out a piece of chalk and drawn a circle on the wood about the size of the face of a large grandfather's clock. Then he screwed in the bit and applied it as it were to twelve o'clock on the clock face.

This wood, also mahogany, was about three-quarters of an inch thick. It was how Paul, who knew a lot about how coaches were constructed, said it would be. This single wooden barrier separated the interior of the coach from the padlocked compartment under the coachman's seat. But the mahogany was hard and unyielding – quite as hard as oak – and to bore a hole needed constant muscular pressure to force the bit to bite. When the bit was unwound and withdrawn it left a hole about a third of an inch in diameter. Stephen began to drill a second hole at six o'clock.

The coach slowed as it attempted the long ascent near Trerule Foot. Some beggar children began to run alongside it, calling out and shouting. One or two tried to get a lift by hopping perilously on the axles but were quickly driven off. Paul unwrapped the rest of his linen packet. Three narrow saw-blades about six inches long for fitting into a wooden handle of the same length; a tin of grease, a bunch of keys, a tiny bottle of 'train' oil, two steel crowbars each about a foot long and screwing together.

By now Stephen had driven six holes.

'Let me take over,' said Paul.

'Wait.'

The coach was slowing as they neared the crest of the hill. Quickly the lining was flipped back into place, the cushion seat replaced, the tools stowed under the cushions. The coach stopped and the outside passengers got down to lighten the load. Jeremy lowered the blind and peered out. Mrs May continued to lie back with closed eyes. The gallant lieutenant opened the window and put his head out.

'Would ye wish me to walk too? It is no trouble.'

'Thank ee, no, sur,' called the driver from his seat. 'We'll manage nicely, thank ee all the same.'

It was no more than a hundred yards to the top, but it seemed a long way.

'Am I disturbing ye, ma'am?' Lieutenant Lean asked. 'Is the air too fresh?'

'No, no,' said Mrs May. 'It is pleasant for a few moments.'

At the top was a toll-bar. Here they stopped a moment to pay their dues. Then the outside passengers and the second coachman and the guard climbed aboard. The coach, with some clucking and clicking and the snapping of the whip, got under way again, the blind was drawn up, and after it the window. At once the lining was bent down again and Stephen snatched up the brace.

'Like me to take over?' Paul asked.

'No, not yet. Put the blade of the saw in, fit the bars together. God's eyes, are we never to be still! It is one thing we hadn't banked on!'

The 'thing' they hadn't banked on was the lurching of the coach. In bad places it jolted and swayed so much that Stephen was off his balance and nearly let the brace fall. Often the hole took twice as long to drill.

Jeremy looked at his watch. 'How many have you done?'

'On my ninth.'

'How is that going for time?' Paul asked.

'Not ill. We might just accomplish it all before Liskeard. It depends on the number of interruptions.'

'D'you wish me to start with the saw?' Paul asked impatiently.

'Certainly not. It's a last resort, that. In any event we have four hours before Lostwithiel.'

'I'd be happier to see it all done this side of Liskeard.'

'Forget that. Take over from Stephen now. Then I'll take over from you.'

They changed places. The space was very confined and they constantly bumped against each other. Stephen began to brush the sawdust together with his hand and put the dust in an inside pocket of his naval coat.

Jeremy watched the others and watched the holes growing in the clock face. In spite of his apparent calm his heart was thumping as if he had run a mile. Paul also was badly strung up; but rather to Jeremy's surprise Stephen looked equally so. Risk and hazard and the illegal act were not nearly so foreign to him as to them, but he had never before run this sort of risk. Danger was to him something to be undertaken in the heat of the moment, violence as its natural expression. This was too cold, too calculating: a burglary taking place in a jolting coach, *surrounded* by other people within earshot, almost within reach, and virtually in the presence of two coachmen and a guard armed with a carbine. He looked sick.

One thing about this scheme – and Jeremy had no idea whether it approximated to the events of the Brighton coach robbery – was that it was, so far, silent. You had to think not only of the coachmen but of the passengers, who could be heard overhead moving about from time to time, scraping their boots on the roof, shouting to each other and laughing. But the brace and bit made virtually no sound at all. If at a later hour the saw had to be used, and later still the crowbar, the inside noise might increase; but even so it should not be above the acceptable level. What passenger or guard was ever likely to hear anything from inside the coach when they were jogging and wobbling and jolting along an ill-kept turnpike road with the horses trotting and a fair breeze blowing over all?

They had come down a gentle incline past Budge's Shop with the occasional squeak and grunt of the brakes, and were now following the path of the valley. The sun shone with a mild warmth though it was the depths of winter; little yellow nosegays of primroses showed on the banks; rivulets of clear water crossed the road; cows and sheep fattened in the lush fields. The coach was a microcosm of civilized life crawling across the smiling, unheeding countryside. All that was different was three young men deep within the coach, sweating at their endeavours, perpetrating, or attempting to perpetrate, a crime that was punishable by death.

Changing places every ten holes, they bored twenty, forty, fifty, sixty. Jeremy, planning it all so carefully beforehand, had measured everything, and reckoned that about ninety holes would weaken the wood so much that it could be gently tapped out. If this were not so, the saw would be used to join one hole to the next until it all gave way. At seventy, when he took over himself again, he tried the wood, inserting his fingertips in the holes, pressing and pulling, but there was no hint of weakness yet. It reminded him of when he was sawing some tree or log at home. You could often saw nine-tenths of the way through and the one-tenth that was left would be as solid and as unyielding as iron. Only at the very last second when the saw had apparently nothing more to work on did the tree suddenly topple. Beads of sweat formed on his upper lip now as the possibility of miscalculation fretted his mind. Suppose this wood was harder than any other. Supposing one got so far and then . . .

'Wait,' said Paul, whose turn it was to keep a look out.

They had come to another toll-gate, where an outside passenger climbed down and two others got on. There was a lot of talk and some raillery. It was in a village, and Jeremy guessed it was Menheniot. If that were the case they would be in Liskeard within the hour. Much still to do. A high blast from the horn set the dogs barking, and the coach jerked into motion.

'Go on,' said Paul.

Drilling again. They had reached seventy-five and were slightly more than three-quarters of the way round the clock. That is to say the next hole Jeremy bored would be at about twelve minutes to the hour. Not every hole could be exactly equidistant from its neighbour: average gap was about an eighth of an inch, but here and there it widened, here and there the holes had actually joined together. Where the gaps were greatest would be the first places to attack, either with the saw or with additional borings, once the circle was complete.

Another hill was slowing them, slowing them to a stop.

'Wait,' said Paul.

Passengers were clambering off the coach. There seemed to be a discussion. Presently there was a tap on the door. Stephen lowered his window and his blind, as the knock was on his side.

Stevens. 'Beg pardon, sur, the bridge be wanting strengthening acrost this yur stream; so if so be as you and th'other gentleman would care to walk acrost the footbridge downstream; we'd not disturb the leddy, sur; she could stay right where she's to; but if you and th'other gentleman would walk; we'd not disturb the leddy.' He peered in at the dark figure in the corner. 'Twill be better when we get to Liskeard, ma'am; the road be not so pluff for a while then. She's . . . no worse, I 'ope?'

'The jolting of the coach is very disturbing,' said Jeremy. 'Dearest, you heard what the coachman said?'

'Yes, yes,' said Paul in a faint voice. 'Pray do as he says.'

The two men got out and joined the other passengers; they crossed the footbridge in a group and returned to the coach when it was safely over. Jeremy knew his face to be sweaty and flushed, and noticed some flakes of sawdust under Stephen's fingernails.

'How long before Liskeard?' Jeremy asked the coachman.

''Bout twenty minutes, sur.'

They all climbed aboard and once again they were off.

Jeremy took the brace from under a cushion and brushed away more sawdust. 'Not be finished by Liskeard – that's certain now. You'd better stay in the coach then, Paul, ask not to be disturbed. I've never known – do they ever come to brush out the interior or anything of that sort, Paul?'

'Never. Lucky if it gets brushed out at the end of the day.'

Eighty-nine, ninety, ninety-one. Four more would complete the circle.

'It's my turn,' said Stephen.

'Let me finish.'

In five minutes he had finished, knelt back in the confined space on the seat staring at the circle. Then he put his hand in the centre of the clock face and pushed. It remained immovable. Not by a single creak did it give the impression of being under strain. Jeremy exerted his strength. No result.

He handed the brace to Stephen. 'Join up some of those early holes around five past and ten past.'

Paul said: 'Let me try the saw at this side while Stephen is doing the other.'

'All right. But use plenty of grease. And go gently.'

'We're *slowing* again,' said Stephen.

'It's a long climb into Liskeard,' Paul said. 'This is the beginning. But the horses will manage it. We don't need to stop yet.'

So for another five minutes they worked. By then the wood between five past and ten past was cut through in a continuous line; and the saw had joined four holes together at twenty minutes to the hour.

'That's enough,' said Jeremy. He gave the wood another gentle push and thought he detected a slight yielding. But if it did yield now it would be an acute embarrassment, for it might want to fall forward into the coach, pressing the lining outward. 'Leave it now. It's a good two hours to Lostwithiel, and we should finish off within an hour. Certain. Important thing now is to get it tidy.'

Four minutes later the shrill note of the horn warned the inn and the post-boys that they were on their way, and a minute or so after that the coach was clattering into the yard of the King's Arms. Then all was bustle and fuss and noise, climbing down, unloading luggage, bells ringing, porters carrying cases to and from the coach, steaming horses being unharnessed and led away, the fresh ones standing stamping their feet and shaking their heads, ostlers holding reins, shouting and joking among themselves, onward passengers trooping into the hotel to be greeted by Mr Webb, the incumbent, rubbing his fat warty hands and awaiting orders for the light meal they would have time to eat before the coach was due to leave again.

From all this hubbub only the inside of the coach was immune; all the noise and fuss and bustle circled and eddied around it. The blinds had of course been lowered, and the two gentlemen were peering out observing the scene. After a decent interval Lieutenant Morgan Lean touched his cap to the lady and climbed out. A post-boy, having lowered the step, was waiting to hand the lady down, but after a conference only the tall clergyman alighted.

'My wife', he said, giving the boy sixpence, 'is not well and does not wish to be disturbed. I will take a light refreshment and have something sent out to her.'

'Very good, sur. Thank ee, sur.'

So the two gentlemen followed the rest into the hotel, were quickly spotted by the innkeeper, who had a sharp eye for quality, and given preferential treatment. Mrs May was sent out a cup of beef tea and some butter biscuits.

A trying time. Nothing would hurry on the dragging minutes. After wolfing some sort of pie and drinking two glasses of French brandy: 'brought over special, Reverend, brought over special, if you d'know what I mean' – Jeremy paid his score and walked back to the coach.

'D'you want to "retire"?' he asked ironically.

'Yes, by God I do!' said Paul.

'Then wait till Stephen comes back. We can't leave the coach unattended. Where are the tools?'

'Still behind my seat. I've wrapped them in the linen but they're bulky.'

'No one will look.'

In about ten minutes Stephen was back, the sweat starting from under his white wig.

'God's death!' he said, when he was told what was proposed. 'We have to risk capital punishment for the sake of your functions!'

'Well, try it yourself!' hissed Paul. 'This whole escapade, by Christ, it is beyond endurance—'

'Quiet,' said Jeremy. 'I'll help you into the hotel and wait for you.'

The tall frail woman was assisted out of the coach. Her skirt and cloak were so full that they easily concealed any change in her size since she left Plymouth.

An anxious five minutes, and then they made a slow

progress back towards the coach. Half way across the yard they observed Stephen and one of the coachmen in earnest conversation, even argument, with a fat elderly man at the door of the coach.

As they came up the coachman – it was Marshall, the senior of the two – said: 'Ah, Reverend May, sur, a little difficulty 'as arose, as you might say. I trust your wife is enjoyin' 'er journey with us, sur? I trust you are finding everything to your satisfaction, ma'am.'

Paul did not reply, but made a noncommittal movement of his head.

Marshall said: 'Ye see, sur, Mr May, sur, as the fourth passenger was supposed t've joined us at Torpoint and then could not and sent a message, t'say as 'ow as 'e were going to join us at Liskeard instead, and seeing as 'ow as 'e 'asn't turned up 'ere neither; and this gent, this Mr – this Mr Rose – thank ee, sur – this Mr Rose d'wish for an inside place on this coach it only seem right that 'e should 'ave it!'

'Mr Jewell is sure to turn up,' said Stephen angrily. 'He told me—'

'Well, there be but two minutes left, sur. And seeing as there is no sight nor sound of 'im . . .'

'Did Mr Jewell pay for his seat?' Jeremy asked.

'Oh, aye, sur, tis a condition of booking, to pay in advance.'

'Then I do not think you can re-sell his seat.'

Mr Rose, who had a mulberry complexion that contrasted noticeably with the silver whiteness of his hair, beamed over the top of half-moon spectacles.

'Beg pardon, Reverend Sir, madam, beg pardon, I'm sure, it is just that as the seat appeared vacant I thought to avail myself of it. Normally I would not concern myself with the cold airs of January but I have a touch of the old cholicky gout and so an interior seat is well worth the extra expense. I trust I shall not be unwelcome in your company or trouble you greatly with my presence. Of course, if the original traveller were still to turn up . . .'

Sixty-odd. Leather breeches, top boots, blue coat with white waistcoat, unstarched white neck cloth, broad-brimmed beaver hat. Jeremy's tongue froze. If this man came with them the whole elaborate plan was doomed. It would even be unrepeatable, for the guard would notice the holes when he came to take out the cash-boxes; they would see that an attempt had been made and failed; no such attempt could ever be made again. And the obstacle, the unforeseen obstacle to all their plans stood there beaming, all 230-odd pounds of him, solid, irremovable, emanating good will – and spelling ill fortune. Of course the original traveller would not turn up, for he did not exist. They had all agreed that to bring a fourth person into their schemes – lacking someone of their own age, disposition and commitment – would be a mistake. Now they found that their decision had been a greater mistake.

Jeremy said: 'I have to tell you, sir, that my wife is with child and has suffered already from the effects of this journey. What alone has made it tolerable has been the room she has been allowed, to lie back and occupy two seats on the journey so far. I personally', he said to Marshall, 'should be pleased to pay something extra to continue to have this additional convenience for my wife.'

Marshall hesitated and coughed into his hand to hide his embarrassment. The fat Mr Rose looked taken aback, for it was clear that his apologies had been merely by way of introduction and had not meant to be taken seriously. No one seemed quite sure what to say next. Mrs May leaned against her husband and looked frail.

454

Stephen said: 'Mr Jewell – when he left word he would not be joining the coach at Torpoint, he said he would *for certain* join it either at Liskeard or at Dobwalls, he said. So you'd not be able to have an inside seat for very long, sir, seeing that Mr Jewell will be surely turning up at the next stop.'

Mr Rose showed his false teeth in another beaming smile. 'But that is as far as I go, sir! That is as far as I *go*! If the little lady would be so kind . . . You'll appreciate that but for this cholicky gout I should not at all think of inconveniencing her . . .'

In perhaps five seconds every choice open – and its consequences – flashed through Jeremy's mind. He turned to Paul.

'My dearest, we cannot be inhospitable to a gentleman in need. Perhaps you may feel restored after your refreshments and your brief rest. At least, let us be accommodating to the coachman and to a fellow traveller. Let us *try*. If you feel worse we shall have to give up our journey and resume it tomorrow.'

His eye met Paul's. They both knew that after they reached Dobwalls there was two hours before they stopped in Lostwithiel. Stephen was not so sure of his geography and seemed about to continue the argument, but Jeremy stopped him with a gracious lifting of his hand.

'Your concern, Lieutenant, is greatly appreciated. But I think in this we must . . . take this decision.'

By now all the other travellers were on the coach. The Reverend Arthur May helped his wife up the step and followed her in. She took the seat whose seat-cushion concealed the tools; he took his place beside her.

'After you, sir,' Lieutenant Morgan Lean said grimly and the fat man heaved himself in and took the seat opposite

Paul. The whole coach creaked with his weight. After Stephen had got in Marshall folded up the step after him and climbed on to the driver's seat where Stevens was already flicking his whip. The post-boys relinquished their grip of the horses' heads and the coach drew out of the yard, lurching and rattling upon the rutted road.

Chapter Eight

I

Mr Rose was a lawyer, and not at all thin-skinned. In spite of his protestations, he did not seem concerned that his conversation might disturb the lady. He lived in Liskeard, he explained, and had been up at five that morning, examining witnesses for the defence in a case of a man recently charged with obstructing a Customs & Excise officer in the performance of his duty, a matter shortly to be heard before a special jury at Launceston Assizes. He was also advising on a case in which two boys were charged with stealing a two-year-old colt valued at £10.10s.0d. and a month-old-calf valued at £2.12s.6d. He was off to Dobwalls now to interview a rich widow of sixty-seven whose affairs he handled and who had set her mind on marrying one of her footmen, aged twenty-two.

Diamond eyes sparkling over the tops of the crescent lenses, he emanated good will but, fortunately, little apparent curiosity as to the business of his fellow travellers. For the most part it was Jeremy he addressed himself to, while Paul lay back under his veil with his eyes closed and Stephen leaned moodily staring out of the window.

Jeremy said, yes, and no, and indeed, sir, and thought: this is a new and unanticipated risk – that this man with his lawyer's eyes will be in close proximity with us as far as Dobwalls, and will be very well able to remember and describe us. It was not just their clothes he would remember,

457

as the coachmen would, but the colour of their eyes, the shape of their faces, their hands, the flaws in their teeth.

Yet somehow he personally was now too far committed to turn back ... How long to Dobwalls? How long from Dobwalls to Lostwithiel? And was there a further risk at Dobwalls of some other interfering fool wishing to travel inside? And if so, how could he best be discouraged? In those split seconds of indecision in the hotel yard he had reasoned that it was better to allow this fat old man to stop their work for forty-five minutes than to rouse comment among the other passengers or thought in the mind of the coachmen or the guard. It could hardly be suspicion, but it might just make them think a little more about the three passengers inside and their exclusiveness and the drawn blinds.

'. . . Failure of all these banks,' Mr Rose was saying. 'The Tamar Bank at Launceston, Cudlipp & Co., Hill & Co., Pearce, Hambly & Co. Caused great distress in the area. Poor people have found themselves altogether without victuals. Many others, hitherto in a respectable way of life, persons who have scraped and saved to gather together a few pounds by frugality and by forbearance from the simplest enjoyment, such persons have found themselves living almost upon *bread* and *water*, bread and water, sir, finding at a single stroke their little all vanished and themselves reduced to the same state as the improvident, the careless, the lazy, the spendthrift, the drunkard and the glutton. D'you know, sir, I blame Mr Pitt for this! If he were alive today he would observe the fruits of his financial contrivings!'

Dobwalls to Lostwithiel. About nine miles. Two hours to work? Much less because of stops. But one hour would suffice – with luck. It would all depend on the strength of the cash-boxes. Cash-boxes belonging to the bank of War- leggan & Willyams – something to give him the extra motive power – perhaps it was emotive power – to undertake this rash and dangerous adventure.

Through the curtains of his bedroom he had that morning seen the boxes being loaded, before the passengers joined and the rest of the luggage. The boxes had not looked too formidable; but if they proved unopenable in the short term it might be possible to carry them away. That would be very dangerous despite travelling rugs and coats and skirts.

Of course there was nothing to prevent them going on to St Austell, or even beyond – except for their infinitely careful prearranged plans. The Reverend and Mrs Arthur May were to leave the coach at Lostwithiel, her condition having become worse, so that they would choose to spend the night at the Talbot Inn and continue their journey on the morrow. After a decent interval at the Talbot Inn for rest they would take a stroll in the late afternoon twilight and would not return. This walk would take them in as gentle a manner as was seemly along the left bank of the River Fowey, a couple of miles downstream until they came to Lantyan Wood, almost opposite to St Winnow. They would find a stone-built folly put up in the previous century and would shelter there for the rest of the evening. In the meantime Lieutenant Morgan Lean would alight as expected at St Austell. There he would stroll a few hundred yards up the little town to Kellow's Hotel where the day before yesterday he had stabled three horses. Having redeemed these, he would ride out and disappear into the night.

In fact he would ride east again by St Blazey Gate, and Tywardreath to Golant. Just before the village he would take a left turn which in a couple of miles would bring him to the folly in Lantyan Wood. Timing was not of the essence here, but when they rehearsed the ride in the daylight it had taken four hours. At the latest he ought to be there by 10 p.m.; thereafter they would have all night to ride across country to the Gatehouse – cloaked to avoid notice of their very noticeable clothing – where they would change into their own things and have their disguises burnt – wigs and all – before dawn.

'Sir?' said Jeremy, aware that he had unexpectedly been asked a question.

'Your benefice, sir. Are you returning to it?'

'No, no, we live in Devonshire. We are to spend a month with my sister in Falmouth. Perhaps we should not have undertaken the journey, but my wife has been very well until a week or so ago.'

Mr Rose tut-tutted sympathetically. 'You have other children?'

'A boy of five.'

'A bonny lad, I'm sure. I have no children myself. My wife died of the smallpox two years after we were wed and I have not cared to remarry. However, my lot has led me into many pleasant places. For instance . . .' He was off again.

Stephen, sitting beside him and facing Paul, was conscious that there was a sprinkling of sawdust on the floor. There had been more sawdust than they had expected. They had not been careful enough. The sawdust looked new, not grey and muddy as it would have done if it had been left on the floor for some time. And yet . . . who could possibly see any cause for suspicion in such a sign? Unless the man were a seer or a thought-reader, how could he conceivably imagine what had been going on before he arrived, just behind where he was sitting, and what would begin again immediately they were rid of him? The greater danger would be the moment when he got out. One of the coachmen bending inwards to put down the step might notice it. Stephen moved his boot, apparently stretching, rubbed the heel of the boot over the floor, dirtying and obscuring the sawdust.

'D'you know, I have a very interesting case in my hands at the moment. One William Allen, a cardmaker, who died seventy-odd years ago, left in his will the sum of five shillings, out of a house in Fore Street, to be given to ten poor widows at Christmas for ever. But there is now a move to stop it, to discontinue it, on the plea that it is contrary to the Mortmain Act. D'you know what that is?'

'No, sir.'

'Allow me to explain . . .'

For God's sake, where is Dobwalls? Stephen thought. He was not sure he agreed with all of Jeremy's arrangements anyhow: they were too *elaborate*, kept too closely to the apparent pattern of the Brighton robbery. Far better for them all to have alighted at St Austell, and, when the coach had gone on, to walk up the street to Kellow's Hotel, pick up the three horses, and bolt off. If they had not been recognized in the coach it was unlikely they should be recognized in St Austell; darkness would all soon after they left; they would have disappeared effectively into the dark, even have been seen riding east so as to put prying eyes off. In Stephen's view, the simplest ways were always the best.

Jeremy was for more carefully covering their tracks. If they left the coach at different times the authorities would be much more confused. Just as when he and his friends had read the account in *The Morning Post*, no one would be able to decide whom to suspect, and where to start looking. Also, Jeremy had argued, if the first robbery became known to the bank – and banks even as far apart as Coutts and Warleggan & Willyams might well have some sort of contact, particularly over a robbery – the almost identical nature of the thefts would lead them to blame the same gang. If the people responsible for the first robbery were caught, no one would believe their denials as to the second. And as anyhow it was a hanging matter, they could not very well be punished more than once for the double offence.

'You should pause on your way home, sir, spend a day at the inn, see Liskeard; it is well worth a visit,' said Mr Rose.

'Indeed.'

'A very handsome church, St Martin's. They tell me it is the second largest in the county. John Hony is the present vicar. Been there more than thirty years. Excellent good man. I am sure he would welcome the opportunity of meeting a fellow cleric such as yourself. Where did you say was your incumbency?'

'Sidmouth.' Jeremy used the first town that came to his mind.

'Ah yes. Indeed yes. Did you also know that Mr Edward Gibbon, the famous historian, represented Liskeard in Parliament nearly forty years ago? Not that he ever saw the town, so far as I know. He stood in the Eliot interest. Don't think he ever made much of a name for himself in the House.'

Paul thought: Damn and rot this man! He stands between . . . between us all and a lot of money. With it, with his share, Stephen would no doubt buy a privateer and put himself in command of it; so hope to make more money while the war lasted. Jeremy similarly was working out some private war in his own mind over the girl Cuby Trevanion. Paul had never believed there could have been that much intensity and bitterness in his old friend. Far from being the 'led' in this dangerous expedition, he was the 'leader'. Not only did the private war involve Cuby, it extended to embrace the Warleggan family. If this robbery were successful the only regret it seemed Jeremy would feel would be that the sum taken would not be sufficient to bring the bank down.

Whereas he, Paul thought, *his* ambition was really the only justifiable one, in that he was engaging in this adventure largely to save his father from a debtors' prison. (Of course he had all a young man's ambitions for fine living and fine clothes; but at least he was not caterwauling after some young woman who had jilted him. 'My lord,' he would say before the judge put on the black cap, 'at least my motives were not frivolous; I was attempting to save my family from penury and starvation.')

'Not that his literary work was faultless,' said Mr Rose, blinking over his spectacles. 'I think Mr Gibbon was by temper incapable of apprehending spiritual aspirations by sympathetic insight, and he assailed with sneer and innuendo what he did not understand in the Christian faith yet feared openly to attack. Don't you agree, sir?'

'Indeed I do.'

'His end was miserable, as you no doubt know. While still a young man he suffered a rupture and thereafter persistently neglected it. In his latest years such was his corpulency and his gout' – Mr Rose briefly looked down at his own great stomach – 'that he developed a varicocele and thereafter was perforce buttoned up in the morning and never opened till he was undressed at night, so that every need of nature was performed in his clothes. I believe he was so noisome that no one could endure to be near him. Eventually dropsy supervened . . .'

'Please,' said Jeremy. 'My wife . . .'

'Of course. I beg your pardon, madam.'

The coach was slowing.

'Dobwalls,' said Stephen.

'Indeed.' Mr Rose beamed again. 'Where I leave you, alas. I may say, sir, and you, ma'am, and you, Lieutenant, that I have seldom known a journey pass so quickly and so pleasantly. I must therefore acknowledge the elegance and the seemliness of your company. I wish you all good day.'

This was a stage merely to take people up and put them down, so there was no blowing of horns or other formality. Mr Rose eased his bulk out of the interior and one outside passenger alighted with him. After he had left there was a pause of a minute or more. Marshall thrust his head in.

'Beg pardon, cap'n; Mr Jewell, your friend, cap'n, Mr Jewell, don't belong to be turning up.'

'It seems not,' said Stephen, bracing himself to fight off another request for the spare seat.

'Well, thur tis, cap'n, thur tis. Some folk do act some strange, wasting all that thur money. Eh, well, we'd best be off now. Looks, ma'am, as if you'll not be disturbed the more.'

He shut the door and climbed up on to the driver's seat. The coach moved on.

II

The little saws were almost useless, for, however much greased, they grated on the wood, and you couldn't keep to a regular rhythm lest the steadiness of the sound should be picked up outside.

The clock face was completely cut through from midday until the half-hour, and again from three-quarters to the end. The wood was moving now; by pressing on it it would bend. Better that it should come out towards them, for if it fell inwards it might clatter. Jeremy got his fingers in the holes around five past and pulled. The wood screeched. He hastily let go and for a minute or so all work was suspended. It was Paul's turn to keep watch but he had been so concerned to see the operation completed that he had not been looking out. The coach slowly stopped.

By now the three young men had slipped into a routine of replacing the lining and cushions and burying the tools so quickly that the interior was set to rights almost before the coachmen got down. Paul lowered the blind and, forgetting his supposed indisposition, lowered the window and looked out.

He quickly withdrew. 'Looks like a fallen tree,' he said in relief. He subsided in his corner, hand over eyes; no one else moved.

Stephen now looked out. 'Aye. Praise to the Lord it is only a *branch*. Sit still! They're shifting it ... Damned thing is still attached to the *trunk*: they'll have to twist it out of the way ... All's well, I believe ... Fools are tidying up some smaller branches! What do they want to do, *brush* the road? What's the time, Jeremy?'

'Quiet,' Jeremy muttered. 'Collect yourself!'

Through the half-open window they could hear the voices of the coachmen and the passengers; it seemed as if they were arguing about something; but presently it ceased. As Stephen shut the window and then drew up the blind there was a clambering on the coach, a crying to the horses, and the coach lurched into motion once again.

'Now!' said Jeremy.

Stephen drilled two more holes and Jeremy clawed with his fingernails again, found a hold and pulled. The clock face was coming, and silently. At the last it twisted in his grasp and clung by three thin strands of wood. Paul passed up the saw. Now the sawing did not resound so much. The circular piece of wood, indented all the way round its edge like a cog-wheel, came away in Jeremy's hands.

He passed it to Paul, his own fingers not so steady; thrust his hand into the cavity now exposed and at once grasped one of the boxes.

It was heavy and he had to get his other hand in and lever it towards the edge of the port-hole they had made; then a firmer grasp and a heave, and it was in the coach.

A box about twelve inches square by six deep and made of thin steel, it had a handle for carrying, and the catch was secured by a stout padlock. It was enormously heavy for its size. Jeremy went back to the seat compartment and groped about inside. He soon found the second box and fished that out too. This was somewhat smaller – about twelve by nine by four – and was quite disproportionately lighter. It also had a steel handle for carrying but was locked with an ordinary built-in keyhole. The metal of which it was made looked similar to the first.

If the coach stopped now the cushion and lining could be replaced as swiftly as ever, but they could only conceal the two boxes under Paul's skirts as best they could, and the circular wooden face somewhere else.

They screwed together the crowbars and Stephen put one end through the loop of the padlock and bunched his muscles. He applied all his weight and force until the veins in his forehead showed and the sweat ran down his face. He gave up with a grunt. At the end he thought he had felt something begin to give, but perhaps it was the steel of the box that was bending, near the staple. In the meantime Paul had taken out his bunch of keys and was trying each one in the lock of the smaller box.

'Let me try,' said Jeremy. He took the crowbar from Stephen and inserted it from the other side of the padlock loop. In spite of his thinness he was muscularly strong; and once again the toughened steel of the crowbar was pitted against the lock. There were two or three curious cracking sounds but the lock held. Jeremy relaxed, slumped back on the seat and let out a breath.

'How long would it take to file it?' Stephen said.

'Too long, I think. And the box is too big to carry away.'

Stephen shook it. There was a promising rattle. 'God's eyes, we got to force it!' He tried again, his wig awry, his hands slippery with sweat. Eventually he sat back, defeated a second time.

'Wait,' said Jeremy. He took up the crowbar and in order to gain greater purchase inserted it into the padlock loop only a couple of inches. It seemed that something was giving at last, but then the crowbar slipped and he caught the knuckles of his left hand a jarring blow on the side of the box. He dropped the bar, sucking his knuckles and cursing. Blood began to well up over three fingers of his hand.

'That's fine,' snarled Stephen. 'If that falls in the coach it'll look as if we've committed a murder!'

It was all the sympathy available. While Jeremy tried to wrap his fingers in his handkerchief Stephen went to work again . . .

'Holy Mackerel!' exclaimed Paul.

They stopped and turned and saw the smaller box open. He showed his teeth in a stark grin.

'The seventh key only! I *thought* these locks were often made to a pattern!'

They stared at four thick piles of banknotes, held by red elastic cord. Paul lifted them out, put them on the seat. His hands were shaking too. Under the notes were other papers: deeds and the like.

The coach rattled peaceably on its way.

'Put 'em away – quick,' Jeremy snapped. His hand was still bleeding but he pulled on his black gloves to hide the injury.

Paul began to stuff the notes into an inner pocket sewn into his skirts. He hesitated about the other papers.

'Those too,' Jeremy said. 'Anything that'll cause War-leggan's Bank more trouble.'

The papers disappeared. Jeremy snatched up the box, shut it, thrust it back at once into the driver's compartment. He blew out a breath, glad to see one piece of evidence out of sight.

'There's a tidy pack of money there, by Heaven!' said Paul. 'I wonder how much. If—'

'Forget it. Look, would any of those keys fit this lock?'

'I doubt it. The tumblers are usually differently placed in a padlock . . .'

While the other two grimly watched he tried one key after another. There were twenty on the bunch, and some were clearly unsuitable as to size.

The coach was slowing. Jeremy prised open the blind.

'It only looks like a hill, but . . . Is there one round here, Paul?'

'I don't think a bad one. There's a fierce one out of Lostwithiel the other side. What is the time?'

Jeremy pulled out his watch. 'Five and twenty past one. We're due in Lostwithiel in about half an hour.'

'They're no cursed use in this lock,' Paul said, stuffing

the keys back in his pocket. 'It's make or break with this one.'

The coach was at a walking pace, but no one was getting down.

'Keep your eyes open, Paul,' Jeremy said. 'We may be coming to some halt unknown to you. We don't – can't take a risk now . . .'

In turn they once again attacked the padlock. It cracked, and the steel of the box bent, but the lock and the staple still held.

'What it needs', said Stephen, 'is a pickaxe. I could burst it open in no time with one of those.'

'So we could with gunpowder,' Jeremy said angrily; 'we could as well use one as the other here.'

Paul said: 'If we keep to the rest of the plan we haven't more than twenty minutes. We could, of course, settle for the one box.'

Stephen paused to wipe the sweat from his face. 'Any notion how much you have?'

'Five-pound notes, twenty-pound Bank of England notes, some Bank Post Bills – a tidy sum.'

'This', said Stephen, 'might be full of copper and small silver pieces. The banks are always short of change.'

Jeremy took the crowbar from him and weighed it in his hands. In fact his gloves gave him a better grip. 'We don't know how many of those notes will be negotiable. And I'll be disappointed and surprised if there is only copper in here.'

'If we ever find out.'

Paul said: 'Why not all stop on until St Austell? We could well file it through in another hour.'

'Or maybe brazen it out and carry it off,' said Stephen.

'You *could* cover it with your scarf. Who is to recollect exactly what we all brought on with us?'

'I shall have enough to carry, for God's sake,' snarled Paul. 'Tools and the rest.'

Jeremy stopped. 'We *have* to avoid panic. At present no one suspects in the smallest measure. Let it stay so! Even if it *means* taking only what was in the small box.'

'After we're gone,' said Paul, 'let Stephen try. There's a good chance of him being in here alone. We could leave him just the crowbar and the file . . .'

The horses were trotting again.

There was a sudden sharp snap. 'By the Lord!' said Jeremy. 'I believe it is giving!' He withdrew the bar and looked at the padlock.

'Here, let me try now,' said Stephen, but Jeremy would not move out of the way. He thrust the bar in from the other side and tugged and strained. Nothing gave. He returned the bar to where it had originally been. The coach wheels suddenly took on a deeper, more resonant sound.

'What's that?'

'A bridge,' said Paul; 'over a valley, not a river. I recognize it: we're about twelve minutes from Lostwithiel.'

The lock cracked again. Jeremy put the crowbar on the seat beside him, fumbled with the steel loop of the lock. It came out of its socket . . .

They pass through a hamlet: dogs barking, children shouting and running alongside, shawled women in doorways. Put the lock on the seat, open the safe-box. In it are four heavy bags of coin, a bunch of keys, a large ruby tiepin, a double ring with diamonds, two gold signet rings, and a seal stamp with the scorpion sign of Warleggan's Bank.

It had been agreed that, as Stephen would be on the

coach for another stage, no incriminating evidence should be carried by him; so the bags of coin Jeremy thrust into the inner pockets of his long black coat. The smaller pieces of jewellery he put in his waistcoat pockets. The keys went in his trouser pocket.

Another hamlet.

'This is Sandylake,' Paul whispered. 'We're almost there.' Shut the safe-box, carefully transfer it through the hole into the driver's compartment. The great clock face gaped.

Jeremy picked up the circle, tried to edge it back into the driver's compartment as the coach again slowed to a walk. The circle of wood stuck. It was smaller than the hole, but the circle was slightly oval and the two ends got wedged.

A shrill blast on the horn. Paul was busy on the tools, wrapping them in their soft linen container, slipping them into his skirt.

They were almost in. Jeremy shoved the wood violently and it went through so sharply that he dropped it. It clattered on one of the safe-boxes.

'Out of the way,' snarled Stephen. Jeremy fell back in the small space almost on top of Paul: Stephen pushed up the thick felt, fumbled one screw between his fingers, put it in its hole but it dropped out. With oaths he scrabbled among the cushions, found it again, put it back, carefully, his fingers trembling as with ague, screwed it tight. Now the other.

'We're here,' said Paul. The coach was going over cobbles, the horn brayed again, the horses were flicked into a last-minute trot to give a smart impression.

Stephen got the second screw fixed, passed the screwdriver to Paul, who pocketed it. They were all feverishly taking stock of the interior. One thing definitely to show was a pronounced crease, amounting almost to a crack, in

471

the lining where the felt material had been persistently bent back throughout the journey. Part of it could be covered by the cushions and the seat, but the rest of the crease must show. So long as Stephen occupied that corner his bulk would almost hide it. But the coachman would have to be very alert to notice it and draw an inference. He was most likely to see it when he came in to light the lantern, but by then they would all be gone.

The coach lurched like a ship at sea as it turned into the yard of the Talbot Inn. Now again all the clatter and bustle of the Liskeard stage. Horses whinnying, ostlers shouting, outside passengers being handed down, two men stamping their feet with the cold, a market woman selling oranges, a twisted idiot boy trying to help with the cases, the smell of horse dung and coffee and dried hay and wood smoke.

It was Stevens, the second coachman, who came to the door. Lieutenant Morgan Lean was the first to get down.

He said: 'I think the lady is serious unwell.' He stretched his big frame and walked slowly into the inn.

The Reverend Arthur May came next. He looked very serious and frowned at Stevens with his lop-sided short-sighted stare. 'I much regret. My wife is feeling very poorly. I think we shall have to complete our journey tomorrow.'

'Oh,' said Stevens. 'Sorry 'bout that, sur. She'm looking some slight at 'Skeard. I'll tell Bob.'

Marshall was summoned. The Reverend Mr May repeated his statement to him. 'I very much fear,' he said, 'I very much fear we shall not be able to proceed today. It is quite possible that a long rest may put my wife in fair enough condition to continue the journey tomorrow. Do you know the innkeeper here?'

'Ais. Mr Roberts you d'mean, sur. Shall I go ask 'im now if 'e would have suitable accommodation?'

'For one of the cloth,' said Mr May. 'Accommodation for one of the cloth. I should consider it a favour if you would do so.'

Marshall bustled off.

'Come, my dear,' said Mr May, extending his hand into the coach, careful not to bang his coat on any projection, 'I trust you will be much recovered by a night's rest. If you are better we can go on tomorrow.'

Chapter Nine

I

Tuesday, January 26th was much like Monday the 25th, except that the cold north-westerly breeze had altogether dropped. The weather, Demelza said, was making up its mind whether to be fair or foul. Anything might occur tomorrow, from a tempestuous westerly gale to a return to northerly airstreams, with snow or hail showers and shivering temperatures. In the meantime Tuesday was halcyon. The sun streamed out of a remote pale aniline sky, so different from the peacock blues of yesterday, the sea had settled, the Dark Cliffs looked pale as bread in the afternoon sun, primroses peeped in the hedgerows and little bristly tufts of future bluebells thrust out among the worn undergrowth of winter. Birds, not totally deceived, nevertheless chirped and twittered and pinked around the house and the stream.

She decided the family should go for a walk. There was nothing but good news everywhere, particularly from Geoffrey Charles. Ever since Christmas her health and energy had been coming back like fresh water irrigating dry ground. She had not had a single night of fever and only one day of uncertain malaise.

They went across the beach. Clowance and Isabella-Rose led the way. Clowance would have been perfectly happy to keep pace with the brisk progress of her parents, but Bella inevitably had to be first. All her life was taken at the run.

So they were half a mile ahead on the enormous smoothly rolled expanse of Hendrawna Beach, Bella skipping sideways and urging Clowance along. Jeremy was still away. He had been gone two nights but had said he would be home sometime today.

'It's a year,' said Demelza, 'just about a year since all the machinery was landed for Wheal Leisure. What was the date, I can't remember, no matter, it was a fine day though dull; only a year ago Henry was not even thought of! So life changes. Isn't it wonderful to feel we have another son, another child! And so like you! What was the word Aunt Agatha used to use? The very daps of his mother. She said that about Julia. Well, Henry is the very daps of his father, don't you agree?'

'We'll have to scratch his cheek with a pin,' said Ross. 'Then there'll be no knowing us apart.'

'But aren't you happy about it, Ross? Aren't you content?'

'I don't know where one ends and another begins! I *think* I'm happy; I *know* I'm content; and I'm *vastly* relieved.'

'That's the opposite way round from me. But you were always of a contrary nature. Relief is such a small thing . . .'

'Not for me it is not. When you were so mopish. And so irritable . . .'

'*Was* I irritable? Yes, of course. I know I was. I don't imagine what got into me. I could not help myself. Well, it is gone now. Now I feel like Bella!' She began to skip sideways like her younger daughter, prancing ahead of Ross, eyes aglint, hair blowing.

'D'you remember one day coming back from Trenwith – that first Christmas when I was expecting Julia – and we walked home singing Jud's song?

"There was an old couple and they was poor,
Tweedle, tweedle, go twee."

'Dear life, it seems a long time since – are we the *same* people, you and I, Ross? All that experience since, of striving and living and loving ... All the stress and the strain and the joy and the pleasure.' She stopped hopping to get her breath. 'So many people dead – Francis, Elizabeth, Aunt Agatha, Mark Daniel, Dr Choake, Sir John Trevaunance, Cousin William-Alfred and ... Julia. So much has happened: two of our children grown up and having love-affairs of their own. Dwight and Caroline married, Geoffrey Charles, then a tiny infant now a gallant captain, so much, so much. Can we *two* be the *same*? Would you know yourself if you saw yourself coming across the beach as you were then? Would I? I doubt it. If I am not cleverer, I *must* be wiser. But do you not love me still? Did you not last night? Are we not somehow, somehow the same?'

'If you proclaim it so loud,' Ross said, 'the gulls will hear you.'

'There was an old couple!' Demelza shouted at the top of her voice. 'Tweedle, tweedle, go *twee-ee-ee*!'

The girls heard her and turned and waved. She waved with both hands held aloft. They stopped, thinking she wanted them, but she gestured to them to go on.

'Come here,' said Ross. 'Sober down. Walk beside me. Take my hand.'

So she did as she was told.

II

They had turned back, leaving Clowance and Bella to go further and further on until they were two dots almost out of sight.

Ross thought: sometimes one speaks the truth on impulse. I did then. I *think* I am happy, I *know* I am content. Everything in the end has moved for us well. (The end? Well, so far.) Thanks to the discovery of the Trevorgie workings the mine will pay out a good dividend next quarter. Not riches like Grace, but a fair enough beginning considering. (Grace is failing, but no matter; perhaps somehow the two may be profitably propped up together.) Must get Ben back soon. He, after all, discovered Trevorgie. His resignation can only be accepted as token. In a week or so, when his grandfather is better, he and I will tackle Ben together. It seems even more stupid of him to refuse to come back now that Clowance and Stephen have *not* been reconciled. Their separation must have arisen from something deeper, some more fundamental disaffection than a crude quarrel and a fight outside Wheal Leisure.

The new young man: does he mean anything in Clowance's life? Is he just a charming, eligible, comforting figure she is, almost without realizing it, using as a reassurance to herself that she is now finally over her infatuation for Stephen? Or by this time next year will he be our new son-in-law?

And Jeremy? Jeremy is more of a problem because he is so much harder to read. Everything *seems* to be going well for him. The opening of the mine is now justified, a new small whim-engine is building, some sort of a reconciliation has occurred between him and the Trevanion girl. And with the total defeat of the French army in the snows of Poland, there is literally far less inducement for him to go to fight. That will make Demelza happy. And now Geoffrey Charles . . .

And for myself? Ross thought. Perhaps I am doomed in some way (or blessed, who knows which it is?) to find a large part of my own pleasure or otherwise in the pleasure or otherwise of my family. I believe I *reflect* more happiness than I generate. This is especially so where Demelza is concerned. But to some extent with all of them. It is not so much that I do not *seek* happiness, as come upon it most often at second hand. Yet I am as selfish as the next man. Poldark is perhaps not a breed to live high and free. How fortunate that I have this woman whose nature is devoted to loving all life, appreciating the small things, seeking them out like a collector seeking a new butterfly, and never allowing any of them to stale. I follow behind her, knowing of my happiness through her.

As selfish as the next man. True enough. For in spite of my total involvement with my wife and children I know that next month I shall go to London, and when that comes I shall know a perverse distress at leaving them, yet a perverse sense of relish at returning to the scene I consciously despise. In spite of being no use in the House I shall be interested in its new composition. It is said that Liverpool has increased his majority by forty. It is also said that five or six of Canning's most loyal supporters have lost their seats because of their devoted allegiance to him. There will be a shifting and a realignment. That will not be without pleasure to observe by one who seeks nothing.

Except the prosecution of the war. If Napoleon is temporarily down we cannot lean back and think our greatest efforts are past. That way we shall lose all our gains . . .

'Who is that coming down the cliff from Leisure?' Demelza asked.

As selfish as the next man. 'What?' Ross asked.

'It's Jeremy. I can tell by his lanky legs. He's back, then. I told them to lay for him for dinner.'

Jeremy waved and they waved back. They approached each other at a rate of about eight miles an hour. They came together and he kissed his mother, shook hands with his father, and they turned for home.

'How long will dinner be? I'm ravenous!'

'Oh, twenty minutes. How was Mr Harvey?'

'Harvey?'

'Yes, you were—'

'Of course. Well enough. Still in straits for money, you know. Until he can pay off his late partners . . .'

'Does he have much to pay?'

'Oh yes . . . Yes, there are considerable sums outstanding. But he will survive and prosper, I believe, for it is his nature . . .' Jeremy frowned across the beach. 'Is that Clowance and Bella?'

'Yes. I think they are just turning back.'

'Did you see Trevithick?' Ross asked.

'No, Father. He was in – in Bridgnorth.'

'Bridgnorth?'

'Some – er – castings that were to have been done for him in Hayle have now had to be transferred there because of the injunction . . . And you, Mama,' said Jeremy with an effort. 'You look *brave*!'

'I *feel* brave,' said Demelza, 'and believe I shall eat just so much as you for dinner.'

All the same she did not think *Jeremy* looked brave. From seeming younger than his twenty-one years he had of a sudden come to look much older. His complexion was sallow, and his eyes dark, as if from worry or lack of sleep. A woman of eccentric perceptions where her own family was concerned, she had a sudden moment of unease, of panic, an awareness of crisis, as if something less tangible than the sensory was warning her of a looming danger, either shortly to come or just past. She looked again at Jeremy, assuring herself, trying to reassure herself that it was only a recurrence of the fever disturbing her blood.

'Reports from Leisure are encouraging,' Ross said.

'I'm glad. I – went up there as soon as I came home.'

'Manny Bice and Toby Martin have had a new find. It should bring them a small fortune before the pitches are agreed again.'

'So – we are in profit.'

'Distinctly so.'

So . . . we are in profit, Jeremy thought, still staring at the sea. In profit two ways – only one legitimate. It had come off. After the early hitches it had all gone according to plan. They were safe. Reasonably safe, anyway. All clothes, wigs, disguises had been burned before dawn broke. What they had brought away with them from the two steel boxes had been assessed, counted, carefully hidden. So long as they all behaved with circumspection and intelligence the risks were now small. There was nothing to identify them. Descriptions were bound to be vague and unreliable. They had ridden away into the night. How could anyone know where they had come from, where they had gone to?

In profit. Yet it didn't feel in profit. The bitter rage that had driven him to organize this thing had burnt itself out in the performance of the act. His anger, his frustration, had blinkered him to normal considerations of right and wrong and risk. Now it was over, and successfully over; yet all that was left in his heart was ashes. It was as if his love for Cuby had been purged by the robbery, had apparently died in the coach. Maybe at some future time it would revive, but at the moment he no longer cared anything for her and only asked himself how he could have been so obsessed, so stupidly obsessed as to take the risks he had done in the hope of gaining so unworthy a young woman. It didn't matter any more. She didn't matter any more. All that mattered was disgust.

Perhaps in a day or two – a month or two – the feeling would wear away; the self-disgust would weaken into some more easily containable emotion. At present he felt he had wakened from a nightmare – to find that the nightmare was true. But all things pass. With time one would no doubt begin to feel and think normally again.

He wondered how his father and mother would react if he said something to them now. The Poldarks, it seemed to him, had often been against the law. But not in this way. They had contrived to pick some sort of a fine line among the 'thou shalt nots' of English and Hebraic decree. Yet Jeremy was aware that the basic emotions which had driven him to do this thing had been stronger than his own common sense. And the angry resolution had never faltered, not even in the long hours of the night before the coach ride. That it had now relaxed its grip in no way minimized the power it had exerted while it lasted. Through what wilder generations had his blood come down? But did that inheritance explain anything, excuse anything? Was not one the possessor of one's own soul?

Oh, nonsense. It would all pass. He gave his shoulders a shake as if to dispossess himself of ugly thoughts.

'Oh!' exclaimed Demelza. 'Seeing you, I had almost forgot! Yesterday we received a letter from Geoffrey Charles! It gave us – well, see for yourself! Do you have it, Ross?'

Ross took a sheet of paper from his pocket, the broken red seal attached. He handed it to Jeremy who read:

Ciudad Rodrigo
29th December, 1812.

My dearest Cousins All,

Do you know what has happened to me? Something quite Spectacular and entirely without Precedent! Can you guess? Certainly you cannot!

No, I have not been made Adjutant General of the Forces Overseas, I have not been knighted for my valour at Salamanca, I have not been singled out by Lord Wellington for promotion to the Chief of his General Staff. Nothing of the sort. But, by a single deliciously Happy Accident, I have become a Married Man!

Do you recollect in my last letter I believe I told you that I was billeted in this town upon a Señor de Bertendona? Do you recollect that I told you he had a wife, two sons and a Daughter? Can you suppose other than that in the course of the last six weeks I have fallen in love with the daughter, Amadora, and – far, far more astonishing – she with me? She is nineteen years of age and beyond measure beautiful and charming, with all the dignity and pride of the Spanish but all the slender elegant beauty of a woman! I must say no more, otherwise you will think I have become a schoolboy again and lost my senses. It is not so. She is all that I could have dreamed of.

I have but a short time to write to you now for I am on Parade Duty this week, but I must tell you simply that we were wed on Tuesday morning, first by our chaplain, the Reverend Mark Foster, and then in the Gothick Cathedral by Father Antonio Carreros, for good measure. Señora de Bertendona is deeply distressed that her daughter should have married a Heretic, as is the elder brother, Martin; but her father is so much an Anglophile in all things that he can see only good even in Me as a Son-in-Law! And Amadora herself, though brought up strictly in the Other Faith, swears to me privately that – well, I dare not tell you what she swears to me privately lest I be considered a man of overweening Conceit – but I trust and believe that with the sort of love we have for each other, tolerance and common sense will smooth over such difficulties as may arise.

I cannot tell you what our plans are, except that for the time being we continue to live in her parents' house along with David Hamilton, Father Antonio Carreros, seven Spanish guerrillas, a Portuguese shepherd-boy and a host of servants! Further plans will be much influenced – for me at least – by the decisions shortly to be taken about our spring campaign by the new Duke of Ciudad Rodrigo, the Generalissimo of the Spanish and British forces, none other than the Marquess of Wellington.

Great Tidings from the Russian front! Perhaps soon it will all be over!

Our most affectionate New Year and other greetings to you all,

from
Geoffrey Charles and Amadora Poldark.

'What *news*!' said Jeremy, again making the effort. 'What *surprising* news! So some day, perhaps soon, we shall have a Spanish cousin at Trenwith!'

'He provokingly says nothing about that,' said Demelza. 'I wonder if she has money.'

'What?' asked Jeremy, startled.

'I wondered if the girl had money.'

'Oh. Oh yes, I see.'

'It would be lovely if she were able to help Geoffrey Charles to restore Trenwith. He will have very little of his own.'

'I know the name de Bertendona,' Ross said. 'I can't remember in what connection, but it is a distinguished name.'

'Well, I hope they will come soon,' Demelza said. 'I am thankful that he says she has a little English, for I doubt my ability to learn anything else.' She stopped. 'Have you hurt your hand?'

'What?' Jeremy stared at his scarred knuckles. 'Oh, that. A lever slipped when I was trying to force something open.'

'When was it done?'

'Yesterday.'

'It hardly looks as if it has been cleaned! Have you put any balsam or ointment on it?'

'No . . . I sucked it clean, but it has got rather dirty riding home.'

'What time did you leave?'

'Where? . . . Oh, Hayle. Soon after dawn.'

'Well, when we get in wash it thoroughly and I'll put a plaster over.'

'It is not necessary to fuss, Mama,' he said irritably. 'It is scarcely painful now. Nature will take its own remedies.'

They had reached the stile dividing the beach from their

own land. She looked at Jeremy again, no longer conscious of well-being and the warmth of the sun.

She said: 'Have you seen Cuby?'

He looked up. 'What? No. Oh no. Not at all.'

'Everything is just the same as before?'

'Yes.'

'No change?'

'No change,' said Jeremy, looking over her head at the distant sea.

The two girls were now approaching rapidly and shouted for them to wait. They waited by the stile, and then went in to dinner all together, laughing and joking, a cheerful and a united family.

WINSTON GRAHAM

Bella Poldark

Pan

'*Now, hurrah, Poldark rides again through the action-packed pages of Winston Graham's long-awaited concluding volume of the hugely popular Poldark saga. From the very first lines we tingle with the sense that we are in good hands, transported by Graham's atmospheric prose back to 1818 and the treacherous coast of craggy Cornwall*' Daily Mail

Graham's magical stories of the Poldark family, together with the much-loved television series, have millions of fans worldwide. Now we continue the story:

Of Ross Poldark, strong, independent squire at Nampara and his beautiful, outspoken wife Demelza. Of Valentine Warleggan, the wayward, perverse son of George, whose existence rubs salt in the war wounds his father and Ross have inflicted on one another. Of Bella, the Poldarks' youngest daughter, who is encouraged as a singer by old flame, Christopher Havergal – this objective being deeply complicated by the appearance of French conductor Maurice Valéry, who has more in mind than simply exploiting Bella's talent. Of Clowance, the Poldarks' widowed daughter, who meets Philip Prideaux, a mysterious figure who emerges from the shadow of the Battle of Waterloo and wishes to marry her. And of a murderer who lurks in the villages of west Cornwall, and is long – too long – in being discovered.

Written with power, humour, irony and elegance, *Bella Poldark* makes a brilliant finale for this distinguished saga.

WINSTON GRAHAM

Memoirs of a Private Man

PAN

'I have always been more interested in other people than myself – though there has to be something of myself in every character created, or he will not come alive...'

Winston Graham's bestselling career spanned more than forty novels, among them the celebrated *Poldark* series, which won him the hearts of millions. When he eventually found the time to tell the story of his own life he produced a wonderful book, free from what he calls 'the fashionable sins' but rich in charm. Witty, eccentric and intimate by turns, *Memoirs of a Private Man* offers an insight into the world of the novelist who rose from the isolation of Cornwall to the glittering London film scene, supported throughout by his lifelong loves: of his wife Jean and of writing.

'To read his memoir is to meet a charming, decent, old-fashioned sort of character with an enormous capacity for friendship and a wonderful interest in other people... Every gentle page offers us a shining example of prolific creativity and a good life well-lived' Val Hennessy, *Daily Mail*

'A must for Poldark fans... His essential niceness shines through in this endearingly self-effacing autobiography' Maggie Pringle, *Express*